RANTHORPE.

GEORGE HENRY LEWES

RANTHORPE.

EDITED WITH INTRODUCTION

AND NOTES BY

BARBARA SMALLEY

OHIO UNIVERSITY PRESS : ATHENS

Introduction © 1974 by Barbara Smalley
Library of Congress Catalog Number 74-82496
ISBN 8214-0167-X
Manufactured in the United States of America by
Oberlin Printing Company, Inc.
Design by Hal Stevens 76-10 56

CONTENTS

INTRODUCTION

It has been suggested by a number of critics that George Eliot's Will Ladislaw, the mercurial, many-theoried suitor and second husband of Dorothea in *Middlemarch*, owes a good deal of his personality to Eliot's own helpmate, George Henry Lewes. There is evidence to back the association, and fresh corroboration for such a view will be found in *Ranthorpe*. *Ranthorpe* is the sort of novel Will Ladislaw (like Lewes an unusual mixture of exuberance and sophistication, of whimsy and intellectual seriousness) would have written—full of self-revelations, full of ingenuity, full of absurdities in its juxtapositions of the real and the ideal, but at the same time reaching forward experimentally in both theme and treatment toward a new era in the history of the novel. Readers of *Middlemarch* are often skeptical of Will's ability to leave his period of experimentation in many fields for a career in politics, but George Eliot assures us in chapter 46, as Richard Ellmann has pointed out,[1] that people like Will can abruptly show powers for intensity their acquaintances had no idea they possessed. George Henry Lewes, for his part, though at least as varied in his interests as Will, had even in his twenties showed unusual energy in nearly all of them. He was later to strike

judges of his many achievements as one of the most
astonishingly versatile men the nation had seen.[2]
Even by the time of *Ranthorpe*, Lewes had explored
subjects as varied as Comte's theories, Shelley's poetry,
Spinoza, the Roman Empire, the Greek chorus, He-
gel's aesthetics, Arabian philosophy, and the business
and the art of acting. He had placed his articles on
such topics with major English periodicals, including
the *Edinburgh Review*, the *Westminster*, and *Fraser's*.
He had published a book on the Spanish drama and a
four-volume *Biographical Dictionary of Philosophy*
that was widely popular. His studies in human psychology, strongly reflected in *Ranthorpe*, dated back
as far as his nineteenth year. He had planned a whole
treatise on "the Philosophy of the Mind" at that early
age, and though he wisely postponed the idea of publication, he did present a series of lectures on the subject in the following year at Fox's Chapel, Finsbury,
a gathering place for intelligentsia, for William Johnson Fox was an eminent liberal and a friend of such
persons as John Stuart Mill and Robert Browning.[3]

I

Ranthorpe as Autobiography

Lewes's rearing, like Will Ladislaw's, had been cos-
mopolitan and haphazard. Born in London on April 18,
1817, he derived on his father's side from a family of
actors. Lewes himself had probably acted in plays before he reached his twenties, and he had written at
least three dramas before he finished *Ranthorpe*,[4] in
which much of the realistic detail of life backstage and
in rehearsal obviously stems from his own experiences.
Lewes's formal education, which had involved much
shifting of location (he was a pupil at different times

in London, in Jersey, and in Brittany), ended when he
was sixteen. For a few years thereafter he tried a succession of occupations—working in a notary's office, a
counting house, a Russian merchant's establishment
(Ranthorpe was to start life as a lawyer's clerk). For a
time Lewes became a medical student (medical students were to figure importantly in his novel), but
then defied poverty, as does his hero Ranthorpe, in an
attempt to make his living at literature. William Bell
Scott, the artist, describes Lewes at twenty when he
was still "in his infancy as a professional literary man."
Later Scott learned to regard Lewes, for all his volatil-
ity of talk and temperament, as one of the most tren-
chant minds in the England of his time, but in their
early acquaintance Lewes had seemed "an exuberant
but not very reliable or exact talker . . . a mixture of the
man of the world and the boy."[5] Even at that time
Lewes had amazed Scott with his precocious command
of literature and of languages. Guests of George Eliot
and Lewes at the Priory a quarter century later were
to describe him as everything from winningly genial
to offensively informal, but nearly all of them remark
upon the quickness of his mind and the wealth of his
ideas.

After nearly two years spent mainly in Germany,
during which he appears to have supported himself
(as does Ranthorpe in a comparable period in Germany) chiefly by giving lessons in English, Lewes lived
for some time, probably in the capacity of tutor, with
the family of Swynfen Jervis of Darlaston Hall, in Staffordshire. Like Ranthorpe's friend Wynton, who was
to serve as tutor for a Gloucestershire family, Lewes
with his bright wit and precocious learning probably
figured as a local celebrity, "treated as an honoured
guest, not as a tutor." Wynton was to fall in love with

the beautiful daughter of the house, and the girl was to
encourage his suit for some time only to reject him at
last under strange circumstances revealing unusual
characteristics in her patterns of thought and motive.
Lewes fell in love with the daughter of the Jervises—
also eighteen and also beautiful—with a different out-
come. In February 1841 he was married to Agnes Jervis, as exceptionally lovely according to general report as Lewes was in universal opinion exceptionally
ugly.

The two settled in London to make a meager living
from their writing, with Agnes contributing by translating articles from the French and from Spanish originals. Lewes by this time or soon afterward enjoyed a
broad range of literary friendships, including the Carlyles, Dickens, Leigh Hunt, Bulwer-Lytton, Thackeray, and John Stuart Mill. Thackeray sketched the
Leweses as Agnes played the piano and Lewes sang.
Mill sent long and carefully considered letters of counsel on the style and matter of articles Lewes had undertaken. The Leweses were frequent visitors at the
Carlyles and at the Phalanstery, a co-operative household of persons of advanced views that was a social
focus for a number of intellectuals.[6] Eliza Lynn Linton
remembered meeting Lewes there in 1845 and the
shock she had felt as a young girl fresh from country
life at the freedom of his conversation. Lewes would
talk without a hint of reticence on "the most delicate
matters of physiology." Nevertheless she found him
fascinating. "In work and in idleness, in the *sans façon*
of Bohemianism and in the more orderly amusements
of conventional society—in scientific discussion and in
empty persiflage, he was equally at home; and wherever he went there was a patch of intellectual sunshine
in the room." Even his ugliness had charm: "The

brightness and versatility of Lewes, and the wonderful expressiveness of his eyes, made one forget the unlovely rest. . . ."[7]

When *Ranthorpe* appeared in the spring of 1847, the Leweses were already parents of three sons. There was, apparently, nothing in their lives to suggest the difficulties that a few years later would cause Lewes to separate himself from Agnes to become the husband in all except legal definition of Marian (earlier Mary Anne) Evans, the future George Eliot. *Ranthorpe* is dedicated to Agnes, the wife "who has lightened the burden of an anxious life."

II

Ranthorpe and Charlotte Brontë

Read a century and a quarter later and judged simply on its merits as a work of fiction, *Ranthorpe* can hardly fail to strike the reader as a flawed and curiously uneven performance. It is clear, however, that in 1847 competent judges of novels viewed it otherwise. Whoever served Chapman and Hall as evaluator of the manuscript must have been considerably impressed with it—enough so for this firm to pay Lewes a round hundred pounds for the right to issue a thousand copies. It was a substantial sum which constituted well over a fourth of Lewes's total income for the year. For one reason or another the novel was to appear anonymously—possibly because Lewes felt (as he was to feel many years later when William Blackwood proposed to use his name in reprinting two of his tales for *Blackwood's Magazine*) that a writer of much sober nonfiction might be damaged with the public if he were identified as a storyteller.[8] If he feared that *Ranthorpe* might damage his reputation, however, the ac-

tual reception must have reassured him, for a year later his second and only other completed novel, *Rose,
Blanche, and Violet,* bears his name on the title page
and specifies *Ranthorpe* as a work by the same author.
Ranthorpe did, indeed, receive a generally favorable
critical reception. One reviewer, to be sure, intimated
that the anonymous author who talked ingenuously in
his preface of having pruned and corrected for the
past five years ought to have kept at the process another
five, but the critic in the influential *Examiner* (it may
well have been John Forster) found the book full of
movement and vivacity and filled with sufficient "original thought, fine reflection, and dramatic point" to
place it well above the main run of ephemeral fiction.
At a time when few novels were yet taken seriously as
contributions to literature, the *Spectator* also treated
Ranthorpe seriously and at length as a work of substance that challenged close criticism. The *British
Quarterly Review* in a critique several months later
pointed out for special admiration the peculiar powers
of the author as an analyst of character and a creator
of highly dramatic scenes.[9]

Edgar Allan Poe, who had no knowledge of the writer of the anonymous novel, read *Ranthorpe* with
"deep interest." Its portrayal of the experiences of a
struggling author struck home to him with force. He
had, he confided in a letter to his friend Annie Richmond, derived "great *consolation*" from the book, and
he urged her to read it "for my sake."[10] Charlotte
Brontë, who did know the author through correspondence with him following the publication of *Jane Eyre*
in the same year, clearly viewed *Ranthorpe* as a work
of unusual meaning and value for her. She was already
aware that Lewes was soon to review her own novel,
but self-serving flattery was something quite alien to

Charlotte's nature. We can hardly question the sincerity of her emphatic pronouncement on Lewes's novel, written to Lewes some six months after its publication:

> I have now read *Ranthorpe*. I could not get it till a day or so ago; but I have got it and read it at last; and in reading *Ranthorpe* I have read a new book—not a reprint—not a reflection of any other book, but a *new book.*
>
> I did not know such books were written now. It is very different to any of the popular works of fiction; it fills the mind with fresh knowledge. Your experience and your convictions are made the reader's; and to an author, at least, they have a value and an interest quite unusual. I await your criticism on *Jane Eyre* now with other sentiments than I entertained before the perusal of *Ranthorpe.*
>
> You were a stranger to me. I did not particularly respect you. I did not feel that your praise or blame would have any special weight. I knew little of your right to condemn or approve. *Now* I am informed on these points.[11]

What made Charlotte Brontë see *Ranthorpe* as a distinctively "new" book full of fresh knowledge was almost certainly Lewes's scenes that break with romantic tradition in the novel to attempt a fresh sort of realism and a fresh emphasis on detailed observation of motive and cast of mind. *Ranthorpe* is a strangely schizoid work of fiction that combines romance and psychological realism, melodrama and minute analysis. If Shelley had undertaken to examine Laon or Cythna's unapparent patterns of thought that lay behind but were traceable in their more sensational actions or if he had halted his narrative at times to give us graphic but prosaic accounts of Laon's difficulties with the publisher of his poems, the effect would not be altogether unlike. In part, the sentimental scenes in *Ranthorpe* surely owe their coloring to the author's unusual familiarity with acted melodrama, but Lewes seems to have had a particular fictional model in mind for many of his sensational incidents. A decade before *Ranthorpe*, Lewes's much-admired friend Bulwer (who in 1843 was to add Lytton to his surname) had written *Ernest Maltravers* and its sequel *Alice, or The Mysteries*; in these novels Bulwer's hero follows a course that in its outlines has a good deal in common with the career of Lewes's hero. Both Maltravers and Ranthorpe early in their histories fall in love with a maiden of great beauty and noble simplicity of mind though she is of humble origin and situation. They are separated from this embodiment of ideal love during much of the narrative while, remote from the scenes they have shared with her, they struggle with the affairs of a sophisticated world—Ranthorpe largely with the graphically portrayed world of publishers, critics, and the stage; Maltravers predominantly with the glamorously painted world of high society. Both are ultimately reunited, amid pastoral surroundings and under implausibly melodramatic circumstances, with the object of their early and only authentic love. This is a narrative that readers of Byron, Scott, and the current sentimental fiction could follow with few surprises; but even in their encountering of the busy world, Maltravers and Ranthorpe pursue somewhat similar courses. Both are poets (a fact that, to be sure, figures much more importantly in Ranthorpe's history), both meet with early acclaim with their first volume of poems; both publish a second volume only to be disparaged by envious competitors. Maltravers, like Ranthorpe, represents a type of *Bildungsroman* protag-

onist who, relatively shallow in youth but extremely
sensitive by nature, grows through chastening experiences until by the conclusion of the novel he has
achieved not merely material success but spiritual
maturity.

The differences between Bulwer's work and Lewes's
are nevertheless pronounced. Bulwer was too practiced
a hand in the writing of popular fiction to mix genres;
Maltravers is a romantic hero from first to last, well
distanced from the sort of detailed realism of situation
or ambitious analysis of motive that Lewes tried to
combine with his melodramatic plotting. Bulwer's situations are often wildly implausible, but the modern
reader's perspective on them, if he reads them at all,
remains unjarred by discordant particulars. Poe, Charlotte Brontë, and the reviewers of *Ranthorpe* were far
less conscious of the incongruities in Lewes's narrative
(as was Lewes himself) than the modern critical reader, because romance or melodrama was still the
groundwork of the general run of contemporary novels
they were accustomed to reading and had for them a
kind of secondary reality of its own. Lewes's portrayal
of the beautiful and spirituelle Isola did not strike
them as especially overdone, and the incident of Isola's
fainting dead away on overhearing Percy Ranthorpe's
declaration of his impassioned love to Florence Wilmington possessed for them a kind of fictional plausi-
bility that is likely to be totally absent for the modern
reader. Charlotte Brontë must have recognized in *Ranthorpe* the same sort of blending of romance and realism that she had herself effected with greater subtlety
and less emphasis on the unpoetic data of daily life in
Jane Eyre.

Even by 1847 Lewes as critic of fiction had shifted
his perspectives considerably from those that had char-

acterized Lewes the novelist, who, he tells us in his preface to *Ranthorpe*, though he had done much condensing and altering in the interim, had written the bulk of his novel five years earlier. By 1847 Lewes had obviously done much to clarify for himself the criteria he was to employ in his judgments of fiction in critiques of the late eighteen-forties and early eighteen-fifties—critiques destined to mark him for later critics, including René Wellek, as "the first English exponent of the theory of realism in the novel."[12] When *Jane Eyre* appeared in October of 1847, Lewes was overjoyed to discover a contemporary who was bringing to English fiction a new and vital realism of the sort he had himself explored ambitiously but with a great deal less sureness of touch in *Ranthorpe*. "The enthusiasm with which I read [*Jane Eyre*]," Lewes later wrote Charlotte Brontë's biographer, "made me go down to Mr. Parker, and propose to write a review of it for *Fraser's Magazine*. He would not consent to an unknown novel—for the papers had not yet declared themselves—receiving such importance, but thought it might make one on 'Recent Novels: English and French'—which appeared in *Fraser*, December, 1847. Meanwhile I had written to Miss Brontë to tell her the delight with which her book filled me; and seem to have 'sermonised' her, to judge from her reply."[13]

Charlotte's reply (still under her pseudonym as "Currer Bell") makes it evident that Lewes had indeed solemnly preached to her the creed that he by now wholeheartedly espoused but that sorts strangely with a part of his own practice in *Ranthorpe*. "You warn me to beware of melodrama," Charlotte wrote, "and you exhort me to adhere to the real. When I first began to write, so impressed was I with the truth of the principles you advocate, that I determined to take Nature

and Truth as my sole guides, and to follow their very
footprints; I restrained imagination, eschewed romance, repressed excitement; over-bright colouring,
too, I avoided, and sought to produce something which
should be soft, grave, and true." The result had been
that six publishers in succession had rejected her manuscript, intimating that it was lacking in "startling incident" and "thrilling excitement." Since much of their
profit came from sales to lending libraries, they could
not afford to consider publishing her. *Jane Eyre* itself
had been objected to on the same grounds but had
finally been accepted. The implication, pretty clearly,
is that without the infusion of the amount of melodrama *Jane Eyre* did contain it would not have reached
publication. Charlotte then takes up Lewes's further
admonition:

> You advise me, too, not to stray far from the
> ground of experience, as I become weak when I
> enter the region of fiction; and you say 'real expe-
> rience is perennially interesting, and to all men.'
> I feel that this also is true; but, dear sir, is not
> the real experience of each individual very lim-
> ited? And, if a writer dwells upon that solely or
> principally, is he not in danger of repeating him-
> self, and also of becoming an egotist? Then, too,
> imagination is a strong and restless faculty, which
> claims to be heard and exercised: are we to be
> quite deaf to her cry, and insensate to her strug-
> gles? When she shows us bright pictures, are we
> never to look at them, and try to reproduce them?
> And when she is eloquent, and speaks rapidly and
> urgently in our ear, are we not to write to her dic-
> tation?
> I shall anxiously search the next number of
> *Fraser* for your opinions on these points.[14]

Miss Brontë was glad to learn on inquiry, from her correspondent Smith Williams, that Lewes was "a clever and sincere man." She would, she wrote in reply, await Lewes's "critical sentence with fortitude; even if it goes against me I shall not murmur; ability and honesty have a right to condemn, where they think condemnation is deserved." Reading *Ranthorpe* not long afterward apparently reassured her and added measurably to her respect for Lewes's opinion, though she had already observed the discrepancy between this critic's advice to her regarding melodrama and his practice in parts of his own novel.[15]

Though Lewes's critique,[16] at the request of the editor of *Fraser's*, covered several novels besides *Jane Eyre*, there is no question as to which is central to what he has to say. Lewes begins with an early and important declaration for the dignity of prose fiction as a form of serious literature. Though many persons despise all storytelling as a waste of time, a really good work of fiction, he declares, can take its place in the very "first rank of literature." Such books are, of course, still rarely produced. His own criterion for excellence in the novel is "a correct representation of life." Fielding and Jane Austen are the greatest novelists in the English language. Scott's romances constitute bad models for later writers, for Scott was "the Ariosto of prose romance." Sensational incidents and eloquent diction cannot compensate for an absence of veracity in the delineation of life and character. Before entering on *Jane Eyre*, Lewes touches on *The Bachelor of the Albany*, an anonymous story he had found amusing but in the end unsatisfactory. He had by now worked out a distinction in regard to proper subject matter for the novel that he had not, it seems, clarified for himself at the time of constructing a considerable part of the scenes and situations of *Ranthorpe*: Incidents suitable for the stage may be unsuitable for fiction. "The drama and the novel . . . with the same end, have very different machinery wherewith to accomplish that end . . . ." *The Bachelor of the Albany*, failing to observe the distinction, lapsed into becoming "stagey" and farcical.

Having prepared the way, Lewes takes up his discussion of *Jane Eyre*: "This, indeed, is a book after our own heart; and, if its merits have not forced it into notice by the time this paper comes before our readers, let us, in all earnestness, bid them lose not a day in sending for it. . . . Almost all that we require in a novelist she has: perception of character, and power of delineating it; picturesqueness; passion; and knowledge of life." Above all, it is Currer Bell's truth to life that lends distinction to her work (for Lewes was already confident the writer was a woman): "Reality—deep, significant reality—is the great characteristic of the book." The "remarkable power" that Lewes finds in *Jane Eyre* comes, he is sure, from her writing on the basis of life she has herself observed and emotions she herself has felt. "The machinery of the story may have been borrowed, but by means of this machinery the authoress is unquestionably setting forth her own experience." Unless a novel "be built out of real experience, it can have no real success. To have vitality, it must spring from vitality." All the ingenious novelties of plot or flowers of sentiment devised for the circulating libraries could not make "that seem true which is not true" or produce a book of any lasting value. In the more effective parts of *Ranthorpe*, Lewes had himself mined his materials from his areas of personal knowledge—from his past experiences as a clerk, a medical student, an inhabitant of rooming houses, an

impoverished student of literature, a writer of plays,
a denizen of the theater both before the curtain and
backstage, a student of French and German life, a tutor in love with a daughter of the family, a journalist.

He had also, as has already been intimated, drawn
upon his not inconsiderable studies in psychology for
his elaborate analyses of his main characters' patterns
of behavior. Much of Lewes's admiration for Miss
Brontë's novel comes from her cultivating of psychological realism—her impressive gift for "connecting external appearances with internal effects . . . of repre-
senting the psychological interpretation of material
phenomena." The weak parts of *Jane Eyre* occurred,
in his opinion, precisely where the author veered toward melodrama and improbability, particularly in
the incidents surrounding the mad wife.

In closing, Lewes addresses Currer Bell directly in
tones of admonishment such as he had apparently
adopted in his letters: "To her we emphatically say,
Persevere; keep reality distinctly before you, and paint
it as accurately as you can: invention will never equal
the effect of truth."

In sending Lewes her thanks, Charlotte emphasized
the seriousness with which she was considering all that
he had said, at the same time making it abundantly
plain that on some of his points she could by no means
see eye to eye with him. "I mean to observe your warning about being careful how I undertake new works,"
she assured him; "my stock of materials is not abundant, but very slender; and besides, neither my experience, my acquirements, nor my powers are sufficiently
varied to justify my ever becoming a frequent writer."
She would try, moreover, to avoid sensational incidents: "If I ever *do* write another book, I think I will

have nothing of what you call 'melodrama'; I *think* so, but I am not sure. I *think*, too, I will endeavour to follow the counsel which shines out of Miss Austen's 'mild eyes,' 'to finish more and be more subdued'; but neither am I sure of that." Writers, at least so far as her own experience told her, could not guarantee to produce according to conscious theoretic plan: "When authors write best, or, at least, when they write most fluently, an influence seems to waken in them, which becomes their master—which will have its own way—putting out of view all behests but its own, dictating certain words, and insisting on their being used, whether vehement or measured in their nature; new-moulding characters, giving unthought-of turns to incidents, rejecting carefully elaborated old ideas, and suddenly creating and adopting new ones. Is it not so? And should we try to counteract this influence? Can we indeed counteract it? . . . Am I wrong; or were you hasty in what you said?"[17]

Lewes's reply must have been immediate and vehement, for within the week Charlotte wrote him again, speaking of his "anger" at her having questioned the greatness of Jane Austen and pleading, half-seriously perhaps, for his "forgiveness" for her not being able to subscribe to all his views.

> You correct my crude remarks on the subject of the 'influence'; well, I accept your definition of what the effects of that influence should be; I recognise the wisdom of your rules for its regulation. . . .

> What a strange lecture comes next in your letter! You say I must familiarise my mind with the fact that 'Miss Austen is not a poetess, has no 'sentiment' (you scornfully enclose the word in in-

verted commas), 'no eloquence, none of the ravishing enthusiasm of poetry'; and then you add, I *must* 'learn to acknowledge her as *one of the greatest painters of human character*, and one of the writers with the nicest sense of means to an end that ever lived.'

The last point only will I ever acknowledge.

Can there be a great artist without poetry?

What I call—what I will bend to, as a great artist, then—cannot be destitute of the divine gift. But by *poetry*, I am sure, you understand something different to what I do, as you do by 'sentiment.' . . .

Miss Austen being, as you say, without 'sentiment,' without *poetry*, maybe *is* sensible, real (more *real* than *true*), but she cannot be great.

More "*real* than *true*": Charlotte is deftly adapting her severe preceptor's own weapons and turning them against him. Lewes had said in his *Fraser's* critique that *The Bachelor of the Albany*, lacking an overall effect of truth, was not saved by the everyday realism of many of its individual scenes—"if *vrai*, it is not *vraisemblable*." Nevertheless Charlotte seems in *Shirley* (1849) to be resolved on abandoning poetry for an excessively flat kind of verisimilitude. It is the theory of Franklin Gary in an extended and well-argued essay that *Shirley* represents a misguided attempt to apply Lewes's dicta. The second paragraph of *Shirley* constitutes, in fact, a manifesto for realism that reads surprisingly like the declaration of intent George Eliot was to make, three years after she had joined forces with Lewes, in the first work of fiction she was to produce. "If you think, from this prelude," Charlotte wrote, "that anything like a romance is preparing for you, reader, you never were more mistaken. Do you antici-

pate sentiment, and poetry, and reverie? Do you expect passion, and stimulus, and melodrama? Calm
your expectations; reduce them to a lowly standard.
Something real, cool, and solid lies before you; something unromantic as Monday morning, when all who
have work wake with the consciousness that they must
rise and betake themselves thereto." The "Rev. Amos
Barton," George Eliot was to write in Chapter V of
The Sad Fortunes of the Reverend Amos Barton
(1857), "was palpably and unmistakably common-
place; . . . was not even in love, but had had that complaint favourably many years ago." A lady reader who
"prefers the ideal in fiction" is imagined as protesting
the direction things are taking at this point, and Eliot
replies that her characters are intended to present life
as it is lived by ordinary Britons, who are, most of
them, "simply men of complexions more or less muddy,
whose conversation is more or less bald and dis-
jointed." There will be nothing in the history of Amos
Barton about deep and liquid eyes, extraordinary
wickedness, sparkling witticisms, volcanic passions, or
thrilling adventures. Lewes was to quote the passage
admiringly in his memorable essay on Jane Austen in
1859.

As Charlotte Brontë knew and George Eliot was
probably aware, Lewes had made ambitious though
uncertain attempts at rendering ordinary life in *Ranthorpe*, where realism and implausible melodrama often rub elbows with ludicrous effect. He had gone farther with attempts at realistic portrayal in *Rose,
Blanche, and Violet*, published in the year following.
In this second and last completed novel of Lewes's
there appears a passage that lacks the graceful touch
of either Miss Brontë or George Eliot but that seems,
for all its awkwardness, interestingly similar. Introduc-

ing Julius St. John, who "had not a person correspond-
ing to the beauty of his name," Lewes addresses a
young lady who has already ventured past his initial
chapters:

> Do not, my pretty reader, turn away your head:
> do not shrug your shoulders; do not skip the next
> page or so, because truth bids me inform you
> Julius was remarkably plain. . . . I am now going
> to demand your admiration for a young man, who
> is undisguisedly, unequivocally plain. Not ugly—
> ugliness implies meanness, or moral deformity—
> yet absolutely without any feature which could re-
> deem him from being familiarly called 'a fright.'
> Strikingly plain is the proper expression; so strik-
> ing as, perhaps, to be the next best thing to beau-
> ty, from the force of the impression created. . . .
> No, reader, no; while I am perfectly aware that
> some plain features are rendered handsome by ex-
> pression, I am also aware that some faces—and the
> faces of very noble creatures—are irredeemably
> plain; and such was Julius St. John's. (I, 76)

III

Ranthorpe, Middlemarch, Daniel Deronda

Franklin Gary argues persuasively that Charlotte
Brontë continued to go to school to Lewes—even after
she had experienced with great bitterness what she
considered his betrayal of her—and that her masterpiece, *Villette* (1853), could be written only after she
had seen both her strengths and her limitations as a
creative genius made excruciatingly clear to her in
Lewes's ambitious *Edinburgh Review* analysis of *Shirley*.[18] The extent and nature of Lewes's influence upon a still more eminent woman novelist with whom he

was on far more intimate terms remains a question of
interest and lively debate.[19] Marian Evans, the future
George Eliot, first came to know Lewes in the fall of
1851 during the unhappy years following his wife's
transfer of her affections to his friend Thornton Hunt
and her bearing of two children by Hunt. Marian had
by then, at thirty-one, achieved a modest reputation as
the translator of David Friedrich Strauss's *Das Leben
Jesu* and as an intellectual of unusual capabilities. She
was soon to become editor of the *Westminster Review*.
By 1853 Marian was speaking of Lewes as a friend who
was kind and attentive and had "quite won" her esteem
after her initial dislike of him. He was "a man of heart
and conscience wearing a mask of flippancy."[20] In July
of 1854 they set out for Germany. They were to spend
the next twenty-four years living together as man and
wife. Lewes had condoned Agnes's adultery; divorce
was impossible.

George Eliot inscribed in her journal under the
heading "How I Came to Write Fiction" the circumstances under which, in September 1856, she entered
upon her career as a creative artist. Ten years earlier
she had composed an account of life in a Staffordshire village, a purely descriptive piece intended for an
introductory chapter. In the intervening ten years,
however, she had never done anything further, and
she had gradually "lost any hope that I should ever be
able to write a novel." When she showed the piece to
Lewes, he was impressed with it. Soon he "began to
say very positively, 'You must try and write a story,'"
and kept on urging her to make her attempt. "He used
to say, 'You have wit, description and philosophy—
those go a good way towards the production of a novel.
It is worth while for you to try the experiment.'" When
Marian had, after several delays, composed her first ef-

fort at narrative, she submitted it to him for his judgment. "The scene at Cross Farm, he said, satisfied him
that I had the very element he had been doubtful
about—it was clear I could write good dialogue." However, there "still remained the question whether I
could command any pathos, and that was to be decided by the mode in which I treated Milly's death."
A short time later Lewes left the house for the evening
expressly for giving Marian a quiet time for coping
with the scene. "I wrote the chapter from the news
brought by the shepherd to Mrs. Hackit, to the moment
when Amos is dragged from the bedside and I read it
to G. when he came home. We both cried over it, and
then he came up to me and kissed me, saying 'I think
your pathos is better than your fun.' "[21]

The pattern thus established during the writing of
George Eliot's first story—the reading aloud of install-
ments of her work to Lewes for his judgment and encouragement—was to continue throughout her career
as novelist. It is unlikely, as Anna Kitchel observes,
that any single tale or novel of Eliot's "ever grew to
maturity without being discussed in all its stages by the
pair."[22] "Hitherto I have read my M.S. (I mean of my
previous books) to Mr. Lewes, by 40 or 50 pages at a
time," George Eliot wrote Frederic Harrison in 1866
regarding legal advice he could supply for *Felix Holt*,
"and he has told me if he felt an objection to anything.
No one else has had any knowledge of my writing
before . . . publication (I except, of course, the publishers)."[23] In 1875, struggling with the problems of *Daniel Deronda*, the last novel she was to write, she confided to a Swiss admirer: "I suffer always increasingly
from doubt as to the quality of what I am actually doing. Just now I am writing a new novel . . . but if it
were not for [Lewes's] firmness of opinion as to the

worth of what is already written I could not carry out
my intention. In this way he has always supported me
—by his unreserved sympathy and the independence
of his judgment."

It was apparently because Lewes praised the piece
of description she had written ten years earlier of life
in a Staffordshire village that Eliot reawakened her
long-dormant or abandoned hopes of becoming a novelist. Probably she did not need Lewes's guidance to
know that she should rely on her own experience for
her proper material—the surroundings she had grown
up among and the sort of emotional situations she had
herself gone through or observed at close quarters.
What is clearer is that Eliot's early novels follow
precepts that Lewes had himself attempted to follow as novelist and had vehemently preached as critic
as early as 1847. From *Scenes of Clerical Life* (1858)
through *Adam Bede* (1859), *The Mill on the Floss*
(1860), and *Silas Marner* (1861), Eliot drew upon
her memories of her own early Midlands life—most
intimately of all, of course, in the autobiographical
parts of *The Mill on the Floss*. Even a decade later in
Middlemarch (1872), her masterpiece, she is employ-
ing the experiences and observations of her Warwick-
shire youth in ways subtle and various, certain to
command delight and admiration from Lewes, her
primary audience, whose responses to her scenes were
registered for the author even as she was in process of
shaping them. George Eliot was so preternaturally
sensitive to criticism that Lewes must be extremely
cautious in indicating the slightest nuance of disapproval or allowing her to receive expressions of disapproval from others. "But do not write me about it,"
Eliot begged an intimate friend on sending her an early
printed copy of an installment of *Middlemarch*, "be-

cause until a book has quite gone away from me and
become entirely of the non-ego—gone thoroughly from
the wine-press into the casks—I would rather not hear
or see anything that is said about it."[24] "Mrs. Lewes is
so easily discouraged and so ready to believe and exaggerate whatever is said against her books," Lewes
wrote William Blackwood, warning him against mentioning any criticism of *Daniel Deronda,* "that I not
only keep reviews from her but do not even talk of
them to her." Eliot suffered even on reading adverse
criticism of the work of others. "I sometimes shrink
from every article that pretends to be critical—I mean
of other people's productions, not of course my own,"
she wrote Alexander Main, "for you know I am well
taken care of by my husband and am saved from getting my mind poisoned with print about myself." Such
evidences of George Eliot's isolation from a larger
body of critical opinion and the degree of her depen-
dence upon her husband as her critical audience ex-
tend throughout her career and begin as early as
Lewes's plea to John Blackwood regarding *Scenes of
Clerical Life*: ". . . unless you have any *serious* objection to make to Eliot's stories, *don't* make any. He is
so easily discouraged, so diffident of himself that not
being prompted by necessity to write, he will close the
series in the belief that his writing is not relished." The
great importance of Lewes in protecting George Eliot
from adverse comment and bolstering her confidence
during her frequent periods of deep depression, in
which she was all but convinced of the valuelessness
of her writing, has been generally recognized. What
has not been adequately taken into account, I would
suggest, is the extent to which her intimate knowledge
of Lewes's particular interests and preferences in fiction, her familiarity with what he would respond to

with special enthusiasm, served to influence emphasis
and subject in what she wrote. "My poem has been a
great source of added happiness to me," she confided
to a friend in July 1868 concerning her recently published verse play *The Spanish Gypsy*, "—all the more,
or rather principally because it has been a deeper joy
to Mr. Lewes than any work I have done before. I
seem to have gained a new organ, a new medium that
my nature had languished for." The instances of her
following his overt suggestions (not all of them fortunate ones)—for creating a "more direct collision" between Adam Bede and Arthur Donnithorne, for example,[25] or for taking up Savonarola as subject—have been
often covered, but there is evidence in *Ranthorpe* to
indicate that his influence on her work was considerably more pervasive than has been generally assumed.

It is in *Middlemarch* that George Eliot finally
achieves her superb handling of psychological narrative, a subject I have dealt with at length elsewhere.[26]
Lewes's own fascination with problems in human motivation—a study that had formed an important part of
his intellectual life ever since he had entered on it in
his youth—was in the foreground of his interests by the
time George Eliot began the writing of *Middlemarch*,
for he was already engaged in preparing the volumes
of his *Problems of Life and Mind* (1874-79), the work
he intended to make the magnum opus of his career.
The shared intellectual life of Eliot and Lewes, a major fact of their experience at all times (as countless
references in Haight's volumes of their letters and
journals make manifest), seems to have been especially
active during the years of the writing of *Middlemarch*.
"Both Mr. Lewes and I are deeply interested in the
indications which the Professor gives of his peculiar
psychological experience," George Eliot wrote in July

1869 concerning an account of a visionary's impressions, "and we should feel it a great privilege to learn much more of it from his lips. It is a rare thing to have such an opportunity of studying exceptional experience in the testimony of a truthful and in every way distinguished mind."[27] It was in the same month, according to Jerome Beaty's calculations, that Eliot entered in earnest on the writing of *Middlemarch* (though elements of it "had been soliciting [her] mind for years"). "I think my affections grow more intense and my interest in [Lewes's] studies increases rather than diminishes," she confided to another correspondent in January 1871. And in September she wrote Alexander Main of her progress on *Middlemarch*: "Perhaps you do not imagine me as a writer who suffers much from self-distrust and despondency. If I had not had a husband who is not only sympathetic, but *so sagacious in criticism that I can rely on his pleasure in my writing as a satisfactory test*, it would be difficult for me to bring myself into print" (italics mine).

References in the letters and journals of George Eliot and Lewes to their daily habit of sharing books are frequent. "We are in our usual train of home procedures," Eliot wrote in November 1872 as she neared the completion of *Middlemarch*, "—thinking, reading, talking much en tête-a-tète, and hoping that there are many others in the world who are as happy as we are."[28] During the three and a half years in which *Middlemarch* was written, the two had spent much time in isolation from the larger world. In October 1870 they "enjoyed three weeks . . . reading and walking together" in their favorite retreat in Surrey, and the next spring and summer they were spending a much longer period away from other companionship in another

rural retreat "like two secluded owls, wise with un-
fashionable wisdom." Eliot regularly read aloud for
their mutual enjoyment and profit "almost all the evening—books of German science, and other gravities,"
books that were, many of them, to be cited early in
the first volume of the first series of Lewes's *Problems
of Life and Mind* (1874), as Haight informs us in a
note providing many of their formidable titles. She
was also reading portions of her manuscript to Lewes,
usually within a short time after she had finished them.
In August, still isolated in the same rural retreat, Eliot
read to Lewes the part of her manuscript dealing with
"Dorothea Married" to his huge delight and "expectation of a great success." Surely during their long evenings together and during the extensive walks they
seem to have shared more or less regularly during their
months in the country they must have talked long and
often, directly or indirectly, of the problems that absorbed them in what they were writing. Exactly how
much Lewes had to do with the particular subject matter of *Middlemarch*—how much Eliot's novel owes to
his own intensive concern with problems of human motivation and patterns of human conduct as he discussed them with her at this period or during the earlier years of their intimately shared intellectual life
—is an extremely interesting question that is not likely
to receive any precise answer.

What is clearer is that parts of *Ranthorpe* read
strangely like rough and sometimes inept sketches for
the sort of consummate psychological narrative that
distinguishes *Middlemarch* and thereafter the Gwendolen Harleth half of *Daniel Deronda*. Lewes had
poured into his first novel all the most original materials for fiction that he could command. A considerable
number of them relate to unusual and often paradoxi-

cal patterns of motivation, observations of a sort Lewes
had probably been accumulating ever since he had
undertaken an intensive study of human psychology
at the precocious age of nineteen. Such observations
are especially rich in the two interrelated subplots
that take up a part of *Ranthorpe*. Both center on a
theme that figures crucially in the Rosamond-Lydgate plot of *Middlemarch* and the Gwendolen-Grandcourt plot of *Daniel Deronda*—the complex and insidi-
ous dangers of a species of role-playing, of acting out
an identity counter to one's basic nature with destructive results to another or to one's self. In the two subplots Lewes attempts to deal with the theme in terms
of psychological realism, with elaborate attention to
analysis of motive. Eliot's Lydgate was to be the dupe
of such role-playing twice, first in actively taking part
in the defense of, and subsequently searching out and
proposing marriage to, the Frenchwoman Laure, literally an actress, the beauty of whose stage presence
and the quiet charm of whose simulation of innocence
thereafter had made him sure that she could not be
guilty of the crime of murder.

It was the role-playing of Rosamond Vincy, however, that was to have greater consequences for him,
to lead at last (he was to say with profound bitterness
of spirit) to Rosamond's becoming the murderer of his
mind. "She was by nature an actress of parts that entered into her *physique*," George Eliot tells us soon after introducing Rosamond; "she even acted her own
character, and so well, that she did not know it to be
precisely her own." (Her "very affectations," Lewes
had written of his comparable character, "seemed to
be natural to her."[29]) The role of pliant "infantine"
flatterer of men, ready to play the piano or sing whatever piece might be preferred ("she only wanted to

know what her audience liked") effectively masked a
basically stupid but almost hermetically self-concen-
tric nature that T. S. Eliot declared frightened him
more than Goneril or Regan.[30] George Eliot's "charming stage Ariadne" (221) possesses in outline much in
common with Lewes's sketch of a young woman who
conceals beneath an acting out of feminine complai-
sance an equally self-centered nature, though Lewes's
development of his conception is indeed awkward by
comparison. To the inexperienced eyes of the young
tutor Wynton, the daughter of his employer appeared
to embody in truth "all that she affected to be, and as
good as she was beautiful." Like Rosamond, who could
always "say the right thing; for she was clever with
that sort of cleverness which catches every tone except
the humorous" (117), Wynton's love possessed "quickness" in affecting attitudes while lacking education or
intellect at any deeper level. She "seemed so angelical
in disposition, her sentiments were so noble," Wynton
recalls to Ranthorpe, "her sympathy so active, and her
person so beautiful, that I soon forgot her poverty of
brain." Moreover, "in spite of her dullness of comprehension, she was the most consummate flatterer. Small
as was her intellect, she seemed to have a more than
animal quickness of instinct in detecting the foibles of
those around her; and utterly destitute of convictions
or earnestness, she could with equal facility adopt any
opinion, any sentiment, or manner of the person she
was conversing with. She was like the chameleon reflecting the colour of every tree under which it reposes;
she passed from the most contradictory ideas, and antagonistical sympathies, in the same evening—the same
hour—with unparalleled ease. She flattered every
body, and cared for none" (88).

Ranthorpe, who is familiar with the woman in ques-

tion and who is having her history recounted to him
for a warning, remarks at a later point in Wynton's
narrative, " 'You have made me sadder . . . from the
hideous picture you have drawn of a woman whom I
always thought a negative kind of being, without
force of character enough to be bad—much less to be
the demon you have drawn.' " But the originality of
the sketch depends, as does Eliot's later superb portrait of Rosamond, upon the sheer negativeness, the
very absence of evil intention, in the character's nature. Rosamond's most appalling speeches are her
quiet statements, from her perspective of nearly absolute self-centeredness, of her utter dissociation from
her husband's sufferings. "What can *I* do, Tertius?" becomes a speech with awesome implications that falls
on Lydgate's senses "like a mortal chill" (434). Lewes
attempts to elaborate a quite similar conception without being able to make it an active part of his narrative: " 'Yet she is not a demon,' replied Wynton; 'believe me she is a woman, and a not uncommon woman.
. . . Experience, and long studies of moral anatomy,
have convinced me of my error. Calm now, I can read
her character in its true light. Shall I read it aloud?' "
And on Ranthorpe's asking him to continue, Wynton
provides an analysis drawn from his extensive studies
in moral anatomy: " 'Well, then, Fanny was simply and
truly a victim of *intense egotism with no intellect to
direct it* . . . she had no malignity, she had not force of
character for any villany that did not spring from the
negative vice of want of principle. Self was her only
consideration, and she was reckless what she sacrificed
to it' " (96).

It is obvious in *Ranthorpe* that Lewes considers his
portrait of Fanny, Lady Wilmington, a high point in
his novel. He returns to discussion of her character

much later in his narrative, speaking this time as omniscient author: "A character like hers, reduced to its strict formula—without heart as without intellect—appears, at first sight, the mere exaggeration of a novelist, and the reader refuses to believe that such a woman could anywhere be tolerated. But, good and gentle reader! I have not been thus minute in painting a mere exaggeration. It is a portrait—taken at many sittings, and under many different lights—a portrait, unfortunately, that might be hung up in many a drawingroom, and pronounced 'most like'" (339). Apparently Lewes himself feels uneasily, however, that his raw data are better than his powers to handle them, for he adds: "And yet is it not strange that the reader should doubt [the portrait's] truth, because, although the features themselves are neither untrue nor exaggerated, yet inasmuch as the *expression* is absent, so the face seems revolting. I have given the moral characteristics of Lady Wilmington: but the *manner*, which was as drapery to her worthlessness—manner by which most people are judged—this I could not give."

The Rosamond-Lydgate story features a heroine who conceals her near-absolute egotism and want of intellect beneath a cleverly acted semblance of tenderness and talent. It is a man of no ordinary powers of intellect who becomes the dupe of her acting. This is also the plan of Lewes's story, and in both the hero interprets the heroine's nature in terms he has learned from sentimental literature. Lydgate, who had once got all of Scott's poems by heart (200), is to read the personality of the criminal actress Laure according to a version of reality he has acquired from such reading and is to envision life with a woman of Rosamond's qualities as a matter of "reclining in a paradise with sweet laughs for bird-notes, and blue eyes for a heaven" (70). In the

early days of their acquaintance Rosamond was to
seem to him a perfect embodiment of "that feminine
radiance, that distinctive womanhood which must be
classed with flowers and music, that sort of beauty
which by its very nature was virtuous, being moulded
only for pure and delicate joys." Not intending to
marry for a long time to come, however, he could return to his scientific studies "bringing a much more
testing vision of details and relations into this patho-
logical study than he had ever thought it necessary to
apply to the complexities of love and marriage, these
being subjects on which he felt himself amply informed
by literature, and that traditional wisdom which is
handed down in the genial conversation of men" (122).
During his engagement to Rosamond he continues to
read her reality in terms of romantic literature: "Ideal
happiness (of the kind known in the Arabian Nights,
in which you are invited to step from the labour and
discord of the street into a paradise where everything
is given to you and nothing claimed) seemed to be an
affair of a few weeks' waiting, more or less" (257).
Lewes's outline for such a conception is brief and
specific rather than, like Eliot's development in her narrative, subtle and pervasive: Wynton explains to Ranthorpe that despite all his unusual erudition and cleverness in more abstract kinds of thinking (he had been
celebrated as "the 'lion' of the county" for his bril-
liance), he "was ignorant enough of human life and
human motives; my ideas of them had been gathered
from poetry and novels (those falsifiers of nature, the
more pernicious because they pretend to truth), and I
had familiarised myself with romantic adventures, the
audacity of love, and the escapes of brides from detested unions even at the foot of the altar" (90). Wynton's affair ends in a series of scenes that ineptly

attempt to combine melodrama with psychological realism. George Eliot would never have countenanced their like. The considerable parallels of plot and theme between Lewes's novel and *Middlemarch*, however, seem more plausibly traceable to George Eliot's intimate familiarity with favorite themes and theories of human behavior of the erstwhile author of *Ranthorpe* than by an accident of simple coincidence.

Gwendolen Harleth, as an Eliot critic has remarked, is "a Rosamond Vincy expanded into a fuller creation, but a Rosamond Vincy still."[31] Though Gwendolen is more volatile and more assertive than Rosamond, she is a sister to Miss Vincy in her essential coldness of heart, her cleverness in acting, and, above all, her egoistic self-absorption. The ironical "drama of incommunicability," in which persons who are pointedly strangers in spirit perform the intimacies of courtship or the shared life of wedlock, constitutes a prominent feature of *Middlemarch*. It is a central fact in the Gwendolen-Grandcourt plot of *Daniel Deronda* and in the subplot Lewes in *Ranthorpe* devotes to Florence and Sir Frederick Hawbucke. Alienation between husband and wife as a subject for extended and intricate analysis was still uncommon to English prose fiction in the eighteen-seventies (though by then such works as Browning's *Andrea del Sarto* [1855] and especially Meredith's *Modern Love* [1862] had rung subtle changes on the theme in poetry). In the eighteen-forties when Lewes wrote *Ranthorpe* the theme was —dealt with at least in comparable terms of psychological theorizing—all but unprecedented in the English novel. Both the Gwendolen-Grandcourt part of *Daniel Deronda* and the Florence-Hawbucke plot of *Ranthorpe* are grounded on a courtship and marriage of

antithetical types. Both present an excessively volatile
and selfish heroine who habitually acts roles to accen-
tuate her high-spirited archness and unusual beauty.
In both, the suitor who becomes the husband is a man
whose eccentric patterns of behavior stem from a paradox of his nature. Grandcourt as well as Hawbucke
faces society with an appearance of phlegmatic boredom, while beneath his show of extreme indifference
each entertains a morbid concern for the world's opinion. It was "perhaps not possible for a breathing man
wide awake to look less animated," George Eliot says
of Grandcourt.[32] His posture, contrary to the forms of
polite bearing, "had no rigidity, it inclined rather to
the flaccid," and he spoke "with a certain broken
drawl, as of a distinguished personage with a distinguished cold on his chest" (79-80). "I can't imagine a
more consummate representation of the most detest-
able kind of Englishman—the Englishman who thinks
it low to articulate," Constantius remarks in Henry
James's charming three-voiced critique of *Daniel Deronda*.[33] "And in Grandcourt the type and the individual are so happily met: the type with its sense of the
proprieties, and the individual with his absence of all
sense. He is the apotheosis of dryness . . . ." Yet for all
his outward show of dryness, Grandcourt is excessively conscious of his audience, a trait he shares with
Gwendolen herself. Though he "went about with the
sense that he did not care a languid curse for any one's
admiration," Eliot tells us, he was in need at all times
of "a world of admiring or envying spectators." For if
you "are fond of looking stonily at smiling persons, the
persons must be there and they must smile" (440).

    Lewes's Sir Frederick Hawbucke is by no means so
intricate or so accomplished a study. Though Lewes is
at some pains to trace the paradox of his hero's nature,

Hawbucke remains largely the outline of a curious pattern in human motivation rather than anything approaching the splendidly individualized portrait of masked brutality that Eliot was to effect. "Sir Frederick Hawbucke was a type of the English gentleman," Lewes tells us. Huge, handsome, and powerful, a fearless horseman and a "dead shot" (Grandcourt had hunted tigers), there was yet "nothing in his manner which in the slightest degree indicated either the roughness of the sportsman, or the pride of physical superiority." In society he was "the quietest and dullest of human beings." But though he appeared wholly impervious to the concerns or good will of others, he was, seen beneath the "same mask of indifference," a person "morbidly alive to the opinion of the world upon the slightest matter connected with himself" (240). Grandcourt was to be, as James's Constantius remarks, "a consummate picture of English brutality refined and distilled." The refined sadism of Grandcourt's nature has a rough parallel in Hawbucke's later scenes with Florence, but it is overt violence that has mainly characterized his moments of brutality when he has in the past broken from his habitual phlegmatism. "There were fearful stories told of him at Eton—of terrible reprisals taken on those who had offended him." He was brave as a lion and equally ferocious, but his "nature was excessively English." He more nearly resembled the English bulldog with its sluggish conduct in ordinary concealing the terrible implacability of its disposition when roused.

Both Grandcourt and Hawbucke, to repeat, are paired with heroines who are markedly unlike them. James's Constantius remarks that Gwendolen Harleth (who is in due course to become Gwendolen Grandcourt) is "perhaps at first a little childish for the weight

of interest she has to carry," but Theodora takes issue
with Constantius: "Gwendolen is a perfect picture of
youthfulness—its eagerness, its presumption, its preoccupation with itself, its vanity and silliness, its sense
of its own absoluteness." Eliot has aptly entitled the
first book of her novel "The Spoiled Child." It is, however, a particular type of spoiled child that we gradually have revealed to us—a ruthless young lady with
an "inborn energy of egoistic desire" and a "power of
inspiring fear as to what she might say or do" in those
near to her (28). She "meant to do what was pleasant
to herself in a striking manner; or rather, whatever she
could do so as to strike others with admiration and get
in that reflected way a more ardent sense of living . . ."
(26). This habit of intensifying her own charm and
presence for herself by displaying her beauty in various roles before an audience becomes an important
feature of her experience. In the opening scene of the
novel she is portrayed quite consciously assuming a
part for an audience even as she explores the excite-
ments of a continental roulette table. She "had visions
of being followed by a *cortège* who would worship
her as a goddess of luck and watch her play as a directing augury." When her luck changes, she shifts roles
but is unwilling to lose her audience. "Since she was
not winning strikingly, the next best thing was to lose
strikingly. She controlled her muscles, and showed no
tremor of mouth or hands" (4). Gwendolen's passion
for such acting is strongly to color intervening scenes,
and Eliot is to sound it once more as a sinister motif in
the moment of Gwendolen's marriage to Grandcourt
—"as she felt herself standing at the game of life with
many eyes upon her, daring everything to win much
—or if to lose, still with *éclat* and a sense of importance" (264).

The relation of Lewes's Florence to Eliot's Gwendolen seems, like that of Hawbucke to Grandcourt, the
relation of a relatively crude outline for a type of personality to a profoundly individualized characteriza-
tion in which, as James's Constantius observes of
Grandcourt, type and individual are superbly joined.
As a "gay, careless, witty" coquette, Florence up to the
time of her marriage has also been in the habit of acting identities not basically her own, but without the
compulsive intensity Gwendolen was so often to bring
to her performances. Both Lewes's heroine and Eliot's
find a false reassurance in the contrast between their
prospective husband's manner and their own. Even as
Sir Frederick is "the least *demonstrative* creature" she
has ever met, Florence writes a friend, so she herself
is "the most demonstrative creature ever born; so that
the antithesis is perfect" (246). Frederick has pursued
her with silent unanimated deference, and she had
come to look upon him "as a sort of tame cat," a persistent but subordinate element in her own brilliant atmosphere. The first weeks of marriage were not to destroy her illusion of his docility. She seemed to have
at her own command "one of the handsomest men, and
one of the prettiest properties in England" (239). As
with Gwendolen, Rosamond, and Lady Wilmington
(who is, in point of fact, Florence's mother), the extreme degree of her characteristic absorption with her
own self precluded love at any depth: ". . . she could
hardly be said to love him, in any earnest sense of the
word" (239) but she admired her husband and congratulated herself. It is only after the two have settled
on Hawbucke's country estate that her new life begins
to pall. She "could not be lively alone; she needed
company," so that she seeks relief from Hawbucke's
dull undemonstrativeness by confiding her ennui in a

letter to her friend Caroline. All her life, she says, she
has been "a spoiled child . . . accustomed to amusement." She must now call on all her resources to keep
from Frederick her state of boredom in their marriage.
She entertains "a *great respect*" for him but "*no sympathy*" with him. "I have often been accused of being
a consummate actress," she continues; "people don't
know the value of that art; I do. *If I were not an actress Frederick would be miserable! If I could not deceive him into the idea that his society is pleasant to
me—is sufficient for me—*" . . . (250).

Florence's letter breaks off abruptly because Sir
Frederick has entered the room. Her embarrassed replies arouse him from his habitual phlegmatism. "He
was a morbidly jealous man," and he is rapidly convinced that Florence is trying to conceal the fact that
she has been writing to a secret lover. Hawbucke demands to read her letter and bears down all her opposition. He has without warning become for her a
stranger and an enigma. Where was "his deep and tender love? where was his quiet idolatry? was that also a
mockery? was he as cold as he seemed?" (254). As so
often elsewhere in *Ranthorpe*, Lewes combines sensational scenes, bordering on or altogether falling into
melodrama, with attempts at realistic analysis of patterns of motive that underlie the action—often patterns
contrary to the reader's casual assumptions. Lewes's
prosaic discussion of Sir Frederick's thoughts once he
has finished his wife's letter makes strange reading following as it does the theatricality of her exit speech.
"It would be difficult to render in words," Lewes tells
us, the state of Sir Frederick's emotions as he laid down
the sheet. Florence was "hopelessly mistaken in her estimate of his character." The idea that such a man
could feel any great depth of love "could only have en-

tered the head of the capricious, wilful, and exaggerated Florence, who, because she knew that her own nature was demonstrative, but not deep, was led to believe that his nature was deep, but not demonstrative!" (255-56). And Lewes continues with a generalization on jealousy: "It is mostly pride that feels jealousy, seldom love. A lover may be jealous, but it is almost always his pride that suffers. . . . When I say, therefore, that Sir Frederick suffered the tortures of jealousy, I do not imply that his love for Florence was more vehement than before stated, but simply that his sensitive pride suffered from a *prospective* jealousy. It was evident that she did not love him. Her love was acting." George Eliot was to make a basically similar observation regarding the origins of jealousy in pride in *Middlemarch*. Sir James Chettam, she tells us, recovered from Dorothea's preference for Casaubon's suit rather than his own with comparative ease because his pride could not be seriously hurt in her making such a fantastic choice. "He had no sense of being eclipsed by Mr. Casaubon" (49), so that there was no occasion for deep jealousy.

Eliot's Gwendolen Grandcourt was, like Lewes's Florence Hawbucke, to receive painful lessons in her husband's real nature. During the months of Grandcourt's remarkably undemonstrative courtship she had felt a growing sense of command over "this silent man seated at an agreeable distance with . . . an attention bent wholly on her" (222). Before long "She was thinking of him, whatever he might be, as a man over whom she was going to have indefinite power; and her loving him having never been a question with her, any agreeableness he had was so much gain" (233). Gradually she began to act with him a little play in which she assumed the role of imperious royalty. Grand-

court, for reasons of his own, willingly assumed the
role of servitor acquiescent to her commands. "The
scene was pleasant on both sides," Eliot observes. "A
cruder lover would have lost the view of her pretty
ways and attitudes, and spoiled all by stupid attempts
at caresses, utterly destructive of drama. Grandcourt
preferred the drama; and Gwendolen, left at ease,
found her spirits rising continually as she played at
reigning. Perhaps if Klesmer [who had assessed her
talents unfavorably] had seen more of her in this unconscious kind of acting, instead of when she was trying to be theatrical, he might have rated her chance
higher" (234).

Behind Grandcourt's amused compliance in his role
as servitor in their little drama lies his sinister aware-
ness that Gwendolen is compelled not by love but by
her poverty to perform her own part. "From the very
first there had been an exasperating fascination in the
tricksiness with which she had—not met his advances,
but—wheeled away from them. She had been brought
to accept him in spite of everything—brought to kneel
down like a horse under training for the arena, though
she might have an objection to it all the while" (237).
With their marriage, Gwendolen's "swift travel from
her bright rash girlhood into [an] agony of remorse"
(522) abruptly accelerates. Her illusion of the power
of her animated nature to dominate Grandcourt's sluggish nature is rapidly dispelled. "Already, in seven
short weeks, which seemed half her life, her husband
had gained a mastery which she could no more resist
than she could have resisted the benumbing effect
from the touch of a torpedo [or electric eel]. Gwendolen's will had seemed imperious in its small girlish
sway; but it was the will of a creature with a large dis-
course of imaginative fears; a shadow would have been

enough to relax its hold. And she had found a will like that of a crab or a boa-constrictor which goes on pinching or crushing without alarm at thunder" (317). Grandcourt had become a "blank uncertainty to her in everything but this, that he would do just what he willed, and that she had neither devices at her command to determine his will, nor any rational means of escaping it" (319).

Lewes's husband is less deliberately cruel but hardly less absolute in his crushing of his wife's volatile spirit. Weeping and hysterics, pleas for reconciliation, fail to melt him. Like the Grandcourts, the Hawbuckes act out for society "the appearances of affection" despite the gulf that separates them in private. "No one imagined but that they were the most enviable couple in England" (259). Whereas jealousy scarcely enters into Grandcourt's tyranny over Gwendolen, jealousy colors nearly all of Hawbucke's ensuing conduct. He has convinced himself that his wife, contrary to all her protestations, has taken a lover. His morbid obsession with maintaining his honor in the world's eyes becomes a monomania. It is specifically with the world's eyes Hawbucke is preoccupied—with society's notion of honor, according to which the husband may have as many mistresses as he chooses without in any appreciable degree staining his name, whereas a wife's slightest aberration will destroy her husband's reputation. "His life, he foresaw, would be a combat; but he savagely exulted in the idea, that at any rate he should not be a dupe" (257). Hawbucke's suspicions were altogether unjustified, as Lewes explains in one of his many running analyses of the motives of his characters. Florence "was indeed the last woman in the world to be afraid of, at that period. Her belief in man's affection was destroyed. She had renounced the idea of

love, and she had no inclination to bring disrespect upon herself by flirting" (260). The story veers farther
into melodramatic incident interspersed with analyses
of motivation—often motivation contrary to what seems
the obvious cause behind the action. Having settled
upon a young Frenchman as the specific threat to his
honor, Hawbucke carefully contrives a quarrel that
will seem to rise from his own feigned attempt to steal
the Frenchman's mistress, and rejoices in killing the
man (he is "in truth, supremely, savagely happy") in
the ensuing duel (267). Under Hawbucke's coldly
deliberate brutality, Florence's life becomes a desperate affair. "If you flirt, I shoot your cavalier," he assures
her without raising his voice; "if you compromise my
name, I shoot you." To her friends she pleads ill health,
"and she looked ill enough to make it plausible" (270).

The perils of acting parts counter to one's true identity, a theme that enters profoundly into the texture of
the Gwendolen-Grandcourt plot of *Daniel Deronda*
and figures importantly not only in Florence's early
conduct but in Hawbucke's complete and largely un-
warranted disbelief in her candor during their running
drama of incommunicability, receives further and more
specific treatment in the final episode of the story.
Eliot's Gwendolen in her distress was to seek out Deronda as an advisor of grave counsel suitable to her
own altered perspective. In what reads strangely like a
burlesque version of that relationship (though I am
not at all suggesting arcane significances in the fact),
Florence in her time of extreme trouble looks to (and
falls in love with) a man who professes to view the
human condition in the gravest of lights. Lewes explains that Hawbucke could not suspect this particular
confidant of his wife as a serious threat to his honor:
"What made him blind to Florence's love was the ab-

surdly mistaken notice he had formed of her. He thought her frivolous, and that, *therefore*, she would only love a frivolous man: strange error! . . . This, which at no time would have been true, was singularly false under present circumstances. Florence was wretched, and needed sympathy, not liveliness" (318-19). Florence's new confidant was Bourne, an inept writer of plays. "Bourne was naturally of a bilious temperament; and continued ill-success, acting upon an idolatry of Byron, had fostered in him a very respectable amount of misanthropy. He was intensely vain; and was incessantly endeavouring to assume some imposing attitude before the world." With Bourne, Florence can experience relief by exploring her own unhappiness in larger terms as a part of the general melancholy of man's lot. "They spoke vaguely of woes which had, in both their cases, embittered an ardent youth—of deceptions which had blighted a believing heart. They were eloquent in scorn of the pretended force of love." Whereas Florence believes in what she utters, however, Bourne is merely attitudinizing. "In this Florence was serious, Bourne acting. Strange that this actress should in turn become a dupe!" (320). Bourne, who has seldom found a willing listener, is delighted with her credulity and begins to entertain hopes of winning not only her attention but her love. He "made up a history of his life, smacking greatly of the circulating library, but avidly listened to and believed by Florence."

Florence thus becomes not only the dupe of Bourne's acting but the dupe of a version of reality modeled on sentimental literature. In a paragraph that depends on Lewes's familiarity in 1847 with patterns of attitude, temperament, and conduct that were later to figure with importance in *Middlemarch* and in *Daniel*

Deronda, Lewes explains somewhat magisterially why this was so. Like Gwendolen, who took for an actuality of Grandcourt's nature his role of amused docility in their little drama during courtship, Florence lacked emotional depth of a sort that could distinguish between genuine and merely acted, superficially simulated, versions of truth: "Florence, as I have more than once intimated, was not possessed of much heart. She had more sensibility than depth of feeling. Her nervous temperament and her education together had made her somewhat romantic—that is to say, avid of emotions; but hers was not a loving nature. She loved with her head more than with her heart. And it was owing precisely to this distinction that she was led away by the vulgar acting of Bourne" (320). And like Lydgate, who had been trained in scientific verities but could not read the reality beneath Rosamond's acting, Florence was unable to distinguish between genuine feeling and sentimental cliché: "Her imagination was inflamed. She seemed in his history to have read the narrative of a life which she was made to render glorious and happy. Bourne was the loving, sensitive, suffering heart, she had been seeking all her life."

Bourne soon avows his love, and with "the terrible figure of her husband" vivid in her mind and the idea of escape stronger than her qualms and fears, Florence flees to her lover's apartment. Her awakening into an untheatrical world of fact is abrupt and painful. Her lover and hero (in one of Lewes's happier juxtapositions of realism and melodramatic incident) is in his bedroom slippers cooking his breakfast eggs and preparing his toast, chuckling meanwhile "over the success of his acting, and framing plans of future delight." In the scene between them Bourne is soon exposed as a timid soul who would not risk taking Florence as his mistress in prosaic actuality on any terms whatever. "She knew herself to have been his dupe. He had only acted love!" (326).

An ironical turn in Hawbucke's stratagems to preserve his honor in the eyes of society releases Florence from her bondage. We see her last as she adjusts her thinking to the prospect of freedom, a prospect which fails, though readers of popular novels might expect otherwise, to give her sudden joy. "Her terrors once banished, her grief returned. But it was a silent grief —a stupor, not a passion."

W. J. Harvey expresses his doubt whether the former "author of *Ranthorpe*" could teach George Eliot "a great deal about her art."[34] Unless we give the meaning of *art* a wide latitude, his doubt is unquestionably warranted, and further familiarity with Lewes's novel serves to emphasize both the superb quality of Eliot's narrative gifts and Lewes's own good sense in shifting his impressive talents into more congenial channels— to achieve no inconsiderable fame in criticism, philosophy, biography, and science. Whether George Eliot ever read *Ranthorpe* and, if so, what she thought of it are extremely interesting questions without much likelihood of receiving a definitive answer. There is no mention by her of either of Lewes's novels in her collected letters. On the whole, however, it seems more reasonable to suppose than not to suppose that in shaping her thoughts to the writing of fiction in the fall of 1856, with Lewes very much in her mind as her counselor and her prospective first audience, Marian Evans would make it a point to read or (more likely) to re-read what narrative works he himself had written. Though Lewes was by then directing his main attention to marine biology, he had within the year figured once more as a published writer of fiction. His extended tale *Metamorphoses* for *Blackwood's Magazine* had in July brought an important fifty pounds into their income.[35] In 1871 James Russell Lowell wrote Lewes of having encountered *Ranthorpe* at a bookseller's in the year of its publication. He had been impressed with the anonymous author's display of familiarity with the writings of Goethe and had bought the book and still had it in his possession.[36] If Eliot (as seems on the whole quite unlikely) had never read *Ranthorpe* earlier, she might conceivably have done so now, her curiosity roused by Lowell's letter. But this is all, of course, mere speculation, and on a question of much interest but no great importance. What seems plain, and of larger import, is that as early as 1847 Lewes was exploring, as a pioneer in English realism in general and psychological realism in particular, themes and patterns of human behavior that George Eliot was to employ with immeasurably greater art but often with curious similarity of outline in her masterpiece *Middlemarch* and thereafter in *Daniel Deronda* during years when her shared intellectual life with Lewes was especially close. The similarities between *Ranthorpe* and the Rosamond-Lydgate part of *Middlemarch* and the Gwendolen-Grandcourt part of *Daniel Deronda* seem to go well beyond the possibilities of simple coincidence. They concern what are generally considered among the most strikingly original characters and situations in Eliot's novels. Lewes had earlier served as a by-no-means negligible influence in the creative thinking of Charlotte Brontë. If George Eliot could consult with Lewes over the "psychological problems" of *Felix Holt* in June 1865 as she shaped her plans for the novel—on one occasion apparently for two hours at a sitting—and look to him for confirmation of her

"choice of incidents" as she progressed with her manuscript in ensuing months,[37] it seems likely that she
looked to him for more than simple encouragement as
she worked with the complex psychological problems
of *Middlemarch* and *Daniel Deronda*. The evidence of
Ranthorpe suggests that Lewes's contribution to George
Eliot's creative life took more forms and was of greater
meaning than has often been allowed. It seems probable that this remarkable pair, the psychologist and the
novelist—"two of the most intelligent people of their
time," as one critic remarks in passing[38]—had much to
say to each other.

NOTES

1. Ellmann, "Dorothea's Husbands: Some Biographical
Speculations," *The Times Literary Supplement*, 16 February
1973, pp. 165-168. The essay has since been incorporated as a
chapter into Ellmann's *Golden Codgers: Biographical Speculations* (Oxford, 1973). Ellmann believes Eliot's impressions of
young John Cross also enter into Will Ladislaw. As early as 1883,
Matthilde Blind observed Will's debt to Lewes. A recent critic
to present Lewes's claims as the original for Will is Ian Milner,
The Structure of Values in George Eliot (Prague, 1968), pp. 82
ff. See also Edgar W. Hirshberg, "George Eliot and Her Husband," *English Journal*, LVI (1967), 816-817.

2. "No man, it is likely, will ever again find it possible to
be a . . . journalist, novelist, critic, biographer, and essayist, and
at the same time to write like a specialist upon chemistry, biology, language, sociology, physiology, and philosophy. In all
these fields Lewes did brilliant, if not always sterling work"
(Fred N. Scott, Introduction to Lewes's *Principles of Success in
Literature* [Boston, 1894], pp. 10-11). See also R. L. Brett,
"George Henry Lewes: Dramatist, Novelist and Critic," *Essays
and Studies*, XI (1958), pp. 101 ff.

3. Michael St. John Packe, *The Life of John Stuart Mill*
(New York, 1954), pp. 120 ff., 135-136. Lewes describes his pursuit of psychological studies since their beginning in 1836 in his
preface to *Problems of Life and Mind*, First Series (London,
1874), I, v ff.

4. Edgar W. Hirshberg, *George Henry Lewes* (New York, 1970), pp. 22-23, 123.

5. W. B. Scott, *Autobiographical Notes* (New York, 1892), I, 130.

6. Anna T. Kitchel, *George Lewes and George Eliot* (New York, 1933), p. 27. Thackeray's sketch appears opposite page 132 in Gordon S. Haight, *George Eliot: A Biography* (New York, 1968).

7. Linton, *My Literary Life* (London, 1899), pp. 19, 25-26.

8. Lewes's record of his literary receipts is reproduced in *The George Eliot Letters*, ed. Gordon S. Haight (New Haven, 1955), VII, 365 ff., a rich storehouse of Lewes's letters as well. Lewes's letter to William Blackwood (17 July 1878) occurs at VII, 43. Lewes did not object to Blackwood's reprinting the stories anonymously.

9. Reviews referred to in this paragraph occur successively in: *The Literary Gazette and Journal of the Belles Lettres*, LXI (1847), 368; *The Examiner* (8 May 1847), pp. 291-292; *The Spectator*, XX (1947), 520-521; *The British Quarterly Review*, VII (1848), 332-339.

10. John H. Ingram, *Edgar Allan Poe: His Life, Letters, and Opinions* (London, 1891), p. 402.

11. *The Brontës: Life and Letters*, ed. Clement Shorter (1908: New York, 1969), I, 368 (22 November 1847).

12. Alice R. Kaminsky, *George Henry Lewes as Literary Critic* (Syracuse, N.Y., 1968), p. 185.

13. Elizabeth Cleghorn Gaskell, *The Life of Charlotte Brontë* (London, 1908), p. 233.

14. *The Brontës*, I, 365-366 (6 November 1847).

15. Charlotte writes Lewes on 12 January 1848 following her reading of his critique in *Fraser's*: "I am glad that another work of yours will soon appear; most curious shall I be to see whether you will write up to your own principles, and work out your own theories. You did not do it altogether in *Ranthorpe*—at least, not in the latter part; but the first portion was, I think, nearly without fault; then it had a pith, truth, significance in it which gave the book sterling value . . ." (*The Brontës*, I, 387). *Rose, Blanche, and Violet* (1848), Lewes's only other completed novel, does by and large follow his theories more consistently, though its subject matter tends to be less highly original and his psychological theorizing less a prominent feature of the work.

16. Lewes, "Recent Novels: French and English," *Fraser's Magazine*, XXXVI (1847), 686-695.

17. *The Brontës*, I, 386-387 (12 January 1848).

18. Gary, "Charlotte Brontë and George Henry Lewes,"

PMLA, LI (1936), 518-542. "The full force of Lewes's criticisms was not felt by Charlotte Brontë, I believe, until she wrote her fourth and last novel, *Villette*, surely her masterpiece. . . . How much Charlotte Brontë would have developed in this same direction in the natural maturing of her powers . . . it is of course impossible to say. But it has seemed to me, going through her letters and novels, that the criticism which she received from him . . . made her artistically more self-conscious, in a way that no other criticism did" (pp. 539-540).

19.   The question of how much and in what directions Lewes influenced George Eliot has understandably been much discussed ever since her novels began to appear. George W. Smalley, London correspondent for the *New York Tribune*, generalizing on the relationship at the time of her death in 1880, spoke of Eliot's often declaring that her "obligations on the intellectual side to Lewes were very great." The impression of others was, however, that Lewes's influence had been actually limited to the kind "a merely clever and studious man of eager and strenuous temperament sometimes exercises on a very sensitive nature." As their joint life continued, Lewes had been increasingly harmful to her. Under his growing influence she had abandoned the early charm of such novels as *The Mill on the Floss* to effect such overerudite productions as *Middlemarch* and *Daniel Deronda*. "She was aware of the change, and took pride in it, and thought her work had gained by it in quality and value. Not a few of her friends and admirers thought it had deteriorated; and that as Lewes's influence became more powerful the change in her method of writing became more pronounced and the deterioration more evident" (*London Letters* [New York, 1891], I, 242-243). Edith Simcox, an intimate friend of George Eliot, writing the year following her death, stressed the great value of Lewes's habitual encouragement of Eliot rather than any special direction it had taken: ". . . we owe to Mr. Lewes the complete works of George Eliot, not one of which would have been written or even planned without the inspiriting influence of his constant encouragement" ("George Eliot," *Nineteenth Century*, IX [May 1881], 773).

Anna T. Kitchel's *George Lewes and George Eliot* (1933) remains a valuable overall view of the relationship as seen in their letters and journals. Kitchel implies that the influence of Lewes was pervasive in the novels, but a day-to-day record of their life together rather than the tracing of any special theme such as the particular direction Lewes's influence took is Kitchel's overriding concern. In the same year, P. Bourl'honne (*George Eliot: essai de biographie intellectuelle et morale 1819-1854* [Paris, 1933], pp. 156 ff.) revived the old accusation that

Lewes had gradually effected Eliot's decline into erudition and was to be held responsible for her later novels' inferiority. In 1955 Alice R. Kaminsky ("George Eliot, George Henry Lewes, and the Novel," *PMLA*, LXX [1955], 997-1013) argued strongly for Lewes's great influence as an exponent of realism upon George Eliot's theory and practice, especially in *Middlemarch*. Gordon S. Haight in "George Eliot's Theory of Fiction" (*VNL*, Autumn, 1956, pp. 1-3) took exception to much of Kaminsky's argument, holding that Lewes had functioned chiefly as agent, guardian, and encouraging audience for a mind of incomparably greater creative powers than his own. Haight's view in his *George Eliot: A Biography* (1968) seems unaltered. W. J. Harvey in *The Art of George Eliot* (1961; London, 1963), pp. 33 ff., assumes that Lewes's influence did not enter significantly into Eliot's artistry. As writer of the George Eliot chapter for *Victorian Fiction: A Guide to Research*, ed. Lionel Stevenson (Cambridge, Mass., 1964), Harvey considers the question of the "particular influence" of Lewes on Eliot a "major issue" (p. 305) but believes that Lewes's importance as a decisive critical influence continues unproved.

In his "Formative Influences on George Eliot, with Special Reference to George Henry Lewes" (Diss. University of Toronto, 1963), Roland Frank Anderson carefully considers aspects of the relationship and concludes that Eliot first rapidly assimilated Lewes's critical theories in regard to fiction and then refined upon them in essays she had written even by the time of her entering on her career as a novelist: "Lewes' ideas started her thinking, and her superior abilities enabled her to develop their implications beyond his intellectual range to the point where she could see how to use her philosophy and experience in shaping the material of life into realistic fiction that would contribute to the improvement of mankind. Lewes' great achievement was to provide through sympathetic understanding just the right emotional and intellectual climate, and the most appropriate guidance in terms of her ideas and experience to bring about the release of her inhibited genius" (p. 266). Hirshberg's view in both his "George Eliot and Her Husband" in 1967 and in his *George Henry Lewes* in 1970 seems basically that of Haight, though Hirshberg provides in his article several interesting examples of Eliot's following suggestions of Lewes's or reflecting his fields of interest in her novels. Hirshberg sees Lewes's influence, such as it was, decreasing rather than growing in her last three novels. Kaminsky in her *George Henry Lewes as Literary Critic* forcefully and more clearly restates in 1968 her contention that the influence of Lewes *as critic* was of great importance for Eliot. The particular direction of Lewes's influence is likely to remain what Harvey considered it in 1964 —a "major issue" on which authorities disagree. The evidence of *Ranthorpe*, I suggest in what follows, is that Lewes did indeed enter significantly into Eliot's creative thinking in ways that have not heretofore been given much attention.

20. *George Eliot Letters*, II, 98 (16 April 1853).

21. Ibid., II, 406-408.

22. Kitchel, p. 172.

23. *George Eliot Letters*, IV, 221-222 (22 January 1866). The quotation that follows this within the same paragraph occurs at V, 109 (3 January 1875).

24. Quotations from *George Eliot Letters* in this paragraph occur successively at V, 214-215 (19 November 1871), VI, 244-245 (2 May 1876), II, 363-364 (12 July 1857), and IV, 465 (July 1868).

25. Eliot's "History of *Adam Bede*" as recorded in her Journal and included in *George Eliot Letters*, II, 504. For Savonarola, see Lewes's journal entry in ibid., III, 295.

26. Barbara Smalley, *George Eliot and Flaubert: Pioneers of the Modern Novel* (Athens, Ohio, 1974).

27. *George Eliot Letters*, V, 48 (11 July 1869). The correspondent is Harriet Beecher Stowe, and the Professor, as Gordon S. Haight informs us in a note, is her husband, who from early childhood "saw phantoms and spirits of various kinds." Additional quotations from the *Letters* in this paragraph occur at V, 16, V, 135, and V, 185. Jerome Beaty analyzes Eliot's progress with her novel in *"Middlemarch" from Notebook to Novel* (Urbana, Ill., 1960); see p. 39. On 19 February 1869 Eliot had written John Blackwood: "I mean to begin my novel at once, having already sketched the plan. But between the beginning and the middle of a book I am like the lazy Scheldt; between the middle and end I am like the arrowy Rhone—unless . . . the difference is that between a languid gutter and a lively one. The various elements of the story [the Vincy-Lydgate part of *Middlemarch*] have been soliciting my mind for years—asking for a complete embodiment" (V, 16).

28. *George Eliot Letters*, V, 326. Additional quotations from the *Letters* in this paragraph occur successively at V, 119; V, 150; V, 179 (the title, as Haight adds in a note, was later changed from "Dorothea Married" to "Waiting for Death"). For mention of their walks in the countryside, see Haight, *George Eliot: A Biography*, p. 435; and for Eliot's reading aloud from her manuscript to Lewes, pp. 431-432. Lewes's "The Novels of Jane Austen" appeared in *Blackwood's Magazine*, LXXXVI (1859), 99-113.

29. *Middlemarch*, edited with an Introduction and Notes

by Gordon S. Haight (Boston, 1956), p. 87. Further quotations will be identified by the page number of this edition supplied in parentheses in the text. *Ranthorpe*, p. 340. Page numbers will be supplied hereafter in parentheses in the text.

30. T. S. Eliot, *Three Voices of Poetry* (New York, 1954), p. 18.

31. U. C. Knoepflmacher, *Religious Humanism and the Victorian Novel: George Eliot, Walter Pater, and Samuel Butler* (Princeton, N. J., 1965), p. 124.

32. *Daniel Deronda,* with an Introduction by F. R. Leavis (New York, 1960), pp. 79-80. Page numbers of this edition will be supplied hereafter in parentheses in the text.

33. James, *"Daniel Deronda*: A Conversation," *Atlantic Monthly*, XXXVIII (1876), 684-694. Five years later in *The Portrait of a Lady* (1881) James was to endow his own Gilbert Osmond with a similar though less phlegmatic affectation of indifference to the opinion of society, behind which there lived an excessive preoccupation with the impression he was producing. He had a watchful "eye to effect, and his effects were deeply calculated." See Barbara Smalley, *George Eliot and Flaubert*, pp. 215 ff.

34. Harvey, *The Art of George Eliot,* p. 36.

35. "GHL's Literary Receipts," *George Eliot Letters*, VII, 374.

36. Haight, *George Eliot: A Biography,* p. 411.

37. Ibid., p. 382.

38. R. C. Churchill, "Charles Dickens," in *From Dickens to Hardy (Pelican Guide to English Literature*, 1958), p. 121.

ACKNOWLEDGMENTS

I wish to thank the Library of the University of Illinois, Urbana, for permission to reproduce the text of its copy of the first edition of *Ranthorpe*, and for a number of additional favors from its staff during the course of preparing this book. Grateful acknowledgment is due also to my husband, Donald Smalley, whose ready help and wise advice have been of inestimable value to me at all stages of my labors.

TEXT

Ranthorpe is reproduced here without change from the first edition. Printer's errors in the 351 pages are nearly nonexistent. Lewes or the printer employs *lead* for *led* on pages 89, 151, and 277, and Lewes typically spells *recall* without a second *l* (as, for example, on page 289) and *alleged* with a *d* preceding the *g* (as on page 331). The use of *headach* on page 221 is probably an error, but the only two instances of spellings that are unquestionably out-and-out mistakes that I have found in the entire text occur on page 315—the initial *o* and the *s* reversed in *bosom* and the *f* failing to show in *foliage*.

RANTHORPE.

J'avais entrepris une lutte insensée ; je combattais la misère avec ma plume.

H. DE BALZAC.

Wie verfährt die Natur, um Hohes und Niedres im Menschen
Zu verbinden ?   Sie stellt Eitelkeit zwischen hinein !

GÖTHE.

LONDON:

CHAPMAN AND HALL, 186, STRAND,

MDCCCXLVII.

C. WHITING, BEAUFORT HOUSE, STRAND.

TO HER

WHO HAS LIGHTENED THE BURDEN OF AN ANXIOUS LIFE,

THIS WORK IS INSCRIBED BY

HER HUSBAND.

PREFACE.

RANTHORPE was written five years ago.

No one will doubt that it has in many respects profited by the delay in publication; yet it has not escaped the evil of that tendency,

> To add and alter many times,
> Till all be ripe and rotten,

of which the most fastidious of contemporary poets complains; and which made Schiller question the advantage of Horace's celebrated *nonum prematur in annum.* So that when I state that the one volume now presented to the public was originally three, the critic will easily understand how certain faults of construction, and sins against *l'art de conter*, arose from so great a change in the structure and proportions of the whole. Of these faults I became aware only when too late—when reading the proof sheets ; and all which now remains is to confess and apologise.

That the faults are not *more* numerous is owing to the
admirable criticisms of two eminent friends, who paid me
the compliment of being frankly severe on the work submitted to their judgment. Sensible of the kindness in
their severity, I have made them—what, for an author,
must be considered as a magnificent acknowledgement—
I have adopted all their suggestions !

London, April, 1847.

CONTENTS.

BOOK I.

THE POET'S FIRST STRUGGLES.

BOOK II.

THE LION.

BOOK III.

THE UNSUCCESSFUL AUTHOR.

BOOK IV.

STRUGGLES WITH CIRCUMSTANCE.

BOOK V.

ISOLA.

RANTHORPE.

BOOK I.

THE POET'S FIRST STRUGGLES.

> How like a younker, or a prodigal,
> The scarfed bark puts from her native bay!
> SHAKSPEARE.

> Mir glüht die ganze Seele bei dem Gedanken endlich einmal
> aufzutreten, und die Menschen in das Herz hinein zu reden,
> was sie sich so lange zu hören sehnen.—GÖTHE.

RANTHORPE.

CHAPTER I.

THE THREE STUDENTS.

By solemn vision and bright silver stream
His infancy was nurtured. Every sight
And sound from the vast earth and ambient air
Sent to his heart the choicest impulses.

SHELLEY.

IT was a cold November night. Holborn was noisy,
murky, and sloppy. A drizzling rain descended through
the haze: the chilling haze of a London winter night.
Streams of brilliant gas, reflected from gilded lamps and
pillars in those splendid mockeries named gin-palaces,
flashed at intervals through the darkness, calling attention
to the orgies there perpetrated: where brutal violence,
sodden depravity, low cunning, vice in all its hideousness,
and poverty in its desperate wretchedness, had assembled
to snatch a moment's delirium or a moment's oblivion of
the bitterness of existence. Omnibuses, cabs, waggons, and
trucks, rolled past with ceaseless rumbling din. There were

B 2

the brawls of miserable women reeling from public houses; and the scuffles with pickpockets emerging from Saffron Hill. The sloppy pavement clacked beneath the feet of the crowding passers-by.

Amidst this noisy, cheerless scene, standing at one of the numerous book-stalls, was a youth of nineteen, who, his hands and feet benumbed with cold, had been standing for half an hour, gloating with hungry eyes upon the treasures there displayed. He was enveloped in a camlet cloak, the scanty proportions of which just sufficed to hide the poverty of his garments, and to ward off the rain. He had no gloves, and his hands were purple from the cold. His hat betokened the fidelity of an ancient servitor; it was scrupulously brushed, and shone from repeated wettings. In a word, the youth looked like a clerk—and was one.

Those who looked a little closer, however, might have seen that there was something in this youth's face which belied his dress—an air of refinement and command—a look of the English gentleman, which is peculiar to our nation, and to one class in that nation. The mouth was very remarkable: it was voluptuous, and yet refined; full, yet delicate—the mouth of a poet. The eyes were of a deep blue; long and somewhat languishing, and shaded with the sweetest fringe imaginable. The forehead was delicately cut; the chin weak and faltering. A physiognomist would at once have pronounced him to be a remarkable person; but somewhat deficient in strength of will.

This youth was Percy Ranthorpe.

His eyes wandered over the titles of the volumes so temptingly displayed; but nothing came within reach of his finances. His was a Barmecide feast; he cared not for rare editions, large paper copies, or sumptuous bindings.

His hunger was for knowledge; he had a passion for books —no matter what editions, what bindings; he cared not even whether they had covers at all. He only thought of the price.

After enviously opening many a volume; with a secret consciousness that his looking at the price was all a magnificent juggle with himself, as he was certain not to be able to pay it, yet still pleased with even an imaginary purchase; he at last came to a tub filled with dirty ancient books. From this tub rose a stick, bearing a piece of cardboard, on which was written:

ALL THESE BOOKS 6*d.* THE VOL.

Here possibilities merged into actualities: he could purchase: to the length of sixpence he could indulge! Accordingly, he began to handle the volumes with a sterner and more business-like air. But he was long in making a choice.

While thus engaged, another young man stopped at the stall. Percy made room for him; but the new-comer only stopped to light a cigar at the jet of gas; and was about to move on, when he was accosted rather boisterously by a third.

"Hollo! Harry, is that you? Well, how are you, old brick?"

"How are you, Oliver? What have you been doing with yourself for the last century?"

"Oh! flaring up!"

"That of course. I was at the masquerade last night— so jolly drunk!" This Harry uttered with the complacency which young men often assume when speaking of their vices; and Percy looked up involuntarily, but soon continued his search, though unable to avoid hearing their conversation.

" Oliver, are you going to the Cider Cellars to-night?"

" Don't know. Short of *tin*. Spent a couple of sovereigns last night."

Two sovereigns in senseless dissipation, thought Percy,
and with two sovereigns how many books might he have
bought!

He again looked up, and this time scanned the friends
more closely. They were evidently two medical students;
and as they are to play important parts in this drama, I
may as well complete Percy's observations, and briefly
paint their portraits for the reader's benefit.

Harry Cavendish was a student of St. George's. In
his appearance there was something at once prepossessing and repulsive: a mixture of the gentleman and
the Mohock. His coal-black hair was trained into
one long curl on either side of his cheeks ; thick black
moustaches graced or disgraced his upper lip; his hat was
slightly cocked to look jaunty; he carried a formidable
stick; and smelt strongly of tobacco. Yet his dark eye was
full of fire and intelligence; his open laughing face was
indicative of malicious mirth and frankness; and the resolution about his brow, and sensibility about his mouth,
redeemed his slang appearance, and showed the superior
being, beneath the unprepossessing exterior.

Oliver Thornton belonged to the Middlesex Hospital.
He was heavy and clownish-looking; with a large, pale,
sensual, and rather placid countenance, the predominant
expression of which was sleepiness, strangely mixed with
cunning. It seemed as if his small twinkling eyes were
in perpetual struggle with the somnolent disposition of his
other features. It was a thoroughly disagreeable face.

The two students—"*arcades ambo*—blackguards both"
—walked on, and Percy felt quite relieved by their absence. Their whole tone was such as could not but be

displeasing to him; and he sighed to think of their money squandered and time lost, both of which, had he possessed them, would have made him the happiest of men!

He had his sixpence, however, and books were before him. An odd volume of Shelley's poems, somewhat tattered, turned up; and now his hesitation was dispelled at once. He marched with it into the shop, paid his money with feverish delight, and hurried homewards in triumph.

As he turned up King-street, his way was stopped by a crowd of people assembled round an athletic costermonger, who was beating his donkey in so brutal a manner that several persons were crying " Shame! shame!" The man only looked fiercely in the direction of these cries, and recommending the interferers, in language not the most polished, to mind their own affairs, continued to wrench the mouth of the animal, whom he almost stunned with a heavy stick. Percy was about to spring forward, when he saw Harry push his way through the crowd, followed by Oliver.

" What's the row?" said Harry; and on learning the state of matters, he went up to the costermonger and said, "Now then, Carrots, none of that. Is that the way you treat a servant and a brother? Have you no feelings—no fellow feelings?"

" I'll split your skull if you give me any of your chaff," retorted the costermonger, savagely.

" No, my friend," said Harry, coolly; " no; you'll excuse my contradicting you—but you won't."

" I won't!" roared the other.

" You must get up much earlier in the morning to do it, I pledge you my word. And now listen to this simple and familiar observation I have to make : if you don't cease maltreating that miserable animal, I shall first give you a drubbing to gratify my own feelings, and then pull you up before a magistrate to gratify Mr. Martin's feelings."

At the word " drubbing" his antagonist threw down his stick and hat, and putting himself into a posture of defence exclaimed, " Come on, come on ; I'll give it yer."

Oliver endeavoured to persuade Harry to decamp ; but Harry took off his gloves with extreme coolness, folded them up, put them in his pocket, and then, without heeding the remonstrances of his companion, quickly knocked the costermonger down. A yell of derision and delight burst from the crowd as they saw the brute in the mud. They had been a little anxious before ; but the coolness, science, and force Harry exhibited, soon quieted their fears; and the pleasure which all men feel in an exhibition of prowess was here heightened by the indignation excited by the costermonger's brutality.

Maddened by his fall and by the derision of the crowd, the ruffian started to his feet and rushed impetuously upon Harry, who, stepping a little aside, to avoid the shock, dealt him so heavy a blow that he reeled and fell sprawling in the mud. He got up again; but he was disheartened ; he felt that he had no chance against the skill, coolness, and strength of his antagonist. Instead of renewing the attack, he skulked away to his cart, put on his hat amidst the laughter and gibes of the crowd which was now large, and taking hold of the donkey's bridle, moved on in sullen silence.

Harry took out his gloves, put them on as if nothing

had happened, and looked round for Oliver, who had slunk off on the first appearance of a danger in which he might possibly be implicated. Several people congratulated Harry, and praised him for his generosity and prowess.

Percy felt as if he could have asked his pardon for the contempt which a little while ago he had felt for him. But the crowd had dispersed, and he was alone.

He continued his walk home, now ruminating on the scene which had greatly affected him, and now peeping into his volume of Shelley, which he hugged as only a poor poet could have hugged it. Under more than one lamp-post did he stop to catch a glimpse at the poems, gathering in those glimpses fresh impatience for the whole.

" What, *more* books !" reproachfully exclaimed his father, as he entered the room. " What he can do with them all, I can't think." This was said to a young girl who was at that moment preparing Percy's supper.

Percy was silent. He had been so long accustomed to the sneers and reproaches of his father on the point, that though he had not ceased to feel them, he had quite ceased defending himself.

" I suppose," continued Mr. Ranthorpe, " you have gone without dinner again to-day, to buy that trash."

" I dined frugally, and bought this book with the money saved."

" Well, if you like to starve yourself, for the sake of the books, that's your affair not mine," rejoined Mr. Ranthorpe. With this observation—his unfailing one— he let the matter drop. Percy exchanged a glance with the lovely girl before named, and in her approving, tender look, read a recompense.   If *she* thought well of what he did, he was satisfied.

And who was she ? asks the reader.   How came she there ?   If he has any sagacity he will at once divine that she is to play an important part in this drama.   She is indeed our heroine, and must have a chapter to herself.

CHAPTER II.

ISOLA.

S' ella ride ella piace ; s' ella parla la diletta ; s' ella tace ell' empie altrui d' ammirazione ; s' ella va ha grazia ; s' elle siede ha vaghezza ; s' ella canta ha dolcezza ; s' ella balla ha Venere in compagnia ; s' ella ragiona, le Muse le insegnano.

FIRENZUOLA: *Della Bellezza delle Donne.*

ISOLA CHURCHILL was an orphan. Her father had been Mr. Ranthorpe's partner and friend for many years, and when he died Mr. Ranthorpe took her to live with him, as a child.

She was exquisitely beautiful. But her beauty was of that chaste severity of style which only strikes connoisseurs. She had few of the charms which captivate drawing-room critics; was neither sylph-like nor sportive, neither sentimental nor voluptuous. Her cheeks were innocent both of roses and lilies. I am not aware of any cupids having taken up their abode in her dimples ; nor did I ever hear any thing of the "liquid languishment" of her eyes. In fact, she was a girl whom seven out of every ten would call "nice looking," or "well grown;" without a suspicion of the other three looking upon her as a masterpiece of nature's cunning hand.

Tall, finely, somewhat amply moulded, with a waist in

perfect proportion, her walk was the walk of a goddess; perhaps for that reason few thought it graceful.

From her mother—an Italian—she inherited a pale, olive complexion, large lustrous eyes, black hair, and a certain look of Raffaele's Sistine Madonna. From her father, the winning gentleness which softened her somewhat stern severity of outline, and converted the statue into a woman. Yet, on the whole, her beauty was more sculpturesque than picturesque.

Her voice was peculiar. Though musical and vibrating, it had that loudness common to Italians, but which in England, amongst a race accustomed to eat half their words, is regarded as ill-bred. But the clear, vibrating, powerful tone of Isola's voice, always seemed to me a witchery the more, and was not inaptly characteristic of her frank, large, and healthy soul. It gave some persons the impression of her not being feminine; and this impression was strengthened by the simplicity of a manner, free from all the permissible coquetry of woman. Yet Isola was exquisitely feminine in soul. She was woman in her gentleness, lovingness, singleness of purpose, and endurance ; only not in coquetry.

To those whose tastes had been kept pure, who could distinguish truth and love it, there was an indefinable charm in her manner. It would have been impossible for the most impertinent of men to have paid her common-place compliments : the quiet simplicity—the grandeur of her direct and truthful bearing—protected her.

If the reader run away with the idea that Isola was an *imposing* woman, he will be curiously misled. It is the fault of language that it cannot convey *manner*, so that the term " grandeur" applied to one so simple and truthful as Isola, may seem ill-applied; because it is forgotten that all grandeur is excessively simple.

Her character will be seen in this story. Her accomplishments were not inconsiderable, since music and painting were her birthright, and Dante was as much her childhood's companion as Shakspeare.

Percy and Isola, living under the same roof, very naturally fell in love. Ignorant of the world, but looking forward to the future, confident that it would bring them the consummation of their desires, they plighted their vows. Nor did Mr. Ranthorpe disapprove of it. This seemed to him the best way of securing Isola a protector should he be suddenly cut off; and he felt Percy would, above all men, need a good, economical, sensible woman for a wife, whenever he should be old enough and rich enough to think of one.

Mr. Ranthorpe had a very special contempt for poets, and never lost an opportunity of expressing it before his son. He himself had been all his life a speculator; and because he had pursued the chimera of making his fortune, he considered himself eminently a *practical* man. A life of unsuccess had failed to teach him. He had no faith in any thing that was not practical, that did not obviously lead to hard cash. His son's poetical tendencies were therefore regarded as alarming symptoms. The old man was, however, somewhat calmed when he saw Percy accept the miserable situation of a lawyer's clerk, and attend regularly enough to business, in spite of his devoting leisure hours to books and poetry.

If his father did not understand and sympathise with him, Isola did. She was the confidante of all his plans; sympathised in all his aspirations; shared all his hopes. She believed with him that the volume of " Poems of the

Affections" which he was preparing, would create for him
a rank in the world of letters, which to them would be
a fortune.

It is necessary that the reader should clearly understand
the position of our hero, which I have briefly indicated in
the foregoing pages.   It is necessary that he should see the
poverty and ambition, the obstacles and the courage, to understand the struggles which are about to ensue.   Few men
have been more unfavourably placed than this young lawyer's clerk; none have ever had a more stirring ambition.
He had but one friend—but one partner in his hopes.   The
rest of the world were all superbly indifferent to him and his
aspirations; except his father, who was indignant at them.

Few sights are more saddening than that of a young spirit
struggling in vain against overwhelming obstacles ; unheeded, unassisted, without friends, without position, and
without advisers.   But this sight, though sad to the casual
spectator, has another aspect to him who looks deeper.   Underneath those thwarted hopes, that wild ambition, there
breathes a free spirit of energetic action; and this activity is
a fountain of delight, as activity always is.   We who see
the struggling boy, and calmly measure the immensity of
the barriers which shut him from success, we may deem him
unhappy, because we foresee that he will be so.   But we do
not feel the rapture of his reveries—the delight in creation
— the transports of anticipated success — transports more
vividly felt at that period when criticism has not detected
weakness, when experience has not chilled flushed confidence with its cold misgivings.

The poet's desire is to " *get published:*" in that anticipa-
tion lies his delight.   He is the lover who is still enamoured,
because still unmarried.   He has the world lying before
him; and it is plastic to his hopes: he moulds it as he wills.

After publication (that marriage with the muse!) he can no longer dream: he must confront reality. The world, before so plastic, is now a rock whereon are wrecked his cherished fancies. The unpublished poet mistakes his aspiration for inspiration. He confounds the excitement awakened in him by great works, with the excitement awakened by self-developed ideas and self-experienced feelings, which imperiously demand utterance. He lives in the circle traced by his own delusions.

Perhaps there has been no author, whatever may have been his renown, who has looked back upon the early years of uncrowned endeavour without envying their freshness of spirit, virginity of soul, and boundlessness of hope. Of the two points in the adventure of a diver,

> One—when a beggar he prepares to plunge;
> One—when a prince he rises with the pearl.*

the first is the happier: the confidence of the beggar exceeds in rapture all the triumph of the prince. The pearl is beggary beside the boundless wealth of imagination.

Percy Ranthorpe was a beggar, and about to plunge!

* Paracelsus.

CHAPTER III.

EARLY STRUGGLES.

J'ai su, pauvre et content, savourer à longs traits
Les muses, les plaisirs, et l'étude, et la paix.
Une pauvreté libre est un tresor si doux !
Il est si doux, si beau, de s'être fait soi-même;
De devoir tout à soi, aux beaux arts qu'on aime.
ANDRÉ CHENIER.

THE " Poems of the Affections" were completed.   Having copied them out, Percy sent them to Mr. Wilson, the publisher, with a note requesting him to read them, and see if he had any objection to publish them ; Percy announced his intention of calling in three days' time.

He did so.   He dressed himself in his best clothes, and set off flushed with triumph.   It was with peculiar, almost awful, sensations that he entered the shop, and inquired for Mr. Wilson.   The three clerks took no sort of notice of him.   One was eating his luncheon.   A second nibbing his pen.   The third tying up a parcel of books.

" Is Mr. Wilson within ?" repeated Percy.

" Do you want to see him?" asked the clerk with his mouth full.

" Yes."

" He's very much engaged."

" Perhaps you will take in my name. Mr. Ranthorpe."

" Jim, take in the gentleman's name, will you?"

The clerk, nibbing his pen very leisurely, laid it down, got off his stool, gave the fire a poke, and sauntered into an inner room, from whence he shortly proceeded with far greater alacrity, and politely requested Percy to step in.

I quite relinquish the attempt of depicting the poet's sensations as he entered the dusky room, where sat the awful Mr. Wilson, upon whose decision his fate seemed to hang. Mr. Wilson motioned him to a chair and said:

" I have read your poems, Mr. Ranthorpe ; and very pretty they are; very."

There was a ringing in Percy's ears ; his face was crimson ; he was speechless.

" They will make an elegant little volume," continued the publisher; " I presume you would wish it handsomely got up?"

" Why yes—that is—of course—I leave that to you."

" Very good. I will get it up for you as moderately as I can, and as well."

Percy did not comprehend this. The publisher thought he was simply requested to publish the poems at the author's expense. Judge, then, of his surprise when asked by Percy timidly:

" What do you think you can give for the copyright?"

" Copy——? My dear sir. There's some mistake. Do you not wish me to publish your poems ?"

" Yes."

" At your expense ———"

" At my expense ! Oh no ! I thought, as you admired the poems, you would purchase them."

C

"Ah, my dear sir, you are young yet, or you would know that we *never* purchase such things."

"But if you admire them?"

"The public won't buy them. Poetry, sir, is a drug; a drug, sir. I couldn't sell 'Childe Harold' if it were now first published."

"Will you publish the poems at your risk?" asked Percy in desperation.

"It is a thing we never do, I assure you; never—never. In fact, we consider it a compliment when we consent to publish *for* an author."

Some feeble skirmishing was kept up; but Percy, seeing Mr. Wilson was pitiless, took back his manuscript and left the shop, gloomy and sick at heart.

"Some other publisher may be glad of them," he said, at last; and this revived his hopes.

But another, and another, and another followed, with unhesitating unanimity declining the honourable risk.

The self-love of the poet was exasperated. He felt towards the publishers a feeling of bitterness allied to hatred. Life was spoiled for him; and by them. A barrier, insurmountable, seemed to rise between him and success.

"I shall die unknown, Isola," he said. "I shall die unrecorded and unread. Oh! if the poems *could* but appear, they would be sure to succeed; I know it; feel it. But these ignorant booksellers, thinking only of pounds, shillings, and pence, know nothing of poetry, and care nothing about it."

"But, darling, you must not blame them: pounds, shillings, and pence are their objects: they are tradesmen, not critics."

"Yes, *tradesmen*," retorted Percy, with bitter contempt. " And by what privilege do they trade in poetry? Oh! that I were any thing but a clerk!"

It was then, for the first time, he felt that he was no-thing. What thoughts then oppressed him! What sad despondency nourished in a soul hitherto so buoyant and so hopeful! What cries of anguish at his social position!

" Genius," said Isola to him one day, " has always to struggle; but it always vanquishes at last."

" If it have courage, Isola; perhaps so."

"It is not genius if it have not. Therefore, Percy, let us hope on."

She rested his aching head upon her bosom, and kissed his hot brow. He looked into her calm lustrous eyes, and in the unutterable love there he read courage to endure. He felt he was not alone in the world. If all else were denied him, she was with him; and her love made life a paradise.

With somewhat of the pride of a martyr, Percy con-sented to accept his obscurity for the present. Meanwhile, his studies went on. He had resolved to fit himself for the rude battle with the world.

At the time I speak of, there used to be in Holborn (and there may be still) a coffee-house, at which the young poet spent much of his time. It was an uninviting look-ing place. Two kidneys placed upon one plate, and one solitary fly-blown chop on another plate, flanking a tin coffee-pot, and a cup inverted in its saucer: such was the symbolical appearance presented by the window-ledge. Over these was placed a printed bill of fare; concluding with this announcement:—" *Daily and Evening Papers: Reviews and Magazines.*"

The interior did not belie the exterior. The long room, with two rows of " boxes" looking like pews, was lit up with gas. The refreshments were cooked at one corner, behind a screen. The tables were strewed with cups of tea and coffee, broken bread, and rashers of bacon. The men seated at the tables were mostly mechanics, snatching an hour from toil, and in all their dirt revelling in newspapers and magazines, of which they were eager devourers; and some " penny-a-liners," and a few of the poorer sort of clerks were also there, joking with the drab who waited on them—a girl all dirt and pertness, well used to the easy and familiar wit of the customers who called her " Mary, dear," or " Jemima, love."

Into this dismal, but not uninteresting place—for there also was the growing avidity of the people for instruction exemplified—Percy was attracted by the reviews and magazines; and made himself acquainted with the ideas the age was putting forth. In the perusal of the criticisms on contemporary writers, he silently amassed a fund of critical ideas, which he endeavoured to apply to his own compositions. One day, after reading some poems in " Blackwood," it struck him that here was an opening.

" I will send one of my poems to ' Blackwood,' " he said; " the editor is a judge; he won't be so stupid as the booksellers. If he prints it, I will send him others, and thus, in time, I may get known."

He did so. The editor *was* a judge, and refused it. Percy was angry, but sent it to " Frazer" with the same result. His poems went the round of the magazines, but appeared nowhere.

Did he despond? Did he for one instant suspect that he was on a wrong path? that nature had not destined him for literary success?—Not in the least. Nothing so pliant as the vanity of an author; no rebuff can break it; it will bend, and bend, and bend, but will not break. Percy consoled himself, and Isola, with the idea that all great men had suffered neglect. It was notorious that all the best books had been refused by booksellers; all the best poems at first condemned by critics. The conclusion was obviously in favour of the excellence of all refused works: they were too good for the age. Percy had often read the sad tale of neglected genius. He was neglected; and logic abetted vanity in jumping to the conclusion that he was " before his age."

This is a common delusion. When a man fails in literature, his inordinate vanity makes him assume that the public is not fitted to comprehend his works. He is before his age. But when the fact of failure has two explanations, why not sometimes suspect the second to be true? Why not assume the works to be behind the age?

Men treat this wondrous age of ours too cavalierly. Depend upon it, our age is no laggard: it advances with giant strides, and is not to be outstripped by one of common thews and sinews. To keep up to its level is a task for no ordinary powers. To rise above it is the rare privilege of few. Various minds are struggling for mastery, and seek distinction in various ways. There are some men who swim with the stream, and some who swim against it: men with their age, " in the foremost files of time;" and men behind it. There is also a third class. There are men *beside* the age. These neither swim *with* the stream; they have not the courage: nor *against* it; they have not the strength. But they sit moaning at the river's side, calling upon mankind to admire how exquisitely *they are made for swimming*. The busy world is deaf; the moaner therefore continues unheeded, except by a few idle or sympathetic souls who gather round him, and admire his make. These at length urge him to take a plunge. He plunges: one splash, and

he rises dizzy from the whirl of waters; sprawls, and floun-
ders till he reaches land, and then meets his admirers by
observing:

" Great swimmers are never in their element in river
water, they want the roaring waves to buffet with."

Percy was a neglected genius, and regarded his neglect as
a token of his superiority. He had before him about this
time an example which went very far towards turning him
from his career. He had made the acquaintance of a brother
poet—a Mr. Wynton—another neglected genius, and who
seemed likely to remain so, for he was old enough to be
Percy's father. He was a fine creature; and a community
of feeling soon established a degree of intimacy between
them. He invited Percy to " look in upon him" some day.

It was a bleak chill afternoon, as Percy was returning
home, that he " looked in upon" Wynton. The room
into which he was shown made a deep impression on him.
Its poverty was hideously distinct ; small and low, it had
no carpet, the coals were contained in a kitchen shovel in
one corner, and the only fire-iron was a poker worn to a
mere rod. Cowering over a miserable fire sat Wynton's
wife, a woman evidently born and bred a lady, and who
seemed meekly to bear her fate. She was rocking the
cradle, wherein squalled a red baby, whose frock was dry-
ing by the fire, the back of a chair officiating as a clothes-
horse. Wynton was worn in appearance, but his manner
was light and buoyant. His eye sparkled with pleasure
as Percy entered, and throwing round him the skirt of an
ancient dressing-gown, which he did with an air as if it
had been the most sumptuous of raiments, said :

" This is a comfortless place to receive you in; but poverty and poets, you know."

This was said with a touch of pride. But in the subsequent conversation which took place, Wynton spoke too bitterly of the deceptions which awaited every man who trusted to literature, for Percy not to see that however he might hug his poverty in certain moments, he deeply regretted it at others. Percy left the house thoughtful and sad. He determined to relinquish literature.

On reaching home, the bright smile of Isola flashed its sunshine across his gloom.

" Have you seen the paper, darling?" she asked eagerly.

" No."

" Then come in! good news! look here!" And she held out the paper to him, pointing to an advertisement of one of the magazines, where, amongst various contributions, he read this:—" *The Poet's Heart. By Percy Ranthorpe*."

" The poet's heart" at that moment beat violently. He read the advertisement again and again, and throwing down the paper, clasped Isola to his arms in transport. His father entered.

" Look here, father, look here!" he exclaimed.

" What, what?"

" See. Read that; I am on the way to fame."

And with supreme triumph he pointed out the advertisement.

"Pooh," said his father, affecting indifference ; but really little less proud than his son. There is in ignorant minds a curious *prestige* attached to print; when they see a name in a newspaper it always seems written in gold. Old Mr. Ranthorpe thought it right not to show his pride, but he *was* proud.

The wise resolution, so recently formed, was utterly forgotten. Such is the poet's nature! The first glimpse of success suffices to arouse all his energies, to excite anew all his old delusions, to restore all his passionate aspirings. He may be baffled, he may be discouraged; he may blaspheme and despair. But, in the storm of his despair, a breath will turn him.

The magazine came out; and Percy saw himself in print. Those who have once experienced this, will remember their delight and pride. Months succeeded, and with each succeeding month appeared some new poem by the intoxicated Ranthorpe. And yet no enthusiastic public had crowned the poet in the capitol; no coterie swore by him; no one wrote for autographs! But the poems appeared: that satisfied our lovers. Hope had hung upon a slenderer thread for it not to hang on this. He could afford to bide his time, when every month brought fresh incense to his vanity. This incense was poison. He became so accustomed to regard the publication of his verses as success, that his clerkship became more and more intolerable to him. He longed to set himself fairly afloat upon the wide sea of literature. He filled so much space in the world of his imagination, that he could not help believing he must be important in the world of reality.

Isola endeavoured to restrain him. She pointed out to him the dangers—his youth and inexperience, and advised him to be patient. He was silenced but not convinced.

CHAPTER IV.

LE PREMIER PAS.

He whose profession is the Beautiful, succeeds only through the sympathies. Charity and compassion are virtues taught with difficulty to ordinary men; to true genius they are but the instincts which direct it to the destiny it is born to fulfil—viz., the discovery and redemption of new traits in our common nature. Genius—the sublime missionary —goes forth from the serene intellect of the author to live in the wants, the griefs, and the infirmities of others in order that it may learn their language; and as its highest achievement is Pathos, so its most absolute requisite is Pity.

ERNEST MALTRAVERS.

" I HAVE brought forward all the arguments I can think of," said Percy, one day to his father; "I am now one-and-twenty, and must ask you to consider my feelings in the matter."

" Your fiddlesticks!" contemptuously retorted Mr. Ranthorpe. "What has a boy of your age to do with feelings ? Have you not to get your livelihood?"

" True; but there are other means of gaining a sub-sistence than as a lawyer's clerk."

" What, literature, I suppose?" asked his father, with a cold sneer.

" Yes, literature," proudly replied Percy.

A loud, contemptuous laugh was all the answer his father vouchsafed. Percy was nettled.

" I know you think authors are a despicable race, living in garrets—"

" *Starving* in them," interrupted his father. " I never said living. Mere hirelings of booksellers and editors."

Percy continued, without noticing the interruption,—

" And however absurd such a notion, I will not attempt to argue you out of it. But I have resolved to quit my office."

" Then you quit my house at the same time. What! am I to see you throwing up a certainty—a livelihood !"

" A livelihood ! you do not imagine that my salary of five-and-twenty pounds a year would support me."

" You may get something better."

" That I intend; and at once."

" Very well; only don't give up your situation till you have got something else."

" I must give it up at once."

" You shan't do any thing of the kind," fiercely exclaimed his father, whose irascible nature was greatly excited by this dialogue.

" Why not?"

" Because I don't choose it, sir."

" Suppose I have done it already."

" Suppose—you're a fool !"

" Then understand me father, *I have done it.*"

" You have !" exclaimed his father, bounding from his chair, " then go this instant and undo your folly, or you shall never set your foot within my doors again."

" I would rather quit the house than stay in it a clerk."

A heavy blow on the face was his father's answer !

Stung with rage at the indignity, Percy sprang from the chair, hurried to his own room, packed up his few clothes, and left the house in silence. When out in the

open street he wandered for some time unconscious of
every thing around him. Bitter feelings assailed him ;
but his haughty and imperious nature found a sort of
delight in the frank struggle with fate and circumstance
which now awaited him. Resolved to owe no more to
his father ; resolved to carve his own path, he trusted in
the strength of his own right arm. The world was before
him, vast as his desires, and he was free !

Free ! what a thrilling sensation is that when the
young adventurer first quits the paternal mansion to carve
for himself a pathway in the world ! How strong the
sense of existence, when he first feels independence !
Boyhood retreats into the past ; manhood begins. The
world's burden rests upon the adventurer's shoulders, and
rests lightly, supported as it is by Hope.

Inexperienced as Percy was, and anxious to play some
part in the world, he looked upon his deliverance from the
paternal authority as a blessing. A load was rolled from
his heart. He began to scrutinise his position as a general examines the plans of a campaign. He had twelve
pounds, ten shillings — a half year's salary — for the
whole of his fortune, and this he had to husband till he
should get employment. He took a bed-room near the
street where Wynton lived. For this he paid five
shillings a week. His breakfast would cost him twopence-
halfpenny, viz., a penny loaf and a cup of coffee; his dinner,
two penny loaves and a bit of cheese or bacon, would
cost threepence or threepence-halfpenny ; his tea the same
as breakfast. Thus for eightpence or ninepence a day
he could exist.

Having made these calculations and set apart the
money in small parcels for each week, he wrote a long
letter to Isola full of regret at being separated from her,

but instilling into her his own confident hopes that all
was for the best, and that they would soon be united.
He asked her to send him his books, and appointed a
place where she could meet him.

" My dearest Percy," she said, when they met, " there
is no chance of your father's relenting unless you apologise to him."

" Apologise for what ?   For his having struck me?"

" Had you given the blow he could not be more indignant," she replied.   And this was true.   Mr. Ranthorpe
quite hated his son at that moment ; hated him as we
sometimes hate those we have wronged.

" Never will I move one step," replied Percy ; " never
will I again live under his roof.   My anger is gone,
perhaps, but all filial respect is gone with it.   Home has
long been irksome to me, now it would be intolerable."

" What will you do?"

" Work.   I have talents.   Hundreds of men whom I
believe to have less than I are earning independence ;
why should not I ?   Literature I was destined to.   I
always wished to try my venture on its seas ; now I am
forced upon them."

Thus lightly and confidently did this sanguine boy
cast himself upon the perilous bosom of that sea wherein
so many brave hearts have been shipwrecked.   It was a
fearful step.   Hundreds of young men take it with the
thoughtless recklessness of youth.   They confound their
desire for distinction with the power of distinguishing
themselves.   Doubtless the temptation is great.   " Oh!
what a luxury is there in that first love of the Muse! that
process by which we give a palpable form to the long
intangible visions which have flitted across us."*   The

* Ernest Maltravers.

delight of appearing in print, of being to thousands of
readers that near and cherished friend which a favourite
author is to us! Is not that temptation enough to seduce
the young and aspiring into any peril? Unhappily none
know the danger save those who have escaped it.

> An author ! 'tis a venerable name !
> How few deserve it, and what numbers claim !
> Unblest with sense, above their peers refined
> Who shall stand up, dictators of mankind ?*

The combat commenced. His pinching poverty was
endured with firmness, if not indifference ; but his repeated ill-success in the efforts he made to get employment was more hard to bear. He wrote tales and
sketches, hoping to get them inserted in the magazines.
All were refused. He then suspected that he should be
forced to *write down* to the magazine readers. Fatal
delusion, which has misled so many ! He tried what he
called the " popular style;" but as writing badly with
malice prepense never yet succeeded with any one, so did
it in nowise profit him. His popular style was as merci-
lessly rejected as his ambitious style.

Many a long night did he sit in his small room reflecting on his position. As his burning head rested upon
his hand, and his eyes mechanically wandered over the
various plans and manuscripts strewed before him, he
sometimes felt a sick despair growing over him. He
counted his finances, and was shocked to find them so
nearly exhausted. A few more weeks, and beggary
stared him in the face. Want had been his familiar
playfellow ; but Hope had been always at his side pointing to the sunny future. Now hope seemed to vanish.
If his small fund were to be exhausted before he got em-

* Young.

ployment, he would have no other resource than to enlist as a common soldier. What a prospect for an ambitious youth !

His prospects shortly brightened a little. Wynton had got an engagement on a weekly newspaper of good repute, and hoped to be able to introduce Percy to the editor, and so manage to find a place for him also.

The sight of Wynton installed in new and well-furnished lodgings, with all the necessaries of life about him, was peculiarly gratifying to Percy, not only because he rejoiced in his friend's fortune, but also because the change in that friend's fortune looked like a harbinger of hope to him.

There remained only money enough for three weeks' penurious existence, when a note came inviting him to dinner at Mr. Rixelton's, the editor of the paper on which Wynton was engaged. He wrote a hurried hopeful note to Isola announcing the event, and set forth with a lighter heart than had beat in his breast for many months.

CHAPTER V.

RANTHORPE BECOMES A JOURNALIST.

If by the liberty of the press we understand merely the liberty of
discussing public measures and public opinions, let us have as much of
it as you please; but if it means the liberty of affronting, calum-
niating, and defaming another, I, for my part, own myself willing to
part with my share of it; and shall cheerfully exchange my liberty of
abusing others for the privilege of not being abused myself.

FRANKLIN.

Je critiquai sans esprit, et sans choix
Impunément le théâtre, la chaire.

VOLTAIRE.

THE dinner was copious; the conversation noisy. If
authors, as a race, do not talk well, they certainly talk a
great deal, especially when together.

Ranthorpe at first was silent: awed by finding himself
amongst acknowledged writers: men who treated articles
and books as matters of course! But his natural vanity
soon loosened his tongue. He wished to shine, and he
shone. With the guests he was in ecstacies.

In the life of an author, there are few events more
highly prized than making the acquaintance of literary
men who have attained some success. People talk of the
envy and jealousy of authors; but it is a vulgar error.
I firmly believe that no author, unless a man of the

meanest and most envious disposition, ever envied the
success of another.   Authors are an imaginative and
sympathetic race.   They gladly associate with each other.
They take keen interest in each other's projects.   And to
an obscure author, the acquaintance of one acknowledged
by the world is always peculiarly fascinating; Ranthorpe
was fascinated.

Of the assembled guests I may introduce the reader to
Mr. Joyce, a middle-aged Scotchman, whom every body
declared to be " a regular trump."   Of Scotchmen this
much may be said: let the national character be what it
may, whenever the individuals free themselves from its
prejudices they are glorious fellows.   When a Scotchman
is a " trump," he is always an Ace of trumps.   Joyce was
an Ace.   His large, round, good-humoured face beaming
with intelligence, was the index of a large, wise soul. His
presence was sunshine in a room.   He was friendly with
all men, whatever their tempers or opinions.   No one
ever quarrelled with him; every body asked his advice,
and what is more, *took* it.   He knew a little of every thing,
and a great deal of a great many things.   He had learning, taste, and supreme good sense.   He had written one
of the most popular books of our day, and had never put
his name to it, although the world attributed it to
another.   He could argue with men, and gossip agreeably
with women.   He was considerably pestered by country
cousins, who absorbed a great deal of his time, but he
bore with them with amazing equanimity.   Ranthorpe
instinctively took to him; and they afterwards became
intimate friends.

Opposite Joyce sat Wynton, and by his side sat Pungent, the editor of the " Exterminator."   Pungent was a
small, thin, sleek-looking man of about forty.   He was

always dressed like a clergyman ; having the two-fold ambition of being taken for a wit, and mistaken for a clergyman. The Rev. Sydney Smith was his ideal. Though overflowing with kindness, he unfortunately mistook asperity for wit; so that in all London you could not find a kinder man, nor a crueller critic. The early pranks of the " Edinburgh Review" had turned his head. In their lively ridicule he saw the perfection of criticism; and he imitated it, unconsciously omitting the liveliness. This sleek, kind, cruel man uttered sarcasms with a breath of tenderness; he wounded your self-love with unspeakable suavity. Ask any thing of him but his good word, and you were certain to obtain it.

Opposite Pungent sat Bourne, a pale, melancholy looking man, doing his best to appear romantic, who having failed to make any figure in Parliament, had thrown himself upon literature for distinction. He was a man of independent property, and could afford the expensive luxury of literature: printing his own works, and being his own purchaser. His great ambition was that of a dramatic poet; he had printed several tragedies and one " ideal comedy." He had been enthusiastically praised by his friends; yet in spite of the eulogies showered on the second Shakspeare, neither managers nor public could be induced to look at his plays.

" Does any one know how the new play went off on Thursday?" asked Joyce.

" What ! haven't you seen the ' Exterminator?'" asked Pungent.

" No."

" No; then do so ; you know I am devoted to the drama, pen and pencil-case." Then, in his blandest tone, Pungent added; " I think I have settled the author."

" Quite right!" said Bourne, vehemently; " such trash! but it's just like the managers to bring out this stuff. What annoyed me was to see a parcel of stupid fellows— friends of the author—who went purposely to applaud. For my part I went to hiss; and hiss I did."

" That was kind," quietly suggested Rixelton.

" It was conscientious. I foresaw what it would be; else how could a manager have been induced to produce it? Managers have an abstract horror of good plays; their ignoble souls delight only in trash."

" How can that be?" asked Joyce.

" *How* it can be I don't know; but it *is*. However, there is always consolation in a play d—d. Every failure is a lesson. Managers, on the verge of ruin, will be forced to produce good pieces; forced to bend an unwilling knee to genius. *I* bide my time. The Ideal must be recognised at last."

" My good fellow," said Joyce, smiling, " do you really think the public cares about the Ideal? It is not the want of our age. The Ideal is only fitted for ages of faith, and ours is an age of scepticism."

" Oh, surely not," interposed Ranthorpe.

" Well, then, of *prosaism*. People now care for Use, not Beauty. It was once otherwise. The Greeks, with all their splendid architecture, never had a bridge. The Italians, who worshipped the delicate genius of Benvenuto Cellini, could not boast of a lock. We have superb bridges and locks, but we have lost the sense of beauty. Out of Leda's egg our age would make—a custard."

" Joyce is quite right," said Pungent. " Poetry, as we are repeatedly told, is a drug."

" Yes, *drug*-poetry," retorted Ranthorpe. " But in spite of what we are perpetually told, our daily experience

contradicts it. Poetry can never die; never become a
drug. It is the incarnation of our dearest hopes, the utterance of our most passionate aspirings. When we have
ceased to hope and ceased to feel, poetry will die, and not
till then."

" I attribute the present neglect of poetry," said Pungent, " to the indifference of critics, who, allowing trash
to pass without reprehension, have corrupted the art. In
your paper, Rixelton, I am sorry to see a want of stern-
ness. You have no epigram—no Attic salt—believe me
you want light and shade—a due blending of blame and
praise."

" That's capital," rejoined Rixelton, " when you never
praise."

" It gives breadth to criticism."

" Shall I tell you the real truth?" said Rixelton. " I
began my career tolerably reckless of the self-love of
others. I scattered, with an unthinking hand, no small
quantity of the Attic salt, you mention, into the open
wounds of authors' self-love. I wrote a book. Gentlemen, I then felt that criticism was not a joke! I was
' cut up.' I had the measure meted out to me that I had
meted out to others. I was humiliated—maddened—I,
who had humiliated and maddened others for so long.
From that moment I was a changed man."

" But," objected Pungent, " it is just as bad praising a
book which does not deserve it. You mislead the public
if you speak of a work as if its few merits were samples
of the whole."

" And," rejoined Rixelton, " does it not still more
grossly mislead the public when a few faults are dwelt on
as if *they* were samples of the whole?"

D 2

"Might one not accomplish the real object of criticism," asked Ranthorpe, "by never blaming without assigning reasons, and never praising without sincerity?"

"An ideal standard," said Joyce, "and not easily reached."

"But to which we should constantly aspire," replied Ranthorpe.

"You will never convince me," said Bourne, "that blame, however just and temperate, will not exasperate an author."

"The surgeon and the assassin both use the knife," said Ranthorpe; "the one with kindness and science, the other with wantonness and malice. The one cuts that he may cure, the other that he may kill."

"Mr. Ranthorpe is right," said Rixelton, approvingly, "and although perhaps the patient might wince under the operation, he would nevertheless regard the operator with respect and gratitude."

A few days after this dinner Rixelton, who was greatly pleased with Ranthorpe, offered him an engagement, which I need not say was accepted with intense delight. He had to write the theatrical critiques, and occasionally review poems. For this he received a guinea a week—to him a fortune!

The world again was bright to him. The cherished ambition of his life was once more possible. Isola smiled at his enthusiasm, and half shared it. But life was extremely sad now that Percy no longer lived under the same roof with her, and she was condemned to hear constant reproaches uttered by his father respecting his unfeeling conduct, mixed with sombre prophecies of his coming to some dreadful end.

The old man continued obstinate. He would not listen to Isola's pleadings in his son's favour. He called him an ungrateful wretch, who repaid kindness with insolence. And as about this time he had entered upon a speculation which promised to be highly lucrative, he felt a savage pleasure in contemplating his success, and thinking that Percy had shut himself from all participation in it. I verily believe that, much as he loved money, he cared more for the success of this new speculation from the triumph it would give him over his son than for the money it would bring. And it was with real pain that he heard of Percy's new situation. This escape from want vexed him. He had gloated over the idea of his son reduced to absolute want, and forced to come to him a suppliant. He knew that nothing short of that could bend him. But he also knew how scanty the sum of money he had in his possession, and greatly marvelled at its not having long been exhausted. This situation on a newspaper, therefore, which Isola told him of with pride, thinking that this first glimpse of success might soften him, was doubly hateful. Hateful, because it was a refuge for Percy, and prevented the necessity of his yielding; and hateful, because that refuge was literature.

Meanwhile, Percy was supremely happy. Passionately fond of the drama, he undertook the task of criticism as a luxury. He scarcely ever missed an evening's performance. Beyond this, conceive the pride of " being on the press !" His pen was a power; at least he thought so. The printing-office, dirty, murky, and ill-ventilated, was a sacred spot to him. He rejoiced in its gaseous-heated atmosphere ; he loved the smell of the ink and damp paper. In a word, all the disagreeable things con-

nected with his office were converted into pleasures, by
the fact of their relation to the great profession of literature: they were *les coulisses* of the great theatre on which
he hoped to play so illustrious a part.

Every Sunday morning the paper lay upon his break-
fast-table, and made him feel that he was " somebody,"
as he cut the leaves and eagerly read over his own contributions.

CHAPTER VI.

THE ORPHANS.

Ah! I remember well (how can I
But evermore remember well) when first
Our flame began, when scarce we knew not 'twas
The flame we felt; when as we sat and sigh'd
And look'd upon each other and conceived
Not what we ail'd,—yet something we did ail;
And yet were well, and yet we were not well,
And what was our disease we could not tell.
SAMUEL DANIEL: *Hymen's Triumph.*

Speed was in my footsteps;
Hope was in mine eye;
And the soul of poesy
Was my dear ally.
Earth was then as beautiful,—
As, as is the sky,
When I look'd beside me
And saw—that *you* were nigh.
BARRY CORNWALL.

PERCY at length got so accustomed to all the work of
the press, that it became a " matter of course " to him,
and ceased to be a pleasure. But as he was writing
another volume of poems, he was glad to be earning a
subsistence until they should give him celebrity.

In the course of a few months he had made several

literary acquaintances, and had gradually been initiated into many of the secrets of the profession. His lust for fame continued unabated. He had before him many sad warnings; but he pursued the course of his ambitious dreams undaunted.

His father fell dangerously ill; but refused to see him. In vain Isola begged that she might send for him. The old man sternly declared he should not enter the house, until he could enter it having renounced literature for ever. Percy was grieved at his father's obstinacy, and at times was nearly yielding. But he cherished his ambition too much; he could *not* renounce it.

Twice or thrice a day he called to ascertain the state of his father's health, which was gradually becoming worse. One day Isola said to him:

" Percy, you know how your father has resisted all my entreaties. Nevertheless, in spite of his obstinacy, he loves you, and would gladly see you. Come with me."

" He will refuse to see me."

" Come with me into the room. Venture it. He will not have the heart to bid you quit it."

" It is worth risking," said Percy.

They agreed that he should enter the room quite as a matter of course, and take no notice whatever of what had occurred.

" How are you now, my dear father?" said Percy, tenderly, as he marched resolutely up to the bed-side, and took the old man's hand.

" Better—better—my dear boy," said the old man, with tears in his eyes.

Isola was right. The sight of his boy was too much for his anger; it vanished at once. There is a chord in a parent's heart which is never touched in vain. However angry we may justly be with a child—he is still our child, and our hearts yearn irresistibly towards him.

The old man pressed his boy's hand in silence; gazed on his exquisitely beautiful face with all a father's fondness and admiration; reading in its lines such grace, beauty, tenderness, and promise, that he wondered at himself how he could ever have felt otherwise than he did then. Percy, touched at his manner, was about to ask forgiveness. The haughty boy, whom no harshness could have moved, was melted by these signs of affection.

" Silence on that," replied his father, mournfully, shaking his head as he interrupted him, " let bygones be bygones. I am not long for this world."

" Oh ! do not say that."

" I would not say it, did I not feel it. But it is too true. I have not long to live. The little time I have yet must be devoted to the future, not the past."

They prayed together fervently. By his bed-side sat Percy three days and three nights, without stirring. He could not be persuaded to leave his father, whom he felt he had not treated with the consideration which was his due. He slept in a chair; or, while he watched the troubled slumbers of the dying man, prayed in silence for his recovery.

As he watched thus one night, he was startled by the expression of agony and the heavy breathing of the dying man, who awoke in terror.

The old man sat up in his bed, looked wildly at his son, then gazing abstractedly at the shadows moving on the wall, as the night lamp flickered, muttered—

" Thank God !—only a dream—only a dream."

He then sank back upon his pillow, and complained of

thirst. Percy brought him some barley-water; which, having drunk, the old man said slowly—

"My dear boy, dreams are sometimes warnings from above."

Percy would not contradict him.

"I have had a warning about you. It seemed to me that—as if—I dreamed—" His voice became inaudible; a sharp pang shot through him; he closed his eyes and was silent.

The stillness of the room—the flickering lamp—the heavy breathing, occasionally swelling into moaning—the distortion of the features—fearfully impressed Percy's imagination, weakened as he was by continual watching. He longed to hear his father's dream. Free from all superstition as he was, he could not shake off an indefinite fear and anxiety respecting this dream.

At length the old man's features became composed—he sank again to sleep. From this sleep he never woke but once, and that was only two hours afterwards.

"Percy—I'm dying—promise me—that—you will— give up literature—my dream—promise me—literature— destruction—scaffold!"

This last word was a hissing whisper; and with it he expired.

Had the old man lived one minute longer, he would have extorted the promise from his son; which would have been religiously kept. Indeed, so impressed was Percy by the scene, that he inwardly resolved to obey his father's last wish, whatever it might cost him.

But resolutions made in such moments are seldom kept. On cooler reflection, he began to see that it was impossible for him to give up his career; and that his father only desired it from a prejudiced and unenlightened view of literature. Yet the hissing of the word "scaffold" ever and anon rung ominously in his ears !

Isola and Percy both grieved deeply. They were now orphans in the world. As the funeral ceremony concluded they clung to each other in a wild embrace, as if each were now the world to each.

When the first flow of grief was passed, and they began to look around them, it was found that, when all debts were paid, Percy's father had left nearly two hundred pounds. This seemed to them a fortune; and when Isola communicated her intentions of earning her own livelihood, as companion to Lady Theresa Wilmington, he said—

"Dearest, you never can think of it. *You*, too, at the beck and call of any one. No! Let us marry at once. We have money to furnish a house, and begin the world with; and, for the future, I am easy on that score."

"No, no, no," replied she, "I must work as well as you."

"But why ?"

"Because we are not rich enough to marry."

"Nonsense ! We have enough to start with."

"Yes; but we cannot live upon that. Darling Percy, you have your name yet to make in the world. You will have to publish ' The Dreams of Youth' at your own expense. When once that work is fairly known, I'm sure you will never want employment; but till then it would be madness in us to marry."

"Do you, then, fear poverty ?"

"That is unkind in you, Percy. You know I should not feel poverty with you. But I prefer feeling the humiliations which I may meet with as a companion, to that far deeper and irremediable humiliation of being a

burden upon you.   Besides, surely we are young enough
to wait."

Poor girl! how little she suspected that one day her
arguments would be turned against her!

Percy was annoyed at first; but he soon saw that her
reasoning was just, and he knew her heart too well to
suppose that her fears were selfish.   He himself, though
violent, and apt to be roused whenever his wishes, however unreasonable, were in the least opposed, was generous
enough to comprehend her generosity.

"I have been thinking," said he, the next day, "of
your going to Lady Theresa's, and cannot reconcile myself
to it.   So I have a proposition to make.   You are some
day to be my wife, are you not?"

She pressed his hand as her only answer.

"Very well; then of course you consider what is mine
is yours.   Now, you shall *not* go to Lady Theresa; but
the money left me by my poor father I hand over to you.
It shall be your support until I can get regular employment to justify our marriage."

"Generous creature," she exclaimed, kissing him.

"You accept then?"

"Do I accept? No, Percy; but it is not pride which
makes me decline.   The money is *necessary* for your
advancement; I will not touch a shilling of it."

"How, necessary? foolish girl."

"First, to publish your poems."

"Well, then, I will deduct the sum necessary for that;
the rest *shall* be yours."

"It will not prevent my going to Lady Theresa's.
Percy, Percy, what extravagant ideas have you got respecting my situation?   It may be irksome, but it has
surely nothing degrading.   Besides, I repeat, the money

is necessary for your pursuit. You must leave the paper, and devote yourself to some work—your tragedy, for instance. This you cannot do, unless you have money to live on. In two or three years you will be famous and rich."

This struggle of generosity was often renewed; but Isola was always invincible. She shared his hopes and aspirations, and, therefore, could not think of, in any manner, standing in the way of his advancement. She said that he was wasted on a newspaper, and ought to accomplish higher things.

She accepted the situation. She had to submit to the too common lot of orphan girls; but she was upheld by the proud consciousness of being no obstacle to her lover's success.

He gave up his situation on the newspaper. He had attained the Archimedean standing point—the $\pi o\hat{v}\ \sigma\tau\omega$ of his career; and to move the world was now his object. And as he saw his poems through the press, and dwelt with all an author's fondness on their beauties, he smiled down the vague fears, which the recurring sound of his father's sombre warning ever and anon called up. A scaffold? What connexion had literature with that?

BOOK II.

THE LION.

To what base ends, and by what abject ways,
Are mortals urged through sacred lust of praise!

POPE.

Er erinnerte sich der Zeit, in der sein Geist durch ein unbedingtes
hoffnungsreiches Streben empor gehoben wurde, wo er in dem leb-
haftesten Genusse aller Art, wie in einem Elemente schwamm. Es
ward ihm deutlich, wie er jetzt in ein unbestimmtes Schlendern ge-
rathen war!

GÖTHE.

CHAPTER I.

THE LITERARY LION.

Les devoirs de la société lui devorent son temps; et le temps est le
seul capital des gens qui n'ont que leur intelligence pour fortune. Il
aime à briller; le monde irritera ses désirs qu'aucune somme ne pourra
satisfaire; il dépensera de l'argent et n'en gagnera pas. Les succès
littéraires ne se conquèrent que dans la solitude et par d'obstinés
travaux.

DE BALZAC.

THE ball was splendid. The rooms were crowded with
lovely women, and distinguished men. Grisi was pouring
forth a torrent of song from her exquisite throat; and the
guests were absolutely listening!

" Sir Charles," said Florence Wilmington (niece of the
Lady Theresa, with whom Isola had been for some
months as a companion); " Sir Charles, you know every
body, do tell me who that is leaning against the piano
talking to Grisi?"

Sir Charles, thus interrogated, put up his glass, and let
it fall carelessly, saying,—

" Don't know, positively."

" Emily, my dear," said Florence, to the daughter of
the hostess, who was then passing, " do tell me who that
young man is, talking to Grisi."

" Don't you know Percy Ranthorpe?"

E

"What, the author of 'The Dreams of Youth?' I thought he was a poet by his beauty. How divinely handsome!"

"Shall I introduce him, Florence?"

"Do, Emily dear, above all things!"

"Take care of your heart, then," said Emily, laughing; "for Apollo himself was not more fascinating."

"Certainly not handsomer!"

"Will you risk your heart, then?"

"Bah! let him beware of his!" said the beauty, with a charming toss of the head.

And yet any girl might have well been warned against so handsome a man as Percy Ranthorpe. He was quite a picture, as he stood there in an impassioned conversation upon music with the lovely young Grisi. Giulia Grisi was superbly handsome at that period, like a Greek statue, in the mould of her head and bust; and was peculiarly attractive to Ranthorpe, from having somewhat of the same kind of beauty as Isola.

Nothing could be greater than the contrast of Ranthorpe's appearance at that moment, with that at the period of his first introduction on the scene of this novel. Instead of the poor, ill-dressed, attorney's clerk, he was now dressed in the newest fashion,—he had become a "Lion."

In a few minutes he was standing up with Florence Wilmington to a quadrille.

"I dare say, Mr. Ranthorpe," said she, with a most winning air, "you will think me very *missish;* but I must tell you, not only how often I have wished for the pleasure of your acquaintance, but also that I at once guessed who you were directly I saw you." A little fib, which belongs to the white lies of society.

Ranthorpe bowed.

" But don't be vain," she said, archly; " for after all you disappointed me. I expected something more tragical and gloomy; something, in short, which should tell of the sadness uttered in your poems."

" Are we unfortunate scribblers then bound to be always in a state of melancholy?" asked Percy.

" Why, you would be more interesting."

" I doubt it. A melancholy moment or so may serve as a condiment; but one cannot dine off spices."

" But I don't see any trace of sadness about you."

" How could I be such a brute as to be sad when basking in the sunshine of your smile?"

" Prettily turned off. But you have *désillusioné* me. I shall no longer believe in *le morne désespoir* of your poems." Florence was fond of studding her conversation with phrases borrowed from French novels.

"If life were a quadrille, and I had you for my partner, believe me there would be no longer any sadness in my muse."

" Oh! don't suppose that I am always gay," said she, bending her long voluptuous eyes upon him.

" Are you ever sad?"

" Yes; and if I had no cause, I would make one. *Toujours perdrix* is unwholesome. Perpetual gaiety is a curry without rice. I see another volume of poems advertised by you. Are we soon to have it?"

" Very shortly, I hope."

" Don't you admire Grisi? is she not *délicieusement belle* ?"

" Like a bit of Greek sculpture."

" Ah! that's so like you authors! As you believe books superior to realities, so you always prefer a statue to a woman."

In this style they rattled on. Florence had made up
her mind to a conquest; and Ranthorpe had shown no
backwardness in replying to her advances. Accustomed
as he had been for some months to the flatteries of drawing-
rooms, he had learned to play the dangerous game of
badinage as a necessary consequence of his position.

He was neither surprised nor intoxicated by Florence's
evident admiration. The success of the "Dreams of Youth"
had been considerable. Indeed the small critics had not
only "hailed the volume with delight," but declared it
"decidedly superior to any of the season;" some going so
far as to pronounce the author a second Byron. Pungent
alone remained true to his character, and was voluble with
ponderous levities respecting the errors and crudities of the
poems. He told Ranthorpe that it grieved him to speak
so of his friend's work; but that he owed it to posterity
to be uncompromising. His friend forgave him.

The sounder critics, though scorning the stereotyped
drivel of the press, and seeing in the "Dreams of
Youth" rather a skilful echo of other men's thoughts, than
original works, yet detected touches of real feeling, lines
of exquisite melody, and images of daring felicity. The
beauties they quoted; the errors were treated leniently.
This is dangerous kindness, and has ruined many. A poet
is naturally vain; and if vain when unapplauded, unappreciated, what wonder if he grow arrogant on applause?
He rushes into the world full of ardour and dreams of glory.
His eyes are so intently fixed upon the star that shines
upon the double-crested mount, Parnassus, that he over-
looks the steep and perilous ascent—an ascent which must
be climbed with toil, and cannot be cleared at a bound.
He attempts to clear it at a bound: and is applauded for

his rashness. Confirmed in his error by applause, and believing success easy, he takes no pains to achieve it.

'Tis the old story of the hare and the tortoise!

Ranthorpe was not only the supreme poet of albums, but the first waltzer in London. His aristocratic air, his haughty bearing, his beauty and success, soon made him a "Lion."

This was his ruin. The poison was offered to him in a golden cup, and he greedily swallowed it. Without positively regarding " moving in the first circles," as the object of his existence, he certainly regarded it as the best means to attain his object. He looked to patronage for success, and forgot the public for a coterie!

Wretched youth! He had lost an author's courage to endure poverty and neglect, to live unnoticed, unflattered, unappreciated; because he had lost that conception of his mission which makes martyrdom a glory. Poverty, then, for the first time appeared in all its terrors. It was not only poverty to him—it was failure. He had lived upon eight-pence a day, and had been rich upon it. He now lived as a prodigal, and dreaded the inevitable termination of his career. In the society he now frequented, he believed personal influence the great requisite for success; and that his "powerful friends" would remove all the barriers which kept him from fortune and renown. He was daily getting more of these friends; fresh houses were constantly being opened to him; his position in society was daily becoming more prominent. But all his little fortune was squandered, and debts were fast increasing. At first the expenses inevitable upon his position wrung from him secret cries of anguish; and his delight at being invited to some country seat was considerably alloyed by the idea of what it would cost him. He soon got over this; and the life of a man about town suited his

disposition so well that he insensibly fell into it, and squandered his money with a poet's recklessness.

"Ranthorpe, can I set you down?" asked Sir Henry
Varden, as he saw Percy about to withdraw.

"Thank you," replied Percy, "if you are going now."
And twining his arm within that of his "powerful friend,"
he descended the stately staircase with a proud feeling.

"Sir Henry Varden's carriage stops the way," roared
one of the servants.

"Sir Henry is coming down," answered another.

The next minute Ranthorpe was reclining against the
easy-cushioned back of his friend's carriage, listening to
his remarks with tolerable indifference, till Sir Henry said,

"By the way, you made a fresh conquest to-night—
Florence Wilmington. Take care; she's a terrible flirt."

"I am in no danger, I assure you."

"Don't you admire her?"

"Immensely. But my heart is elsewhere."

"So much the better; you may defy her, for she in-
tends to lay siege to your heart, I'll swear, by the triumphant smile with which she learned that you were to be
at Rushfield Park during her stay there. By the way, I
shall be going down the day after to-morrow, why can't
you accompany me?"

"Let me see. The day after to-morrow—well, I see
no obstacle—I certainly will avail myself of your offer."

"That's settled then. But here we are at your door."

The carriage stopped at a house in Dover-street, where
Ranthorpe had apartments. Bidding Sir Henry adieu,
and again engaging to accompany him to Rushfield Park,
he opened the door with his latch key, and proceeded to
his room.

" Only twelve," said he, looking at his watch. " I must do a little work, for to-morrow I breakfast out, and that will be another day lost."

Another day lost! He actually regretted it, and did not see that his whole life was a series of such losses.

He opened his portfolio, and endeavoured to work at his tragedy. In vain. His brain was sluggish, or wasted itself on chimæras and air castles. When he attempted to write, the sound of music was in his ears, and the forms of fair women amidst brilliantly-lighted saloons were before his eyes distracting his attention. The real poetic fire that once ran through his veins, no longer gave vitality to his literary projects. He was consumed by a factitious excitement ; a hectic and unnatural heat burnt out his energies.

Upwards of an hour he sat there, his head resting on his hand, and his pen vacantly drawing figures on his blotting paper. He vainly endeavoured to arouse the tragic inspiration by thinking of the necessity of soon finishing his play. But the very current of his thoughts was sufficient to destroy all genuine enthusiasm.

I cannot better paint the situation of his mind than by indicating the current of his thoughts on this as on all other occasions when his play was the subject. He thought not of the passions and motives of his characters ; but of the worldly success of the piece. He saw, in his mind's eye, gigantic placards announcing that success. The words EVERY NIGHT and OVERFLOWING AUDIENCES for ever floated before him. He read imaginary reviews, wherein the critics welcomed his piece as a revival of the intellectual drama, and were sensitively alive to all its subtler beauties, as to all the splendour of its poetry. He held imaginary interviews with rival managers hungering after his next play. He imposed on them exorbitant terms. The money was already laid out: he would start a cab, and remove to the Albany. He should be able to continue the career of a man about town; and be on a footing of equality with his acquaintances.

Last and fatal symptom!—he never thought of Isola as the sharer of this splendour!

CHAPTER II.

THE POET OUT IN THE WORLD.

> Se oggidi vivesse in terra
> Democrito, (perchè di lagrimare
> Io non son vago, e però taccio il nome
> D' Eraclito dolente,) or, se vivesse
> Fra mortali, Democrito, per certo
> Ei si smascellerebbe della risa,
> Guardando le sciocchezze de' mortali.
>
>   CHIABRERA.

How came the poet so transformed?

This question, so naturally asked, and so difficult to answer, is important for the future interest in my hero. Let me beg, therefore, some attentive consideration of the causes which influenced him; let me trust the reader will be as ready to detect the real force of such circumstances on such a nature, and by imagining himself in the same position, extenuate the errors of a youth.

Poets are proverbially vain, impressionable, and luxurious; working by fits and starts, as the impulse moves them; and hating all continued toil that is not forced upon them by some overmastering idea; very sensible to all the refinements of luxury; and very liable to act upon their hopes as if they were established certainties.

These general qualities Ranthorpe shared; and added thereto certain peculiarities of position and education which made his fall the easier. He had been bred amidst pinching economy, with the constant dinning in his ears of maxims relative to the omnipotence of wealth; he had dined for weeks together on dry bread, to be able to purchase some envied book; he had known all the miseries of being placed at the bottom of the social ladder; and now he dined off the rarities and delicacies of the season, and drank the costliest wines: things which had a sort of poetical magnificence to him, who had only dreamt of them in reveries.

The fascinations which daily tempted his soul, and finished by subduing it, *were* fascinations to him. To those born to splendour—to those even who had known the ease and comfort of moderate incomes—the things which affected Ranthorpe would have had little attraction. But he had been poor, and was suddenly plunged into society where every one was rich; he had been a miserable attorney's clerk at a salary of ten shillings a week, and was suddenly elevated to the society where his family—nay, where his former master—would not have been admitted on any sort of plea.

It is necessary to remember this if one would understand the sort of intoxicated vanity which filled him, as he lounged into the large and splendid rooms, or rolled along in the luxurious equipages of his friends. The respect which footmen and hall porters (those incarnations of fat insolence) invariably paid the man—in whose face a little while ago they would have slammed the door—pleased him no less than the flattery of the drawing-room. The sensations which he felt as he was driven through the parks, seated beside some dandy, or some lady of fashion, it is impossible to describe!

He gazed upon the foot passengers with a serene good nature. He was sure they must be envying him. Yet, he had no carriage—his genius alone gave him the seat he occupied!

And, then, the contrast between the manners of his new friends and those of the society he had been bred in! The low soft voice, the easy carriage, the constant courtesy of manner, even in uttering the greatest impertinences—the thousand indescribable nothings, effects of long habit and education, which distinguish well-bred people, compared with the loudness, blunt coarseness, undisguised impertinence, and inelegance of his former associates, made a very strong impression on him. He felt a childish delight in wearing yellow kid gloves in the street, on reflection that formerly he had seldom worn gloves at all. Every way his senses tempted him. What wonder he succumbed! Was he not luxurious, and a mere boy?

One had need be both, to be so intoxicated!

The society he mixed with flattered all his propensities. To please his friends he had no need of study—and he was idle. Their admiration gratified his vanity, and their wealth ministered to his luxury.

This was the fruit of his lionism. People were pleased to have him at their parties; he amused them. But these very people would not have given him a sixpence; could not have assisted him in the world of literature. The unfortunate poet had renounced the dream of being, like a second Petrarch, crowned in the Capitol, for that of being crowned in the drawing-room.

And was not his love for Isola strong enough to save him? Alas! no. That, too, had not escaped the contaminating influence of his ambition. At first he had regarded his elevation into a higher sphere of society as a triumph which he should one day call her to share. But, as the purity of his intentions became effaced by contact with impure ambition, he began to blush for her! He felt that the social inferiority of his future wife would be an insuperable barrier to her admission into "circles," where he fancied he was admitted solely for his genius; not reflecting that handsome young men, of gentlemanly bearing, and living in a certain style, are always gladly invited to parties; and that he, in spite of his genius, would not have been admitted, had he not appeared in a decent coat and cravat.

He struggled and sophisticated with himself; he would not own that his engagement was irksome, but he felt it deeply. He felt that, with Isola, he had nothing but a laborious and precarious existence to look forward to.

" Are all the energies that pant within me to be frittered away," he would ask himself, "wasted in the desperate struggle for daily bread? Must I renounce my dreams? Must I abjure the doctrines which I burn to teach, for those only that *will sell*? Must I, too, *write for the market*? Horrible! horrible!"

And the coxcomb, who had no convictions of his own, shuddered at the idea of writing for the popular wants. The adventurer, who had abjured his mission to maintain a wretched place in society, cheated himself with these high-sounding phrases. Thus must we ever cheat ourselves with the image of virtue, even when our baser impulses plunge us into vice.

It is one of the peculiarities of imaginative natures, that they are so prompt to furnish the instruments of their own destruction. They are so dangerously fertile in excuses for their own acts! They are so dangerously

endowed with the faculty of turning their *weaknesses* into
apparent *calculations*—their *wishes* into *necessities,* that,
for an act which a well-principled but duller man could
find no excuses, and would therefore shun with horror,
they can invent such imperious justifications, such magnificent sophisms, as, instead of turning them aside in horror,
urge them to pursue their course in triumph. Imagination
creates idols, and then falls down to worship them.

Ranthorpe was sincere, even in his falsehood. He was
his own dupe. It should also be added, that he very
seldom saw Isola; so that the evil influences of lionism
were not counteracted by her presence. Other thoughts
effaced her image from his heart. She was not often
enough by his side effectually to renew the impression.
He was unworthy of her; and this made him feel uneasy
in her presence. He felt lowered before her. The
sophisms which deluded him never withstood the limpid
clearness of her good sense. Her intellect was too upright
and truthful to accept the excuses which to him were
valid. She did not tell him so; but he felt it. He felt
that the reasons which to him were irresistible, to her
were not even plausible ; and he felt considerable anger
at her not sharing his illusions. Men resent nothing more
than contradiction on a point, which they themselves feel
uneasy about. Truth may be disputed with impunity;
a sophism can only be torn from out the mind with a
violence that lacerates and embitters.

CHAPTER III.

THE MEDICAL STUDENT.

Son los estudiantes, madre,
  De muy mala condicion;
Que al mirar una buena moza,
  Mas no estudian la leccion.
Song of the Sevillian Students.

Est enim leporum
Disertus puer ac facetiarum.
                    CATULLUS.

The strawberry grows underneath the nettle,
And wholesome berries thrive and ripen best
Neighbour'd by fruit of baser quality:
And so the prince obscured his contemplation
Under the veil of wildness.
                    SHAKSPEARE.

ISOLA was waiting for Ranthorpe by the Kensington
Gate of Hyde Park. He had written to appoint this
meeting, to say adieu before leaving town. As her
duties were not very absorbing, she easily escaped, upon
some plea of shopping, which Lady Theresa always accepted; and this was the only means she had of speaking
with her lover.

A weary half hour past the appointed time—which
was quadrupled by her anxiety—had she waited, and

still no sign of her lover. She felt this neglect the more, not only because she knew he was master of his time, but also she had observed of late that his manner was greatly changed towards her. Ready enough to make excuses for him, she could not help feeling hurt. While musing on this, she suddenly heard quickened footsteps behind her, and, thinking it was her lover, turned round a beaming face of welcome. To her surprise and annoyance, she met the smiling glance of a young gentleman who was following her with strictly *dis*honourable intentions.

Blushing at her mistake as much as at his insulting glance, she walked rapidly on. In an instant he was at her side; and addressed to her, between the puffs of his cigar, various jocular pleasantries touching her charms, and his very discriminating appreciation of them. Without daring to look up, she hastened her pace.

" Don't hurry, my little divinity," said her tormentor, " and pray don't be alarmed. What can make you fly from such a lamb as I am?" and a voluminous column of smoke issued from his mouth.

This lamb was Harry Cavendish, the medical student whom we introduced to the reader in the first chapter of this tale.

His not very prepossessing exterior, joined to the easy impertinence of his address, so terrified poor Isola, that it was some time before she could summon courage to answer him.

" Now, my inestimable *bandbox*, don't be modest," said he; " you're really very handsome."

" I beg, sir, you will cease addressing me," she said, calmly; " I do not know you."

" Exactly ! the very reason why you should remain quiet

till you do. Running away is not the readiest method of
forming a lasting acquaintance; nor is silence the most
satisfactory sort of eloquence. Restrain your paces, my
angel, and listen. I am Hyacinth Napoleon Potts, heir
to an earldom, fortune unknown. You are—"

" Are you a gentleman?" she inquired, with some
effort.

Harry puffed forth a column of smoke, and said,

" Do I look like a tailor?"

A tailor, be it observed, is the last degradation humanity can reach in the opinion of medical students; and it
is probably owing to this contempt for their persons, that
arises the indifference to notice their bills, which has
been remarked as characteristic of the students.

" I ask you, sir, if you are a gentleman?" she pursued,
her voice regaining its accustomed power. " Not how
you look, but how you feel. If you *are* one, you must
see that your language is an insult, and an insult to a
woman who cannot repel it!"

Harry gazed at her for a moment incredulous; but
though a " rip," he was a gentleman, and struck by the
unmistakeable sincerity and dignity of her manner, and
the earnestness of her tone, raised his hat respectfully,
and replied,

" Since you are serious, I can only apologise for my
mistake."

She bowed and passed on. He watched her till out of
sight, and then resumed his promenade.

This incident represents two phases of his character;
and as he is about to occupy a large portion of this history, I may as well pencil his prominent peculiarities.

Harry Cavendish was, to most people, a mere medical
student, of ebullient animal spirits, extreme good nature,

somewhat slang and dissipated. To those who knew him as did Ranthorpe (with whom he had recently become acquainted), he was a very different being; though the mixture of slang and sentiment in his composition was a perpetual puzzle. He was certainly not one of those who " wear their hearts upon their sleeves, in compliment externe." Nothing could be finer than his real nature; but it was somewhat tarnished and distorted by his education, and by habits picked up from his fellow-students. The unpretending heroism which pulsed beneath that extravagant exterior and dissipated habits—the delicacy and generosity of feeling which distinguished him, this tale will fully exhibit. He was really as romantic as he aspired to be rakish; he was not a " rough diamond," but never was diamond set in more extravagant bad taste. His virtues were his own; his vices he owed to his position as a student.

CHAPTER IV.

THE LOVERS' MEETING.

How her heart beats!
Much like a partridge in a sparhawk's foot,
That with a panting silence does lament
The fate she cannot fly from.
                              MASSINGER.

NOT unobserved did Harry quit his pursuit of Isola. Ranthorpe entered the park in time to see him raise his hat and depart. A feeling of jealousy first shot across his heart; but the respectful manner in which Harry had taken his leave, soon suggested the thought of his being a stranger. But when did he learn to know her; and how?

These and other thoughts assailed him, as he walked rapidly towards Isola, whose agitation, when they met, puzzled and irritated him. He resolved not to begin upon the subject, that he might see whether she would refer to it.

The air was warm, and lazily fanned their cheeks; the sky was cloudless, and dim with heat; every thing without bespoke calmness and happiness—a painful contrast to the " world within" of these two lovers.

She met him with a palpitating heart—a heart wounded by neglect, yet fluttering with its love. He came haggard, despondent, and bitter. At the first glance of his wretchedness, she forgave him; her pangs were forgotten in her sympathy with his.

After a few questions and answers—excuses mostly,—he could no longer restrain himself from asking how long she had known Harry Cavendish. She did not understand him. He then told her how he had seen Harry bid her adieu but a few minutes before. She related what had happened.

Ranthorpe was silent. His brow was so gloomy that Isola dared not question him; so in silence they walked on. He was suffering a martyrdom of vanity at the thought of his affianced bride's social position. "To be spoken to by every *roué*—to be treated as a milliner," he said to himself: "no more free from insult than the humblest of her sex; and perhaps my friends will recognise in my wife, the girl whom they have attempted to seduce!"

These thoughts irritated him. So keen was the expression of pain upon his countenance, that Isola attributed his silence to physical suffering. She ventured timidly to ask him if he were ill.

"Not precisely ill," he said, "but jaded. Late hours—heated rooms—dissipation," he was glad of the excuse, so continued: "moreover, the sad necessity of mixing in the ruinous frivolities of society."

"Why mix in them?" she asked, with divine simplicity.

But this home-thrust of natural logic pierced not the thick shield of vanity. She could not understand how men cling to follies which they see through, and which they abuse in bitterness of spirit. As the drunkard in his sober moments curses wine, so could Ranthorpe curse society.

"I must court it," he said, "although I despise it. In London there is no success without friends. Every thing is got by interest. Patient merit must be content with its patience."

"But can you not rely upon yourself?" said she.

"No," replied he, "I cannot in England; elsewhere I might. In England, merit unheralded wins no victory; unpatronised, gains no attention: the soldiers win the battle, but the generals get the fame. If genius be struggling and starving, it may struggle and starve; but if it seems to have no need of the world, the world is at its feet."

"But, dearest, are you not already known? Your poems have been wonderfully successful; and your society is sought by those you call influential; will they not assist you?"

"Assist!" he said, bitterly. "Yes—yes—the *assistance* of friends—we know that!"

"How bitter you are."

"Bitter? Ay, lessons of adversity are bitter! Is it not bitter to find youthful dreams nothing but dreams? To find all your hopes unrealised, thoughts misunderstood, friends false, and fame a mockery? Is it not bitter," he continued, grinding his teeth, "to see the courageous heart of man cowed into nothingness by the swart shadow of Respectability? Is it not bitter to see the tinsel of the gauds of life fixed on the pedestals where should stand the men of genius? Is it not bitter to discover that the grand mistake in life is sincerity, and that one had better have every vice, and agree with the world, than every virtue and differ with it?"

He was acting. Instinctively, but dimly, Isola felt it.

These phrases, however, affected her, not in themselves, but as indicative of the state of his mind. Oh! how unlike had he become to that young poet, who on eight-pence a day had looked cheerily in the face of the world, and—

"Strong in will
To strive, to seek, to find, *and not to yield.*"*

" The seal is taken off my eyes," he continued. "The veil is lifted which concealed the world ; I see it now in all its shivering nakedness—*for I am poor.*"

" You have been poorer," she mildly suggested. "Oh! Percy, do not despair. Think not so ill of the world: it is full of love and kindness, and will cherish its teacher."

" Cherish? Yes: when I am *dead!*—They break the poet's *heart*; but ; oh! good people! they honour his *ashes.* They throw the living man into prison; or let him starve and rot. The dead man is placed in Westminster Abbey, under Latin inscriptions. The workhouse and a monument—these are the poet's rewards!"

" You exaggerate."

" No; I speak but the truth. We authors live for humanity: if we fail, men laugh at us; if we succeed, they envy and malign us; if we differ from them, they trample on us!"

She made no reply. Her truthful nature, however unsuspicious, could not accept his acting as natural feeling. She felt that there was something beneath his words and manner, though she knew not what.

" I must maintain my footing in society," he said, shortly afterwards, " at the cost of the greatest privations. In England to *seem* poor is to *be* poor. And of all curses poverty is the worst."

* Tennyson.

" You did not always think so."

" Not when I was younger, less experienced. Besides,"
he added, and his voice faltered, " I had only then to
brave it for myself. Now I have to think of you; and
to think of you in want, is fearful to me."

" And is it for me?—" she began, with a look of
triumphant tenderness.

" For you—for you," he replied, " I would have all
that wealth can bestow."

" And what is this boasted *all* that money can bestow?" she said, with enthusiasm, quite thrown off her
suspicions by that one hint. " Money can furnish pa-
laces, but it cannot fill the heart; it cannot purchase the
supporting strength of love. It can make the brow glitter
with jewels ; can it make the cheek glow with ruddy
health? Can it chase the quivering from an anguished
lip—a tear from the burning eye? Can it give health—
repose—content? Not one of these! Then what a
splendid braggart is this wealth !"

He smiled mournfully at her enthusiasm, and said,
" You think so because you are young."

"I think so because I love !"

" Frankly, then, do you not dread poverty—if not for
yourself, then at least for your children?"

" No. I have courage. Poverty is the least evil
that can affect me. Love makes life's burdens light."

" Truly ; but it is no shield against misfortunes."

" Yes, Percy, against every thing. We have in this life
all to struggle, and much to endure. Life's harmony must
have its discords; but as in music, pathos is tempered into
pleasure by the pervading spirit of beauty, so are all life's
sorrows tempered by love."

" Then should that love be very certain," he said, fixedly.

" Who doubts ours?" The calm trustingness with which she said this, made Percy wince; looking into her exquisite face he saw an irresistible commentary on her words. He was silenced. His silence awoke strange misgivings in her breast. " Surely, Percy, you have no doubts of me?"

" Listen, Isola; and listen calmly. We are now at a point in our lives when a false step will be irrecoverable. You are still very young, and may not know your own heart. Mind; I do not doubt your love. No! But how often is a first love succeeded by a second, and a third—when wider experience—but, good heavens! you are crying!"

Crying! her young heart was breaking! One flash of light had revealed to her the abyss on the brink of which she was standing.

" Isola, Isola! Do not weep. I was talking but of possibilities—things which may never be, but which *must* be looked in the face. Come, come; don't be foolish."

" I foreboded it," she sobbed.

"Foreboded what?" he asked, with some irritation.

" That it would come to this."

" Come to what?"

" You do not love me!"

" Very well! very well! Directly I wish to talk reasonably, I am supposed to love you no more! Just like women! But you will not hear me!"

" I have heard too much already for my peace. Our engagement alarms you."

"It does—but on *your* account. You know how I have faced poverty; you know how little I care for the

world. But you do not know how hideous poverty is,
when you see it brought upon another by your means!
I dread it, because it would destroy that which gives life
its value—love!   Think of us, married, and poor.   My
temper is irritable—want sours the best of tempers.   I
should be cross to you—and then the necessity for in-
cessant labour will keep me perpetually away from your
side.   Oh!" he exclaimed, passionately, "love never could
survive that!   Love, which lives upon perpetual kindness,
which is grace, beauty, happiness—could not survive the
blistering curse of poverty."

Isola continued weeping, but made no reply.

" Then, to think of you in want—your beauty tarnished
by suffering—your hands hardened by labour—and our
children, so many silent reproaches on the parents who
brought them into the world, without the means of feeding
them when there.   The thought is appalling!"

She had checked her sobs, and dried her eyes.   A
sudden resolution had given her fortitude.   In a calm,
low, but unfaltering voice she said:

" Percy, you are right.   Our union would be cursed
with poverty; and that, as you say, is the worst of ills;
and I agree with you—when love is absent.   I should be
a burden to you.   I should have blighted your prospects.
Think no more of it.   From this moment consider me as
a sister."

The agony which distorted her face belied the calmness
of her manner.   Percy felt it—and felt a sudden sense of
humiliation, at having given one who loved him such
pain.   He could not continue the part he had assumed.
He unsaid all that he had said; he protested that his
fears were dissipated by her confidence; he conjured her
to forget them—to think only of his undying love; to

hope in the future. He was passionate—eloquent—and in earnest. She was too willing to believe him; and they parted with mutual vows and mutual protestations, that the future must bring them happiness, if they could await it courageously.

Percy returned home in a state of great excitement. This soon wore off; and he almost repented of the termination to their interview, when he came calmly to look at his condition. He did not know it, but the truth was, that his love for Isola was stifled by other feelings. It was a love which had its roots in the heart of the manful, struggling, dreamy poet; but which was altogether out of place in the heart of an idle, intoxicated, feverish Lion!

CHAPTER V.

FIRST LESSONS OF ADVERSITY.

Viendole asi D. Quijote le dijo: yo creo, Sancho, que todo este
mal te viene de no ser armado caballero.

CERVANTES.

> What a bridge
> Of glass I walk upon, over a river
> Of certain ruin, mine own weighty fears
> Cracking what should support me.

MASSINGER.

Voilà, disais-je, un homme qui s'est donné le temps de penser
avant d'écrire; et moi, dans le plus difficile et le plus périlleux des arts,
je me suis hâté de produire presqu' avant que d'avoir pensé."

MARMONTEL: *Mémoires.*

RANTHORPE had soon to learn the bitter lesson of how
impotent were all his " powerful friends," to bring him
one step nearer to the goal of his ambition.

This announcement appeared in the papers:

" On Monday next, the 15th, will be published, in one
vol., 8vo, 10*s.*,

LYRICS,

By PERCY RANTHORPE, ESQ.,

Author of the 'The Dreams of Youth.'

Also, DREAMS OF YOUTH. Third Edition.

'Exquisite imaginings.'—*Morning Paper.*

'A volume of lofty ideality. Mr. Ranthorpe will take rank beside the most intellectual of our poets.'—*Evening Paper.*"

Those who read this announcement were naturally prepared for a volume of some pretensions. Reviews were awaited with impatience. It was a publication of some moment: it made or marred the poet.

Authors do not sufficiently consider this. Instead of surpassing themselves in their second attempt, they generally produce something inferior to their first. But if the second be really equal to the first, it will be thought inferior, because the public expect more.

The "Lyrics" were confidently, carelessly written: products of necessity, not of inspiration: written because the poet wanted to bring out another volume, not because feelings and thoughts within him struggled for utterance.

With this inferiority in poetical value, the "Lyrics" had to contend against the severity of a watchful criticism, which the "Dreams of Youth" had disarmed. Those who were really influential—who had spared the youth and inexperience of his former volume—who had cheered him to fulfil the promise he had given, recommending study and care—these men were all against him. Whether some feeling of indignation at having been deceived, or of his not having taken their advice, mingled with their feelings of distaste at the carelessness and conceit exhibited in this volume, I will not say. Critics, like other men, resent their prophecies not being fulfilled. Certain it is, however, that this volume plainly told them that here also was another noble spirit ruined by success. The cutting severity of their reviews was heightened by the evident sorrow which accompanied their blame.

One sentence from a review I may here transcribe, as falling in with the moral lesson meant to be conveyed by this tale:

"Mr. Ranthorpe has mistaken the conditions of rapid writing. The history of literature would convince him that no one ever produced excellent works in quick succession, who had not qualified himself by many years' study and reflection. He who has accumulated stores of experience may write rapidly, because the interval which must elapse before his materials are exhausted will itself be long enough for him to accumulate fresh materials. The neglect of this obvious rule is the ruin of so many young men, who, after giving splendid promises, dwindle into insignificance: buds that never become flowers; fruits that are rotten before they are ripe."

Not only were the serious critics severe; but the " small fry " were outrageous. The volume was received with universal condemnation.

Ranthorpe suffered deeply, horribly. In vain did he endeavour to console himself by saying these criticisms were the productions of " envy"—in vain did he try to shut his eyes to the failure manifest before him. In vain did he exclaim, " these criticisms live only for the day; my poems will survive them." In vain did he sophisticate; there were not forty copies sold.

What then became of his "powerful friends?" They had been his flatterers; more they could not be. " Powerful friends" could not give him genius, could not endow his verse with vitality and beauty. " Powerful friends" were not reviewers—" powerful friends" were not the public.

Too many aspirants share this idle delusion about powerful friends for me not to insist upon it here. One illustration, striking and conclusive, will suffice. It is this. When noblemen, as they often do, enter the field of literature, all the prestige of their names, all the influence of their " powerful connexions," can neither force their works upon the public, nor redeem them from ridicule and contempt. Hundreds of instances might be quoted: but the fact is sufficiently patent in itself. I would ask the aspirant, therefore, this simple question: If " the great" cannot help one of themselves, what likelihood is there of their succeeding for a protégé?

But worse than all, " powerful friends" not only give no laws to the public, but absolutely receive its verdict; and what it refuses to accept as poetry, they regard as trash! Ranthorpe was shorn of his glorious mane: he went into society, and found himself no longer a Lion!

He had to learn, not only the impotence of a coterie, but the serious truth that literature is not a field to sport in: that there, insolence and audacity are quickly crushed; and that a man is not, there, accepted for what he holds himself. He had to learn that puffery or luck, though it may give a momentary success, cannot sustain it: real ability alone does that. Sooner or later, the puffed-out wind-bag, floating so buoyantly aloft, is pricked by a pin, and then tumbles into the mire, never to rise again. A first success is the *premier pas;* but in literature, it is not the *premier pas qui coûte.*

At any other time, this failure might have opened his eyes to his true position. But alas! his eyes were dazzled, his head was turned, his heart was intoxicated. Love abetted vanity in deceiving him.

Yes, love!—He had fallen into the snares of the fascinating Florence Wilmington; fallen slowly, unconsciously, but irretrievably. He had been much thrown with her during his stay at Rushfield Park. She had determined to captivate him, and succeeded. Since his return to town, he had been a frequent visitor at Lady Wilmington's; and had drunk deeply of the poisoned goblet which the lily hand of Florence held up to him.

CHAPTER VI.

THE TWO SISTERS.

Sweet alluring eyes; a fair face made in despite of Venus, and a stately port in disdain of Juno ; a wit apt to conceive and quick to answer. What of this ? Though she have heavenly gifts of beauty, is she not earthly metal, flesh, and blood ?

LYLY: Alexander and Campaspe.

> But the heaven-enfranchised poet
>   Must have no exclusive home.
> He must feel and gladly show it,—
>   Phantasy is made to roam :
> He must give his passions range,
>   He must serve no single duty,
>   But from Beauty pass to Beauty,
> Constant to a constant change.

MONCKTON MILNES.

FLORENCE WILMINGTON was a flirt—that is to say, she had great animal spirits, great vanity, and as a spoiled child, had never been taught to heed consequences. Ranthorpe was handsome, celebrated, and lively; he was, therefore, a very proper flirting companion. She began to throw her spells around him at first innocently enough; but when she found that the impassioned poet was becoming serious, and supposed her to be so, she thought of putting an end to the game. Just as she was about to

quit Rushfield Park, however, Sir Henry Varden warned
her not to lose her heart to Ranthorpe, as *his* was engaged
elsewhere. She was surprised; scrutinised Ranthorpe's
manner closely; and jumped to the conclusion that he
was an adventurer feigning love in hopes of making
her a stepping-stone. Her vanity was piqued, and she
resolved in secret to punish him, by making him really
and desperately in love with her. Accordingly, on reaching London, she began a system of alternate coolness and
tenderness, irritating and maddening the unhappy poet, by
keeping him in a constant fever of suspense and doubt.

Ranthorpe long endeavoured to hide from himself that
he loved her. He juggled with his conscience; and tried
to convince himself that it was only her lively manners,
which made him prefer dancing with or talking to her;
and he thought of Isola, and tried to make her image
drive that of Florence from his heart ; but in vain. He
seldom saw Isola; and when he did, he was always
despondent. Florence, on the other hand, always either
animated him beyond expression, or made him jealous and
exasperated. Do what he would, Florence alone occupied
his thoughts.

While he was thus carried away by the fascinations of one sister, another sister was silently che-
rishing a secret adoration for him. Fanny was very
unlike Florence. Without being plain, yet her complexion was so sallow, and so lined with illness and
melancholy, that she seemed plain at first sight. Those
who loved her, thought her beautiful. There was a deep
quiet in her hazel eye, and a winning sweetness in her
smile, which few could withstand. But she had no admirers
among young men, she was so shy and reserved. Elderly

men, with whom she felt more at ease, pronounced her a paragon.

In character she was as earnest as her sister was frivolous. Ill-health had greatly secluded her from society, and had thrown her upon the society of her books. In the solitudes of her library she had formed her heart and mind. The result was an excessive shyness, which veiled with coldness a warm, loving, and romantic nature. Her days were usually spent with her aunt, Lady Theresa. There she learned to know and value Isola, for whom she conceived a strong sisterly affection. Fanny understood Isola; Isola understood her, and loved her.

Between these two beings there never was a suspicion of "the difference of station." From the first, their relation towards each other had been divested of all conventionality. One secret alone was ever kept from each other—their mutual love for Ranthorpe.

Yes, Fanny loved Ranthorpe, though she knew it not. He had been the first young man whom she could admire, who had vanquished her diffidence. A few interviews with him, in which they, unrestrained, poured forth all that was in their hearts, had completely subjugated her. In such natures love is of sudden growth; and Ranthorpe, quite unconscious of the poison he was instilling, pleased at having a listener who so well appreciated him, sought her society whenever he could not engross that of Florence. As Fanny always saw him so very lively when with Florence, she did not suspect his attachment. Love to her was always serious.

Ranthorpe had no suspicion of the love he inspired. In fact, he had eyes for no one but Florence—no thoughts for any one but for Florence, and she made him mise-

rable. Remorse for his treachery to Isola, and doubts
respecting Florence, tortured him.

At this juncture, Wynton one day called, and finding
him in a very excited state, began talking on his prospects.
From several incoherent remarks, Wynton at length
divined the real cause of his unusual excitement, and
said abruptly to him :

" Percy, you are in love with Florence Wilmington."
He started, and coloured.

" Do not deny it," continued Wynton ; "look your
malady boldly in the face, and I will help you to cure it."

" Malady !—cure !"

" Malady, yes—poison !   There, go and blow your
brains out at once.   Do any thing but give up your
heart to be gnawed by the cruellest of all vultures—a
coquette."

" You are raving, Wynton."

" I am horribly serious.   It is my friendship for you
makes me so ; if my manner is a little wild, it is owing to
recollections which . . . .   Enough ! I tell you, in sober
sadness, that your passion for Florence Wilmington, if
you do not conquer it, will be the greatest misfortune
that can befal you."

" Do you know her?"

" I? No. But I know . . . I know what *I* suffered. Percy, I have never told you the history of my
early life—and I rejoice at it; for now that history may
serve as a warning to you, which you need. Will you
listen to me calmly?"

" Certainly.   You pique my curiosity."

" I shall not be long ; and you will see how nearly it
concerns you."

CHAPTER VII.

WYNTON'S STORY.

With that low cunning which in fools supplies,
And amply too, the place of being wise,
Which Nature, kind, indulgent parent, gave,
To qualify the blockhead for a knave.

CHURCHILL.

Thou art not fair; I view'd thee not till now—
Thou art not kind; till now I knew thee not—
And now the rain hath beaten off thy gilt,
Thy worthless copper shows thee counterfeit.
It grieves me not, to see how foul thou art;
But mads me, that I ever thought thee fair.

ARDEN OF FAVERSHAM.

" On leaving Cambridge," began Wynton, " I was, in common with so many thousands of young men, a social anomaly, in a country where wealth or rank are the only passports to society. To the cultivation and education of a gentleman, I added the patrimony of a beggar, and the prospects of an adventurer.

" My father was a clergyman, with a living of five hundred a-year, and nine children to absorb it. He pinched himself, to give me a college education. His pride lay in my talents; and to give them a fair development, he willingly deprived himself of every comfort. I was sent to college. I gained there some distinctions ; and left it with the firm conviction that I was to make the fortune of my family.

" Filled with classic lore, and minute scholarship, I went to London, expecting to find employment and emolument at once. You may measure the extent of my simplicity by that one fact. My dear father was, however, equally simple. London, the great mart for talent of every description, seemed merely necessary to visit, and ' *something* would be sure to turn up.' He recalled all the illustrious names of men who had risen from nothing,— forgetting the thousands who had perished in the struggle ! We repeated all the commonplaces about force of merit, and certainty of protection, and doubted not but that I should soon be sought out by the rich and powerful.

" Thus confident, I went to London; I will not detain you with a description of the gradual breaking up of my illusions. You can fancy how soon it was that I discovered my social insignificance in that vast centre of talents; how soon I felt the insufficiency of a scholarship equalled by hundreds, and surpassed by scores; how soon I felt the meagreness of that knowledge which had hitherto been my boast—the *knowledge of books*—compared with that far deeper *knowledge of life*, with which I saw so many gifted. The young student with the classics at his fingers' ends, soon finds himself a child in comparison with the man who has lived, and reflected on his experience.

"A knowledge of the sciences is comparatively easy, and may be acquired by very ordinary intellects. Though it requires a great intellect to originate profound views, a child may learn them when originated, and therefore

ordinary intellects can acquire considerable knowledge of
the laws of nature; but a knowledge of life is the result
of abundant experience drawn by a reflective mind. The
labours of philosophers, extending through centuries of
observation and experiment, are amassed in books. There
the student may find them, question them, and having
furnished himself with their results, begin the study of
nature, rich in the experience of ages. Not so the student
of mankind. He is almost like a philosopher who should
set to work to observe phenomena, without having studied
the results obtained by others. No amount of experience
is stored up in books for him to consult. He must study
the living subject. He must draw his own conclusions.
The works of poets and moralists, indeed, contain the results of great experience; but unfortunately these are of
little help; we are unable to appreciate them till we ourselves have discovered the same truths. A man shall
read Shakspeare for thirty years, and at the end of that
period shall detect truths of human nature, which escaped
him before: and why?—because he himself, not having discovered them before, could not recognise them when he
saw them written. From poets, we learn confirmations of
our views—never the views of human nature themselves.

" The knowledge of life is marvellously complex: its
materials are drawn from past experience, present observation, and prevision of the future. In youth, we are
subject to deceptions as much from the boundless confidence of hope, as from the dazzling novelty of our impressions. We have no standard to test things by. We
have no experience to correct the rashness of our wishes,
and the immaturity of our judgment. In youth, we can
seldom judge men aright; for to judge men aright, we
require to be arrived at that age when experience is

weighty enough to balance the inventive nature of hope, and capable of analysing all impressions in the crucible of the understanding. In truth, a knowledge of men is always difficult and rarely certain, for men themselves are ever vacillating between new ideas and ancient prejudices; between their interests and passions.

" In London I found myself a child. I might be great at Cambridge—honoured amongst silk gowns—immortal amongst gerunds—but in London I was a cypher. I could find no employment. I knew no one in the world of letters. I had done nothing to justify my pretensions. I was in that crowded city, anxious to get my bread by honest employment of my talents; and found thousands eager in the same pursuit. Ah! how I longed to get an opening!

" I sent articles, tales, and poems to every magazine then published. I lived month after month upon the delicious cozenage of hope that one of the editors would at last have taste and judgment enough to recognise an unknown genius. You know enough of literature to judge what success I met with. I clung to my hopes tenaciously; but at length, in despair, I accepted a situation as private tutor in a rich Gloucestershire family.

" To this, then, after a few months of glorious illusion and painful humiliation, had my boasted talents brought me! To rust my energies, to waste the verdure of my life in a country house, instructing a heavy youth.

" Yet my father never lost courage. *He* could not renounce his illusions. He could not admit his error of judgment. To have admitted it would have been to admit that he had wronged his other children by that error. He was forced to hope. I should distinguish myself even as a tutor! Many a man had started from a less favourable point; with my talents I was sure to excite general admiration and respect. I did so. I was the 'lion' of the county. You know how little it would require to be the wonder of a county, so that I need affect no modesty on that point.

"I was a wit, a scholar, and a gentleman: so said the county. The clergymen declared my scholarship considerable; and in return I admired their sermons. The men thought me a wit and a philosopher; and the women adored my verses. I was treated as an honoured guest, not as a tutor. My society was sought. I was intoxicated with my success, and began again to hope.

"You may here, my dear Ranthorpe, trace the generic resemblance of our fates; what you were in London society, I was in Gloucestershire. Both of us exalted beyond our merits, and both of us nourished in presumptuous thoughts. But now attend! and you will see a still closer resemblance to your history.

"The sister of my pupil was then eighteen; and I fell in love with her. It would be impossible for me to paint her portrait, because I have since seen how false was my view of her; and if I were to paint it according to my present knowledge, you would never believe in the sincerity of my affection for her. Let me therefore rather say that, to my inexperienced eyes, she was all that she affected to be, and as good as she was beautiful.

"It was a mad thought, in such a country as England, for a poor tutor to aspire to the only daughter of a wealthy gentleman: but what will not youth and passion dare? What anomalies will they not reconcile in fiery imagination? I loved Fanny, and I never doubted that her father would consent to our union, *in time*. I loved her to distraction, and it was not long before I *knew* she had remarked

my passion.   Would she return it?   That was my perplexity.

"Return it she did, as far as in her nature lay. Flattered
by the passion she had excited, it was evident to me that
she returned it as much out of vanity as real affection; but
I was too enamoured, and too young to be scrupulous as to
the *means* whereby I gained her love.   She was deplorably
ignorant; all education seemed useless with her; she had
quickness, but could never learn.   This want of intellect
shocked me at first; but she seemed so angelical in disposition, her sentiments were so noble, her sympathy so
active, and her person so beautiful, that I soon forgot
her poverty of brain.   Alas! I loved her too well to
detect the faults so glaring to others.

"And then, in spite of her dulness of comprehension,
she was the most consummate flatterer.   Small as was her
intellect, she seemed to have a more than animal quickness
of instinct in detecting the foibles of those around her;
and utterly destitute of convictions or earnestness, she
could with equal facility adopt any opinion, any sentiment, or any manner that would fit the opinion, sentiment,
or manner of the person she was conversing with.   She
was like the chameleon reflecting the colour of every tree
under which it reposes; she passed from the most contradictory ideas, and antagonistical sympathies, in the
same evening—the same hour—with unparalleled ease.
She flattered every body, and cared for none. For none—
no, not even for me; beyond the gratification of her vanity,
which was pleased with the idea of the cleverest man in the
county being her slave.   I did not know this at that time
—I did not suspect it. She was all enthusiasm, tenderness,
and melancholy grace; the tears would come into her eyes
if I recited verses to her, or if I complained of a headache·

She seemed 'wrapt in adoration.' I believed all this; the fumes of vanity intoxicated me—delirious presumption distorted my judgment.

" Ah! those were days of rapture and torture, such as I have never since experienced. Glorious visions of future happiness and greatness floated before my eyes. Intoxicating hopes and burning passions were the will-o'-wisps that lead my heart astray. And yet amidst these raptures were the poignant doubts which my social position generated; the fears that I was indulging in a dream from which I soon must waken!

" These fears became at last realities. A wealthy nobleman came to pass a few months at the house where I was tutor. He was evidently struck with Fanny, and she was as willing as usual to listen to his flatteries. The coquette! how bitterly I cursed the vanity which could thus torture another's heart, as she knew she tortured mine. I reproached her with it. She wept—affected innocence—said it was only her *manner*—and that she *meant* nothing—vowed that she loved none but me. I was but too willing to believe her!

" All rapture now had fled, and grim despair seemed rooted in its place. Perpetual quarrels when alone ; perpetual jealousy when in company : this was my life. I could not be blinded to the fact that she encouraged her admirer ; but, at the same time, I was too young to understand how she could reconcile it to her reiterated assurances of undying affection for me.

" The mystery became greater when the nobleman proposed, and was accepted! What ! said I to myself, actually accept him, and only last night she swore that I alone should ever have her love! Great God ! is she a demon, or is she an idiot?

"We had a violent altercation directly we were left alone. I heaped the bitterest reproaches upon her, which she received with forced playfulness. She persisted in vowing unalterable love for me; and declared that she had only accepted his proposal out of policy—her father being so bent on it that she feared her refusal might have ruined our prospects.

" 'But you will marry him?' I exclaimed.

" 'I will marry none but you,' she replied; ' you have my heart, you alone shall have my hand.'

" 'But how?'

" 'Leave all to me. You look incredulous? *What motive can I have in deceiving you?*'

" ' None,' I replied, sorrowfully; for I had often asked myself the same question, and could never devise an answer.

" Her caresses and promises dispelled my fears during the rest of the interview, but I became sombre and sceptical immediately afterwards. I was ignorant enough of human life and human motives ; my ideas of them had been gathered from poetry and novels (those falsifiers of nature, the more pernicious because they pretend to truth), and I had familiarised myself with romantic adventures, the audacity of love, and the escapes of brides from detested unions even at the foot of the altar. I did not see how these were to operate in my favour; but Fanny seemed so confident that I trusted blindly to her ingenuity.

" Thus fretful and sophisticating, I passed the time allowed for the marriage preparations. I saw her *trousseau*, sometimes with a grim irony, sometimes with a sad foreboding, according to the view I took of the probability of her being true or false to me. At length the last week arrived, and Fanny seemed as gay and bustling as any

bride could be. I began to suspect that she was deceiving me, and would continue to do so to the very day.
The thrilling horror of this thought almost maddened me.
I rushed forth into the park and wandered distractedly
about. Desperate thoughts, and violent plans, crossed
and recrossed my brain; and I returned to the house so
exhausted with emotion, that they all remarked my sickly
appearance. I pleaded illness, and went up to my own
room, where I dined by myself. That evening the whole
party were going to a ball, given by one of their neighbours. I rejoiced in the idea of being left alone.

" To quench the burning flame of jealousy which was
devouring me—to deaden the conviction that I had wasted
myself on a coquette—to stupify the wounded pride revolting at the thought of my having been made a dupe—
I drank largely of the generous claret. I remember with
horrible distinctness my sensations : they were a mixture of
keen anguish and heavy insensibility; of vivid conception
and sottish brutality; the external universe seemed pressing upon me with an intolerable weight ; and the vigorous
mind seemed struggling to free itself from the oppression.
I was not drunk, but besotted. Gross and brutal feelings
seemed urging me to some desperate act.

" About half-past ten I rose from my seat and left my
room. The house was empty, and I wandered vacantly
through the rooms, a sort of life-in-death. I know not from
what motive, but I soon found myself in Fanny's bed-
room. This seemed to have a sort of quieting influence over
me; my ideas became more vivid and less fantastic, less confused. It was her bed-room! I had never crossed the
threshold before, and now I was seated in her very chair;
turning over her combs and brushes, her trinkets, and

scent bottles; touching the counterpane of her bed; kissing the curtains; looking in her glass; and picturing her also in the room!

"While thus yielding to delicious reveries I heard footsteps approaching. Alarmed at the idea of being detected there, I hid myself behind the ample curtains of the bed. The house-maid entered, finished her work without detecting me, and left the room.

"This put strange thoughts into my head. I examined the position of the bed and the amplitude of the curtains, and from every part of the room viewed the capabilities of the hiding-place; and having satisfied myself on that score, I determined to await Fanny's arrival.

"'I will endure this suspense no longer,' said I, 'this night shall decide my fate.'

"The time dragged heavily onwards after this resolution; but I grew more and more confirmed in it, as the time for its execution approached. The fumes of the wine had not yet gone off, but they did not stupify me so much as they had done. My head seemed as if bound with a wreath of burning iron; the blood burnt along my veins; a quenchless thirst scorched my palate; and a dull, dogged sense of resolution filled my mind. When the party returned home, I felt capable of any crime.

"Fanny came up to bed, chattering incessantly to her obsequious maid. I could not see her, but I recognised in her voice and manner an excitement produced by the flatteries and frivolities she had been enjoying. I heard her tell her maid all the persons she had danced with, all the dresses she had admired, or laughed at, and all the inanities of which balls are composed.

"At length, her maid finished her hair, placed every

thing ready, and departed. I no sooner heard the door shut, than I peeped cautiously out, and saw Fanny turning over some letters—they were mine!

" In spite of my half-intoxication, and the dogged resolution it inspired in me, I had not courage to step forward; a fire burnt up my veins, but a cold perspiration covered my body. I watched in breathless silence, till my situation became insupportable, and I determined to venture forth. The house was silent, every one was abed, and, probably, after the fatigue, sound asleep; so I murmured, 'Fanny,' in a gentle tone. She started; and again pronouncing her name, with a caution to her not to be frightened, I stepped forth.

" She was surprised, terrified, and indignant; and ordered me to quit the room instantly, or she would alarm the house.

" ' Alarm the house!' I replied, brutally, ' and let your future husband know *why* I am here.—This is folly! Let us be calm and rational. You, alone, can suffer from any discovery. You *dare* not alarm the house: you know you dare not.'

" ' That makes you courageous.'

" ' No; it makes me resolved. Therefore, sit quiet, and listen to me. I am to be trifled with no longer. Tell me you do not love me, and then—'

" ' What then ?' she said, haughtily.

" ' Why, I may kill you for your falsehood! Do not be terrified—I know not what I am saying; but release me from this agony of suspense; do you love me ?'

" ' You know I do,' she answered, reproachfully.

" ' How can I know it, when I see the preparations for your marriage with another ?—preparations, which you take as much apparent delight in as the happiest of brides. You do not answer?—Beware, oh! beware!'

" ' You terrify me so that I have a good mind to punish you, by not telling you my object in appearing a happy bride.'

" I was softened in an instant. I wanted an excuse for her, and she was going to furnish it. I entreated her to tell me what she meant.

" ' Why, as you know, my father would take no denial in private. He wishes the match; and, in his house, his wish is law. But he is very anxious to make a good figure in the eye of the world. Now, at the wedding, there will be a large assembly of our relations and friends, and if before them all I declare that my affections are another's, my father will not dare to force me; and to prevent his forcing me, I intend at the altar saying, ' No.' This will create grand scandal; but the magnitude of it will be our safety. My hand will never be forced, when they see how determined I am.'

" ' But why not elope?'

" ' For your sake. I am under age. You would be accused of abduction. No; my father shall give me to you.'

" I allowed myself to be convinced; and kissing her on the eyes, I crept to my own room.

" The marriage bells were pealing; the day was bright and sunny. The bells seemed to mock me: I thought I could distinguish voices in them. The day was hideously glaring: I thought it also a mockery of my inward gloom. I had horrible misgivings. Fanny's plan was wild and romantic. I had *read* of such things, and they seemed probable; but when the plan was about to be *acted*, it seemed impossible. Obedient to her wish, I did not attend the ceremony. But I could not forbear skulking about the outside of the church, with anxious ears awaiting some confusion to betoken an interruption of the ceremony. I expected every minute to see the doors open and people rush out.

" All was silent: painfully silent.

" I crept into the church, unable to endure the suspense, and felt the world turn giddily round me, as I saw the bridegroom in the act of passing the ring on the finger of his radiant bride. I staggered from the church. The soft breeze revived me for an instant. I wandered on, brooding thoughts of vengeance. I felt a sudden sickness and a film overspread my eyes. I sank senseless on the grass.

" When I recovered, the sun was pouring his intolerable rays upon me; the birds were twittering in the trees; the blue sky above me was dotted with lazy clouds. For a moment I knew not where I was.

" The pealing bells awakened me to consciousness.

" I returned home as the ' happy pair' drove from the door, upon their marriage tour. The drama had ended; my deception was complete; and Fanny became *Lady Wilmington.*"

" Lady Wilmington!" exclaimed the astonished Ranthorpe.

" Yes, Lady Wilmington," bitterly repeated Wynton. " And now you see the closeness of our fates. What Fanny was, her daughter is—a coquette. She plays with you, as her mother played with me. You may fancy she loves you; perhaps she does, but that will not prevent her breaking your heart, for her love will not be a feather's weight upon her conscience!"

There was a pause, during which each was absorbed in

his thoughts and recollections. Wynton was moved with the ripping open of old wounds; and Ranthorpe was astonished at the wondrous history, and its connexion with his own.

"You have made me sadder," said he, "from the sufferings you have endured, and from the hideous picture you have drawn of a woman whom I always thought a negative kind of being, without force of character enough to be bad—much less to be the demon you have drawn."

"Yet she is not a demon," replied Wynton; "believe me she is a woman, and a not uncommon woman. When I was your age I thought as you do. Experience, and long studies of moral anatomy, have convinced me of my error. Calm now, I can read her character in its true light. Shall I read it aloud?"

"Do so—but no paradoxes I beg!"

"None that I can help. Well, then, Fanny was simply and truly a victim of *intense egotism with no intellect to direct it;* weak, vacillating, and unprincipled, she had no malignity, she had not force of character for any villany that did not spring from the negative vice of want of principle. Self was her only consideration, and she was reckless what she sacrificed to it. She was gratified by my love in many ways. By her vanity she lived; to gratify it was, therefore, to give her a vivid feeling of her existence. Hence her delight in my passion.

"She could not break off our intercourse when once her future husband had dazzled her with the prospect of a wealthy 'establishment.' I say she could not, and for these reasons:

"She would never sacrifice a gratification merely at the expense of another's suffering; and my love was a gratification, and I was easily deceived.

" She could not bear to be *thought ill of*, by any person, no matter by whom; it tortured her. She lived as I said by her vanity, and this vanity was inordinate; the praise of the meanest was food to her; and hence the pliancy with which she suited herself to every body's way of thinking.

" But if to be thought ill of, even by a servant, was a pang to her, what would she have suffered if the man who then adored her were to turn his adoration to contempt? How much pleasanter to prolong that adoration till the last minute!

" As she never for an instant contemplated becoming my wife, she knew that I must detect her some day; all her art was required to delay that moment until she should see me no more.

" Now, in supposing that I have read aright the motives of her conduct—stripped of the palliations and sophistications of her own conscience—we have, as a result, the portrait of a very unprincipled *woman*, sacrificing every thing to her intense egotism; but no *demon*. A demon, in our conception the incarnation of malignity, is not so odious as the incarnation of egotism. Malignity is respectable in comparison: there is force and energy in it; there is a defiance, and a power which extorts sympathy from us. As the highwayman is less contemptible than the pickpocket, so is malignity less odious than egotism. The cruelty of egotism is not less than that of pure malignity; but the motive is more contemptible. Satan is grand, terrible, sublime; Iago is utterly despicable. Moloch is loveable in comparison with Blifil.

"Fanny was no demon, but an egotist; this explains her actions. Wherever you see intense egotism, you see more or less want of moral principle; for whatever principle the

H

egotist exhibits, is only such as will keep him from the bar of justice or of public opinion. His real standard is not a moral, but a purely selfish one. Wherever you see a want of moral principle arising from a weakness of character (more than from defiance of society, or misdirected energy), there you will be sure to find a being capable of acts similar to those of the miserable girl we speak of.

"Now," added Wynton, "tell me whether my story has been of any use to you, Percy?"

"It has, indeed," said Ranthorpe, mournfully; "you have saved me from destruction."

CHAPTER VIII.

POOR ISOLA.

Je pense en vous et au fallacieux
Enfant Amour, qui par trop sottement
A fait mon cœur aymer trop haultement;
Si haultement hélas! que de ma peine
N'ose espérer un brin d'allégement.

CLEMENT MAROT.

You held your course without remorse
To make him trust his modest worth,
And last you fixed a vacant stare,
And slew him with your noble birth.

TENNYSON.

My ears
Receive, in hearing this, all deadly charms,
Powerful to make men wretched.

MASSINGER.

WYNTON's story had certainly made Ranthorpe very unhappy; but it had not cured him, it had not convinced him. This is one of the sad conditions of life, that experience is not transmissible. No man can learn from the sufferings of another: he must suffer himself; each must bear his own burden.

The reader will not wonder, therefore, if, the first time

Ranthorpe saw Florence, after Wynton had distressed him with his story, all the doubts which that story had aroused were at once dispelled. One quadrille, one tender smile, sufficed to make him scorn the idea of Florence being at all like her mother. The more he thought of Lady Wilmington, and compared her with Florence, the more was he struck with the differences; and they were really many and important. Lover like, he only saw the best side of his mistress—he only perceived the differences between her and her mother, without also noting the resemblances.

In truth, he was in such an unhealthy state of irritation, intoxication, piqued will, and fascinated senses, that his mind could not have fairly apprehended the truth, however clearly it might have been placed before him. He yielded himself up to the charm of being deceived, and would have thanked no one for undeceiving him.

Wynton grieved to see the little influence he had exercised; reproached him gently with it; but Ranthorpe had only one answer—Florence is not at all like her mother.

Wynton rather angrily retorted: "Declare your love, then, and try her."

"I will," was the haughty reply.

The next day he was alone in the drawing-room with Florence.

"You look ill," she said, with feigned anxiety.

"I am unhappy."

"Oh, if it's only that," she said, relapsing into her usual playful manner, "I have no pity. . . . . Poets, you know, must be unhappy, to make the world believe in their poems."

"That, perhaps, is the reason," he said, somewhat bitterly, "why the world ill-treats poets. It fears we may not have *cause* enough to weep, and so heaps scorn, envy, and neglect upon our sorrowing heads. We are the singing birds whose eyes men put out, to give more touching plaintiveness to our song."

" *Ah ça! vous allez donc faire le Byron?*"

" I am serious."

" What, *you* complain of the world?"

" I complain of the *one*."

" Oh, then there is *one*. . . . . . I thought so! Now you must make me your confidante. . . . . . She must be very charming, to have captivated you; but still more hard-hearted to have been *cruel* to you. *Voyons, Monsieur le poète* . . . . . Who is *la belle perfide?*"

" Do you not know her?" he asked.

" I cannot guess," she answered, with an air of utter unsuspiciousness.

" Can you not read the feelings written o'er the face? Can you mistake the eyes?"

No one could have mistaken his eyes, or the tone of his voice, or his manner; but the persistent blindness of a coquette is one of the peculiarities of the race. Florence replied—

" Who could not mistake eyes? They are *such* deceitful things! Then, too, one never knows when you poets are in earnest—"

" Are there not," he replied, passionately, " looks which utter what the faltering lips recoil from? Are there not *tones* which pierce the husk of conversation, giving a meaning to unmeaning words? Is there not the fret—the anxiety—the fever—the jealousy—the flushed cheek and eager eye, to mark the true love from the feigned?"

" Yes—but you men! Really you are *such* creatures!"

" Dare I proceed ?"

" *Assez—brisons là-dessus!* You have been eloquent enough;—and eloquence is dangerous."

" You—*understand* me—then ?"

" Perhaps—" Then, feeling that she had got to the uttermost limit, and that it was necessary to change the subject before it went further, she added, carelessly, " Have you seen the 'Puritani?' Delicious, isn't it? Bellini is such a love of a composer!"

" Pray do not trifle with me. Answer me, dear Miss Wilmington; do you—do you understand me ?"

" *Allons, pas de sentiment!*—I hate it.—Don't be theatrical, *mio caro poeta.* Let us change the subject."

Ranthorpe, stung by her manner, passionately replied, " Change the subject—I cannot change it! It haunts me like a dream.—It is all I ever think of.—My existence is bound up in it!"

" You forget yourself," she answered, rather haughtily;—somewhat uneasy at the declaration she had drawn forth.

At this moment Isola was coming up the stairs, to seek a book in the drawing-room for Lady Theresa; and hearing Ranthorpe's voice, in tones she knew too well, her footsteps were arrested at the threshold, and unconsciously she became a listener.

" Forget myself!" replied he, bitterly. " Yes—that is the word—that is my reward! I cannot help it!—My heart is at your feet, trample on it, Florence—trample on it, and crush out every feeling—or breathe into it the breath of new and vigorous life! Florence, I love you!"

" Mr. Ranthorpe!" she exclaimed, rising with feigned astonishment.

" I love you—love you!" he fiercely reiterated.

A low and stifled scream startled them both. It was followed by a heavy fall on the ground. They looked, and beheld the senseless form of the broken-hearted Isola.

"O God! O God! O God!" exclaimed Ranthorpe, hiding his face between his hands, agonised at the sight of his wrong.

"Miss Churchill has fainted—ring the bell," said Florence.

"Fainted!" he replied, in a hollow tone—"She is dead! dead—and I have killed her!—Said I not that my heart was at your feet? There it is," pointing to Isola, "there! I have sacrificed *her* to my mad passion—I have filled my soul with horror and remorse to gain a smile from you.— And now, here, over her corpse—here, at my feet, this victim of my love—here, with *her* between us, do I repeat ' *I love you!* '—what is your answer?—You are silent! You love me not!—You have played with me!—Behold, at your feet, your deed!—O God! O God!"

He rushed out of the house; wandering through the streets, with the prostrate form of his once-loved Isola ever before his eyes, goading him to madness.

He returned home weakened, and almost deadened to external impressions, while internally the Eumenides goaded him to despair. His first act was to write to Isola, imploring forgiveness;—telling her that the last chord that had bound him to a false ambition was snapped; —and that he had seen his error.

His messenger returned with the information that Miss Churchill had left Lady Theresa, and no one knew whither she had gone!

BOOK III.

THE UNSUCCESSFUL AUTHOR.

O, my blessing!
I feel a hand of mercy lift me up
Out of a world of waters, and now sets me
Upon a mountain, where the sun plays most
To cheer my heart, even as it dries my limbs.
THOMAS MIDDLETON.—*No Wit like a Woman's.*

CHAPTER I.

THE ARISTOCRACY OF INTELLECT.

When there is no difference in men's worths,
Titles are jests.
                              BEAUMONT AND FLETCHER.

Jung und Alte, Gross und Klein,
Grässlickes Gelichter!
Niemand will ein Schuster seyn,
Jedermann ein Dichter!
                              GÖTHE.

For there is no power on earth which setteth up a throne in the
spirits and souls of men, and in their cogitations, imaginations, opinions,
and beliefs, but knowledge and learning.
                              BACON.

RANTHORPE stumbled at the threshold of his career.
His mistake was fatal, though common. He misconceived
his own position in the world: he belonged by nature to
one aristocracy, and he aspired to the other ; born a
member of the great aristocracy of intellect, he misconceived his rank, and yearned for recognition and fellowship
in the great aristocracy of birth.

Let me explain.

Birth was in antique times the ensign of command.
Those only who belonged to the aristocracy were free.

To be born under a certain condition was to be a *thing*, not a man ; it was to be a slave, progenitor of slaves ; a slave, with no hope of freedom, but from the master's caprice or avarice. To be a man—to enjoy man's imperious will and proud prerogatives—it was necessary to be born free.

Birth was then indeed glorious ; no misfortune could obscure it ; no rivalry could equal it ; without it, men were the *property*, the goods of another. To be a slave was to be branded, even in enfranchisement, with contempt : the slave might be freed, but he could not with his servitude shake off the stigma of his birth. He might, in corrupt ages, become the emperor of the world— but not even the imperial purple could hide the original stain ; and a Diocletian, a Pertinax, a Probus, or a Vitellius, never escaped that bitter reproach.

Birth was all-important. A man might have senses, apprehensions, affections,—but he was a *thing*, unless he belonged to the privileged few. No wonder that the pride and exclusiveness of the few became outrageous !

Things have changed since then. Christianity, by its institutions, no less than by its doctrines, abolished the great distinction of races, noble and servile. Slavery, which to the wisest and humanest of the ancients seemed a necessary condition of society, became abolished. Industry, in the hands of these enfranchised slaves, became a power. The people was created—society was changed.

Yet in those antique times, side by side with this most haughty aristocracy of birth, arose the haughty aristocracy of mind. Like its rival, this, too, was essentially *oligarchical*, tyrannical, and, like it, was also scrupulous to keep the profane vulgar from its circle. Philosophy was confined to a few teachers and their disciples ; and to keep its secrets from the world, the Egyptian priests invented their hieroglyphics, symbolical instructions, and mysterious ceremonies.

So long as mind was the vicegerent of religion, so long was its power, even over birth, acknowledged ; but when its office changed—extended—then its power fell.

This power it is fast regaining. Mind holds the supremacy once held by rank, though not so exclusively.

Mind, so jealous when it first felt its power, that it employed every machination to keep that power in the hands of the few, has now, because for the first time it truly recognises its own mission, become, instead of a waxen taper shining in a cell, a glorious sun giving the whole world light. The learned languages are no longer written; the living speech utters the living thought; and cheap literature, in some of its myriad channels, conveys that thought even to the poorest cottage.

Learning no longer rules supreme, but must give place to *knowledge :* the owl has become an eagle !

The aristocracy of birth is not the figment certain democrats proclaim. A thorough-bred hunter is not a hack. The members of a jealous aristocracy preserve their social preponderance, not only by their fortunes, but also by the purity of their race. They have purer blood—more beautiful persons—greater refinement of manner. These things have their influence, because they are *qualities*, not accidents. Your true nobleman remains such, through every misfortune.

> " Licet superbus ambules pecuniâ,
> *Fortuna non mutat genus.*"

Strip your banker-lord of his wealth—and where is his nobility ?

But the aristocracy of birth is no longer the power which it was formerly. The real government lies in Intelligence. "*Le Roi règne et ne gouverne pas.*" To Intelligence both Rank and Wealth must bend the knee—and do bend it.

"*Si on annonçait M. de Montmorency et M. de Balzac dans un salon,*" says Jules Janin "*on regarderait M. de Balzac.*" Who occupies the foremost position in the world's eye—the lord or the admired author? While the most potent Marquis of Fiddle-faddle, with all his untold wealth and line of ancestry, "dies and makes no sign"—the house, the room where the author lived, the chair wherein he sat, or the desk on which he wrote, are treasured as national relics unto which thousands of pious pilgrims make journeys from year to year; and libraries are full of "Lives," "Memoirs," correspondence, anecdotes, and criticisms of this one man ; no mention being made of my Lord Marquis. The haughty Duc de St. Simon could say of Voltaire, "that is the son of my father's notary;" yet that notary's son was the most potent man in all France—in all that France had produced for the century; and in his eighty-fourth year, on his visit to the capital, was received like some Julius Cæsar in his triumph. Rousseau was the son of a watchmaker—D'Alembert was picked up in the streets—Burns followed the plough. Had these men no nobility? Were they not of the ἀριστεια ?

Whatever future changes may produce, there are at the present day two potent aristocracies, both swarming with presumptuous parvenus, despicable and despised : parvenus (let it never be forgotten) of intelligence as well as of station : men who aspire to qualities they have no claim to: eunuchs of ambition !

Society is brimful of absurdities, which no ridicule will

*re*wither; and of this kind is the absurdity of the members of *one* aristocracy consenting to become parvenus in the *other:* authors degrading themselves into parvenus of station, and lords descending into parvenus of intelligence—this indeed is a misconception sometimes fatal; always ludicrous. Lords, consent to be lords; and, before attempting to be authors, rigidly scrutinise your claims and title deeds! You are proud of your own blazonry, and ridicule the pretensions of the parvenu; but you become equally ridiculous when aiming after the blazonry of mental aristocracy—the titles of books; unless, indeed, you have the gift of genius to secure your position.

Authors, consent to be authors; and before attempting to " move in the first circles," unless your position call you there, rigidly scrutinise *what* it is you want : what is your aim, and whether this society and its demands be compatible with the mission of your lives. Do not degrade yourselves by abdication of a rightful throne for a baffled attempt at usurpation of a foreign one.

Either there is dignity in intellectual rank, or there is not : if there is, no other rank is needed ; if there is not, no other rank can give it ; for dignity is not an accident, but a quality.

CHAPTER II.

PRIEZ POUR LUI.

> Full little knowest thou that hast not tried,
> What hell it is in suing long to bide;
> To lose good days that might be better spent;
> To waste long nights in pensive discontent;
> To speed to-day, to be put back to-morrow;
> To feed on hope; to pine with fear and sorrow;
> To fret thy soul with crosses and with cares;
> To eat thy heart through comfortless despairs;
> To fawn, to crouch, to wait, to ride, to ronne,
> To speed, to give, to want, to be undonne.
>
> SPENSER.

Oui, mon ami, le véritable et la plus digne ressource d'un homme de lettres est en lui-même et dans ses talents.

VOLTAIRE.

A PRISON stared Ranthorpe in the face when he awoke to the stern realities of life. Duns beset his doors, and made him deeply feel the humiliation of his lot. He had abjured his pilgrim's scrip and staff, and now was stumbling over the path to ruin. One bitter lesson he had learnt:—to trust only to himself. Bitter, but beneficial; for it served to bring his mind back again to the right disposition, and served to unveil to him the utter folly of his previous hopes.

In his rage he first cursed the world and its falsehoods, —he pictured mankind in all the despicable colours of resentment; he scorned them with a scorn of rash-judging youth, and hated them with the hatred of one just deceived. All this was beneficial, for it threw him upon himself; and made him look only to himself, and his profession, for his support and glory. He learnt the feeling of majestic self-reliance;—too often but a pitiable self-reference!

And yet, in moments of despair, this feeling of self-reliance seemed to him a mockery, and the world a huge distorted farce. Self-reliance!—what could come of it? Was he not without friends—without money—without work? Would superb self-reliance procure him the meanest necessaries?

The book of life had lain open before him, and on its fair pages he had scrawled the characters of folly and misery; were it not better at once to throw that book into the flames, than tear those blotted pages out?

His situation was indeed pitiable; and yet he could do nothing to better it. He mused and mused over his past folly, and his blighted prospects; but he could only muse: his thoughts were directed to the past and future.

The truth is, he was unfitted for work; his previous habits and his present melancholy equally interposed. The life of an author, when he sets himself to work, must be placid and contemplative; he who has to live in an ideal world, should be tranquil as regards the real. He should know the *real* world—he should have suffered in it— and experienced all its phases, grave and gay, rich and poor; but this experience, which is to be the fountain of his inspiration, must not mingle with the current. The stream flows bright and limpid over its sandy bed; but if you disturb that bed, the sand mixes with the water, making it thick and undrinkable. Experience is the bed over which must flow the lucent stream of poetry.

The poet can no more write without having suffered and thought, than the bird can fly in an exhausted air-pump. He must *learn* the chords of the everlasting harp, before he can draw sweet music from it. But he cannot play while he is learning—he cannot write while he is suffering—he cannot sing while his heart is bleeding. If he attempt it, he will but utter incoherent sobs. He must wait until that suffering has passed into memory. There it will work, fortifying the soul with its examples, not tearing it with thorns. He must wait till suffering has become spiritualised, by losing every portion of the sensuous pain, before he can transmute it into poetry: because in the divine world of art all is ideal, even tears; and in its battles no *real blood* flows from the wounded soldier, but celestial *ichor* from the wounded god.

CHAPTER III.

EXPIATION.

Sans avenir, riche de mon printemps,
Leste et joyeux, je montais six étages,
Dans un grenier qu'on est bien à vingt ans.

BERANGER.

Les larmes troublent la vue.

ALFRED DE VIGNY.

Juste ciel! tout mon sang dans mes veines se glace!
O trouble! ô desespoir! ô déplorable race!

RACINE.

RANTHORPE renounced society. The friends whom he had courted, to whom he looked for patronage and success, were now regarded by him in their true light. He saw that genius, however great, has nothing in common with the drawing-room, unless it dwell in the mind of a man bred up in drawing-rooms; he began to heartily despise the people by whom he had a little while ago aspired to be treated as an equal; he rushed into the other extreme, and thought society synonymous with frivolity. Florence he cursed in the bitterness of his heart, though he had really no one but himself to blame; he was furious at her treatment of him; filled with remorse at his treatment of Isola. He was as one awakened from a debauch, whose brain, no longer troubled with the fumes of wine, clearly apprehends the folly of his acts.

But amongst his old friends he found true friendship—
ready sympathy. Wynton sincerely felt for him; he had
cause to do so.   Joyce was foremost in his offers of ser-
vices, and soon procured him several means of lucrative
employment; he was, however, too much depressed to
write.   Harry Cavendish instantly remembered that his
" rooms" were too large for him; and that, having a spare
bed-room, it would be both pleasant and economical if
Ranthorpe would lodge with him.   This offer was accepted the more joyfully because Ranthorpe felt the want
of Harry's liveliness as a preservative against despair.

Harry's " rooms" were not illustrious for their elegance.
They consisted of a first floor in Hans Place, Sloane
Street, comprising a drawing-room, and two bed rooms;
but, although Hans Place is dull and murky enough,
No. 7 was a lively house—the cage might be dark, the
birds within sang merrily.

The furniture of the drawing-room was not exactly in
accordance with Ranthorpe's newly-awakened luxurious
taste, but his position prevented him from fastidiousness.
One stout mahogany table covered with a very dingy
green cloth, variegated with figures of gentlemen in hunt-
ing costumes, dogs, and birds as large as the men; four
dusky-looking chairs, from the seats of which the horse-
hair bulged in various places; one discrepant sofa, a well-
used drugget, a ricketty cheffonier upon which were ranged
a few medical books, two meerschaum pipes, an instrument case, and a pair of boxing gloves; one green flower
stand, with the paint much peeled off, containing one
solitary myrtle pot: such were the articles of use.

Elegance, however, was not unattempted, as Mrs. Captain Wilson, their landlady, piqued herself upon her
" taste," and, although " misfortunes" (not specified) had

reduced her in circumstances, yet nothing she declared could "make her forget she was a lady!" Now Mrs. Wilson thought that "a few elegant little knicknacks," always made a room look well, and "so much depended on appearances!" Such was her theory; her realisation of it may be gathered from the inventory of the knick-nacks gracing the drawing-room. Three large shells placed on the ledge of the cheffonier, were balanced by the charms of the mantelpiece; viz., in the centre one French cup and saucer, with a landscape and windmill painted on either side, from which rose to some height two peacock's feathers—very graceful, indeed; the cup was flanked on the one side by a tiny wax figure with tremulous head, carefully protected by a glass shade, with a rim of cut velvet round the base; and on the other side lay an alabaster poodle, with stiff curls and staring eyes; a cup, inverted in its saucer, stood by the poodle and wax figure; two enormous shells followed; while at each extremity were two chimney candlesticks with glass drops (mostly broken), and *save-alls* in them to represent wax-ends. An ancient glass, with a diagonal crack, in a pauperised frame, hung over these ornaments; and over the glass hung a portrait of Mrs. Captain Wilson herself, in a low dress, with very long curls, as she might have appeared some twenty years before; one hand resting romantically on her bosom, and the other on the head of her daughter, a bony dabby child of six or seven, with flaxen ringlets and snub nose, holding in her hand a hoop of gigantic dimensions, while a blue scarf "carried off" her white muslin frock. A miniature of "the Captain," in brilliant regimentals, and highly pacific countenance, graced the space between.

I forgot to mention a stuffed blackbird in a glass-case which had a very lively effect on a side table.

Harry rebelled against these ornaments at first, but Mrs. Captain Wilson assured him that they gave such a finish to his room when any body called; and, in fact, so overwhelmed him with her experience as a woman and a housekeeper of many years' standing, that he was perforce obliged to let her have her way.

Here Ranthorpe found an economical home, and a joyous companion, whose unflagging spirits served in a great measure to correct his despondency. But when Harry was absent, the fits of melancholy would return; and the unhappy poet was unable to find refuge in the only direction where it could possibly be found—in work.

And why was he unable?

In the whirl and giddiness of his lionism, he had contracted debts with the same recklessness as he had done every thing else. But his sense of honour was now galled when these debts were to be paid, and he found himself without money to pay them. He had been corrupted—not hardened. His great anxiety was how to free himself from debt. He tried to write; but his brain was sluggish. He was too unhappy, too melancholy, to write. He had lost his ambition, he had lost his illusions, and more than all he had lost his self-respect. The excuses, which I formerly endeavoured to make for him, did not occur to his mind. He only saw the facts and their results; saw how he had wasted his money, his time, and his affections; and lost his position, his ambition, and his now doubly-dear Isola.

He threw down his pen and strolled out. His way led

him into Hyde Park. A sudden pang shot through him as he saw Lady Wilmington's carriage driving slowly along. To avoid all possible rencontre, he turned into Kensington Gardens. There he wandered about gloomily, retracing the history of his acquaintance with Florence; and it was in this mood that he was startled and annoyed to find himself standing face to face with Fanny, who, blushing and smiling, held out her hand to him. The carriage had brought her there, and was waiting till she had concluded her walk.

He was very agitated; and his agitation communicated itself to her; though in general she was not at all shy with him.

" How is it that we have not seen you?" she asked, at length. " Two whole months to-morrow, since you last called! Is this kind?"

Ranthorpe looked at her wonderingly.

" I thought you considered us as friends," she continued, looking down.

" I have been ill," he said, at last, anxious to make some answer.

" Ill? oh .... not dangerously?" she said, eagerly.

" I fear incurably," he said, without intending it.

She raised her large eyes to him; they were full of tears.

He felt uneasy. He could not understand her. She must surely know of Florence's rejection of him—and yet her manner seemed to show that she wished to be considered his friend as heretofore. They walked on together for a few yards in silence.

" I hope you have the best advice," she said, timidly.

" The very best—my physician is Sorrow. His drugs are bitter, but they either kill or cure."

" Sorrow ?—oh ! what cause can you have for sorrow ?"

" Many; above all, the loss of my own respect—the sense of my own weakness—madness."

" What weakness can a mind like yours have—oh ! how can you, who have the world's respect, be wanting in your own ? This is some momentary despondency."

" Are you then ignorant—is my secret a secret to you ?"

She blushed deeply, and looked down. He misinterpreted her blush.

" I see you know it; well, then, is it not weakness to forget your *station*—to raise your eyes to one who can never look down upon you, so far are you beneath her in the social scale ?—Is that not weakness—madness ?"

Her eyes filled with tears; but they were tears of joy. A suffocating sensation—dim, but intense—rendered her speechless. She felt he was on the eve of declaring his love for her.

" Oh," he continued, without noticing her agitation, " what a mockery it is to talk of genius—to declaim about the supremacy of mind—when the strongest mind is borne along by the wayward gusts of passion and vanity. We are the slaves of our passions; and our intellects only serve to make us aware of our slavery, without being able to burst its bonds. Miss Wilmington, you and I have often talked with enthusiasm about poets, yet, if you look into their biographies, you will find that one and all have suffered from ill-placed affection; they have raised their eyes too high above them, or too low beneath them. This has been my misfortune, and I rue it now. I have been too ambitious. I have been misled by vanity to place my affections where they could only meet with scorn."

" No—no—no—no !" eagerly answered Fanny, " not with scorn."

" Then, with worse—with ridicule."

" Ridicule!" she said, looking at him, tenderly, " you are not serious—you are trying me; you—" she paused, and then, with a sudden effort, but in a low and scarcely audible tone, blushing deeply as she spoke, " You cannot have misunderstood me ?"

Ranthorpe trembled; he understood her *then*, and his heart throbbed violently, as the wild thought flashed across his brain. She loved him !

In another instant he chased away the thought as the suggestion of his vanity. But one look at the agitated girl beside him, who, trembling, with downcast eyes, stood fluttering, like a new caught bird, awaiting his reply, convinced him that he had not misunderstood her. It was a moment of strange emotion. A young, rich, noble, charming girl, avowing her love to a poor, melancholy, ruined man, and that man one who had so recently been rejected by her sister, would at all times have been perplexing; but to him it was doubly so, from his anxiety as to how he should escape from the dilemma. He dared not deceive her; he dared not undeceive her. To tell that she had misunderstood him, would have been excessively painful; to tell her that he had loved her sister, would scarcely be less so.

Besides, in his heart of hearts, he was not a little gratified at her affection. I must do him the justice to say, that he never once thought of availing himself of it. He did not love her. Her rank and wealth were no temptations to him; although these things had certainly unconsciously added to Florence's charms. Nevertheless, his vanity was pleased—his wounded self-love was soothed at the idea of her affection for him.

His silence only increased her agitation. He saw that

it was necessary to speak; and justly deeming that plain avowal of his situation would on the whole be the least painful, as it would enable him to affect a misunderstanding of her words, he thus addressed her.

"My dear Miss Wilmington, I am sure you are a sincere friend, and I will therefore confide in you that secret which your sister appears to have concealed."

She was amazed and somewhat alarmed at this commencement ; the introduction of her sister was peculiarly unpleasant to her.

"You are good enough to think that my affection would not be treated with scorn or ridicule ; because your own excellent heart assures you, that were *you* so placed, the refusal would at least be kindly. But your sister is different, as I, unhappily, know too well. She won my heart—but she won it for her amusement ; and when I earnestly, but humbly laid it at her feet, she scorned me! You weep—you feel for me ! Thank you for those tears. I, too, have wept over my folly—and this has been the malady I spoke of ; my weakness was love; my madness was loving one who could not, *would* not love me !"

Her tears fell fast; her pale lips moved, but no word issued from them. The blood left her cheeks and rushed to support her sinking heart. She had been dashed from her pinnacle of joy, and was stunned by the fall.

"This is the reason of my ceasing visits, which to me were once so delightful," he added, in the hopes of giving her time to recover herself whilst he spoke. "Of course I could never meet *her* again. Indeed, I have given up society altogether; although there are some few whom I shall regret—yourself among them. There has always been the purest sympathy between us; and I shall always preserve a delightful recollection of you. But you must see how imperative it is on me not to waste any more time in society where I have no rightful place. I have now to devote myself solely to art."

They were at the gates. He conducted her to the carriage, took a respectful but friendly leave of her, and saw the carriage drive off with peculiar satisfaction.

When Fanny found herself alone she threw herself back and indulged in a paroxysm of grief. There was one ray of comfort—she had not betrayed her feelings—Ranthorpe had misunderstood her! This was something; it was a small ray of sunshine edging the thunder-cloud; but the cloud was not less dark and oppressive, because its edge was tinged with light.

Ranthorpe walked home pensive.

CHAPTER IV.

NEW HOPES.

He arose fresh in the morning to his task; the silence of the night
invited him to pursue it; and he can truly say that food and rest were
not preferred to it. No part gave him uneasiness but the last, for then
he grieved that the work was done.

BISHOP HORNE.

O pouvoir merveilleux de l'imagination! Le plaisir d'inventer ma
fable, le soin de l'arranger, l'impression d'interêt que faisait sur moi-
même le premier aperçu des situations que je préméditais, tout cela me
saisit et me détacha de moi-même au point de me rendre croyable tout
ce que l'on raconte des ravissements extatiques.

MARMONTEL: Mémoires.

RANTHORPE had recovered his self-respect.   The interview with Fanny Wilmington had this effect at least upon
him : that it taught him, firstly—how easy it is for those
in love to fancy their passion returned (and thus excused
his weakness in supposing Florence loved him); secondly—
it made him aware that his love for Florence had not been
an adventurer's love—that her rank and wealth alone
would never have dazzled him—never made his heart forget
its allegiance to Isola.

The reader may perhaps fancy that Ranthorpe needed
no monitor to convince him of this; but we must understand that he believed Florence to be nothing more than

a worthless frivolous, coquette. Accordingly, when in the severity of his self-examination he found that his love had been rather the result of a feverish excitement, than of real sympathy, he accused himself of having been dazzled by her extrinsic advantages, because he could then see nothing intrinsically worth loving.

Fanny's love thus reinstated him in his own opinion. He felt that if he had erred, it was from no unworthy motive : the inexperience of youth, his extreme susceptibility, and Florence's art, were to blame; and Isola herself, he thought, would pardon him if she knew all !

His spirits revived, and he began to write with vigour. Some miscellaneous contributions to the magazines had put a little money in his pocket, and he resolved at once to write a tragedy upon which he would stake his chance. Harry warmly applauded this resolution; and having determined himself to work a little more steadily at his profession, declared they would be " models to the young generation."

Ranthorpe then set vigorously to work. Oh ! how happy were the quiet days he now passed ! How calm and full was his content, contrasted with the unsettled feverish excitement of his former life !

There was but one sorrow—but one dark, ineffaceable spot: that was the remembrance of Isola, and the fruitlessness of his search after her. No clue whatever was afforded of her whereabouts. At times he shuddered as he suspected her of having committed suicide. But this suspicion was soon dispelled, by the reflection that her suicide would assuredly have been known; and moreover, that she was too strong-minded to yield to any weakness of the kind. Her absence was the only drawback to his happiness.

He used to rise early and strike across the fields for a long walk, during which he planned the scenes of his tragedy. The bracing air gave him such an appetite that Harry Cavendish, whose nightly dissipation destroyed his morning appetite, was ceaseless in his jokes at the poetical voracity of his friend.

Truly, the haycocks of bread-and-butter, and indefinite quantities of eggs, vanished with marvellous rapidity, while joyous conversation made digestion light.

His mind recovered its elasticity, and his work advanced rapidly. Pungent and Bourne vainly endeavoured to dissuade him from so wasting his time; he treated all their objections, founded on the ignorance of actors and managers, with the specific levity which characterises the poetic race.

" It is useless for Bourne to talk," he said to Joyce one day ; " I know very well that a good play is sure to succeed, and of course I fancy my play will be good. Bourne's plays have been unanimously refused, no doubt. No wonder; but I cannot see how what holds good of him, must necessarily hold good of me !"

Bourne, however, was prodigal of his experience. He inveighed against Macready, because he would not play "*Rodolpho the Accursed*," a part written for him, and calling forth all his peculiarities, with a mad scene and a murder. Bourne's tirades fell flat upon the ear of his friend, who, having *read* " Rodolpho," could not but applaud the taste of the actor. He was not at all surprised at the treatment Bourne had received, nor at all disposed to think it could possibly apply to his play.

" You are young and enthusiastic," said Bourne; " you love poetry—especially your own—you have confidence in its success; but let me tell you, that managers and actors are equally leagued against all dramatists; the former have an abstract horror of fine plays; their penchants are for pageants—their souls are drunk with sumptuosities and 'gettings up.' Actors are no better: they think of nothing but their ' parts,' which they *never* understand— no, not even when drilled by the author. All they care for is salary and applause."

"Surely you libel them."

" I don't, indeed; I flatter them, on the contrary."

In spite of this advice, Ranthorpe continued, and constantly sat up all the night ere he could lay down his pen. This Mrs. Captain Wilson thought very extraordinary; but what struck her as still more so was the declamation which he so loudly indulged in, " frighting the dull ear of the drowsy night." While writing, he was often so excited, that he would rise, and twining his fingers in his hair, would stride about the room, declaiming the verses as they were flowing from his brain, in that state of poetic exaltation, so well named by the Greeks, *enthusiasm*—a being full of the God. Now, although Mrs. Captain Wilson had the very profoundest respect, and some regard for Ranthorpe, yet she could not consent to have her slumbers broken by these fits of enthusiasm. She could not understand, she said, " why he did not sit quietly at his table to write, as she did when she wrote a letter, or made out the washing-bill;" and at last she was forced to remonstrate with him on the necessity of so doing.

He apologised, and promised reformation. To carry this plan into efficient execution, he went to bed early. The next night he sat up, however, and wrote in silence till twelve o'clock. He then, quite unconsciously, began

to pace the room.   To declaim to himself in an undertone was, of course, the next step—and to be carried away
by his feelings, and to raise his voice to ranting pitch, was
a natural consequence.

Mrs. Wilson turned uneasily in her bed, and had "no
opinion of authors."   At length, to his great joy, and
hers, the tragedy was finished.   He read it over with
considerable pride, and saw in it the sure foundation of
his fortune.   He then invited several of his friends to
a reading of this play, that he might profit by their
suggestions.

CHAPTER V.

THE READING OF THE PLAY.

Le Marquis. Quoi! chevalier, est ce que tu prétends soutenir cette pièce?

Dorante. Oui, je prétends la soutenir.

Le Marquis. Parbleu! je la garantis détestable.

Dorante. Pourquoi est elle détestable?

Le Marquis. Elle est détestable, parcequ'elle est détestable.

Dorante. Après ca il n'y a plus rien à dire; voilà son procès fait. Mais encore instruis nous, et nous dis les défaults qui y sont.

Le Marquis. Que sais-je, moi? je ne me suis pas seulement donné la peine de l'écouter. Mais enfin je sais que je n'ai jamais rien vu de si méchant, Dieu me damne!

MOLIERE: *La Critique de l'Ecole des Femmes.*

Bayes. You must know that I have written a whole play just in the very same style; it was never acted yet.

Johnson. How so?

Bayes. Egad, I can hardly tell you for laughing: ha! ha! ha! It's so pleasant a story, ha! ha! ha! Egad, the players refused to act it, ha! ha! ha!

Johnson. That was rude.

Bayes. Rude, ay, egad, they are the rudest and uncivilest persons, and all that, in the world. I've written, I do verily believe, a whole cart-load of things, every whit as good as this, and yet I vow to Gad these insolent fellows have turned them all back again upon my hands.

The Rehearsal.

THE piece was to be read to a few " literary friends," *i. e.* gentlemen who expect boxes on the first night, and

K

presentation copies; in return for which they are ever ready to enlighten their circle of acquaintances with information as to " what—is doing now;" together with many interesting particulars of the opinions, habits, looks, and domesticities of the celebrated author; which particulars have their origin mostly in conjecture or exaggeration, but being uttered with confidence to a gossipping world, are received as unquestionable truths. From these unsullied sources certain weekly newspapers are supplied, and evening parties enlivened. Thus the world becomes aware of the singular facts that Wordsworth likes the lean of mutton chops, and that Bulwer does *not* write his own novels.

To such an audience, relieved by Pungent and Bourne, Ranthorpe was to read his play. Joyce and Wynton had seen it in manuscript. The candles were snuffed—the author coughed—the manuscript was bent backwards—and the auditors looked becomingly serious. The subject was announced as " Quintus Curtius."

" Roman costume?" asked Bourne.

" Of course."

" Oh! I only asked; you know, I suppose, that Roman costume is in very bad odour at the theatre. Several first-rate plays refused solely on account of the toga. I know it from *personal* experience."

The poet replied that he was sorry to hear it; but as he had no great faith in such obstacles, with " Virginius" before his eyes, he was not much alarmed.

The reading commenced.

The opening speech had scarcely been finished, when Pungent observed,

" Pardon me the interruption—but you know my frankness—I may perhaps say fastidiousness—but don't you think the epithet '*pregnant* danger' rather indelicate?"

"To the pure all things are pure," replied Ranthorpe.

"True," added Pungent; "to the *pure*—but not to the *pit*. I daresay it may pass as a metaphor, but still you know the public is as censorious as a prude, and as sharp-nosed—I only give you my opinion—"

Authors! if ever you desire to appreciate the extent of men's impertinence, ask them for their opinions. Many many things they dare not utter spontaneously, are brought out by this inconsiderate candour.

"Why—since you ask me my *real* opinion," they observe (glad to escape the hypocrisy of politeness), by way of preface to their malice. Oh! it is a glorious opportunity. Never did they relish honest candour so much before.

This Ranthorpe experienced. Pungent's objection was but the key-note to a chorus of carpings. His friends did not listen—they watched for words or metaphors to object to. They had come there to give their opinions, and nothing but discovery of faults could have reflected on their judgment.

So annoyed was the unfortunate author, that he several times offered to cease the reading, but his " friends" were too anxious to exhaust their triumph, to consent to any cessation. At the end of the fourth act these judgments were severally passed:

" I think it wants action."

" No: but situation and variety."

" Some comic characters would enliven it."

" It is so very ill-constructed."

" You have no villain—tragedies never succeed without villains."

" It is much too long."

In spite of opposition the fifth act was clamorously
solicited.   During the perusal, the " literary friends"
were observed to yawn, to read the titles of the books on
the shelves, to examine the nature of their boots, and to
be curious about their nails.

They did not spare the fifth act ; the first four had
hardened them in impertinence, and the taste of honest
candour had been so inviting, that they surfeited themselves at last with it.   They advised him " as a friend"
not to send it into any of the theatres.

Bourne declared that if the piece were five times as perfect, he would have no better chance of getting it produced,
or looked at.   He (Bourne) knew *something* of theatres,
and Ranthorpe would *one* day tell him he had been right.
For *his* part, he had quite given the drama over as hopeless; and until pageantry ceased, and the true intellectual drama, with purity of purpose and legitimacy of
means, again arose, he (Bourne) should have nothing to
do with it.   With these, and many similar remarks, his
friends took their leave, having taught him a lesson he
was not likely to forget.   He packed up his manuscript
with offended pride, and reproached himself for having
solicited their attention.

" Had I merely shown my play to a few of my real friends,
like Joyce and Wynton, I might have been spared this
evening; I might have received hints from which to profit.
But these fellows are now rejoicing in having sat in judgment on a work they cannot comprehend.   Should it
succeed, they will exclaim on all sides, ' Yes, he read it to
me in manuscript; I took the liberty of suggesting some
alterations.'   Should it fail, they will declare that they
predicted it ; that they offered some remarks, but my

vanity would not allow me to avail myself of them. I will appeal to that sole critic, the public."

Reader, are you of a " literary turn?"—if so, let me hint a word of counsel. Before you submit a manuscript to a friend for his opinion, be very sure he *is* a friend. It requires great confidence in a man's friendship and rectitude, to place your self-love thus at his feet. The temptation to exhibit his cleverness at your expense is irresistible. If not that, then there is the other temptation, of winning your good-will by unhesitating cajolery. Depend upon it he will see nothing good in your work, or every thing— unless he is really your friend, in which case he will not be deterred from very plain speaking; he will not deceive you by flattery; he will point out the portions he objects to, with manly confidence in your appreciation of his motives.

In this latter case, a friend's eye is, indeed, invaluable; he alone can distinguish between intention and execution, and can tell whether what is clear to you, is also clear to the reader. But, as I said, you must have confidence in his judgment and his friendship before you risk his " friendly malice."

CHAPTER VI.

COSA SCABROSA.

O, but man, proud man!
Drest in a little brief authority;
Most ignorant of what he's most assured—
Like an angry ape
Plays such fantastic tricks before high heaven
As make the angels weep!

MEASURE FOR MEASURE.

O, it is excellent
To have a *manager's* strength; but it is tyrannous
To use it like a *manager*.

IBID: *variorum edition*.

ABOUT three hundred plays are every season sent in to each patent theatre—about three or four plays are produced !*

Those who shout their approbation of a dramatist on the successful " first night," naturally think that it must be a glorious thing to sway the multitude of hearts then jubilant with enthusiasm; but little do they know *all* that the happy dramatist has undergone, before his play could

---

* It must be remembered that this was written five years ago; now there is not one patent theatre in which the legitimate drama is performed. But the *cosa scabrosa*, noted in this chapter, remains the same as ever.

be produced; little do they know his petty vexations and serious alarms—the hopes and fears that have haunted his harassed brain—the " suing long to bide," and the " insolence of office," to which he has been subject!

Ranthorpe thought, that having written his play, the great obstacle was overcome; he knew not that he had three hundred rivals, and an ignorant judge: he soon unlearned his error.

Ah! glorious shout that betokens success! How it thrills the heart!—how intoxicating is this feeling of success! A thousand hands stirred by a thousand hearts, give my creation their approval!

Sweet, no doubt! but *it* would never repay the toil, anxiety, and distress which every dramatist must undergo. Ah no! success has no such price; the poet must be content to draw repayment from the delight he experienced in the elaboration of his work, in all the blissful thoughts which it inspired, and in all the activity which it provoked—only thus can he be repaid!

Ranthorpe had yet to learn the conditions of success. Having copied out his tragedy with scrupulous neatness, he packed it up in a neat little parcel, and enclosed a neat little note, informing the manager he gave him the *first* offer of his play, which seemed perfectly adapted for the present company; and requesting, that in case of its not being considered suitable, the manager would return it to him as early as possible.

This precious parcel he took himself to Covent Garden Theatre, for fear of any accident; and it was with extreme nervousness that he entered at the " stage door," and found himself in a dark, low, dismal-looking passage, where two actors, and some " understrappers," were engaged in a little playful conversation. He asked if

Mr. —— was within. One of the actors turned to the porter, and said: "Walker, here's a gentleman wants Mr. ——; is he in?"

Walker was at that moment superintending the cooking of a chop, and without raising his eyes from the gridiron, replied: "No—won't be here to-day."

"Then," replied Ranthorpe, "I'll leave this parcel for him." He blushed, for he felt that every one present must have detected him to be an author, and his parcel to contain a play. He hurried into the street again, and felt a load was off his mind. His play was presented; the next step was to have it produced. He invented several forms under which the flattering admiration of the manager would be expressed, in the note which would follow his first perusal. Then he doubted, perhaps, whether the manager would not be *too cunning* to express *all* he felt, for fear of raising exorbitant demands from the author. Before he reached his home, he had already signed his agreement with the manager, who all this time was as innocent of any intention of reading his play, as he had been of the two hundred and ninety-nine others!

A week passed, and another and another; yet no answer from the manager. Very strange! he must have had abundance of time to read the play. Another week passed; still no answer. Annoyed at this silence, Ranthorpe addressed him a long letter: equally unanswered. Exasperated he wrote again in a very angry style: no answer!

He called at the theatre: the manager was out. He called again: the manager was engaged. He called a third, fourth, fifth, and sixth time, and Mr. —— was always out, at rehearsal, or engaged. The season closed, and Percy had received no answer.

Deeply mortified, he wrote a very peremptory letter

demanding that his play should be instantly returned to him: and asking Mr. —— if he knew *whom* he was treating in that ungentlemanly manner. He received no answer!

Taking his horsewhip with the firm intention of applying it to the back of the insolent blackguard, who had treated him with such utter want of respect, he arrived at the theatre and found it *closed.* The manager was on the continent " during the recess."

I know not whether " they manage these things better in France," but I am sure that they cannot manage them more unfeelingly. There can be no doubt that managers are a harassed race; but their own interest no less than the respect due to all men, requires that they should adopt some better mode of treating with authors.

CHAPTER VII.

THE DRAMATIST WITH THE MANAGER.

Il est vrai qu'il les connait mal, mais il les paie bien, et c'est de quoi maintenant nos arts ont plus de besoin que de toute autre chose.

Pour moi, je vous l'avoue, je me repais un peu de gloire. Les applaudissements me touchent; et je tiens que c'est un supplice assez fâcheux que de se produire à des sots. Il y a plaisir à travailler pour des personnes qui soient capable de sentir les délicatesses d'un art, et par de chatouillantes approbations, vous régaler de votre travail.

MOLIERE: *Bourgeois Gentilhomme.*

Y escribo por el arte inventaron
Los que el vulgar aplauso pretendieron;
Porque como las paga el vulgo, es justo
Hablarle en necio, para darle gusto.
LOPE DE VEGA: *Arte nuevo de hacer Comedias.*

IMAGINE Ranthorpe's surprise when, some time afterwards, Joyce called on him with the information that the manager of Covent Garden had desired to see him the next day at two o'clock.

" I see your surprise," he added, " but it is a fact. I have some influence at the theatre, and interested myself about your tragedy. After persisting with savage energy for some time, I succeeded in making him read it: directly he had read it, he said he would put it on the stage, and he wishes to consult you on some alterations."

Ranthorpe forgot his anger in the pleasure of this news.

He no longer thought of horsewhipping the manager who admired, and would produce his play.

" I suppose," said Joyce, " you wont object to make such alterations he may suggest."

" That depends upon the things suggested."

" Of course .... of course.   But the fact is, you know, that people in the theatre have advantages which authors want; they have great *practical* experience—they understand the public taste."

" Amply do they show this—by repeated failures," said Ranthorpe, laughing.

" Why, I suppose like other men they make mistakes sometimes."

" The exceptions are *too* numerous to prove the rule."

" Nay, you are hard.   What I was going to say was, don't reject their opinions."

" I won't .... when they agree with my own.   I can't be more impartial."

There was a drizzly rain falling, and a keen wind blowing, as Ranthorpe set forth, the following day, for Covent Garden theatre; but the exultation of his mind prevented his noticing the inclemency of the weather, and he walked along holding imaginary conversations with the manager, and stoutly resisting imaginary alterations.   On arriving at the theatre he was shown into the " waiting-room" while the " call boy" took up his card.   The waiting-room of Covent Garden is not illustrious for its elegance.   It looks as dismal and despairing as the poor poets and unengaged actors condemned to wait there.   Two or three ricketty cane chairs—one table—and a very ancient carpet, constitute the permanencies; while variety is given by an occasional violincello case, a roll of music, a wet umbrella, or a paper of sandwiches, belonging to one of the gentlemen of the orchestra.

Seated on those chairs, or looking from the window out upon the paved court-yard, may at all times be seen various poets and farce-writers waiting to see the manager—to have an answer to their letters, or to get back the unread play; together with actors and " artistes," wives of chorussingers, attorneys' clerks, and creditors.   Every one looks furtively at his neighbour, and wonders " who the devil he can be ?"   Silence is mostly kept;—especially by the authors, who are afraid of betraying their secret.

Ranthorpe had not waited long before the " call boy" announced to him that Mr. —— was ready to see him. He followed him, accordingly, up a murky stone staircase, on which he met several of the actors whom he recognised, and soon put his foot upon the boards, having been duly cautioned " to look out for traps."   He had never been behind the scenes before; and as he marked the daubed and dirty canvas which crowded the back part of the stage, he wondered at ever having been delighted with such things.   As he passed down to the front, and saw the actors at rehearsal, his disenchantment was complete.   He had believed that rehearsals were studies: that actors there made the experiments in their art, which were to be consummated on the stage.   He was not a little disgusted to see them with their hats and bonnets on, their " parts" in their hands, gabbling through their speeches, like boys and girls impatient to be out of school. But this disenchantment was not without good effect: it was the key note to his interview with the manager; and prepared him to listen with more patience to the technical suggestions which were offered.

He was shown into the manager's room, with the information that Mr. —— would be with him at once.   He cast his eye around him, had only time to notice a cheval glass, over which hung an embroidered dressing-gown, and against which leaned a stage sword; a sofa strewed with newspapers and play-bills; a stage edition of Shakspeare, Oxberry's Acting Drama, some old plays, and a London Directory, huddled together on a shelf.   Scarcely had he scrutinised these, than Mr. —— appeared, and shaking him warmly by the hand, declared he was delighted to see him.

" Well, Mr. Ranthorpe," he said, as he seated himself, " I have read your tragedy with attention—very great attention—and I can truly say, that I was charmed with it—quite charmed.   It is quite a treat to me to see such a play, I assure you.   Fanciful dialogue—*ideal* dialogue—" and he looked at him to mark what effect this flattery might have.

" Ideal dialogue," he continued, " powerful language, and all that sort of thing—but rather too long."

" Too long?"

" Rather—for the stage.   But that can be easily altered; and the parts quite suit our company."

" I shall be happy to shorten it."

" There will be a great many trifling alterations necessary—mere trifles—but very important trifles on the stage. Some of your situations, for example, are *impracticable*." Here he detailed some.

" Impracticable!" exclaimed the astonished poet, " why they have never been tried—they are original!"

" Yes: perhaps so," resumed the manager, with complacency, " but original situations are always dangerous.

Keep to what has been tried, and proved successful—it will prove so again: that is my maxim!"

" But unless certain things are tried, you will never know whether they succeed or not."

" They would have most probably been tried before now, if thought well of. Our house is too expensive to be a school for experiments ; we cannot afford to fail. I always wait till some other house has risked a novelty: if it fails, I rejoice at my escape; if it succeeds, I imitate it, and work it till the public declares ' hold, enough.' "

Ranthorpe certainly could not object to a manager's taking his own measures for making money, but he rebelled against the idea of making art subservient to them.

" What you say is perfectly just," replied Mr. ——, " respecting the play as a literary production; but for the stage, other necessities are to be attended to. Now you have three Roman soldiers, who only come on in one scene, but that scene is important. Nevertheless it cannot be played, because I should have to put three understrappers, at a shilling a night, into those parts, and their very appearance would d—n them."

" But could you not have three good actors ?"

" Impossible: they would not play the parts: *not their line!* Believe me, you have too many subordinate characters."

" Not more, I think, than the artistic construction requires."

" For the stage, unquestionably. Allow me to assure you, as the result of long experience, that minor characters are the ruin of half the plays. Badly performed, the audience never takes any interest in them. The laugh which precedes damnation always begins with them. Depend upon it, sir, that Understrappers are the Small-pox of the drama: where they fail to *kill*, they leave indelible *scars!*"

Ranthorpe laughed.

"I am serious," continued the manager. "What happened to us the other day? That booby B—— was cast for *Ratcliff*, in 'Richard the Third.' You must know that one of his illustrious predecessors playing the part, instead of answering Richard's 'Who's there?' by

> 'Ratcliff, my lord, 'tis I. The early village cock
> Hath twice done salutation to the morn.'

was so troubled by Kean's ferocious look, that he said,

> 'Tis I, my lord, *the early village cock!*'

which brought down the house in one shout of laughter. Well, B—— was warned of this mistake, and the warning only served to puzzle him the more, so that when he got on the stage, and Richard screamed 'Who's there?' he blurted out—

> 'My lord—*there are cocks in the village!*'

to the convulsion of the audience."

"That only proves the necessity," said Ranthorpe, laughing, "of having well-trained actors to support the minor characters, and not the necessity of expunging minor characters from the drama."

They then went over the play together, Mr. —— insisting on immense alterations; the effect of which was to cut out all originality, and reduce it to a piece, as much as possible, like every other play that had ever been acted ; and having lopped off all that had not been represented before, the manager was confident of success!

The poet contested several points very stoutly; but he

was forced to succumb, because he could only get his tragedy performed on condition of its being what the manager wanted, and not what had been written. With a heavy heart he took back his manuscript to use the pruning knife, and make " the necessary alterations," and almost doubted whether it would be worth his while to have a mutilated fragmentary play produced at all.

CHAPTER VIII.

REHEARSALS.

O, there be players that I have seen play—and heard others praise—
not to speak it profanely, that neither having the accent of Christians,
nor the gait of Christian, pagan, or man, have so strutted and bellowed
that I have thought some of nature's journeymen had made men and
not made them well, they imitated humanity so abominably.

HAMLET.

To please in town or country, the way is to cry, wring, cringe, into
attitudes, mark the emphasis, slap the pockets, and labour like one in
the falling sickness: that is the way to work for applause; that is the
way to gain it.

GOLDSMITH.

RANTHORPE spent many a sleepless night in effecting
the alterations in his tragedy. Managers fancy that
alteration must be an easy matter, as all would fancy
who had never tried; but every work that is really a
work of art, costs infinite labour in the altering. I do not
here speak of the repugnance to distort the work for
the sake of theatrical precedent. I mean the absolute
intellectual labour of re-arranging materials, or piecing
in new portions with the old. When once a conception
has been incarnated, and developed in all its ramifica-
tions, so that it has expanded into a vital whole, the

L

parts of which are *dependent* yet *constituent* — then indeed to " alter;" to wrench out one scene or character ; to give a different turn to this and that incident; in order to " bring them up to situation," and from this mosaic to produce a whole; is not only difficult, it is almost impossible.

Thankless was the toil he underwent; but it made him forget his sufferings; it directed his whole thoughts to his play, and to the prospects for his future career opened by that play. His alterations completed, he again presented himself at the theatre, and was received with the same warmth by Mr. ——, who now declared the play was certain of success. It was read in the green-room, and the actors were all in its favour. Nothing could exceed their enthusiasm—every one was confident that " the town" would be in raptures. In short, as so often happens, a second Shakspeare was about to revive the drooping drama. Theatrical gossip was full of the new play, and the " Dramatic Intelligence" in the Sunday newspapers was in mysterious ecstacies of anticipated delight.

No prospects could have been more brilliant than those of our hero for the success of his piece, and he smiled a calm reply to all Bourne's insinuations respecting its not coming out at all.

" For my part, I tell you frankly," said Bourne, "that you may consider yourself a lucky dog to get your play read; but—" here he dropped his voice to a mellifluous whisper; " I think they must be insane if they bring it out. It will never do—Roman subjects don't do. Besides, your play wants situation. My *Rodolpho* had a *tableau* at the end of each act—and a murder—yet they said it wanted situation !"

Now came on the harassment of rehearsals. He was

forced to attend them all for his own sake, as he had to instruct some of the actors in the right pronunciation of the Roman names, and some few English words. There was one most desperate cockney who could not be induced to call "Fulvia" any thing but "Fulv*ia*r;" another had got irrev*ò*cable in his head, and couldn't get it out. Whenever Ranthorpe quietly suggested a correction, the invariable reply was:

" Oh, yes! I'll be sure to remember it."

There was another who could not be made to deliver correctly this passage, to be said in agitation:

> Fulvia is my sister—true—
> But why am I—her brother—to be mixed—
> In all her headstrong plans?

This he delivered, as,

> Fulvia is my sister—true!
> But why am I her brother?—to be mixed
> In all her headstrong plans?—

" I beg your pardon," observed the author, biting his lips; " but you have mistaken my meaning in that passage. " But why am I? a slight *pause* after ' I,' if you please, to denote the flurry of his thoughts, and then resume ' her brother'—then another slight pause. "

" Oh, I know what you mean—

> Fulvia is my sister—true!
> But why? am I her brother?—

" No, no," shouted Ranthorpe; but his anger was inaudible in the laughter with which this reading was received.

These were not the only torments: positive blunders of pronunciation or of grammar can be corrected; but blunders of emphasis, and more especially of conception, are very difficult to correct in an actor who, as he regards the

literature of the drama solely as "*the words*," deems his
duty done when he has learnt those words.

A queer-looking old gentleman in a scratch wig was
generally present at these rehearsals, which he seemed to
inspect with great interest, though he never made any
remark. But he used to eye Ranthorpe with a rigid
scrutiny, that made him feel very uncomfortable. He
asked one or two of the actors who this old gentleman
was; they only knew his name was Thornton, and that
he was a great play-goer. This information did not satisfy Ranthorpe, who could see no connexion between
being a play-goer, and always watching him so strangely.

Nevertheless, all the uneasiness and anger provoked by
the various blunders at rehearsal, were dispelled as the
poet walked home and saw underlined on the play-bills
the magic words:

In rehearsal, and will speedily be produced, a new TRA-
GEDY, *in five Acts.*

There was a significant mystery in the announcement,
and as he saw the people stop to read it, he moved away
with a sort of uncomfortable consciousness, not unmixed
with a notion that every body *must* recognise him as the
author of that tragedy; and when any body in turning
from the bill looked him in the face, he blushed involuntarily.

To have a play in rehearsal! Who is there that has
not speculated on the glory and delight of such an event?
Who has not pictured to himself what his feelings would
be on such an occasion?

It would be a curious morsel of moral statistics to calculate the number of human minds annually inflated with
such a desire. If we consider that every man who writes
at all, or even dabbles in literature, has at one period of

his life essayed a play, and then take pencil and slate, and calculate the enormous amount of authors, scribblers, and " gentlemen of a literary turn," we shall be able to work out a tolerably startling sum of would-be dramatists.

Every one of these men has had more or less the idea of having his play performed; and although many plays are " written solely for the closet " (when the stage has refused them), yet the idea of a rehearsal must have been unanimously entertained. To the Thousand and One Knights of the Drama, therefore, I appeal for sympathy with Ranthorpe's feelings, which can be so much more easily " imagined than described."

It was indeed a glorious time for him—so glorious as almost to make him forget the want of *her* sympathy with his hopes which alone could have made his felicity complete. The public were now informed that *The new* TRAGEDY *of*

QUINTUS CURTIUS

will be produced on Thursday next; supported by the entire strength of the company.

On Wednesday afternoon, however, the rehearsal did not go off so glibly as was to be desired, so the public was " respectfully informed that, owing to the indisposition of a Principal Performer, the new Tragedy of QUINTUS CURTIUS is unavoidably postponed till Saturday next; when it will positively be produced, on a scale of unexampled splendour!"

CHAPTER IX.

THE TRAGEDY IS PERFORMED.

Now sits Expectation in the air!

HENRY V.

How like a younker, or a prodigal,
The scarfed bark puts from her native bay,
Hugged and embraced by the strumpet wind!
How like a prodigal doth she return;
With overweather'd ribs, and ragged sails,
Lean, rent, and beggar'd by the strumpet wind!

MERCHANT OF VENICE.

THE Saturday night arrived. There was considerable agitation in the green-room, as is customary on " first nights," and considerable excitement on the part of Ranthorpe, as is customary with authors. He flattered some, and counselled others. Fulvia's brother absorbed a good deal of his attention; and he endeavoured to make that gentleman clearly understand that there was no sort of question *why* he was Fulvia's brother.

The afternoon had been rainy, and had only cleared up towards sunset. Every cloud had been scrutinised as an omen, and resented as an insult; every streak of blue perceptible in the sky was exaggerated into certain evidence of clearing up; till at last the weather did clear up; and

Pungent told him that was a most fortunate occurrence, that afternoon shower.

" Fortunate! pray how?"

" Why it will prevent your friends from being re-marked."

" Really, my dear Pungent, I don't comprehend you."

" Why, of course, you have a tribe of friends coming to support you, and whatever the weather, friends always bring umbrellas. Now the rain will bring a number of umbrellas, and thus conceal your friends in the crowd."

" Ha! ha! well thought of, Pungent ; but I have no friends in the house."

" *No* friends !" said the incredulous critic.

" None: I determined to give no orders—to ask no friends. I want to have the unbiassed judgment of the public. I want the success of my first night to be as genuine as the others."

" My dear Ranthorpe, your romantic notions have un-done you. Friends are the necessary counterbalance to the malevolence always awakened on a first night."

" I have few enemies."

" Personally, perhaps; but dramatically a vast number. The case stands thus: not to mention personal foes, there are always a number of envious rascals glad to d—n, they care not whom; to these add all the d—d dramatists—and all the friends of the ' other house,' anxious to prevent the success of a rival; and you will find yourself with a toler-able and formidable host of opponents."

" But the public ?"

" Why the public is an ass, and will be lead ' as tenderly by the nose as asses are.' The public is neither for you nor against you. If you strike its fancy, it exaggerates your merits; if you happen to be above it, or below it, you are lost. But I was hasty in saying the public is neither for nor against you. It *is* against you. You appeal to its *judgment*—your fate is in its hands—the temptation to exhibit their judgment and power is irresistible."

" How then do plays succeed?"

" By friends: judicious friends. Not those asses who applaud right and left: but friends who know the good parts, and shout themselves hoarse at them. You have exhibited a passion—the public wavers—knows not exactly whether to applaud or condemn—let some one commence the bravos, and down comes the storm. This is the use of friends: they give the public courage to applaud: they spur hesitation."

There was some truth in this, but his friend could not see it; he trusted to the force of his play to carry the audience with him; and cared little for *claqueurs* or cabals.

Bourne always went to hiss: and every " first night" he was to be seen in a side box, very enthusiastic in disapproval, so that actors,

> " Dreading the deep damnation of his ' Bah!'
> Soprano, basso, tenor, and contralto,
> Wished him five fathoms under the Rialto."

Ranthorpe felt very uncomfortable as he caught the sharp peering glance of the queer-looking old man whom he used to see at rehearsals. He could not account for the uneasiness he felt at his appearance: the more so as the old man's glance, though inquisitive, was kindly.

The overture commenced; the theatre began to fill; intellectual heads were sprinkled in the boxes; critics nodded to each other and smiled; ladies adjusted their shawls, and crumpled the play bills; box doors opened and shut with slams, and dandies looked round the theatre with their opera-glasses. The curtain rose, and the audience hustled into their seats. The first scene was between two women, and was accompanied by perpetual opening and shutting of doors, varied with exclamations as to " First party"—" Second row"—" One front and one second." " Take a bill, sir?" " That seat is taken, sir." " Silence !" " Hush !" Of course this scene escaped unheard.

In the second scene Quintus Curtius appeared. Mr.—— the tragedian being a great favourite, was listened to with attention. The lady who played the heroine was new to the London boards, and was consequently very timid. Ranthorpe was in a fever of impatience, and only consoled himself by the rounds of applause which greeted two or three bursts of poetry.

The act ended, leaving the public in a pleasant disposition towards the author. There had been no action; descriptions, and one love scene, had occupied the act: but audiences are tolerant early in the evening, and consent to be amused with poetry alone; and it was confessed on all sides that " Quintus Curtius" was full of stately and elaborate poetry, often rising to impassioned eloquence.

The regular enemies, and malicious friends, contented themselves with remarking the want of action, and looking forward to the third act.

I may as well here give a slender outline of the plot, that the reader may the more clearly understand its progression. In selecting the historical anecdote of Quintus Curtius, he had availed himself of the dramatist's privilege to surround that anecdote with what circumstances he pleased. He, therefore, made Quintus in love with a noble Roman maiden. This with some minor details occupied the first act. In the second the earthquake occurred, and the consternation of Rome was at its height as the curtain fell. In the third act the oracle declared that the earth would only close over the body of some Roman, and Quintus offered himself as the sacrifice. The fourth act was occupied with the grief of his mistress and his mother at the thought of his self-immolation, and their attempts to dissuade him from it; he remaining immoveable in his design, yet bowed somewhat by his sorrow. In the fifth act some of the people taunted him with the delay, and told him that the earth still yawned. He parted from his love—more like one going to conquest. The leap was not represented, but described by the mother of Quintus looking out: the heroine listening to her narrative in agonised suspense. A shout proclaimed the leap to be taken, and the curtain fell.

This is the skeleton of the play. The reader sees how deficient it is in substance for five acts; a deficiency Ranthorpe himself would have seen, had he not been deluded by his own delight in the mere poetry, and believed *that* to be an efficient substitute for action.

We may now let the curtain rise for the second act. This, though written with the same vigour and beauty as the former one, was received with visible weariness; people had got tired of speeches and descriptions, and showed such signs of this, that some of the enemies thought a hiss might be ventured upon it.

" Silence! silence! turn him out," instantly resounded from all parts of the house, as the ill-timed hissing began. The public had not yet rescinded its judgment; and though not approving of this act, yet (when the hissing commenced,) it applauded vehemently, out of contradiction. Upon this applause came a magnificent description of the earthquake, which made the " umbrellas" uproarious ; and when the consternation and well-grouped confusion of the Roman citizens, escaping from the yawning horror, formed a " situation" for the act to end with, then indeed were the umbrellas excited—then did the sticks approve dogmatically, and hands tingle with real admiration, and voices were husky with bravos!

" Wait till the third act," replied the adverse party.

The author's feelings during the second act it would be difficult to paint. It is a bitter lesson of his errors that a man learns when first he sees his play represented. When he sees the weaknesses which he had slurred over with impatience, and which he would not see to be weak, now brought before the audience in all their nakedness. Passages which he had qualified as those of " necessary repose," becoming on the stage those of unnecessary tediousness—the " quieter parts" becoming the sleepy ones. This the poet now for the first time felt; he saw his error, and cursed it, because now irretrievable; and he noted the silence and impatience of the audience, by no means grateful for " the repose" he had afforded them.

What made it worse, was, that the actors saw this also. They are the first to feel whether a play is going well or ill, and are the first to be depressed. By the end of this second act, they had very strong suspicions that this " new Shakspeare" was a nobody.

The third act—*the* act began—enemies were eager and expectant. It opened with " repose," and the enemies chuckled, making very audible references to bringing night-caps, and to the effect of narcotics. The public was also somewhat impatient. At this period Fulvia's brother appeared, and the author trembled. This unfortunate actor was gifted with a pair of cruelly bandy legs, and a broken nose; so that the Roman costume did not become him, or rather he did not become the Roman costume. The audience giggled; when he spoke, they laughed—for his helmet was fastened so tightly that he could scarcely move his chin, and his elocution suffered from its effects. Being laughed at does not increase an actor's confidence, and our friend had become highly nervous by the time he arrived at the dreaded passage, and he stuttered forth:

> Fulvia *is* my sister—true !
> But—am I her brother? To be mixed—

A yell of derision interrupted him, and Ranthorpe sank back in the box in utter despair; he felt that now the laughter had begun, nothing could save his play.

It was in vain that Quintus himself appeared, the tittering continued, for Fulvia's brother remained upon the stage, and the very sight of him was the signal for laughter. Now the storm began, and ridicule and insult followed every speech; the piece was fast falling, when it was saved by the energy of Quintus, offering himself as saviour of his country. This was a fine situation, and gloriously acted: the splendour of the diction, the earnestness of the sentiments, and the force of the acting, quite turned the tide in its favour, and the curtain fell amidst prolonged shouts, which drowned the groans and hisses of the enemies. The pit became the scene of animated discussion during the *entr' acte*, and the adverse party had a desperate battle to fight.

The fourth act began with animation, and soon changed into pathos; but it fell off subsequently, and when the mother and the mistress of Quintus began their lamentations, the weakness of the scene was again heightened by the inefficacy of the acting, the giggling recommenced. This giggling agitated Fulvia so much, that she lost all confidence,

and with her confidence all remembrance of her part.
Small blunders passed unobserved — greater ones were
laughed at—but the " worst had still to come." When
Quintus replied to her entreaties that he had sworn to
fulfil his vow and sacrifice himself, she forgot the speech
of passionate entreaty which was to follow, and exclaimed:

What, leave me!—oh!

She then stopped, unable further to improvise, and too
agitated to hear the prompter; urged by the tittering
public to proceed, she added—

Oh!—please, don't!

and " inextinguishable laughter shook" the house.

From this moment there was no cessation; the storm
raged with all the violence of a public that has found out
its mistake, and is anxious to atone for it. Peals of
laughter, yells, shrieks, shrillest whistling, hooting, slang,
popular catchwords, mocking " bravos" and " go its,"
accompanied every scene. That great Leviathan, the
public, took a savage pleasure in tearing the author to
pieces. Many causes might have been detected for the
violence of the uproar. First, seeking that sensation in
damning the play, which the play itself had refused to
excite; secondly, there was the exaggeration of emulation
in obloquy—there was revenge, for having paid their
money for amusement, and not being amused; and,
thirdly, there was the delight in an uproar, which is
always grateful to human beasts of all ages and nations.

The actors came on, and opened their mouths, and
" sawed the air with their arms," but not a word was audible; for the thunder of the gods and the yells of the

pit drowned every noise but their own.   Thus ended
the fourth act, to the great amusement of the audience.

Ranthorpe was nowhere to be found!

The curtain rose for the last time, but it was only the
signal for the storm to recommence.   In vain did the
manager step forward and request the audience to suspend
their judgment till the play was ended; they applauded
him, and laughed at the actors.

Louder and louder grew the storm with every succeeding scene, and the din became so fearful, that many left
the house, and some of the bawlers could not hear their
own voices.

Amidst this uproar the curtain fell; and then arose a
mocking shout for "the author! the author!"   After
which the delighted damners rushed into the Albion, to
discuss the exquisite joke over "kidneys and a pint of
stout;" or went home to report the failure to their wives
and families.

The manager was sick with disgust; resolved never to
burn his fingers again with "that d—d humbug, the
legitimate drama," but to spend his money upon spectacles
and ballets—a resolution he faithfully performed, till the
Bench relieved him of his arduous duties, and Basinghall
Street released him from his creditors.

CHAPTER X.

ASPIRATION AND INSPIRATION.

For when sad thoughts perplex the mind of man
There is a plummet in the heart that weighs
And pulls us, living, to the dust we came from.
                    BEAUMONT AND FLETCHER.

Hence doth spring the well from which doth flow
The dead black streams of mourning, plaints and woe.
                    FERREX AND PORREX.

What mortal in the world, if without inward calling he take up a trade, an art, or any other mode of life, will not feel his situation miseable? But he who is born with capacities for any undertaking, finds in executing this the fairest portion of his being. Nothing upon earth without its difficulties! It is the secret impulse within; it is the love and the delight we feel, that help us to conquer obstacles, to clear out new paths, and to overleap the bounds of that narrow circle in which others poorly toil.

                    WILHELM MEISTER. (Carlyle's translation.)

AND what were the author's feelings on hurrying from the theatre ? He wandered, unconscious whither his footsteps led him, brooding on the sadness which assailed his heart. All his brilliant visions were shattered like glass—all his ambitious hopes were crushed.

His tragedy, upon which so much was staked, had failed; and although he knew that much of the disapprobation had been excited by the absurdities of the actors, yet he could not lay the whole burden of the failure upon them. Had they been competent, had they known their parts, his play would have been received with more kindness, perhaps, but would not have succeeded. He had seen the torrent of ridicule arrested by a single speech, and laughter converted into enthusiastic applause by the conclusion of the third act. The fault of his play was in its not having sustained interest. When the minds of the audience are uninterested, they are ready to pounce upon any imperfection, and convert it into amusement.

Ranthorpe felt that he had failed because he deserved to fail. His reflections were most poignant. No failure is so palpable, crushing, irredeemable, as the failure of a play. Other works are neglected; plays are energetically said to be d—d. Ranthorpe's self-love was therefore sorely lacerated. But this was not all: something far deeper than literary vanity was hurt. The failure seemed to him a revelation of the inanity of all his dreams—an irresistible proof that he had mistaken Aspiration for Inspiration.

This mistake is common enough, and dangerous; but when the unhappy wight awakens to a sense of his error, it is fatal. So long as the delusion be continued, it will be a fountain of happiness to sustain the thirsting heart. A man will bear all privation and all neglect, if he can but believe himself to be simply neglected, not *wasted*. But once let him perceive that his life has been wasted on a chimera—that his energies have been squandered to make him ridiculous—that the light he has followed is no real star glimmering in the heavens, but only a will-o'-wisp dancing over murky fens and bogs—once let him perceive this, and the bloom and beauty of life is shrivelled up for ever.

Yet there have been few men of genius, I fancy, who have not had their moments of despondency. Exalted by the contemplation of Beauty, and the harmonious witcheries of Proportion, they have looked upon their own efforts with disgust; aspiring after perfection they have doubted their capacity to attain it, and questioned themselves narrowly as to whether they have not mistaken the aspiration, common to so many, for the inspiration given to so few. The very superiority of mind which enables them to conceive perfection, only the more readily detects the distance which separates their works from it.

In these moments of despondency, when with bitter irony a man interrogates himself and says—Am I what I thought myself? and receives only dark, vague answers— then, should failure come as confirmation, the thought of suicide arises, and is eagerly clutched at by despair. To such despondency a few noble spirits have succumbed: spirits who had endured the goading evils of poverty, envy, and neglect—endured them to a frightful extent, but never suffered them to quell their giant energies.

They wrong us who believe we quail before the ordinary ills of life! We have more than a common courage to endure; the history of our heroic predecessors amply shows it. Our lives are chequered; but because our path is on the stony highway, where thorns and flints pierce our bleeding feet, have we turned aside? Have we ceased the combat when wounded? No; if the path

M

be stony, are there not flowers growing on the hedge? If the path be dark before us, have we not an inner lamp to guide us safely onwards? Ay ; a lamp whose smallest glimmer irradiates the world with beauty ! By its light we walk, and walk cheerily; by its rays we are warmed and gladdened in the depth of winter nights, when perhaps the last dying embers flicker on our desolate hearths. We may be poor, but we are never abject; we may be neglected, but we are not unhappy until we neglect ourselves ! It is only when this inner lamp is quenched, or when we look on it as some false will-o'-wisp, that all the glory of our mission fades away ; and then what wonder if we arrest our steps and die blaspheming ? Answer, Chatterton ! Gilbert ! Haydon !

To have passed a life of cherished hopes and visionary efforts, and to find at last that they were based on air ! To have forsaken all this bounteous world affords, to feed the hungriest vanity, or greediest sense, and to find that you have been a dupe, a miserable dupe ! To hear the ceaseless roll of waters as they break upon the shore, and know how great the busy joyous world they speak of ; yet to feel like some poor stranded bark that had tempted the rough waves in youthful confidence, and now lies broken and deserted on them ! To feel that everywhere around you, men are happy, busy, and you alone without an aim— you alone purposeless, hopeless, joyless—you alone *wasted !* And in this despondency to recall the delicious reveries and bounding hopes which once were yours; to recal the lonely walks, on summer eves, along sequestered streams, where your busy fancy struck out many a gilded pageant of the future ; to recall your midnight studies, when with burning head and aching eyes you peered into the secrets of the great Departed; and then to look upon your present state, aimless and joyless! To awaken from the dream of life to find that inner lamp was false, a mockery of your hopes! This is misery—this is despair mighty enough to quell the stoutest heart!

And this despair seized Percy Ranthorpe, and he resolved to die!

CHAPTER XI.

DESPAIR.

A me non ride
L' aprico margo, e dall' eterea porta
Il mattutino albor; me non il canto
De' colorati augelli, e non de' faggi
Il murmure saluta: e dove all' ombra
Dell' inchinati salici dispiega
Candido rivo il puro seno, al mio
Lubrico piè le flessuose linfe
Disdegnando sottragge,
E preme in fuga l' odorate spiagge.
GIACOMO LEOPARDI: Canti.

THE streets were noisy; life, in its myriad aspects, appeared to the wretched poet, insolent and hideous. He strode along the streets with bitterness at heart, and defiance in his look. Several chemists shops had he passed, because in each he saw some customer, and he felt ashamed to ask for poison in the presence of another.

Having in his wanderings reached Wellington Street, he at once bethought him of the Thames. He passed on to Waterloo Bridge, and sat himself down in one of the recesses, to wait until midnight had cleared the bridge of all passengers.

The night was dark and cheerless. The rain began to

pour down with steady vehemence. The passengers became rarer and rarer. The hour drew near.

The time flew rapidly for him, although he was waiting. Plunged in thought—and that of the bitterest kind—he conjured up before him the phantoms of departed hopes, contrasting them with the realities which subdued him. His lot seemed hopeless. Isola lost. His literary career was blighted. He had failed; and justly. He felt that he had not genius enough to cope with the world, and had not strength enough to endure failure.

The clock struck one, before he was aware of its being already midnight. This recalled him to himself. Looking carefully around him, and seeing no one on the bridge, he climbed upon the parapet. In another instant he would have quitted this intolerable world; and the thought was bitterly sweet to him!

Before he could take the fatal leap he was pulled violently to the ground, and on springing to his feet again, found himself face to face with the queer looking old man whom he had seen so often at the theatre.

" Young man," said he, brusquely, " before you quit this world so ignominiously, answer me: have you done any thing which could make your life more ignominious still ?"

" What right have you to question me?" answered Ranthorpe, angrily and haughtily.

" Never mind the right, say it is *might*. I choose to do it."

" Leave me, sir, I insist upon it."

" Not I. You shall listen to me."

" Are you insane that you would trifle thus with a desperate man?"

" Bah! You know that if I choose to alarm the police

you will be taken before the magistrate for your present attempt. You see I wish you well; so be quiet. Now answer me: have you dishonoured your name? have you done that which should make you shun the society of honest men? If so, quit this honest world at once. I will not bid you stay! Bah!"

Ranthorpe's anger was roused, and yet he felt strangely subdued by the old gentleman's sharp, short, brusque, honest manner. There was something at once command-ing and amiable about him, which made Ranthorpe listen to him.

" Come, answer me."

" Well, then, no: I have done nothing dishonourable."

" Then what makes you quit an honourable world?"

Ranthorpe was silent.

" Well, what answer?" imperiously demanded the little man.

" I am weary of life," replied Ranthorpe, forced to speak.

" At your age? Bah! Your play has failed, and you fear the ridicule attached to failure?"

Ranthorpe assented.

" And don't you see that you make yourself ten times *more* ridiculous by taking failure to heart? If to fail is weak—what is it to commit suicide on that account? Pitiable! Contemptible! Bah!"

And in spite of Ranthorpe's mingled anger and shame, the old gentleman put his arm within his, and hurried him away, talking all the time in an energetic abrupt manner.

" Don't let me hear of such trash! Failure, what is it? A proof of incapacity? No; not a bit! only a proof that the audience and you are in different regions, and don't understand each other. Yours may be the region of darkness, certainly; but it may also be the region of such brilliant light that the boobies can no more see in it, than they can in darkness: too much light is intolerable to owls. Who knows whether your failure be not more glorious than success? Bah! Did not the whole of the Philharmonic orchestra burst out into laughter the first time they played Beethoven? Was Beethoven then a paper-blotter, or a genius? What did their laughter prove?—Their ignorance! Bah!" And with this short, sharp, " bah!" the little man seemed to settle the whole question.

" But, alas! I have not that consolation," said Ranthorpe. " I feel that my tragedy deserved to fail."

" Pooh! you *don't* feel any thing of the kind! No author ever did. The more the people damn, the more the author prizes his work. So do you; bah!"

" I assure you I speak truly. Performance destroyed my illusions; made me distinctly see the feebleness of my play. This tells me that I have mistaken my calling. I have a poet's ambition, but not the poet's genius."

" Wrong! If you really see the faults of your play, that proves that you are superior to it. Understand! *superior* to your failure—*ergo*, capable of success! I had a play d—d once myself; didn't like it—but didn't despair, bah! Try again; and don't be a coward!"

" A coward!"

" Coward! I won't eat my words. A man who cannot endure failure, is an ass; the man who cannot face adversity, is a coward. You are neither; you are only led away by a moment's ill-temper. That's paltry, pitiable!"

Ranthorpe felt he was at a disadvantage, and to excuse himself in the opinion of his strange antagonist, he informed him that the failure of his play was only the last drop that had filled the measure of his cup; and that life had now no charm, no hope for him.

His voice was so sad as he said this, that the little old man stopped suddenly to look at him; and then said:

" That's different. Open your heart to me. Tell me your story. I'm but a poor comforter; but there is always comfort in talking of one's sorrow. It makes the heart wander from its deeper woe; as somebody says. Here we are at my house. Accept my hospitality, will you? That's right."

Marvelling at the power acquired over him by this strange being, and at the curious denouement which seemed to present itself, Ranthorpe ascended the stairs with his new friend, and entered a handsomely furnished but somewhat bachelor-looking room, adorned with engravings, busts, casts, and books which indicated a certain culture in the possessor.

" Bring tumblers and hot water," said the little man to the servant; and when she had left the room he turned to Ranthorpe, and said, " you smoke?"

Ranthorpe nodded; but was perfectly amazed at the calm, matter-of-fact manner in which the question was put. He began to have suspicions of the little man's sanity. But he saw him proceed about every thing in the most orderly style. The spirit decanters, lemons, sugar, and all necessary materials for making punch, were soon on the table. A box of excellent cigars was produced. In a little while a bowl of punch, *brulé*, was flaming on the table; and the little man ladling it out calmly, bade Ranthorpe taste it.

" It's from a famous receipt I got in Germany. Nothing like it elsewhere. Bah !"

Ranthorpe tasted it; pronounced it delicious; lit a cigar; ensconced himself in an easy chair, and was surprised to find himself in a most unromantic and undespairing mood of mind! He had been gradually dragged down to earth, by the sharp good sense and imperturbable calmness of his new friend. And the soothing influence of tobacco, quickly completed what the old man had begun.

Yes, there was no disguising it from himself,—he was saved. The idea of suicide was supremely ridiculous in a man thus enjoying the common enjoyments of the world. And as he gazed at his queer looking friend, upon whose face the purple flames of the burning punch threw a fantastic light, and saw the calm content with which he was inhaling the fragrance of the soothing weed, he felt that, for the present at least, he must relinquish all idea of suicide. To rush from the scene of your ruined hopes, and in desperation die, is a foolish, but at least intelligible act. But after failure, to sit quietly down in an easy chair with a bowl of punch between you and your companion, and a cigar in your mouth, and to rise from this to commit suicide, would be too supremely laughable and contemptible. He felt this; for the ridiculous side of things rarely escapes imaginative people; and no man intentionally would mar the solemnity of his suicide.

And well aware was the little old man of the inevitable effect of his manœuvres; for a more sagacious head was never united to a kinder heart, than in the person of Richard Thornton. As I said, he was a queer-looking little old fellow; and queer were his ways. A scratchwig, which had never exhibited any lofty pretensions to verisimilitude or coquetry, sat carelessly upon a large head, the face being somewhat wizen and wrinkled. His eyes were brilliant, and shaded by thick shaggy brows; his nose would have been handsome, had it not been so pinched in at the nostrils; his mouth was small, the upper lip short and curved, betokening a turn for irony. His complexion was somewhat snuff-coloured; his coat was of a dark snuff-colour; his waistcoat ditto; and altogether his appearance was quaint, yet prepossessing. His manner was a strange mixture of fidgettiness, imperiousness, and tenderness. He was evidently an old bachelor — had been a spoiled child—and had an overflowing source of benevolence in his heart.

The sympathy he had from the first felt with Ranthorpe, when he saw his play rehearsing, had been increased by finding that he was the author of " The Dreams of Youth," which were favourites with the old gentleman; and his own experience of failure made him at once the friend of every unsuccessful dramatist. This will explain the scrutiny with which Ranthorpe had been so displeased during rehearsals. He was trying to guess what strength the poet showed capable of supporting failure, if he should fail; and the result of his scrutiny was so unfavourable, that he watched Ranthorpe from the theatre, and followed him, shrewdly suspecting his intention.

They discussed the punch and the cigars, and talked of Germany, as if they were old friends. Mr. Thornton had lived at Weimar, and had known Göthe, of whom he loved to speak.

" Ah! he was a man; emphatically a man. He looked like a god, and the people always spoke of him as the German Jupiter; not simply because of his majestic presence, but because of the calm mastery over all the storms of life which was written on his brow. Napoleon, when he saw him, said with reverence ' *C'est un homme.*' "

" He seems to have been cold and calculating," said Ranthorpe.

" Seems to *you;* perhaps so ! Göthe was no whining poet. He knew what sorrow was—knew what dark thoughts assail the despairing soul—but he was not one of your weak set, who whine, and whine, and despair, and die. Göthe wrote ' Werther,' but he did not *act* it ! He struggled with his grief—threw it off from him—conquered it—trampled on it like a strong man. No thoughts of Waterloo Bridge could gain mastery over him. Bah !"

This was galling to Ranthorpe ; and was dangerous policy of the old man's. But he knew that nothing sudden could be done, and determined to root out the idea of suicide.

" Göthe, my young friend, was the last man in the world to deserve the epithet cold. What makes boobies call him so, is the magnificent supremacy which his reason always exercised over his passions; because he was not as weak as the weakest of poets and women would have wished him to be, he is said to have been cold. Bah ! He was a loving friend—a generous enemy—an inimitable poet—only not a Werther. Take him as a model; see how he lived and worked. From a wild youth growing into a great man, and till his eighty-third year preserving an unexampled intellect amidst almost unexampled activity. That is the man you authors should venerate and imitate ! He understood the divine significance of man's destiny—which is work. Man the worker is the only man fit to live. Work is the great element in which man breathes freely, healthily. Work is inestimable delight — that which distinguishes us from the brute is our capacity for mental activity — and in this activity we find our greatest and purest pleasures."

This was striking a responsive chord in the poet's heart. He saw the effect, and followed it up. Having gradually excited the poet's enthusiasm to the requisite pitch, he then abruptly asked him:

" And *now* what do you think of suicide?"

" That it is ignoble—contemptible !" exclaimed Ranthorpe.

The little old man jumped up from his seat, hurled his humble scratch-wig up at the ceiling, capered about the room in an extraordinary manner, and then seizing Ranthorpe's hand in both his, pressed them tenderly, and said:

" Young man, young man, you have won my heart; you have done a good action; you have—"

Here he was obliged to cough to conceal his emotion, and uttering his favourite " Bah !" picked up his wig, and reseated himself.

He really felt that Ranthorpe had conferred an immense favour on him by consenting to live. If this should appear strange to any reader, he knows little of the benevolent heart. Mr. Thornton, whose fortune had been literally given away in charity, was too great an epicure in goodness not to feel keen delight in having been the instrument of Ranthorpe's preservation ; and when he had finally succeeded, he felt grateful for the delight received. He was, indeed, one of those rare but inestimable specimens of humanity who seem to have taken as their motto the lines of La Mothe:

" Pour nous, sans intérêt obligeons les humains;
  Que l'honneur de servir soit le prix du service;
  La vertu sur ce point fait un tour d'avarice,
      Elle se paye par ses mains."

A race not yet extinct, whatever may be said by the commonplace declaimers respecting the egotism of our age; a race which may boast of a living representative, in the wise, the happy, the benevolent Dr. Neil Arnott.

BOOK IV.

STRUGGLES WITH CIRCUMSTANCE.

I will stand no more
On others' legs, nor build one joy without me.
If ever I be worth a house again
I'll build all inward.

G. CHAPMAN: *Cæsar and Pompey.*

CHAPTER I.

ISOLA IN HER RETREAT.

The pleasure that is in sorrow is sweeter than the pleasure of pleasure itself.

SHELLEY.

> Sorrow, they say, to one with true touch'd ear,
> Is but the discord of a warbling sphere,
> A lurking contrast, which, though harsh it be,
> Distils the next note more deliciously.

LEIGH HUNT.

BUT all this time I have been neglecting Isola: not
because I had forgotten her, but because sometimes, in
the confidence of love, one treats friends with less attention than acquaintances; and so I consented to keep my
heroine in the background till I could have a clear space
for her to fill.   This now is found.

Nightingale Lane used to be one of the prettiest lanes
about London.*   It turned from the Kensington high-
road, and ran up to Holland House, after which it branched
into two paths, one leading to the Uxbridge Road, the

---

* Used to be, but is so no longer. It has recently become as prosaic
a lane as London's environs can produce; at least until it reaches Holland House.

other leading to Camden Hill. In this sweet lane, so
poetically named from the number of nightingales,

> " Singing of summer in full-throated ease,"

the delightful spirit might really—to use the popular
phrase—" fancy itself *miles* in the country:" it was, in
truth—

> " A most melodious plot
> Of beechen green, and shadows numberless—"

where foliage of every tint and shape, through which the
sun streaked splendour—where

> "Verdurous glooms and winding mossy ways,

enticed the sauntering footsteps to those

> " Murmurous haunts of flies on summer's eves."

As you turned up from the noisy, dusty road, into this
cool and leaf-strewed path, your eyes and ears were constantly delighted; you caught occasional glimpses through
the trees of Holland House, with its quaint architecture,
looking a living record of the past, and strong with all
the associations of a line of wits; your eye rested upon the
lawn stretching its rich verdure before the house, giving
pasture to

> " A few cattle, looking up aslant,
> With sleepy eyes and meek mouths ruminant."

The birds were in the trees, making them " tremble
with music," and the " heavy-gaited toad" hopped across
the path.

I know not why it is that lovely scenes—or even a bit
of sunshine on a spot of green—or the gush of a rivulet
through a deserted lane, always curiously affect me.
These things " overcome me like a summer cloud"—stir-

ring the depths of my soul; and yet so vague and sha-
dowy the impressions, that they seem more like the broken
memories of many dreams uniting into one, than any distinct reminiscence.   Are others so affected?   I know not.
To me it seems as if all the happiest, idlest moments of
my boyhood were dimly recalled; intense, although too
dim for the mind to give them form.   The murmuring of
water recals fragments of many scenes where that murmur
had before been heard; recalling, also, all the youth and
buoyancy, the unused sensibility, the trusting affection
and unfastidious taste, ready to be pleased, and pleased
with all it saw; recalling the delicious loneliness of youth,
when solitude was sought to people it with forms of the
imagination—when the unspeakable emotions of a heart
too full, could only be relieved by solitary brooding—when
the melancholy of a mind, without a purpose, served to
identify itself with the ongoings of external nature.

These, and a thousand different associations, are ever
recalled to me by the mere aspect of external beauty.   On
those occasions, as Wordsworth sings of the daisy,

> " Oft on the dappled turf at ease,
>   I sit and play with similes,
>   Loose types of things through all degrees,
>   Thoughts of thy raising.
>   And many a fond and idle name
>   I give to thee for praise or blame,
>   As is the humour of the game,
>   While I am gazing."

Some such process of association was going on in the
mind of Isola Churchill, as she slowly sauntered up
Nightingale Lane, with a placid smile on her pale and
delicate face, weaving " fancies rich and rare," or watching the green frog springing into the lush weeds that grew

on the hedge side; or allowing her thoughts to lead her
to the happy past.

She thought of her childhood and her early love; with
this love her memory wantoned, and would not quit its
sweet familiar details; till, at last, her thoughts were irresistibly driven to the subject of her first and lasting
misery—her outraged affection. Ah! what a change!
from thoughts of bliss suddenly recalled to that state
Coleridge so finely describes as

> " Grief without a pang, void, dark, and drear,
> A stifled, drowsy, unimpassion'd grief,
> Which finds no natural outlet, no relief,
> In word, or sigh, or tear."

This sudden recollection of a constant grief, from whose
oppression she had escaped for a little breathing time, made
Isola turn into her house with a shiver; and without taking
off her bonnet and shawl, she threw herself into a chair, to
probe the depths of her own wretchedness, and thus find
out its limits, or else to wring a pleasure from her pain.

The " luxury of grief" is a curious paradox; but it is
an incontestable fact. The morbid dwelling on some
hateful matter is a diseased delight; but it is a delight.
In certain natures the craving for sensation is so intense,
that if pleasurable sensations are unattainable, painful
ones are sought, for the sake of the sensation. In moral
pain, there is a feeling of existence, which, on some frames,
acts pleasurably. This is a fact, explain it as we may.

I have no doubt that *sulky* people, from the constant
brooding over the offence they sulk at, extract a real
pleasure, greater than any reconciliation could afford.
They hug themselves in their martyrdom—they make
themselves miserable, and delight in the sensation. They
stimulate their minds to activity by the constant pricking
of a sore place.

When we have real cause for grief, we are too apt to accept of the excuse it affords for the indulgence of this morbid feeling; and hence the profound advice of Jean Paul, that the first thing to be conquered in grief, is the *pleasure we feel in indulging in it.*

This curious fact explains how many people of extreme sensibility have been thoroughly heartless, and how it is very easy to shed floods of tears over the loss, over the misfortune of another, without ever having really loved the person.

The tendency to dwell on grief is greater in women than in men: firstly, because of their greater sensibility; and secondly, because of the monotony of their lives. In the hurry of business, or in attention to study, grief is quickly blunted and forgotten; but, in the monotony of women's lives, the indulgence serves to fill the weary hours with a vivid sensation.

Isola had this malady of the mind, only in a slight degree; but she had real cause for grief, and her solitude excused it. Forlorn and without hope, she found herself wronged and deserted by him on whom she had bestowed her heart. She toiled for her daily bread; and knew not why she toiled, for life to her was cheerless.

Yet, no: not cheerless! She said so; but it was not so. She had still her quick-pulsing youth and ardent faculties; she had still her dreams and her remembrances; when she read *his* verses her heart fluttered as of old—and life to her was precious! On that day which I selected as proper for her re-appearance on this scene, and while probing with relentless hand the wounds of her affections, her eye mechanically wandered round the room, and rested on the various water-colour drawings which adorned the walls; and as her eye thus rested on the work of her own industry, the current of her thoughts was changed, and flowed into that art she loved so well, and to which she owed her modest subsistence.

Art is a perpetual blessing—a household god of peaceful, holy influence—chastening the worldly, and exalting the aspiring; as Keats sings,

> " A thing of beauty is a joy for ever,
> Its loveliness increaseth;"

and with its increase grows its divine influence. No one accustomed to sit surrounded with books and pictures can have failed to remark the influence they exercise upon the currents of thought; whichever way the eye is turned those objects meet it, and their inexhaustible associations fill the mind with beauty.

Isola felt this influence as she gazed, and the Ithuriel spear of beauty healed her wound at a touch. In a few minutes, her heart was light, her mind active, and her face quiet with smiles.

The history of her life, from that fatal day when she overheard Percy declare his passion to Florence Wilmington to the period at which we again meet with her, is briefly told.

In her despair, she left her situation, without communicating to any one her design or her destination. It pained her to be separated from Fanny; but she wished to separate herself from all that could recal her passion, and from all that could possibly lead to the discovery of her retreat. She took an humble lodging in Nightingale Lane; and, when the first torrent of her grief had passed, debated what course she should pursue. An orphan, she had no one to guide her, no one to protect her.

After a little while, she wrote to Fanny, disclosing the secret of her sorrow and present condition. In an instant,

Fanny was by her side, and had to make *her* confidence. Strange tricks of fate that had made these two young creatures waste their hearts upon an ingrate! I need not say this new confidence forged another link of sympathy and affection between them.

Isola had determined to turn her wonderful power of drawing to account; and Fanny gladly undertook to get these drawings sold, and sold well, amongst her connexions.

Thus Isola became an artist, and created for herself a slender but sufficient subsistence.

CHAPTER II.

THE ARTIST.

Handelt einer mit Honig, er leckt zuweilen die Finger.
REINECKE FUCHS.

> My Dionyza, shall we rest us here,
> And by relating tales of other's griefs,
> See if 'twill teach us to forget our own?
> SHAKSPEARE: *Pericles of Tyre.*

BY the pencil Isola lived; by the pencil she contrived to satisfy her wants. Small indeed must those wants have been to be supplied from such a source; but she was as prudent as she was diligent, and seldom knew the sharp pangs of hunger, except when she purchased them by a weakness for—art.

She was a true artist, however humble her talent of execution; she had the genuine feeling and o'ermastering enthusiasm which only artists know. Whenever she had succeeded in executing a painting of more than ordinary beauty—whenever she had thrown more of her own feelings than usual, into any work—she could not prevail upon herself to part with it; and although the need for the money she might receive for it, was often very great, yet she could not let her prudence overcome her enthusiasm, she could not consent to *sell* her poetry, to part with her creations as merchandise: so she kept it, and lived upon a crust till another was finished.

Many will sneer at this as folly, some will sympathise with it as rarest wisdom. When the time of want had passed away, the "thing of beauty" remained to her, and was a "joy for ever." It graced her walls, and gladdened her thoughts. There are thousands who pinch themselves for the sake of a little extra ostentation, and may not one poor enthusiast do the same for beauty, without a sneer ?

Think of this lovely creature, with no companions but her books and pictures, and ask yourself: was she not wise thus to store up enjoyment for herself? Think of this enthusiastic girl dwelling for hours delighted over her own creations—expressing the unspeakable tenderness of her soul in the handling of a flower, or in the branches of a tree rustled by the wind ; think of her using her art, not for the poor recompense of money, or adulation, but as the process whereby she symbolised her innermost feel-ing—feelings she would shrink from expressing otherwise —thoughts which she dared not utter, but which in the unreserved confidence of art she could form into symbols; think of her fondly watching this creative process and loving her realised self: and then think of the pangs it caused her to part with these symbols when perfected; never to see them more, knowing that they were to go before eyes that could not read them, minds that could not comprehend them ! With the painter it is otherwise than with the poet: the latter does not sell away his work, but only the right of printing and publishing his work; he has it always with him ; the painter parts for ever from his work. To those who look on art as a clever manipulation—as alas ! too many are inclined to look on it —this conduct will seem ridiculous, and this symbolising

of her feelings a mere phantasy: it is so to *them*.   Only so
much as the mind knows can the eye see; only so much
as the mind perceives in any object, can it attempt to
represent.   Some painters talk fatiguingly of the "imitation of nature;" whereas art is not a daguerreotype, but
the reproduction of what the mind sees in nature.   It is
in proportion to the faculty of poetic vision, that a Claude
transcends a mere *tableau de genre*.   As an *imitation* of
nature in the literal sense, all landscapes are bungles ; in
the poetical sense there is no question about imitation, but
about reproduction.   I once saw a sketch by Salvator
Rosa of a mere ravine, with one stunted tree bursting
from a mound, and twirling its branches round a piece of
rock, that has haunted me ever since, while of five thousand so-called "landscapes" no glimmering remains.

There is a sentiment in every picture, however rude,
that comes from the hand of a true artist.   A cottage, with
the smoke curling from its small chimney, losing itself in
a clear atmosphere, may be either very poetical or very commonplace, according to the mind of the painter.   All the
correctness of tone, colouring, and perspective in the
world, are nothing, unless the poet's magic give the whole
that grace, impossible to be defined, but by all distinctly
felt.   The difference between an imitation of nature, and an
artistic conception of nature, may be stated by two examples: Denner and Raphael.   Denner copied every hair
and freckle; looking at the human face with a microscope, he
anticipated the effects of the daguerreotype: his works are
glorious specimens of *industry*,   while those of Raphael are
the most glorious specimens of *art*, and are truly "joys
for ever."

So when I say that Isola in her humble way *created*—
that she, too, was a poet—it is intelligible how she should

love her pictures which were symbols of her feelings. Art was her passion: it was

> "That blessed mood
> In which the burthen of the mystery,
> In which the heavy and the weary weight
> Of all this unintelligible world
> Is enlightened."

This passion served at least to soften the pangs of wounded affection and to reconcile her to life. Time, the consoler, poured his balm upon her wounds, and she became at last almost happy; only recurring with bitterness to the past, upon peculiar occasions, when she would brood over her sorrow, till called insensibly away again by her pictures.

She had renounced the world, and the world's pleasures, for the solitary, happy, active life of an artist. And she *was* happy with her books, her pictures, and her dog. I have as yet had no time to say a word about the faithful Leo, a superb Newfoundland dog, who as a pup had followed her home (she had not the heart to prevent him), and who had now grown into a noble companion and protector; but though I have till now neglected him, he occupied too large a place in her quiet existence for me to pass him over entirely. There was something about the calm grandeur and candid lovingness of the dog, which accorded marvellously with the bearing of his mistress; and as she stood sometimes with her hand upon his upturned head, they formed a group which a Phidias might have envied. Leo was of course the companion of her walks; and while she read or painted he sat at her feet, watching her with calm lovingness, and occasionally thrusting his head into her hand to solicit a caress. He not only alleviated her sense of loneliness, but often prevented her sitting at home all day, instead of taking invigorating exercise, for she oftener went out on his account than on her own.

CHAPTER III.

WOMAN'S LOVE.

As mine own shadow was this child to me,
A second self far dearer, and more fair.
    *   *   *   *
This playmate sweet was made
My sole associate, and his willing feet
Wander'd with mine, where earth and ocean meet.
    *   *   *   *
And warm and light I felt his clasping hand
When twined in mine.   We, two, were ne'er
Parted, but when brief sleep divided us.

SHELLEY.

BUT, after all, the artist cannot live wholly for his art :
human affections and human infirmities irresistibly chain
him to the world from which he would flee.

So Isola could not live without affections.   However
the peculiarity of her position might induce her to shun
communication with all former friends, yet the very sympathy and sensibility which made her an artist, made her
pant the more for human intercourse.

The heart of woman is a fountain of everlasting love;
without love it dies, with love alone it rests contented.   It
craves some object on which to pour the pent-up floods of
its affection.   The object may be fantastic, the passion may

be curiously distorted; but the craving must be satisfied in some way. Observe how in old maids this distorted affection, cut off from its natural channel, manifests itself in the extravagant attachment to some cat or parrot: this has its ridiculous side, but it has also a poetical one, for it is a symbol of that undying love women were created to perpetuate.

Isola loved her art, but she panted also for something human; something whose wants and infirmities, appealing to her pity, would stir the sacred waters of her heart; something to protect with lavish love. This she found in a neighbour's child, a chubby boy of five years old, with sparkling eyes, dimpled cheeks, and ringing laugh. Women are by nature fond of all children; and when these youngsters are well behaved and pretty, they are so fascinating that one may really be excused any extravagant dotage.

Who can refuse the petition of a chubby boy? Who can resist the stammering request? Who can be angry at a spirited petulance, which, though loudly qualified as "very naughty," is secretly admired? Who can help being moved with the sharp joyous laugh, the inexhaustible faculty of amusement, the absorbing curiosity and astonishing impudence of children? It is impossible; you can never yourself have been a child to do so; or else you have been crammed with hornbooks and instructive dialogues in the nursery, till you became dyspeptic and premature.

In the lane where Isola lived, she had often met with a chubby, rosy boy, of five years old, whose beauty and winning ways had gradually won her affections. Meeting him almost daily, she began to look upon him as a younger brother. Having nothing else to love, she soon loved him, and with an absorbing affection. He always called her " sister Isola," was always the first to greet her when she came out, and in a little time had established himself in her heart, no less than in that of Leo.

Little Walter became Isola's joy and idol ; on his education and amusement she expended all her leisure hours; and the little fellow touched, as are all noble boys, by kindness, used to obey her to the letter. She had rarely to scold him: to tell him he had done wrong was enough to send tears into his eyes; and even if he repeated the offence—and what child does not? he was always more sorry at having disobeyed her, than at the standing in the corner to which she condemned him.

Touching it was to see the affection of these two creatures for each other—both so young and loving; the one with sunshine always in his face, the other with a cast of pensiveness, which gave

"Elysian beauty, melancholy grace,"

to her sweet countenance. Hers was essentially a motherly heart. Her own strong nature did not need that protection for which woman mostly looks to man; but needed, on the contrary, something feebler to cherish and protect. Her love for Ranthorpe had always been greatly mingled with this feeling; she had early divined his weak, wayward, and somewhat womanly nature, and in their childhood and youth had been an elder sister to him. She foresaw dimly that he would need her support in his battle with the world ; and with all her veneration for his intellect, she felt somewhat towards him as a mother feels for an idolised child of genius. His weakness and waywardness, which would have shocked, perhaps disenchanted another woman, only made her heart yearn more towards him.

Conceive then the delight she must have felt in little Walter. She was now no longer *alone* in the world: and if, as they wandered through the lanes, his tiny hand in hers, or as she watched him romping with Leo, she sometimes sighed to think she had not for him a mother's claims as she had a mother's tenderness; still the constant delight of being with him, thinking of him, purchasing toys for him, and telling him stories, kept her feelings in such active play, that she soon recovered her former elasticity of spirits.

Walter's mother was in narrow circumstances, and had three other children, and she was very sensible of Isola's kindness to her boy—what mother is not so? and was always pleased that he should be with her. Isola taught him to read. Great was her delight at his pride when he jumped about or strutted with importance " worn in its gloss," as he informed every body, that " he knew another line, and could spell it all."

With Isola he rambled through the lanes and fields, weaving fantastic garlands of wild flowers, or showering them upon her in his sport. With her he sat while she was painting, and in grave silence daubed some paper with paint brushes, that he might imitate his darling sister (as he called her) and " play at painting." Often would she look up from her work, and catch the little fellow mocking her attitude with sly gravity, while laughter peeped from under his eye-lids; and then she could never resist pinching his chubby cheeks, and throw aside the pencil for a game of romps.

Or on a summer's evening, after their usual stroll,—or when the rain kept them within doors, she would amuse him with those stories which captivated *our* infancy, but which the next generation stands a fair chance of not hearing; unless a stop be put to the monstrous pedantic

absurdities now in fashion with respect to education:*
absurdities promulgated by the greatest set of dolts that
ever obtained a hearing; which hearing they obtained by
dint of a rotten sophism.

It is not enough that " Goody Two Shoes," " Jack the
Giant Killer," or the hero of the " Bean Stalk," should
ruthlessly be converted into *moral* tales—(as if children
were to be made virtuous by maxims—and, ye gods! *such*
maxims!)—it is not enough that men should so grossly
blunder as to suppose life a scheme that could be taught,
instead of a drama that must be acted;—it is not enough that
the affections, sympathies, and imagination are considered
" frivolous," and reading or hearing stories " sad waste
of time;"—these are trifles, " the worst is yet to come."
Children must be taught "sciences and useful knowledge;"
babies of three or four years old are to have the "steam-
engine, familiarly explained." Infants are to be called in
from trundling the hoop, to con over the mysteries of che-
mical and astronomical phenomena "adapted to the meanest
capacity." As in Hood's exquisite parody of George
Robins' advertisement, the pump is enumerated as having
" a handle, *within reach of the smallest child,*" so do our
illustrious educators wish to place the pump of knowledge within reach of the meanest capacity, that infants may forego the mother's milk to drink of its Pierian
spring.

Is this credible? In a sane country is it credible that
chemistry, geology, astronomy, and theology should be

* Since this was written a change has taken place and in the right
direction, headed by the active and tasteful Felix Summerly. Thanks
to him, and to Mr. Cundall, the publisher of children's books, in Bond
Street, we have now the best old stories illustrated by artists of reputation, and excellent new stories written by men of genius.

" adapted to the infant mind," and the infant mind embedded in this mass of indigested nonsense ?

Most wise doctors! Most credulous parents! Most unhappy children! To you all, a blessed millennium of science is coming, wherein imagination and emotion will no more vitiate the mind ; wherein " prejudices" will be matters of research, and the differential calculus be expounded to the infant in the cradle!—A time when " gentle maidens reading through their tears" will feel their hearts tremble over—conic sections; romantic youths will feel their breasts inflated with the mystery and magic of—the composition of forces; and happy men have all their sympathies enlarged by eccentric orbits! Then will the air be filled with sighs of " definite proportions;" and the dance—theatre—and pic-nic, give place to scientific meetings. Then will the budding rose of womanhood meet her chosen one, beneath the mystic moon, and pour forth her feelings on the atomic theory: her lover answering in impassioned descriptions of stalactite and strata !

This millennium is still, however, distant: as we thankfully acknowledge. Isola had no sort of sympathy with it. Her instinct, rather than her reason, told her that the child must *feel* before it can *know ;* and that knowledge, great and glorious as it is, can never be the *end* of life: it is but one of the many means.

She, therefore, fed his insatiate appetite with stories of human sympathies, sufferings, virtues, and prowess—fairy tales, and legends gay and sad. He listened with open mouth and staring eyes, occasionally filled with tears: precious drops! so necessary to encourage in the egotistical period of infancy; which is egotistical because it knows no other joys and pains than those it suffers; and when she ended, he would exclaim, " Tell it again ! tell it again !"

Tell it again!—what a contrast with the listless, restless mind which a few years afterwards cannot read a book nor hear a story told a second time;—which craves for something " new," though the only novelty be in the title!

Tell it again!—In those words the riches of childhood are revealed; it is in childhood only that we do not weary of the twice-told tale or the twice-felt emotion.

" Let us go and kill giants," he would say, after listening to the exploits of that Achilles of private life, "Jack the Giant Killer." " *Buy* me a fairy, sister Isola, will you?" he often entreated. " I'll be very good."

And thus they lived and loved. They were the world to each other, and beyond that world they did not care to move. There was in her love an intensity—an anxiety which differed, in its unhealthiness, from a mother's love. Isola loved a child that was not her own, and that might at any time be separated from her: no wonder, then, that she was fretful and anxious.

CHAPTER IV.

THE WOOF IS WEAVING.

> Miserable creature,
> If thou persist in this 'tis damnable.
> Dost thou imagine thou can'st slide on blood
> And not be tainted with a shameful fall?
> Or, like the black and melancholic yew-tree,
> Dost think to root thyself in dead men's graves
> And yet to prosper.
>
> WEBSTER: *The White Devil.*

WHEN Ranthorpe awoke, the morning after the night of his failure, he felt almost angry with Mr. Thornton for his benevolent interference. He awoke to find himself once more robbed of his illusions. He had again failed; his greatest effort to win a name had been received with derision. Would it ever be otherwise? Had he sufficient courage to act upon Mr. Thornton's advice?

He doubted his own energy. The intense excitement of the preceding night had now, in its reaction, unnerved him. He felt listless, hopeless, lifeless. Mr. Thornton called early. His conversation for a while revived the drooping spirits of his young friend; but on his taking leave, they sank again. Harry had made one or two efforts at consolation; but soon gave up the attempt as

o 2

fruitless.   He was, in truth, himself too much distressed at his friend's failure, to be an effectual consoler.

In the course of the afternoon a letter was put into Ranthorpe's hands: a mere glance at the superscription made his heart and temples throb violently, and he held it some minutes before him, unable to open it.   It was from Isola, and ran thus:

" MY EVER BELOVED PERCY,—I was at the theatre last night !   That will tell you how much I suffered and still suffer.   The manner in which your play was acted, would have ruined the finest work ; and I perfectly hated the actors !   Every applause made my heart beat; every hiss made it sick; and when I left the house—but I cannot write of it !

" Now, Percy, now do you most need all your strength —now must you wrap yourself up in the proud consciousness of your genius, and the assurance of its ultimate recognition, and not suffer failure to daunt your aspiring soul.   Despise the injustice of the world; do not let it make you swerve one inch out of your path.   Last night I felt despondent—unutterably despondent.   To-day I feel that despondency is weakness, even in me; and that you will not, cannot, let it prey long upon you.   Think of how often the greatest men have been misjudged, but how surely has the world revoked its hasty verdict.   Think of your own works, and compare them with works which have succeeded, and then see how little the accident of one failure can affect your hopes.

" Above all things resist despondency.   Wring what lesson you will out of this unhappy night, but only beware of attributing too much importance to it.   Rise up against it ; look it courageously in the face, and say: I have failed, but I *will* succeed.

" *Will* to do it, and it is done. That you have genius you cannot doubt; but genius itself is powerless, unless accompanied by strength of will. Fortitude of mind is perhaps the greatest characteristic of every great man; and that you will be great I feel deeply convinced, if you can but summon sufficient courage to trust wholly to yourself.

" This was all I intended to say; but it is in vain I strive to master my feelings. While pointing to the future, I cannot help recurring to the painful past. Besides, it would look unkind. If I made no allusion to the past, you might fancy it was from coldness, or pride, or anger. I feel nothing of the kind; and be assured that whatever it may have cost me to own myself no longer your affianced bride, I have now learned to endure my lot with patient calmness. I forgive you, Percy; I have long forgiven you. It was no fault of yours that I was less loveable than another.

" Be great, be happy! that is the constant wish of your devoted *sister*, ISOLA.

" P. S.—You will understand my motives in keeping my present residence a secret. Do not endeavour to detect it. I *could not* see you; I have not sufficient strength. When you are married—then perhaps ; but *now* I feel that I must avoid your presence. God bless you !"

This letter, meant to be so calm, was scarcely legible from the tears she had let fall upon it; and Percy felt as he read it a mixed sensation of pain and rapture: of pain, because he felt how much she suffered; of rapture because he felt she loved him still.

It awoke him from his lethargy; it gave life a value, and a purpose. He would not rest until he had discovered her, and not only obtained her pardon, but her hand.

He, who a few minutes ago was despairing of ever gaining a livelihood by his pen, was now all eagerness to gain a wife.

The post-mark was Camberwell. He instantly set off for Camberwell, and went to the various post-offices there, certain to learn from the letter-carriers Miss Churchill's address. After many disappointments, he at last was told where a Miss Churchill lived. He went there, and found an old maid, who received him with some embarrassment, but whose embarrassment was ease itself compared with his, when he discovered the mistake, stammered an apology, and rushed out of the house.

His search was fruitless. He became at length convinced that Camberwell had been chosen as the place for posting the letter, simply to mislead him as to Isola's real abode. How was he to discover it?"

Every day of the ensuing fortnight, at the top of the first page of the " Times," appeared this advertisement:

" ISOLA *is solemnly implored to communicate with* P. R."

But Isola never saw the " Times ;" never saw any newspaper. Had she seen this advertisement, she would assuredly have written again; but Percy, exasperated by her silence, which he could not understand—never suspecting that she had not seen his advertisement—resigned himself to his fate.

Her letter had, however, produced the desired effect. It had drawn him from brooding despondency—it had restored him his former energy and ambition. Mr. Thornton had, in his benevolent desire to secure the safety of his new *protégé*, offered him the situation of private secretary at a salary of one-hundred-and-fifty pounds a-year. Mr. Thornton dabbled in literature, and had made collections for a " History of the Drama," which he proposed that

Percy should assist him in arranging in due order, and seeing through the press. The proposal was accepted with thankfulness; and leaving his old lodgings, he was quickly installed in Mr. Thornton's house.

He was as comfortable in his new situation as it was possible, considering his uncertainty about Isola. After a little while, he followed Mr. Thornton's advice, and accepted Rixelton's offer to write again the theatrical critiques in his paper. Ranthorpe wished to study the art of the stage, and this office of critic, would, he thought, be beneficial to him in that respect. How much he really learned in this way it is impossible to guess; but he was very assiduous in his attendance, and very careful in his criticisms.

Let us leave him at his new avocation to return to a personage introduced early in this history, but of whom we have hitherto had no interest in following through the downward stages of dissipation and blackguardism. Oliver Thornton—the medical student, whom Ranthorpe saw in company with Harry Cavendish, in our first chapter—was the nephew of old Mr. Thornton. He now re-appears upon the stage as a confirmed specimen of the genus blackguard.

When first we saw him, he was to all appearance no worse than his fellow-student Harry. Both were " fast fellows." Both spent more time in saloons and cider-cellars than in the lecture-room or hospital. But now, while Harry had gradually been emerging from the slang and coarseness of the medical student, and, growing older, had grown more like the gentleman nature intended him to be, though still with too much of the old leaven in him; Oliver had been as gradually sinking deeper and deeper into the mire, till his only fitting atmosphere seemed to be that of night-houses and gaming-tables. In that foul marsh, where Harry, like so many of his comrades, had, in the exuberance of youth, "sown his wild oats," Oliver had rooted his whole existence.

Mr. Thornton was one evening sitting alone (Ranthorpe was at the theatre), discussing a tumbler of his famous punch, when Oliver, who had not been near him for some months, walked into the room. He was not very well pleased to see his nephew; he never was. But a well directed compliment respecting the savour of the punch, caused him to ring the bell, order another tumbler, and prepare to be as amiable as his knowledge of the character of his nephew would permit.

" Pray, when do you intend to pass the college?" asked the uncle, after a while.

" Oh! very shortly. I shall '*grind.*'"

" Grind ?"

" Yes; go to Steggall—he grinds chaps for the college in no time. Never fear! I shall work like a beggar."

" Had you not better work like a surgeon ?"

" You know what I mean. I suppose you intend to stand the needful, uncle ?"

"Not I. Your ways of life have displeased me.— Bah!"

" What ways of life ?"

" *Your* ways ; debauchery, idleness, dishonour. You stare;—you try to look like indignant virtue. It won't do. I have heard all about you."

" What have you heard ?"

" Why, one thing as a sample, you seduced a servant girl. Don't deny it! It is not that I blame so much. I have been young myself, and servants are not Lucretias."

Oliver's face brightened. It lowered again as his uncle

proceeded—" But if an excuse can be found for that, none can be found for your subsequent treatment. She had a child; that child you disowned; you refused to give a farthing towards its support; and that, too, at a time when you were constantly wheedling me out of money to feed your extravagances. Bah! pitiable!—contemptible! You see I know all. Don't wonder then, if, from this moment, my purse is shut against you as my heart is. Extravagance—folly—debauchery, I could forgive, as the wild errors of youth. But unkindness—dishonourable conduct —and to a poor, wretched victim whom you had ruined— that, sir, neither belongs to the errors of youth, nor to the organisation of a gentleman.—Bah!"

The old gentleman had warmed himself into a passion at the mere contemplation of his nephew's conduct. Oliver was silent, uneasy.

" You have lost all claim upon me, sir; except that of being my brother's son. What little I can leave you when I die, may be yours, if you reform; but if I find you pursuing your present career, be assured that I shall leave that little to a more worthy man."

" To your secretary, perhaps," suggested Oliver, with a sneer.

" Yes: in all probability. I have a real regard for him; for you I have none."

" Thank 'ye," said Oliver, rising, and taking his hat. " Then I suppose I may look upon the succession as booked ? Your brother's son, of course, can't pretend to so much regard as a stranger ?"

" Oliver, I do not forget you are my brother's son ; do not *you* forget it. Let his name be preserved from disgrace. I repeat it : if you reform, you shall not want.

What I can leave shall be yours. I do this for your father's sake—not yours. But continue to lead your present life, and I disown and disinherit you. Bah !"

Oliver felt a strong temptation to commit some violence; but restraining himself, as he saw the impossibility of escaping detection, he held out his hand, promised reformation, and quitted the house in a fit of sullen rage.

" **D**—n him !" he muttered, " I shall be done, if he doesn't shortly *hop the twig*."

And he continued his walk, grimly speculating on his uncle's death.

" He knows too much "—thought Oliver—" a great deal too much. If he should find out that affair at Epsom" (he alluded to a disgraceful case of swindling in which he had been implicated), " it is all up with me—no legacy. D—n him ! What an old frump he is ! And to think that I am his heir. If he *would* only break his neck !"

He continued his walk homewards, occupied with these dark thoughts; speculating on the advantages he should derive from his uncle's death ; and on the danger he incurred of being disinherited, if his uncle did not shortly die. On awaking the next morning, the same thoughts presented themselves to him. They pursued him through the day. That night he dreamt that his uncle had been murdered. He awoke greatly disappointed.

All that day, and all the next, this one current of thought was scarcely interrupted. His uncle's death soon became a fixed idea with him. It fascinated him— haunted him. Vague thoughts of murder had tempted his soul, but were shudderingly evaded. They returned, again and again, and at length were evaded without horror. They became familiar: from that moment they became dangerous!

The idea of murder, which had become familiar to his mind, was soon to be converted into a resolution. He tampered with his conscience and his fears ; he fought against the growing resolution, feeling that it would be fatal to him ; he endeavoured, in new orgies, to drown the desperate thoughts which haunted him. But it was too late. The idea had become a fixed idea. He must either become a murderer or a monomaniac!

The tyrannous influence of fixed ideas—of thoughts which haunt the soul, and goad the unhappy wretch to his perdition—is capable, I think, of a physiological no less than of a psychological explanation.

Some fearful thought presents itself, and makes, as people figuratively say, a deep impression. By a law of our nature, it is the tendency, almost invincible, of all thoughts connected with that fearful one—either accidentally or inherently connected with it—to recal it whenever they arise. This association of ideas therefore prevents the thought from evanescing. In proportion to the horror or interest inspired by that thought, will be the strength of the tendency to recurrence. The brain may be then said to be in a state of partial inflammation, owing to the great affluence of blood in one direction. And precisely as the abnormal affluence of blood towards any part of the body will produce chronic inflammation, if it be not diverted, so will the current of thought in excess in any one direction produce monomania. Fixed ideas may thus be physiologically regarded as chronic inflammations of the brain.

Reader! this digression is not idle. If you find yourself haunted by any ideas which you would fain shake off, remember that the only effectual way to rid yourself of them is one somewhat analogous to that practised for inflammation of the body. You must draw the current of your thoughts elsewhere. You must actively, healthily, employ your mind and your affections. You must create fresh associations with such things as have a tendency to recal the thoughts you would evade. Let the mind recover its elasticity by various activity, and you are safe.

Had Oliver plunged into fresh dissipations before the idea of murder had become a fixed one—before the inflammation had become chronic—then he might have been saved. But he tried it too late. The dull mornings following debauchery only left him an easier prey to his fierce thoughts; while the extravagances which made money more and more necessary, served to place his uncle's death in more advantageous colours to him.

I cannot follow him through all the struggles his fears and conscience held with this fascinating idea of murder. Enough if I state that it at length subdued him. It seemed to him as if there were no alternative between his going to the dogs, and murdering his uncle. But of course his uncle's death was a means, not an end. He had no vengeance to satisfy; he had no particular hatred towards his uncle; he only wanted his money. His object therefore was to remove an obstacle, without drawing any suspicion upon himself.

Oliver was extremely cunning, and as unprincipled. His whole thoughts were now directed towards forming some plan whereby he might escape suspicion. Poison in any shape would not prevent suspicion, because he would not be able to prove his absence from the scene. To hit upon some plan which should absolve him from all danger, and, the more effectually to do so, to throw the suspicion upon another, was the problem to be solved. Many plans were thought of; but none were free from danger. " Murder will out," and in so many ways, that the most ingenious cannot foresee all the trivial circumstances which give the clue.

At length his plan was perfected.

CHAPTER V.

Threescore and ten I can remember well;
Within the volume of which time I've seen
Hours dreadful and things strange; but this sore night
Hath trifled former knowings.

SHAKSPEARE.

"SAD piece of extravagance, that of wearing pumps in
the day-time," said Mr. Thornton to his nephew, as they
were sitting together awaiting tea, on that evening chosen
by Oliver for his desperate act.

Oliver smiled as he answered: "Oh, they're an old
pair, quite unfit for parties, and the weather is so warm."

"Well, well, it's no business of mine, to be sure; only
as you have determined on a thorough reformation (excellent determination, too, and will gain your uncle's heart),
it seems to me that extravagance in dress—"

"But, my dear uncle, it's economy. You would not
have me throw them away because they're too shabby for
dinner-parties and 'hops,' would you?"

Mrs. Griffith, the housekeeper, entered at that moment,
to say something to Mr. Thornton.

"Good day, Mrs. Griffith," said Oliver, glad of this
opportunity of procuring a witness of his amity with his

uncle. "Come, look approvingly, Mrs. Griffith—encourage me in virtue. See how good uncle is! I have commenced my reform—am going to become a respectable member of society—and uncle's going to celebrate the prodigal nephew's return with a bowl of his inimitable punch!"

Mrs. Griffith was all smiles. She always knew Mr. Oliver was a good young gentleman, and told Mr. Thornton so. She thought that young men *would* be young men; but that Mr. Oliver would be sure to be steady, after a while.

"Thank ye, Mrs. Griffith," replied Oliver, highly pleased with his success; "but now I must give you a little trouble—and that is, to find my ' Astley Cooper's Lectures,' which I left here some months ago, and you said you had put away for me."

"That's true, Mr. Oliver; I'll get it immediately."

Mrs. Griffith returned empty-handed, declaring that the book was not where she fancied she had placed it, and that it must have been put away somewhere else.

A strange look of triumph might have been observed in Oliver's eyes at this point. He wanted to search the house, in company with one of the servants, as a proof that no one could have been *concealed* there.

"Well, before I go I will have a rummage with you, Mrs. Griffith," he said; "don't trouble yourself now. I shall know the book among a thousand—a mere glimpse is enough for me."

A merry evening was spent over the punch. Oliver was all amiability, and contrived to draw his uncle into telling many of his famous stories, at which both laughed heartily. Oliver was determined the servants should hear the laughter, so kept the door open, on pretext

of the heat. He succeeded; for when Mrs. Griffith
came up again, she remarked upon their merriment.

" By the bye, now, Mrs. Griffiths, if you are at your leisure we will have our rummage."

The proposal was accepted; the house was searched;
every cupboard was opened, they looked under every
sofa, and into every hole and corner. The book was not
found, simply because Oliver had already abstracted it.

But something else was found—at least by him. As
Mrs. Griffith went up to look in one of the attics, Oliver
darted into Ranthorpe's room. He opened the drawer
of the looking-glass, and took a razor out of its case.
He then carefully shut the drawer, concealed the razor in
his pocket, and hastily followed Mrs. Griffith.

Giving up the search as fruitless, they returned to the
drawing-room, where Oliver said he would take one
more glass of punch with his uncle, and then go home,
as it was getting late.

The punch was drunk; Oliver rose to depart, shook
his uncle's hand warmly, and ran rapidly down stairs,
opened the door, and slammed it with some violence.
But he had shut himself in! The servants would all
swear they heard him go—heard him " shut the door
after him." Yet he had simply shut the door *before*
him. Creeping stealthily into the back parlour (the use
of his thin pumps is now betrayed!) he noiselessly concealed himself under the sofa.

His uncle retired to bed ; the servants followed—the
housemaid alone was waiting up for Ranthorpe, who was
at the theatre. Oliver waited in fearful impatience.
Every thing had succeeded hitherto; his plan seemed to
succeed even in its smallest details. But the perilous
moment was to come; his heart throbbed violently as he

heard Ranthorpe's knock—heard the servant let him in
—heard him take his candle, and walk up stairs to bed—
and heard the housemaid lock the street door, and put up
the chain.

He breathed freely again as the last sounds died away.
Every one was by this time in bed. He would wait an
hour or two longer, to allow sleep to dull their senses; and
then the fatal, perilous blow should be given! The clock
ticked audibly; and struck the hours with horrible distinctness. Oliver trembled beneath each stroke. It seemed
to him so loud, that every one in the house must be
awakened by it. But it ceased, and a dead stillness succeeded. Then twelve sounded; then one; and then two.
But these sounds seemed so loud to him that he could not
venture forth—he could not believe they were unheard
up stairs. In this state of fear and suspense he remained
till three o'clock.

He was right in believing that the sounds were heard.
One at least heard them; and that was Percy Ranthorpe.
On entering his room he had thrown himself upon his
sofa instead of undressing; and there had yielded up his
imagination to the delights of dramatic composition. He
had come from seeing Macready in a new tragedy; and
his own dramatic ambition had received a powerful stimulus. Walking home he had sketched the large outlines of
a tragedy, and he was now thinking over some of the
scenes. While thus scheming, he sank asleep upon the
sofa; or rather let me say he dozed and dreamed.

At length he heard the clock strike three, and became
aware of his position. He determined to undress and go
to bed. But whoever has fallen asleep in a chair, or on a
sofa, knows how reluctantly one moves from it—how the
exertion of rising and undressing is shirked as long as

practicable. This reluctance—this stupor of sleep was felt by Ranthorpe. He lay there making up his mind to arise, and making up his body to continue where he was.

From this half-waking state he was startled by a low, creaking sound, as of a step. In such moments the sense of hearing is very acute. The sound was repeated, and repeated. Some one was slowly stealing up stairs. He sat up, and listened. His heart beat so loud, that he could hear it. He was a brave man; but he was nervous and imaginative. His imagination always converted nightly sounds into some exaggerated horrors. Aware of this— aware of how often he had alarmed himself with puerile terrors, aroused by trifling sounds at night—he refused to credit the suggestions which crowded upon him. Who could be up at this hour? Might it not be a sound from the next house? Another step scattered such reasonings, and redoubled the throbbings of his agitated heart. There was a robber in the house! "And yet," he thought, "how absurd to suppose a robbery committed in the midst of London, in a house, too, where all the servants are old and faithful!" But the beatings of his heart could not so be quieted! All was silent again. He listened intently. He was averse to go down stairs, and see if any one really were in the house, lest he should needlessly alarm the sleepers. But the sounds he had heard were so exactly like those of some one creeping up stairs, that he could not be calmed by the present quiet, and listened therefore for some new indication. He sat motionless; holding his breath, and trying to master the nervous beating of his heart, that the noise might not interfere with his catching any other sounds. But the nervous agitation he was in, made a "ringing" in his ears, which exasperated him.

At length the continuance of the silence—only a few

minutes, but to him they seemed almost an hour—
caused him to smile at his suppositions. He accused himself of again allowing his quick imagination to play tricks
with him. He was about to get up and undress, in the
full assurance that he had needlessly alarmed himself,
when he fancied he heard a door gently opened. His
nerves again trembled; the ringing in his ears came back.
Could he again be cheating himself? Was he but the
victim to acute senses, and over-active imagination? Unable to bear the suspense, he arose, determined to go down
stairs, and satisfy himself. He was scarcely on his feet,
when a muffled sound underneath made his heart leap
against his breast—a low groan pierced his ear, and filled
his mind with images of horror. He dashed down stairs
—burst into Mr. Thornton's room—where he had only
time to see his venerable friend half-lying out of bed,—a
fearful gash across his throat,—and to see the assassin leap
out of the window. A wild cry burst from him, as he
sprang to the window, and overturned a table, which
fell with a crash. Without thinking of what he was
doing, he darted after the assassin. He leapt down upon
the leads, and from thence into the garden. He was in
time to run along the party wall, and meet the ruffian
on the roof of the stables, which were at the back of the
garden.

Oliver seeing himself so closely pursued, turned and
grappled with Ranthorpe. It was a terrible struggle.
Both were young and powerful; both were animated by
fierce passions. The slated roof upon which they stood,
was but a precarious footing, and one slip would be fatal.
But they closed! Ranthorpe was too fiercely bent upon
capturing the assassin, and bringing him to justice, to
think of the most obvious means of doing so; that is, of

calling out lustily.   In terrible silence he grasped his antagonist.   His heart bounded as he heard the sounds of
alarm proceeding from the house.   Mr. Thornton would
be attended to!

The struggle, though long to recount, was brief to act.
Oliver was the more powerful of the two ; and he had to
struggle for life.   With one gigantic effort he disengaged
himself from Ranthorpe's grasp, and with a sudden blow
on the chest, sent him reeling over the roof.   Ranthorpe
fell into the garden, and was stunned by the fall.

On returning to his senses he found himself in the
parlour surrounded by policemen, servants, and strangers.
Conceive his horror and indignation at finding that he
was supposed to be the murderer!

He tried to spring up, but his bruised frame refused.
He sank back upon the sofa and sobbed like a child.   Well
as he was assured that his innocence must be proved in a
little while, he gave himself up solely to his grief at the
thought of Mr. Thornton's dreadful end.   All that the unfortunate old man had been able to articulate when the
alarmed servants found him, was " Ranthorpe;" and with
that he feebly pointed to the window and expired.

This last act, and this last word of one who loved him,
were interpreted into an accusation!   "Mrs. Griffith,"
shrieked Ranthorpe, " where is Mrs. Griffith?"

" Here," sobbed that lady.

" You, Mrs. Griffith, cannot you free me from this loath-
some, this insulting suspicion?   Cannot you testify how I
loved that dear old man—how he loved me?   Cannot you
tell the world how impossible it is that I could have
thought of such a crime?   What ! silent? weeping, yet
silent?   O God! O God! even she believes me guilty!"

"No, no, no, Mr. Percy," sobbed Mrs. Griffith—her

suspicions banished in an instant by the pained innocence of his voice: " No, I do not believe you guilty; never will I believe it; but appearances are *so* against you, my testimony cannot shake them."

" And they are?" he asked haughtily.

" They are," interposed one of the by-standers, " tolerably strong. There was no one in the house but yourself and the servants. Mrs. Griffith had searched every hole and corner in company with Mr. Thornton's nephew. No one, therefore, was concealed. Yet the house was locked up—no entrance had been forced; consequently, the murderer must have been one of the inmates. The circumstances which point to you are these: The razor with which the murder was committed was yours."

" Mine—how can you say that?"

" Because your razor-case was found open and empty !"

Ranthorpe stared bewildered. The man continued:

" Your bed was found untouched; you had not slept in it."

" True. I had fallen asleep on the sofa."

" You never did so before?"

" No."

" Exactly. It looks very suspicious that you should have done so then. You were found lying in the garden, having, it is presumed, fallen in an attempt to escape. The last words of Mr. Thornton are enough to convict you."

Ranthorpe sank back again. He saw what a fatal chain of circumstances encircled him; but he felt that whoever had done the deed, had marvellously planned it; and that at present, at least, he must endure the suspicions of the world.

Led before the magistrate, he underwent the examination with great calmness and haughtiness, which were mistaken for hardened guilt. There again he heard the damning evidence detailed. The servants all swore that Oliver had left the house. The housemaid swore she put up the door-chain, which was found untouched when the alarm was given. The evidence to the murderer being one of the inmates was conclusive; the evidence against Ranthorpe was scarcely less so. It was contradicted indeed by the testimonies of the affection which existed between Mr. Thornton and Ranthorpe; and by the proofs that no ill-will had been apparent on either side, nor had there been any symptoms of a quarrel. These were strong presumptions against the evidence. There seemed no possible motive why Ranthorpe should have committed the act, and every motive why he should not. Nevertheless, the facts were so damning, that the magistrate was forced to commit him for trial.

The papers were full of it. London was divided into two parties, one for and one against Ranthorpe. All the literary men were indignant at any one's believing him guilty. Was there ever known, they triumphantly asked, a single instance of murder committed by a literary man? Not one. And was it probable that a sane man, a man like Ranthorpe, should do that to a benefactor, which no literary man had ever been known to do to his bitterest enemy, his worst wronger?

CHAPTER VI.

THE PURSUIT.

Not a word!
It is beyond debate; we must act here
As men who clamber up a precipice.
GUIDONE: *a dramatic Poem.*

IT was a fortunate illness that kept Isola to her bed at this time; she thus heard nothing of the murder, or of Ranthorpe's perilous situation. His other friends suffered greatly on his account. They all believed him innocent, but no one saw any means of proving it.

Harry, Wynton, and Joyce discussed the whole question.

"A thought occurs to me," said Harry, "one of the worst appearances against Ranthorpe is the razor. Now if we assume that he is innocent, it follows that the razor must have been abstracted from his room on the very day, since he himself must have used it in the morning."

"Certainly, certainly. A clue!" exclaimed Wynton.

"We have then to ascertain who were the people known to have been in the house on that day."

"Exactly," said Joyce, "I happen to be one; but I hope I'm not implicated."

Wynton then said:

" I was also there. But Mrs. Griffith told me that the old gentleman's nephew spent the evening there."

" He's our man !" exclaimed Harry, striking his hand upon the table.

" But he was on the best possible terms with his uncle," said Wynton.

" But he is an arrant scamp," retorted Harry, " and I feel a perfect conviction he is the murderer."

" Yet the servants heard him go out."

" I don't care. I don't know how he did it, but I am sure he's the man."

The three then went to the house; and while Joyce and Wynton talked to Mrs. Griffith, Harry examined the house, with a view of ascertaining how an entrance could have been made. He then went to the stables; but they betrayed nothing. As he was looking about, him, however, he discovered behind a dung-heap a man's hat. He picked it up; it was not Ranthorpe's. He looked at the maker's name; and telling Joyce that he believed he was on the scent, jumped into a cab, and drove to Oxford Street. He entered the hatter's shop, and having ascertained that Oliver dealt there, which confirmed all his doubts, he ordered the cabman to drive to Mornington Place, Hampstead Road, where Oliver lodged.

He asked to see the landlady.

" I must request profound secrecy of you, madam, as the life of a fellow-creature depends on it," he said to her. She was considerably alarmed at this opening. " But will you do me the favour of telling me if Mr. Thornton stayed at home on Monday evening last?"

" No, sir, he never stops at home."

" Humph! Do you happen to know what time he came home?"

" I do not, but I can ask the servant; she let him in. It certainly was not before one, because I had some friends, who did not leave me till then."

" Not before one," said Harry to himself, " and they said he left the house about eleven; good." Then addressing himself again to her, " Do not, I beg, speak to the servant about it—she may blab."

" I suppose I dare not venture to ask the reason of this inquiry?" she said, with some curiosity.

" My dear madam, you shall very quickly know all; but at present I must not only be secret myself, but most earnestly request you not to mention a syllable to any one respecting this visit. And I need only tell you that by so doing you will prevent the officers of justice coming here and bringing scandal upon your house."

This threat was well devised, and had full effect. The old lady exclaimed: " Officers of Justice!"

" Hush!" replied Harry, " not a word. My visit will render theirs unnecessary; that is, if you second me."

" Oh! by all means, and with thanks—with thanks!"

" Good; then will you let your servant have a holiday to-morrow evening? She will ask you to go to the theatre, and say she has got orders. You will not refuse?"

" Certainly not; but what can she be wanted for?"

Harry laid his finger on his lips with grave significance, and then said:

" Enough, she is wanted. Do not appear to know any thing, and you will save yourself a good deal of trouble. And I forgot to add, that should you notice any men hanging about the neighbourhood, and watching the house, do not be alarmed, they will be police in plain clothes. Make no observation."

He left the house well satisfied.

The art of courting maid-servants and milliners is an art much cultivated by medical students. It is an art by itself. The man who understands all the labyrinths of a lady's heart, who is irresistible in the drawing-room, would miserably fail in the kitchen. *Filer le parfait amour* is not the art of love known by the Ovids and Gentil Bernards of the lower regions. Fun there takes precedence of sentiment; a knowledge of the life of the lower classes is more necessary than a knowledge of books, which is useless.

Deeply skilled in this art was Harry Cavendish; he was, in fact, a distinguished victimiser. His plan was to get the servant of all work at the house where Oliver lodged, to accompany him to the theatre, confident that if he once got her out, he should be able to learn all she knew.

I cannot detail the progress of the siege. Suffice it that Mary was easily captivated by Harry, and was delighted at the idea of going to see a play, " a thing of which she was pertiklar fond."

The reader is requested, therefore, to accompany them to the pit of the Adelphi Theatre, where John Reeve and Buckstone are making them shout with laughter.

" Oh! he's a funny feller, that he is," said Mary, as the act-drop fell.

" That's just it," replied Harry, " Lord, you should see him do the ' Medical Student;' to the life, and no mistake."

" Lor !"

" You know what a queer chap you've got among your lodgers, don't you?"

" What, Mr. Thornton?"

" Yes—you'll have some oranges, Mary? Pooh! don't be modest. Here, you princess!—he! oranges!"

This was addressed to a stout old woman who was crushing the knees of the audience as she wedged herself between the seats with the melodious cry of " Oranges, ginger-beer, bill of the play!"

" Now, my *fat friend*," said Harry, as she came up, " let's see what you've got in the way of oranges."

This playful address made the old woman grin, and Mary stuff her handkerchief into her mouth to hide her laughter. Some oranges were bought, and while Harry was peeling one, he continued,

" Well, this Thornton was a fellow lodger of mine once. Oh, wasn't he a queer chap!"

"Oh! ain't he still! Oh, no! Lord, I could tell you such larks of his!"

" Do, there's a dear. Here's a delicious orange; you have it, Mary; yes, do. Well, I was going to say that one night when I sat up for him because the servant refused, how d'ye think he came home?"

"How?—Do tell us."

"Why, with his coat slit up the back, and without his hat. He lost his hat in a scuffle, and scampered home without it."

"Lor, how odd! I've a good mind—— I say, you won't tell, if I tell you something?"

" Oh! here's a juicy one : do taste this, Mary, dear. Isn't it famous?—Well, you were going to tell me something."

" But you promise not to tell? 'cos he'll give me half-a-sovereign not to. But then, to be sure, he only meant that I wasn't to tell *missus*, or the lodgers, 'cos he would look ridiklous. But don't you say a word ;—he came home t'other night in a cab, without his hat, and in such a flurry !"

" Ha ! ha ! ha !" laughed Harry, trying to conceal his triumph in boisterous mirth. " Well, that *is* a good one. Didn't you laugh, Mary ?"

" That I did ! ' Lawk ! Mr. Thornton,' says I, ' why where in 'evin's name is your hat?' says I ; so says he, ' Mary,' says he, ' I've been in such a spree, but I've had the worst of it,' says he ; ' two chaps pitched into me,' says he, ' and I was 'bliged to cut and run for it. Couldn't stop for my hat,' says he, ' 'cos it was a old 'un,' says he. ' Quite right, too, Mr. Thornton,' says I. ' But I say, Mary,' says he, ' don't you say any thing to your missus about this, nor to the lodgers. Be sure you don't say any thing about my coming home without my hat,' says he, ' 'cos it would make me look so precious ridiklous.' So, says I, ' That I won't,' says I. ' Well then,' says he, ' if you *don't*, Mary, I'll give you half-a-sovereign at the end of the month,— if you *do*, I shall certainly *not*.' ' No fears,' says I, and gave him his candle."

" Devilish good !" said Harry, laughing. " I wonder whether it was on Monday night, after he left me ?"

" Tuesday *morning*, if you please—and precious early, too ! It was nearly four o'clock, I'll swear."

" Ha ! ha ! ha ! and was he much pummelled about ?"

" No ; he was in a pickle, but not bruised ; 'cos he says he's a first-rate boxer, and had tapped one man's claret,—some of the blood was on the front of his shirt."

" Well, he is a rum one! But the second act is going to begin."

Harry had accomplished his object : he had obtained conclusive evidence, so allowed Mary to enjoy the play as she best could, and left the conversation almost entirely in her hands. She noticed this ; but he pleaded headach. He was too occupied with his own thoughts, to support any longer the character he had assumed. He was considering whether the evidence he had collected would be considered as only presumptive ; and fearful lest it might not be sufficient, he resolved on an attempt to make Oliver confess.

The next day he went to Mornington Place. Oliver was at home ; indeed, he kept himself shut up, pleading the great shock which his uncle's death had given to his nerves. He remained in his room, a victim to the avenging Eumenides. His conscience would not be stifled. His fears were terrible. Every knock at the door went to his heart, as if it announced his arrest. Every noise in the street sounded like the mob coming to seize him. He read the morning and evening paper with horrible eagerness. Every line respecting the murder made him thrill. Every surmise seemed to him growing into a certitude that he was the guilty wretch. Every word in Ranthorpe's defence seemed to him as if it must point him out to justice. If his landlady came to speak to him, to ask him how he felt, or if she could get any thing for him, he thought her motive was to spy upon him. If Mary spoke to him, or looked at him, when she came into the room, he thought she was watching the expression of his countenance, with a view to read if he were guilty.

When he was facing others, and had to assume a

character, the energy and attention necessary for him to perform the part, made him forget his horror and his fears. But left alone to himself, in company with his fears, existence was torture to him. He had thought of flying to America, but was afraid, lest it should look suspicious. He had tried to forget his thoughts in one of his favourite night houses, but before he had been there three minutes, the subject of the recent murder was spoken of, and he was forced to hurry away.

He scarcely slept; and when he did sink into an uneasy doze, horrible dreams tortured him. Thus night and day, and day and night, he was racked by the most wearing of agonies—suspense and fear!

Such was his suffering, that he was often on the point of blowing his brains out, and so ending his misery. He had, in fact, made up his mind to do so, and would probably have done so, on the very morning when Harry, without undergoing the formality of announcing himself, walked into his room. He started, as usual, when any one put a hand on the lock of his door.

" Oh! it's you, is it, Cavendish?" he said. " Well, any news about your friend?"

" Yes," replied Harry, carelessly seating himself, " very good news for us; the murderer is discovered." As he said this, he raised his eyes full upon Oliver, who vainly endeavoured to withdraw all expression from his face. He cowered beneath Harry's gaze, and faltered out: " How—discovered?"

" By very simple means—from the description of his person given by Ranthorpe, which was not very accurate, and from some other suspicious circumstances, I thought I could name the man. His hat was found in the stables, which had been dropped in the struggle,"

—(Here Oliver glared upon him like a wild beast)— "and I found the maker's name. You will naturally suppose I lost no time in asking that maker if he made hats for the person I'm speaking of, and his reply was satisfactory."

"Go on!" hoarsely whispered Oliver.

"The rest of my story is too long to relate in detail. Enough, that I ascertained from the servant who let him in, that the individual I speak of came home on Tuesday morning *without* his hat." Oliver's breath was suspended; his eyes were bloodshot with suppressed rage. "Not only without his hat, but with blood upon his shirt; and, to crown all, he promised the servant half a sovereign.—You need not fix your eyes upon that knife! Take it, if you please; you *dare* not use it against me. And if you dare—if your murderous heart has sufficient courage, your murderous hand has only strength enough to cope with sleeping old men."

This was said with such crushing scorn and loathing, that Oliver bounded like a panther upon him—the knife flashed in the air—and had Harry been less active or less prepared, it would have entered his breast; but, accustomed as he was to single-stick, his quick eye and ready arm saved him from the danger. A sharp blow with an oak-stick upon the ruffian's wrist, made him drop the knife.

"I told you it was useless," said Harry, coolly.

"You know my secret!" yelled the exasperated Oliver, snatching up the knife again—"and you shall pay for it."

"This time I warn you," replied Harry; "I shall not content myself with disarming you." And he placed himself in an attitude of defence.

"This time!" said Oliver, grinding his teeth—"I may as well swing for two as for one."

A rapid blow on the elbow made his arm fall useless at his side, and at the same instant the door was flung open, and two policemen rushed in. At this sight Oliver made an attempt to escape out of the window, but the attempt was fruitless. He was soon handcuffed, and borne off to prison.

"Mary," said Harry, "I've deprived you of half-a-sovereign—but there are two halves as compensation; besides the satisfaction you must feel in having been the instrument of this ruffian's conviction."

"Lawk! well, who *would* have thought it!" was the reflection of the consoled Mary.

CHAPTER VII.

THE TURNING POINT.

To-morrow to fresh woods and pastures new.
SHAKSPEARE.

RANTHORPE was released, and in due time Oliver was executed. But although our hero had escaped the peril, he had not escaped the curse of notoriety. The tragical events in which he had been implicated were of themselves distressing enough. His friend murdered—that kind, good, strange old man, removed for ever from his love—this alone was sufficient to depress him. But to this was added the painful curiosity of strangers, which not only kept his wounds open, but made him feel himself an object of notoriety.

One incident I cannot omit, it is so illustrative of theatrical life. A fortnight after his acquittal, the manager of a minor theatre, which shall be nameless, called upon him, and with inimitable effrontery proposed that Ranthorpe should sustain his *own* character in a new piece about to be produced, entitled " The Dark Deed; or, the Knightsbridge Murder."

" If you will undertake this slight part," continued the manager, " I can offer you a splendid salary—fifty pounds a week, sir; fifty pounds a week !"

Q

Ranthorpe was half irritated, half amused; but shook his head, negatively.

" Don't refuse it, pray, sir; consider fifty pounds a week —come, I don't mind if I say seventy pounds—and absolutely nothing to do but to rush into the room—give a start—look aghast—and shriek, ' *Ha !*' and to re-appear as the accused murderer, with your dress a little disarranged—that's all, sir."

" I fear," replied Ranthorpe, smiling, " that all would be far too much for me. I must decline being any further mixed up with this matter."

" Timid, I suppose; but you'll soon shake off that."

" No, sir, I shall never shake off my disgust at the infamous desecration of the privacies of life, which that system of dramatising recent events fosters. It is bad enough to see the newspapers pander to the vile appetites of the blood-loving public. The stage has not the excuse of the papers."

He rose as he said this, and the manager was forced to take his leave. He returned, however, speedily, and said: " Mr. Ranthorpe, I appreciate your motives, you don't like to appear before the lamps. But you can still assist me; and I will pay for the assistance. Sell me the razor with which the murder was committed—I'll give fifty pounds for it. All London will flock to my theatre to see the *real* razor ! Think what posters I could give ! " *Every Night*—' THE DARK DEED.' *In which the* REAL *razor used by the murderer will be introduced. Come early.*"

The manager was quite exalted at the imaginary prospect of such an attraction; but he quickly scampered down stairs, as he saw Ranthorpe approach him, breathless with indignation.

Harry laughed heartily when he heard of it, and declared the manager was a knowing fellow, who rightly appreciated the public.

But Ranthorpe could bear this notoriety no longer. He resolved on quitting England. He was unhappy; he was purposeless. To be always regarded as the Mr. Ranthorpe, who had figured in the papers as the murderer of his benefactor, was peculiarly galling to him.

It had been his day dream to have his name in everybody's mouth; that dream was now realized in a hateful shape. He had aspired to celebrity, and had been forced into notoriety.

He thought of Germany. He could teach English there, as a means of livelihood; and while doing so, not only would the public forget him, and his history, but he would also be preparing himself more fitly for his career. Germany would afford him subsistence — study — and oblivion.

A day or two before his departure, he read with strange agitation the announcement of the marriage of Florence Wilmington with Sir Frederick Hawbucke, Baronet.

" So, the coquette married at last !" he said, as he laid the paper down, " and to that rich fool, Hawbucke. Well, they will both be miserable."

The train of thought which this incident awakened was extremely painful to him. The past rose before him, and it was full of reproaches. He saw himself again the happy boy, elated by ambition, undaunted by poverty—he saw himself a lion, and dazzled by a small success—he reviewed the progress of corruption, as it had contaminated his mind, and deadened his feelings—he saw himself ensnared by the arts of a coquette—lived over again the humiliation of his rejected love, the failure of his tragedy, and his last misfortune.

"Well, I shall leave England," he said, "and leave behind me the memory of these errors. A new epoch opens. In Germany, I shall learn not only to forget the follies and errors of my youth, but, by being removed from every thing that can recall them, be enabled to work out a path for myself undisturbed. Driven from England, in Germany I shall gain quiet contentment."

Self-exiled from his native land, he has now reached the great turning point in his career. How will he prosper?

CHAPTER VIII.

THE MISERIES OF GENIUS.

We poets in our youth begin in gladness;
But thereof comes in the end despondency and madness!
WORDSWORTH.

And mighty poets in their misery dead!
IBID.

D—n the Muses! I abominate them and their works; they are the nurses of poverty and insanity!
CHATTERTON.

There is not in all the martyrologies that ever were penned, so rueful a narrative as that of the lives of poets.
BURNS.

Most wretched men
Are cradled into poetry from wrong;
They learn in suffering what they teach in song.
SHELLEY.

Gli scrittori grandi, incapaci, per natura o per abito, di molti piaceri umani; privi di altri molti per voluntà; non di rado negletti nel consorzio degli uomini, se non forse dai pocchi che seguono i medesimi studi; hanno per destino di condurre una vita simile alla morte, e vivere, se pur l' ottengono, dopo sepolti.
GIACOMO LEOPARDI.

THUS has Percy Ranthorpe struggled and suffered. He is now sailing on the restless bosom of the sea, and filling the monotonous hours with his retrospections. They are bitter. His lot has not been happy; but with whom lies the fault? Does he, like so many of his kindred, throw the burden of his woes upon his genius? Does he attribute to his genius those sorrows which, properly speaking, have been caused by his want of genius? No; he does not juggle with himself; he feels that he has been weak and has been punished; he feels that the common cant of genius being a fatal gift—a Nessus-poisoned shirt, that consumes the wearer, is a cant, and nothing more. It is an error founded on the most superficial indications, founded too often on the complaints of genius itself.

Genius miserable! Genius a fatal gift! O miserable philosophy that can *so* construe it! Genius is the faculty of creation, of admiration, of love. It creates, from the merest dross, spirits of beauty which haunt the soul through life. It peoples the world with lovely forms, exalted hopes, skyward aspirings, and everlasting joy: and, because the sensibility, which is its condition, subjects it to petty annoyances, annoyances unfelt, or not so keenly felt, by others; because its enthusiasm carries it oftentimes from the path of prudence ; and because the punishment which follows all error is not for it suspended, but falls as upon an ordinary nature's; because, with the precious faculty of giving an utterance to all its pains and pleasures, it *sometimes* breaks forth into a low plaint, or bitter irony, or wild despair, and in those moments curses the very source of all its greatness; because, I say, these things are found accompanying genius, like shadows of its glories, is genius therefore to be called a fatal gift ? Is it not genius, great majestic genius, in spite of all? The sun " kisses carrion," but is not less the sun !

For shame! ye coward and blaspheming souls, who

bowing under a *present* affliction, have cursed your lives, as if they were made up of affliction ! For shame ! ye poets, who have carried within you an exhaustless mine of wealth, yet knowing one day's poverty, have lifted up your desperate voices to swell the universal cry of pauperism ! For shame ! ye rashly-judging critics who have seized upon this single cry, and exclaimed, Listen ! such is the expression of a life !

We are mortal men—erring and infirm; there are miseries awaiting us under every form of life; errors beset every profession, and unhappiness darkens the prospect of the most fortunate. Shall we then drag from the hospitals of the world all the squalid sick, and holding up their miseries, exclaim—" Behold : such is life !" forgetting all the health and strength, the beauty and enjoyment which surrounds us ? Because poets have been poor, and have been driven by poverty to irregularities, and sometimes to despair, thus wasting their lives in infamous debaucheries, or in squalid misery—is therefore genius a fatal gift? If so, then where are all the outcasts of society, the disappointed men in other ranks of life, men not endowed with genius ? Whence come all the moral and social miseries endured by those who have no claim to genius ? Does the physician never starve ? Is the barrister never briefless ? Has the clergyman always a living ? Do these men never *complain* of their hard lot ? Yes, they complain, but their complaint is drowned amidst the multitude; and neither they, nor the world, attribute their misfortunes to their talents !

Observe, that all the *events* of an artist's life become public, and are exaggerated by publicity; whereas the events of other men's lives rarely gain attention. Suicide is daily committed, and statistical tables show a frightful amount of human life thus sacrificed, which never occupies the public mind ; but when (as has happened perhaps half a dozen times) some disappointed genius madly rushes from the world to hide in eternity his sorrow and despair, then the sad news rings through every country, and is deplored on all sides, serving for ages as an example of the "fatal gift!"

So, if a genius suffers the envy, hatred, malice, and all uncharitableness which man heaps on the head of his brother, then we have a vehement protest against it in written works; he bares his bleeding wounds to public gaze, and bids the world observe the reward he has reaped —and he is pitied!

But do not *others* daily suffer this? Is there no lacerated self-love moaning in privacy, without the power of a picturesque appeal ? an appeal, recollect, that is *itself* an exquisite gratification! Other men, besides Lord Byron, were deformed, ill taught, deceived, ill-used by friends and relations, and suffered from these affronts as keenly : but Byron could fuse the passion of defiance and the pathos of his sorrows into splendid verse, and so draw down the pity and the admiration of all Europe. Nor was this pity and this admiration all the consolation he received ; with it he received intense delight from the exercise of his poetic faculty: there was a rapture in thus sublimating his sorrows into monuments of beauty, to which few joys were comparable. His sorrows, in a great part, made him what he was: without his melancholy and defiance, his scepticism and misanthropy, his wrongs and insults, what would he have been? He differed from other men in being able to give his sufferings a picturesque expression, not in the sufferings themselves.

It is because the *events* of an artist's life are made public,

that his sorrows and errors are brought into undue prominence, casting shadows on all the sunshine of his private
joys.   Whatever arouses him to defiance, whatever wrings
from him complaint, the world is called upon to notice.
But all that stirs his soul to rapture—all the intoxicating
visions of beauty and of glory which exalt his mind—all
the secret reveries (coquetries of thought) which haunt
him in his solitude—all the passion of aspiration, and the
delight in creation—these the world can never know:
these are locked in his own breast: these form *the element
in which he lives*, and from which he is only wrenched
by those occasional misfortunes, over which he weeps so
melodiously.

Genius a fatal gift?   Ah, no! it is the greatest and
the happiest of endowments.

> " Oh ! who would lose
> Though full of pain, this intellectual being,
> Those thoughts that wander through eternity?"

Conceive the intense delight genius must feel when
creating forms of everlasting beauty? Who shall estimate
the rapture which glowed in the mind of Shakspeare when
he created Viola, Imogen, Perdita, or Juliet—or of Göthe
when he drew Gretchen, Clärchen, Mignon, or Faust?   I
sometimes feel, while listening to Beethoven, a rapture so
intense, absorbing, suffocating, that it verges upon pain,
and is only relieved by sighs; at such times I ask myself:
" *What could have been passing in his soul when he conceived
such unutterable tenderness and beauty?*"   Only think of the
visions he must have had before he could have written his
Pastorale! what thoughts must have oppressed him before
they found utterance in his *Symphonies* of C minor and B
flat! What gloom—sublime, mystical, terrible,—must have
visited him before he could have written the *Marcia sulla*

morte d'un Eroe! What witcheries of grace and beauty must have haunted him before he could have thought of his *Septuor!* Such raptures—if enduring only for a moment—were worthy of years of suffering!

Genius is the happiest, as it is the greatest, of human faculties. It has no immunity from the common sorrows of humanity; but it has one glorious privilege, which it alone possesses; the privilege of turning its sorrows into beauty, and brooding delighted over them! The greatest that ever breathed has said,

> " Sweet are the uses of adversity;
> Which like the toad, ugly and venemous,
> Wears yet a precious jewel in his head!"

But it is only genius that can extract the jewel, and walk the path of life illumined by its light.

Adversity is an outrage to the common man, an experience to the thinking man, a source of pleasure to the man of genius. The one revolts against, or else sinks under it; the second grapples with it, and wrests some compensation for its pains; the third transmutes it into beauty, and places it in the storehouse of sweetly-pensive memory; and thus

> " Spät erklingt was früh erklang,
> Glück und Unglück wird Gesang."*

Perhaps, by reason of its very unworldliness, genius is oftener labouring under the ban of poverty, and the miseries which poverty will bring, than regulated dulness or presumptuous mediocrity. But can we therein forget the exquisite enjoyment—the passion and the rapture which constitute its daily food? for genius is fed by rapture, and transmutes all its pains into pleasures.

That the lives of men of genius are embittered by many

* Göthe.

miseries, it would be folly to deny. Bad health—bad habits, and mistaken aims—as well as those more common " ills the flesh is heir to" are not without their stings: but these are the *accidents* and not the *consequences* of genius. Double them, treble them, and you will still be unable to counterbalance with them all the pleasures of a life of thought!

BOOK V.

ISOLA.

Soothe her with sad stories,
O poet, till she sleep!
Dreams, come forth with all your glories!
Night breathe soft and deep!
Music round her creep!
If she steal away to weep,
Seek her out—and when you find her,
Gentle, gentlest Music, wind her
Round and round,
Round and round,
With your bands of softest sound.

BARRY CORNWALL.

CHAPTER I.

THE HAWBUCKES.

La reine en cette cour qu'anime la folie,
Va, vient, chante, se tait, regarde, écoute, oublie.
ANDRE CHENIER.

THE stage is clear; I may, therefore, bring forward Florence in a new character, and allow her husband to make his *début*.

Florence Wilmington has become Lady Hawbucke; that is to say, mistress of one of the handsomest men, and prettiest properties in England. Few brides could have been happier, more beautiful, or more buoyant. She admired her husband more than she had ever admired any one before; and although she could hardly be said to love him, in any earnest sense of the word, she felt that she must be supremely happy as his wife; and the gay volatile creature thoroughly enjoyed all the preparations for her wedding, as more amusing even than the preparations for her " coming out."

Sir Frederick Hawbucke was a type of the English gentleman. His Herculean frame, which would have been clumsy in a clown, was carried with such ease and simplicity that his height merely added to his dignity. Supreme in all corporeal exercises—a bold rider—a dead shot—there was nothing in his manner which in the slightest degree indicated either the roughness of the sportsman, or the pride of physical superiority. He had been the same as a boy—quiet and inoffensive in ordinary, but terrible in passion, and irresistible in a struggle. There were fearful stories told of him at Eton—of terrible reprisals taken on those who had offended him. Brave as a lion, and as ferocious, his nature was excessively English, and might be compared to that of the bull-dog, which, as connoisseurs well know, is the dog of dogs for the strange union of inoffensiveness and implacability. To see Sir Frederick in a room, you would fancy him the quietest and dullest of human beings. In action, of any kind, he was the promptest and bravest: cool, resolute, and irresistible.

He was very handsome, but not in the least conceited. Morbidly alive to the opinion of the world upon the slightest matter connected with himself, and wholly indifferent to every thing concerning others; but he concealed the former under the same mask of indifference as the latter. Indeed, so extraordinary was his self-command, that people never divined when they tortured him with their remarks; his stoicism forbade his admitting the possibility of any thing wringing a cry from him.

When Ranthorpe called him "that rich fool," he judged him superficially. Sir Frederick's intelligence was somewhat above the average; he had cultivated it; but that want of impulsiveness which distinguishes the Saxon—that heavy, phlegmatic organisation, which gives its peculiarity to the English standard of good breeding, and which regards the demonstration of any feeling whatever as bordering on vulgarity—that very English virtue, " reserve"—made Sir Frederick always appear to his disadvantage. He was voted dull by lively asses, and ignorant by ostentatious pretenders.

When this large, solid, quiet creature first saw Florence, he became enamoured of her. The contradiction of her character to his own was the great source of attraction, as is usually the case. The heavy, solid giant, with a brain as solid, but as unwieldy as his arm, was ravished— if so strong an expression may be applied to so circumspect and reserved a nature—by the gay, careless, witty, fragile, haughty, coquettish Florence. His plain commonsense had its sparkling antithesis in her playful nonsense. He could have taken her in his hand like a toy, and he crouched at her feet like the timidest of her spaniels. She seemed so light and airy a creature, that an embrace of his would have crushed her; and yet he felt as awkward and powerless in her presence, as if his giant strength had passed to her.

Bashful and silent, he followed her wherever she went. At every party she was sure to meet Sir Frederick; in every country-house where she went, he was sure to be found. But a thought of his affection never presented itself to her. He was always so placid, so dull, and so very indifferent, that his manner justified her saying, " I like to have Sir Frederick in the house. He's always about me ; I look on him as a sort of tame cat. You can't consider him a companion, but you like to hear his purr, and like to admire his beauty."

This silent courtship continued for some time, and was in progress during her flirtation with Ranthorpe, which gave Sir Frederick such alarm, that he more than once thought of challenging his happy rival; which he certainly would have done, had the flirtation not ended.

Indeed, I see not how the ice could have been broken

by any effort on his part. Florence never could suspect
that the quiet, gentlemanly, indifferent person, who, though
always at her side, never seemed roused by her liveliness, or
charmed by her beauty, had any love for her. If she occasionally talked more to him, or paid him more attention than
usual, the only effect produced was that of increased dulness in Sir Frederick. For, in truth, his invincible shyness paralysed his tongue; and because he wanted above
all things to stand well in her opinion, he was unable to
venture beyond commonplaces. Directly she approached
him, he shrunk under the mask of reserve, as the tortoise
shrinks under its impenetrable shell.

His aunt came to his relief. She knew his character,
and divined the state of his feelings; and knowing that
he would never venture without great encouragement to
give a hint of his affection, she one day said to Florence,
as they were walking about Rushfield Park, where they
were all three staying on a visit:

" Well, my dear Miss Wilmington, now do tell me
how long you intend keeping Sir Frederick in his present
suspense ?"

" What do you mean ?"

" When is he to be made a happy man ?"

" Sir Frederick Hawbucke ? I make ?—*ah ! madame,
j'y vois quelque mystification.*"

" Not in the least. I am serious, I assure you."

" *Allons donc !* What, my *tame cat !*"

" You may joke as you please, but you will not convince
me, my dear, that you have not long been aware of his
attentions."

" His attentions! *le mot est joli, vraiment !*—attentions, which consist in standing by me without opening
his lips, dancing with me without an extra sparkle in

his eye, riding with me without a single pretty terror, without one *prévenance*, living under the same roof with me, and never thawing into lukewarm interest."

" Does he not always follow you about ?—Is he not always sitting next to you ?"

" *Précisément!* like a tame cat; and I like him for it. But you do not mean to assert that *that* is his mode of paying his addresses—*hein ?*"

" I do. Allow me, who have known him from childhood, to assure you that underneath that silent, reserved manner, there beats the most passionate heart in the world. Still streams, you know, run deepest. His nature is as deep as it is silent; so deep, indeed, that though I have watched him from childhood, I have not yet sounded the bottom. He has the most superb contempt for all the little nothings which young men in general conceive themselves bound to display for our amusement. He hates affectation; he hates any thing like a demonstration to others of what is passing in his own heart. He is shy; and this makes him silent and embarrassed. Now when I saw him following you from place to place, sitting by your side, more silent to you than to any one else, I was convinced you had captivated his timid, passionate heart. I have since been confirmed in this."

" And did he employ you to make the declaration, which he dared not make himself ?"

" Not in the least. He never mentions you. He would not whisper his affection to any human being; his pride would forbid it. But, my dear Miss Wilmington, if you doubt what I say, observe him closely—see if he is not more reserved with you than with any one—yet, he is always seeking to be near you."

" And when I have discovered his affection, what am I to do with it ?"

" Not trifle with it—why should you not return it ? He is worthy of you, and he would be an excellent match."

" *Hé bien ! nous verrons. Après tout, il n'y a pas du danger—pour moi, du moins !*"

And Florence watched him.   The result may best be read in her own words.

Florence Wilmington to Caroline Fullerton.

" My dearest Carry,

" I have the prettiest bit of intelligence in the world to send you. Prick up your sagacious ears to receive it ! I am engaged to be married ! Actually engaged; have interchanged vows; and am now busy over my *trousseau.*

" But this, as a fact, is too commonplace to deserve much attention—though common as the fact is, we women never lose our interest in it—but it receives extra *éclat* from this other fact, that I *love* my husband elect ! Yes, *love* him ! ' Very natural too !' will perhaps be your reply.—' Not if you knew the man,' I retort.—' Who is he ?' you ask. And as he is the very last person you would ever guess, I may as well relieve your perplexities by naming him. Well then—Sir Frederick Hawbucke ! What think you of that ? I read the astonishment in your face; but you could not be more surprised at the discovery than I was at first.

" You remember when we were at school together, how we used to aspire after some *grande passion.* Our ambition was to inspire an attachment something like that inspired by the favourite heroines of our favourite novels —a passion disinterested as it was exalted, fiery as it was profound. How often has that engrossing subject defrayed our conversation!—how often has it inflamed our innocent imaginations!—how often has it filled us with delicious dreams! And how bitter was my disappointment, when I first awoke from the illusion, to find that in real life such passions were impossible; that men were insolent and selfish, brutal in their thoughts, though polished in their manners; tyrannical, suspicious, and inconstant! The effect upon me was very decided. Violent and impetuous as I am, I suddenly changed from the little *tête exaltée* you knew me, to the flirt you may have heard of. I treated men as they deserved.

"But in the midst of my flirtations I found at last a real heroic heart; at the height of my incredulity respecting man's capability of a great passion, I was amazed to find that I had inspired one of those deep, silent, tenacious, all-absorbing passions which makes man a timid devotee, rather than a coxcomb regarding victory as certain. You may conceive how the *tête exaltée* was intoxicated with vanity at the discovery! I do believe I fell in love out of pure gratitude and enthusiasm! Though as you know my Frederick, I need not tell you that he is worth loving for himself, however surprised you may be at *my* being captivated with one so opposite. But love delights in antitheses. I should hate a man as lively as myself.

" When I think of the lovers I have had swearing they adored me,—or looking it, it's all the same—and compare them with Frederick, I feel that it was my instinct made me only *flirt* with them, because nature had *made* me for him. In none of our novels, I verily believe, did we ever meet with such a profoundly passionate nature, subdued as it is with such magnificent self-control; and I quite tremble sometimes when I think of the force of his passion, and think how he hid it from the eyes of every one, except his aunt! He is the least *demonstrative* creature I ever met; and I am the most demonstrative creature perhaps ever born; so that the antithesis is perfect. But cold as he seems to others, I know that all the warmth which others expend in enthusiasm, in talk, and demonstration, he cherishes in his heart. Conceive how proud I am of him, and how happy I am and shall ever be!

"FLORENCE WILMINGTON."

In due time the marriage of Sir Frederick Hawbucke and Florence Wilmington was solemnised, and the "happy pair" set out for the wedding tour through Switzerland.

Their honeymoon was a honeymoon; that is description enough. They were supremely happy. They were proud of each other—loved each other. Nothing like a disagreement occurred. Florence, indeed, was occasionally made very impatient at the imperturbable phlegm with which her husband visited all the ravishing scenes which lay in their route. Neither mountain nor valley, neither glacier nor lake, could wring from him a cry of admiration. He contented himself with pronouncing the Alps "imposing," and Lake Leman "pretty." He was always willing to make a fresh excursion; but was as willing to quit each lovely spot, as he had been to go to it. He was never seduced into a touch of romance; never came home fatigued with the emotions excited by the scenery. Nothing wearied him, nothing bored him, nothing enchanted him.

For a lively, impressionable girl like Florence, this was, it must be confessed, sufficiently provoking. At first she attributed it to his undemonstrative depth of feeling; she thought he was too much affected to express his emotions. But so flattering an interpretation could not resist the daily contradiction of his insensibility. He was too measured in his language and in his manner, for her to suppose him struggling with unspeakable emotions. He criticised too coldly, to be admiring heartily.

She was impatient at his insensibility, and showed her impatience; but finally making up her mind that he was destitute of all poetry, she ceased to torment him and herself about it. If he could not admire passionately, he could love! That was Florence's consolation. And when she compared him with the French and Germans—nay, even with the English they met on their journey—when she contemplated his manly beauty, and thought how he worshipped her, like Hercules spinning with Omphale, having laid his strength at her feet, she could not but feel a mingled pride and gratitude, which amply compensated for any reflections on his want of poetry.

As for Sir Frederick, he looked upon her enthusiasm as fresh proof of her superiority over him. He knew that he could not understand her; he felt she was a creature of another order—that she did not belong to the same race as himself; and in his affection believed that she belonged to a much more elevated order.

This continued till they entered Italy. There a change took place. There she was as cold, or colder, than he had been in Switzerland. She knew nothing of art, though fond of poetry. Painting and sculpture she thought all very well in the *Exhibition*. There she saw portraits of her friends, there she met a crowd of well-dressed people, who went there, not for the pictures, but for the Exhibition. Sir Frederick had some taste, and more knowledge; was fond of old paintings and statues;

was not without a smattering of archæology ; and knew the history of the Italian Republics with tolerable accuracy. His astonishment may be imagined when Florence assured him, that she took no pleasure whatever in the " dirty brown things" he called old masters; and that she thought Chalon infinitely more agreeable as a painter of women portraits than Titian !

In Rome it was still worse. While he was either placidly examining the wonders of the Vatican, and feeling as much enthusiasm as his nature was capable of, or enjoying the classical associations awakened by the relics of ancient Rome, she was lying on the sofa reading French novels, or paying a round of morning visits, just as if she were in London.

He began to suspect that his wife was not the " superior " creature he had believed her. This suspicion was slow in growing, and was often banished from his mind, but it would force itself upon him. He consoled himself, however, with the reflection, that her education had not fitted her to relish art or antiquities, but that her nature was brilliant and poetical.

These were the only clouds in the serene heaven of their felicity ; and they returned to England as much in love with each other as when they left it. But the terrible mistake was committed of secluding themselves from the world, of shutting themselves up in the old manor-house of an estate in Wales, where they proposed to live like turtle-doves. This at such a time was fatal. For the first week every thing went on smoothly enough. Florence found plenty of amusement and occupation in visiting all the farms, going over the estate, and making excursions to the environs. But when the novelty wore off, she began to get tired of the monotony, and was annoyed to see the placid pleasure her husband continued to take in every detail. Their evenings were horribly dull. The day had furnished no subject of conversation, the monotony of their lives furnished no food for reflection, no points of interest; and between them there were too few subjects of sympathy to supply the place; their educations and their dispositions had not fitted them for mutually enlivening the most depressing of all solitudes—that of a country house. The charm of Florence was her liveliness, but she could not be lively alone; she needed company, new scenes, or new incidents to stimulate her animal spirits. As for her husband, he was a damper rather than a stimulant. His phlegm, which had rendered her impatient on their wedding tour, exasperated her in a country-house. In travelling she could take refuge in her own enjoyment, or in the society of fellow-travellers; but here she had no refuge, and the days were oppressively monotonous. Had she not been convinced of the depth of his affection, she never could have borne with her husband in such a situation; but she was too grateful to murmur ; and he, finding her get more serious, mistaking her ennui for reflectiveness, actually had the naïveté to compliment her on the change—to rejoice that she was becoming a serious woman!

The following letter will convey her feelings at this interpretation.

Florence Hawbucke to Caroline Fullerton.

" My dear Carry,

" If you love me, do persuade your husband to bring you here for a fortnight or three weeks. I am dying of ennui; my heart is ossifying. I, who never was alone before in my life, feel that I cannot support this

solitude. It may be all very well for Frederick; he rides
out, visits the farms, discusses the state of crops, considers
improvements, eats, drinks, and sleeps. That suffices for
his quiet nature; but I perish here. Not a soul in the
neighbourhood, not a human being to laugh and talk with.
You will ask me if Frederick is not enough—Alas! the
truth must be told—he is an inestimable creature, and that
is why I cannot estimate him; I respect the depth of his
nature, but his silence, his undemonstrative, unimagina-
tive, unimpulsive soul, makes him a most uncompanion-
able companion. He is clever, clear-sighted, instructed;
but his brain is unwieldy, and his pulses scarcely beat.
I would not hint such a thing to any body but you; and
I would not have you suspect me of a *complaint;* but
I really feel, as I say, a *great respect* for him, but *no sympathy* with him. *He doesn't amuse me*, in short; and I have
been a spoiled child, all my life accustomed to amusement.
Poor fellow! if he suspected this, it would break his heart,
I know; so you may be sure I keep it carefully concealed
from him. I have often been accused of being a consummate *actress;* people don't know the value of that art;
I do. *If I were not an actress Frederick would be miserable!* If I could not deceive him into the idea that his
society is pleasant to me—is sufficient for me—"

At this moment, she was interrupted by her husband,
who, opening the door, stood outside with his hand on the
lock, and said—

"Did you order the carriage for this afternoon?"

She started; did not at once reply, but shutting up
her writing-case in some agitation, turned round her
head, and then said—

" I really forget."

" Shall you want it ?" asked Sir Frederick, now coming into the room, and shutting the door.

" Well—I scarcely know. Yes, I may as well take a drive."

" What are you doing?"

" Oh! merely writing a letter." She coloured as she spoke.

" To whom?"

" To Caroline Fullerton."

" Remember me to her."

" Certainly."

Florence breathed again. She thought her husband had now quitted the subject, which was peculiarly unpleasant to her; and imagined he would soon leave the room. But he remained looking out of window, to all appearance as calm as usual. He made no signs of going away; and yet there seemed no reason for his staying. He was perfectly silent, motionless. His eyes were fixed upon the undulating lawns spread out before him. He was abstracted.

The truth is, that his wife's manner—her agitation about the letter—had roused painful suspicions in his breast. He was a morbidly jealous man; and he could not resist the inspirations of the demon which now tormented him. As he stood there gazing out of window, he was revolving in his own mind the names of all the young men his wife had seen recently; but he could not single out one upon whom to fasten his suspicions. And yet wherefore this agitation? Could she really be writing to Mrs. Fullerton? If so, why shut up her writing-case?—why colour?

Florence began to feel marvellously uneasy at her husband's silent presence. She sat drawing figures on the blotting-paper, counting the minutes of his stay. She wanted to say something to him, but could think of nothing. The silence was as a spell upon her, which she could not break.

Sir Frederick at length moved away from the window, and lounged to the other end of the room. He took up a volume which was lying on the table : it was the " Dreams of Youth," by his old rival, Percy Ranthorpe. Florence was surprised, beyond measure, to hear him humming a tune, in a low voice, occasionally interrupting it with that sharp breathing which is to whistling what humming is to singing. She had heard him do this but once before, and that was when he heard of a relation of his having been accused of cheating at cards, in one of the London clubs. What could it mean now ? He was reading and humming.

" If you have finished your letter, perhaps you will stroll with me down the shrubbery ?" he said, in his usual tone.

" Very well," she answered.

" Have you then finished it ?"

" No ;—but there is no hurry."

He was silent. She rose to put on her bonnet.

" By the way," said he, " give me your letter—I will finish it. I want to say a word or two to her."

" Then why not write yourself ? I shan't allow you to spoil my letters."

" Let me see what you have written, at any rate," he said, advancing towards her escritoire.

" Nonsense, my dear," she said, swiftly interposing, " you know we women have secrets, which you have no share in."

" Secrets !"

" Yes : all sorts of little nothings."

" Now you pique my curiosity. I must see it."

" No, no, no ; don't be absurd, Frederick."

" To *oblige* me."

" Nonsense."

" I am serious."

" How can you ask such a thing! Who ever heard the like !"

" I have a motive."

" A motive! what motive can you have ?"

" That is my affair ; enough that I have one."

" You are not jealous, I suppose ?" she said, scornfully.

" Why not?" he retorted, calmly.

" This is too ridiculous !" She was moving from the room.

" Florence, I am not so to be put off. I wish to see that letter. No matter what my motive—whether stupid curiosity, or stupider jealousy—enough that I wish it. Will you show it me ?"

" No, I will not," said Florence, drawing herself up to her full height, and endeavouring to crush him with the haughtiness of her indignant look.

" Beware! beware! you are strengthening suspicions. I may be foolish to suspect ; but you are mad if you confirm my doubts!"

" Is it to me you address this insult, Sir Frederick ? Is it your wife that you presume to dishonour by suspicion ?"

" Show me that letter."

" I will not!"

" You fear to do so."

" Put what construction you please upon my refusal.

I will not stoop to excuse myself." Her face was flushed with anger, and her eyes were filled with tears.

" Do you not see that your refusal puts the very worst construction possible ?"

" Let it do so. I am above suspicion."

" Then you brave me?" he said, fiercely.

" No—I despise you !" And with this insult she passed into her bedroom, with the most scornful look that her outraged feelings could call up.

He was stung to the quick; but remained where he stood. Some step was to be taken, but he could not decide which. His own conjugal felicity seemed staked upon the present quarrel. It was not simply a disagreement between man and wife; it was a struggle for mastery, at the very least; and it was probably the detection of some clandestine correspondence.

Had he chosen, he could at once have gone to her writing-case and read the letter; but he determined she should give it to him.

Florence had thrown herself upon a sofa and had given vent to a flood of tears. She was angry and wretched. To be suspected by him—and on such evidence ! So newly married, and so bitterly initiated into the petty world of bickerings and jealousy ! And where was his deep and tender love? where was his quiet idolatry? was that also a mockery? was he as cold as he seemed? She threw herself back upon the sofa in agony at the thought.

Half-an-hour afterwards she rose and walked to the door of her boudoir. Looking in, she saw her husband in the same position as that in which she had left him; his eyes were fixed on the ground, and he was whistling with a sort of ghastly resolution. She walked up to him, saying gently:

" Frederick, we have been very childish. I am sorry for what I said, but you provoked me beyond my power of restraint." She held out her hand to him, " You forgive me, don't you."

" If you show me the letter."

" What! still at your suspicions?"

" Until they are removed."

She turned haughtily from him; and taking her letter from the case presented it to him, saying:

" Since you persist, read. If its contents displease you, it is your own fault. But having read it, burn it; *that* can never go. When next I write about you, it will be in *another* style." And she left the room.

He took the letter and read it with tolerable *sang froid.* From her manner he felt convinced that it was not so important as he had dreaded; and yet it contained something likely to displease him, as she acknowledged.

It would be difficult to render in words the state of his feelings as he laid it down. Had he really loved Florence with that passionate depth she believed him to love her with, this letter would have driven him wild. But she was hopelessly mistaken in her estimate of his character; she had exaggerated it beyond all bounds. Because, in his shyness and self-control, he had concealed his affection for her from every eye, she imagined that his affection was unbounded; because she had discovered some warmth under the snow, she jumped to the conclusion that it must be a volcano. Sir Frederick certainly loved his wife; but it was a very measured, reasonable passion—it was thoroughly " respectable." He would have made her a good husband: kind, considerate, respectful. But the idea of this quiet, gentlemanly, phlegmatic Englishman feeling any of the delirium of passion, could only have entered the head of the capricious, wilful, and exaggerated Florence, who, because she knew that her own nature was demonstrative, but not deep, was led to believe that his nature was deep, but not demonstrative !

It is mostly pride that feels jealousy, seldom love. A lover may be jealous, but it is almost always his pride that suffers. When a husband ceases to love his wife, he does not cease to feel the pangs occasioned by the suspicion of her preference for another: which is enough to prove my position.

When I say, therefore, that Sir Frederick suffered the tortures of jealousy, I do not imply that his love for Florence was more vehement than before stated, but simply that his sensitive pride suffered from a *prospective* jealousy. It was evident that she did not love him. Her love was acting. She confessed it. He wearied her; she wanted some one to amuse her. That one would be found —that one would be preferred ! He felt that, although his rival had not yet a *name*—yet the *place* in Florence's heart was ready for him !

" So !" he muttered, " I am no longer a companion— I am a tyrant to be flattered with simulated caresses. The system of deceit has commenced. She avows it ! Avows to *another* that she deceives her husband !"

His face was deadly pale, and his lips were violently compressed, as this last reflection presented itself. Yes, there was the pang—that *another* should know what passed in his family—that *another* should know his wife loved him not !

What was to be done? He could think of nothing. He could only await the enemy's approach, and then defend himself. His life, he foresaw, would be a combat; but he savagely exulted in the idea, that at any rate he should not be a dupe.

At first he thought of returning at once to town, and allowing his wife to resume her accustomed gaieties. There she would be amused; there, perhaps, the germs of evil would have no leisure to develope themselves; she would not be tired of him, and would not cease to love him. This, indeed, was the wisest course he could have pursued—the only course. But his pride intervened—as it always does—to inflict its own tortures, rather than allow another to ward them off. If he was to owe her affection to *such* means, he would rather be without it. Better at once, he thought, to know the extent of his danger, that he might prepare for it. Thus resolved, he waded deeper into the torrent, that he might know its depth, when there was no necessity for him even to wet his ancles!

Florence was a good deal puzzled at his manner, when she met him, after he had seen her letter: he merely said, in his calmest tone:

" My dear, your complaints of the country are natural enough; but would it not have been better to make them to me than to a third party?"

She had expected a burst of anger; this mildness disarmed; and throwing her arms round his neck, she weepingly begged to be forgiven.

The wound seemed healing; for a few days they were together as heretofore—more affectionate, perhaps, if any thing. This did not last long; quarrels succeeded quarrels. She was more and more *ennuyée;* he was silent, sulky.

A letter from Florence to her mother will, however, save me a long description.

"MY DEAR MOTHER,—We return to town on the 17th. I quite pine for that day. I am very unhappy here; never thought I could be so wretched. But my dear mother will understand what I must endure, when she learns that I have been altogether mistaken in the character of my husband. My last illusion respecting him is gone. I thought, at least, that he adored me, but find his love was as common-place and cold as his other feelings.

"Now we are always quarrelling. I don't know who begins, or whose fault it is; but we quarrel and quarrel, for all the world like man and wife. Then he is always so exasperatingly cool! One knows not how to get the better of him. The other day I tried hysterics, and all he did was to take up the newspaper and read it till I came to! Conceive, my dear mother, what it must be to have a husband whom hysterics cannot move!

"But I shall never finish, if I get on the chapter of his vices. They are all comprised in one phrase—he is a domestic tyrant!

"When we are in town, I sha'n't care. There one can amuse oneself; here we are thrown upon each other for society—*c'est rejouissant!* He will never catch me again alone with him in a country house!"

CHAPTER II.

JEALOUSY.

En parlant ainsi, je vis son visage couvert tout-à-coup de pleurs : je m'arrêtai, je revins sur mes pas, je désavouai, j'expliquai. Nous nous embrassâmes : mais un premier coup était portè, une première barriére était franchie. Nous avions prononcé tous deux des mots irréparables; nous pouvions nous taire, mais non les oublier.

Il y a des choses qu'on est longtemps sans se dire, mais quand une fois elles sont dites, on ne cesse jamais de les répéter.

BENJ. CONSTANT : *Adolphe.*

Indeed such love is like a smoky fire
In a cold morning; though the fire be cheerful,
Yet is the smoke so sour and cumbersome,
'Twere better lose the fire than find the smoke.
Such an attendant then as smoke to fire
Is jealousy to love; better want both
Than have both.

CHAPMAN : *All Fools.*

THE Hawbuckes returned to town. Although Florence had completely given up her illusion respecting her husband's love, and with that illusion had, of course, vanished all the romance of her attachment to him, she continued to show him the proper respect, and kept up at least the appearances of affection. No one imagined but what they were the most enviable couple in England.

Lady Hawbucke's gaiety returned after a very short enjoyment of society. Her house was splendid, her enter-
tainments sumptuous. She passed as thoughtless and
giddy a life of it as if she had never married, or had
never been deceived.

Sir Frederick saw that she was happier in the society
of many men than in his; but even his jealousy could
find no excuse in her conduct with respect to any one
man. She was indeed the last woman in the world to be
afraid of, at that period. Her belief in man's affection was
destroyed. She had renounced the idea of love, and she
had no inclination to bring disrespect upon herself by
flirting. No one young man was, therefore, sedulous
enough in his attentions to justify Sir Frederick's jealousy.
But this was no alleviation of his condition. He would
rather have had one rival than a host of rivals. He knew
his wife was indifferent to him, that she preferred the
first comer's society to his, and this to so proud a man was
terribly galling. He endured it all, however, without a
complaint; without once indicating, by word or gesture, the
jealousy which consumed him.

Just towards the close of the season a young Frenchman,
M. de la Rivière, excited Sir Frederick's suspicions by the
assiduity of his visits. In him he anticipated a successful
rival. M. de la Rivière, though not handsome, was an
accomplished dandy, and possessed that liveliness of animal
spirits which so often passes for wit, and is, indeed, superior
to it in attraction. He was just the man to captivate
Florence's attention; the last man upon earth to captivate
her affections, for he resembled her too much. Sir Frederick never suspected this distinction; he saw that his own
sober nature was not fitted to charm Florence, and very
easily persuaded himself that M. de la Rivière, from his

liveliness and frivolity, must have every advantage over him

He endeavoured, by various pretexts, to warn Florence; but as he dreaded her suspecting his real motive, he was obliged to submit to a defeat in all their conversations on the subject; he could bring forward no good, ostensible reason.

" In a word, I do not like him!" he impatiently exclaimed one day at the close of a discussion.

" *Tant pis!* I do ; and as he never favours you with his company your good opinion is superfluous. *Est ce logique ?*" He was forced to hold his tongue. Her last speech seemed to him like an open avowal of her encouragement of De la Rivière's attentions.

They went to Baden-Baden—M. de la Rivière was only a day or two behind them. He became more and more attentive ; but Sir Frederick's utmost vigilance could not detect the slightest appearance of any understanding between him and Florence. He lived in a perpetual fever of expectation. It was the occupation of his life to guard his honour from the stain he deemed would inevitably be cast upon it, were he not vigilant. Her love was gone, he knew ; his own had given place to contempt. But in the silent defence of his honour—in the gradual development of this internal drama, he felt all the keen delight which ever accompanies strong passions. In this state of mind every trifle had terrible significance ; every word was commented on in a hundred different ways ; every look was interpreted. He stood in presence of a deadly enemy, waiting till he should safely strike the first blow, before one could be aimed at him.

They went to Paris—M. de la Rivière followed. One evening, at a ball, Florence was dancing with him, quite unsuspicious of the watchful gaze of her husband, who was leaning against the door of one of the inner salons. She was in high spirits. As the dance concluded, Sir Frederick, who was watching her narrowly, saw her give a slight start, imperceptible to any but a jealous eye, and saw the colour mount to her cheek. His heart beat wildly, but he preserved the calm nonchalance of his position, rivetting his eyes on his wife. De la Rivière bowed and withdrew. Sir Frederick saw him glide from the room, to which he did not return. Meanwhile, Florence was playing with her bouquet, and dexterously contrived to slip into her bosom the tiniest note conceivable : a manœuvre that did not escape the vigilant scrutiny of her husband.

It was observable that Florence lost her gaiety for the rest of the evening. During their ride home, she never opened her lips, though in general she was voluble enough in her quizzing of the company. Thrown back into a corner of the carriage, she seemed absorbed in her thoughts. The heart of Sir Frederick throbbed fiercely; and a grim smile played on his lips; but he also was silent. The time for action was come! He only waited to see if Florence would mention any thing about the letter, which he thought, if she were innocent, she assuredly would. Her silence was to him convincing proof.

Was then Florence really in love? No. Yet she received a billet from a young man, which she knew must be a declaration, and she had neither virtuously rejected it, nor communicated its contents to her husband. The reasons are simple. Her morality was somewhat lax—her love of any thing romantic very great—her abhorrence of " scenes" was profound—and she dreaded her husband. Without feeling the least affection for De la Rivière, she was flattered at the little bit of romance—she was pleased with his audacity—and had she been offended at it, she was too well bred to have made a " scene." Her intention was to answer the letter by polished coldness in her manner, which should sufficiently express her sense of his forgetfulness of the respect due to her.

The next afternoon, Sir Frederick astonished De la Rivière beyond expression by asking to be allowed to join the dinner which he was to give that day at the *Café de Paris* to some actresses and their " protectors"— *un diner de jeunes gens*, in fact.

" With the greatest pleasure, my dear fellow," replied De la Rivière, overjoyed. " I should have asked you before, but I thought that as an Englishman—*un homme à principes !* — you would scout the idea of such very *décolletée* society as ours."

" I shall be but a poor guest," replied Sir Frederick, calmly, " but I want to see this aspect of Paris life. We have nothing in England like it. Besides, I have heard such praises of your Florine."

" I feel flattered. But you must not expect great things. She is the prettiest actress in Paris—that is why she is my *chère amie ;* but she will not stand comparison with your charming Englishwomen."

De la Rivière was highly pleased at the prospect of making Sir Frederick a *roué.* It would be such a weapon in his hands. What would Florence say when she heard of her husband dining with actresses ! He chuckled prodigiously at the thought.

Little did he know the fierce, implacable, irresistible antagonist he fancied he was leading by the nose ! That calm, polished Englishman, whose name he expected to dishonour, was accompanying him to a battle-field, not to an orgie. The dinner was but an excuse. Sir Frederick

was too self-possessed to think of quarrelling with De la
Rivière on his wife's account. *That* would have been
publishing to the world the very intelligence he meant to
bury in De la Rivière's death. And he was too cool to
make such a mistake.

Thus, while the lively Frenchman thought Sir Frederick
was walking blindfold to his ruin, he himself thoughtlessly
walked into the trap laid for him by his supposed dupe.

The dinner was sumptuous, and boisterous. Four of the
most piquant actresses of Paris, four of the charming
young men, whose ambition is to revive the dissolute
orgies of *la Regence*, were the guests. Sir Frederick sat
next to Florine, to whom he paid marked attention. He
—the shyest, proudest man in London, paid chivalrous
attention to an actress at the *Variétés!* Such is the force
of passion.

Florine was prodigiously flattered. She was moreover
piqued into being fascinating, by the insolent remark of
De la Rivière. When first Sir Frederick entered the
room, she was greatly struck with his beauty.

" Sais tu, mon enfant," she whispered to De la Rivière,
" que ton milord est fort bel homme."

" Le fait est qu'il n'est pas mal," replied De la Rivière,
carelessly.

" Comme tu dis ça ! Tu n'as pas peur, toi?"

" Moi? Bah !"

" Mais je serais très capable de m'amouracher de lui !"

" Possible !"

" Après?"

" Tu y seras pour tes frais !"

" On dirait que je suis laide à faire peur."

" Non; on dirait tout simplement qu'il est Anglais."

The little Frenchwoman's vanity was roused. She determined on the conquest of this supposed impregnable fortress—an Englishman's heart. She exerted all her coquetries. To the increasing surprise of De la Rivière, Sir Frederick became more and more gallant—fixed his eyes upon Florine in an ardent manner—paid her extravagant compliments, which, though they wanted the *finesse* of the Frenchman's, compensated for that deficiency by the ardour with which they were uttered. De la Rivière became jealous.

The champagne flowed—the guests became excited—the fumes of the wine, and the intoxication of talk had begun to operate upon all of them, except Sir Frederick, who, though he drank bottle after bottle, seemed quite above the influence of wine. The only effect was perhaps that of a greater clearness in his ideas. He alone was unabsorbed in the merriment around him. He sat there drinking and making love, but with his ears open to every remark, his eyes catching every change of his enemy's countenance : calm amidst the unrestrained licence of this orgie, steadily pursuing one object.

Florine was so excited by the wine and by her success with Sir Frederick, that she forgot the presence of De la Rivière entirely, and almost turning her back to him, entered into a long and sentimental dialogue in an undertone with Sir Frederick. De la Rivière saw that he was placed in a ridiculous light, and catching an interchange of glances between two of his friends, which exasperated him to the utmost, he resolved to put an end to Florine's flirtation. This was not easy. He had swallowed several bumpers, which completed his intoxication, before he could hit upon a proper plan. At last, with an uneasy attempt at banter:

" Take care, take care, Sir Frederick. You are a novice as yet, and will lose your heart before you know it."

" No great loss," replied Sir Frederick, taking Florine's hand, and pressing it tenderly, " and I should be content to lose it here."

" Bravo! bravo!" retorted De la Rivière, ironically, " Lovelace himself could not have said a better thing. But you forget,—ha, ha, ha!—that you may turn poor Florine's head. She has a passion for Englishmen."

" Perhaps so," calmly answered Sir Frederick, seeing the storm louring.

" You know I shall be forced to be jealous,—ha, ha, ha!"

" Perhaps so. I dare say you would not enjoy losing so incomparable a *chère amie.*"

" Oh! oh! you think then that I should lose her?" retorted De la Rivière, with insolent irony, his eyes flashing as he spoke.

The women trembled. The men held their breath. " When France presumes to cope with England," replied Sir Frederick, with unutterable scorn, " she *must* lose."

This sarcasm was doubly insulting: as a Frenchman and a lover, it was felt by De la Rivière, who started to his feet. The guests all did the same, with the exception of Sir Frederick, who sat pouring out a glass of wine with the most insolent coolness. All eyes were fixed alternately upon the two antagonists, in consternation at the issue of the dispute. De la Rivière raised his wine-glass in the air, and livid with rage, said slowly:

" England is a nation of shop-keepers and clowns, we all know. The mission of France is to instruct the world. Whenever she meets with a *mal-appris*, she gives him a lesson in *savoir-vivre*. She does so *now !*" and he dashed the contents of the wine-glass in Sir Frederick's face.

Sir Frederick had expected this—desired it; he made no effort, therefore, to avoid it; but quietly knocking De la Rivière down, as he would have felled an ox, he turned to the guests, asked which of them was to be De la Rivière's second, and walked calmly out of the room.

At the Bois de Boulogne they met. Sir Frederick was no longer the phlegmatic being his friends had known him. A triumph sparkled in his eyes, which explained the elastic lightness of his step. He came to the rendez-vous more like a bridegroom going to the altar. He was, in truth, supremely, savagely happy; he came to kill his rival!

De la Rivière fired. Sir Frederick staggered. He was hit; but soon recovering his position, levelled his pistol, and taking deliberate aim, shot his antagonist through the head. De la Rivière fell. Sir Frederick walked calmly up to him; saw that he had only a few moments to live; and as neither the seconds nor the surgeon understood English, he addressed these words to the dying man in the politest tone imaginable:

" That is the answer my wife sends to your letter."

The dying man glared fiercely at him—attempted to speak—but his lips only moved feebly, and he expired.

Sir Frederick's strength was now spent, and he fainted from loss of blood. He was borne home insensible.

His wound was not dangerous. Florence, really afflicted, was prodigal in her attentions to her wounded husband. She believed, as every one else believed, that the cause of the quarrel had been De la Rivière's jealousy; but as she had long since ceased to think much of her husband's affection for her, and as she was not herself of a jealous disposition, it affected her very little that he should have been fascinated by an actress. Her attentions to him were however horribly misinterpreted by her husband: he imagined that she had divined the real cause of the duel, and that remorse was the source of her tears—hypocrisy the source of her attentions.

One day, as she sat alone with him, and he reclined upon a couch, having nearly recovered from his wound, she laid down the paper she was reading, and said, laughingly:

"So your Florine is not inconsolable, I see. The *Charivari* informs us that she has left France for Russia, in company with Count O——f."

"My Florine!" he answered, scornfully.

"Yes, yours. Don't be uneasy, I'm not at all jealous, and have known the story a long while."

He fixed a penetrating glance upon her, and said:

"Why must you be such a hypocrite, even when you must know it is useless?"

"Sir Frederick!" she exclaimed, haughtily.

"Let us understand each other. You *know* that Florine was a mere pretext."

"A pretext! and for what, pray?"

"Our duel."

"Pray be explicit; I hate innuendoes."

"I will, since you force me. You kept up a correspondence with De la Rivière."

She sprang to her feet. Then suddenly checking herself, she said scornfully:

"You are misinformed. I received, indeed, one letter from that unfortunate young man."

"And I took upon myself to answer it," retorted he, grimly smiling.

The whole truth was revealed to her as in a flash. For some moments she stood there speechless, bewildered. He watched her in silent scorn: he believed her to be acting. With inconceivable dignity, she turned from him, and swept out of the room.

From this time all disguise was impossible. They mutually read each other's hearts. They hated each other, and they knew it.

Florence would have forgiven any jealousy from a lover; but her husband she knew loved her not, and his suspicions were therefore simply debasing. Conscious not only of her own integrity, but of the care she had taken not to bring the slightest slur upon his name, even by flirtation, she was the more insulted at his groundless jealousy. On the other hand, the systematic manner in which he had avenged an imaginary wrong, seemed to her so diabolical, that his presence became odious.

She proposed a separation. He refused peremptorily.

" I will have no scandal," he said.

" Very well, then," she replied, "if you prefer the scandal of seeing me surrounded by lovers."

" That I shall not see. Every man who approaches you in that character meets the fate of De la Rivière."

This was said so coolly, yet with such determination, that a shiver ran over her.

" I give you due warning," he added. " If you flirt, I shoot your cavalier; if you compromise my name, I shoot you !"

She bowed her head, and wept. There was something in the tone of his voice which gave terrible assurance to his threat. She felt that she was in the power of a man as cool as he was implacable. The bloom of her life was gone; she felt that a miserable fate awaited her, and in conscious impotence she wept.

It was then that the pangs she had read in Ranthorpe's face—as he stood over the prostrate Isola, and passionately declared his love—arose before her in mournful reproach. She had tortured him without remorse; she had shaken off the recollection of his agony, as an uneasy thought is shaken off; she had smiled at his presumption, and thought no more of him. But now, in the depths of her own affliction, his anguished face was before her eyes, and she thought how much happier she should have been as his wife, adventurer as he was, than as the wife of the jealous and implacable Sir Frederick. He would have loved her! There was deep sadness in the reflection, and it seemed to her a punishment for previous recklessness.

The Hawbuckes returned to London. Every one observed the change in Florence; her spirits were invariably either sorely depressed or extravagantly elated. Ill health was her excuse, and she looked ill enough to make it plausible. Sir Frederick was as calm, handsome, and dull as ever.

In this state we must leave the " happy pair," to occupy ourselves about the other, and more interesting persons of this history.

CHAPTER III.

THE SURGEON.

Il vivait jadis à Florence un medicin
Savant hableur, dit on, et célèbre assassin.

BOILEAU.

Thou knowest that in the state of innocency, Adam fell; and what should poor Jack Falstaff do in the days of villainy? . . . . If to love sack and sugar be a fault, God help the wicked.

SHAKSPEARE.

HARRY CAVENDISH, having passed the College of Surgeons, had taken a house in Edwardes Square, Kensington, shaved off his moustaches, renounced his former pursuits, and seemed fast settling into a respectable member of society. People still thought him "too slang," but acknowledged the improvement. It was the turning point in his life. He had " sown his wild oats;" and what he might hereafter become, depended on the goodness of his disposition, and the circumstances which surrounded him.

Too little heed is taken of this critical period in a young man's life. It is a common remark, that the wildest youths turn out the best men. Dissipation, though an evil, is an evil best got through in youth. If there are

wild oats to sow, let them be sown early; for bad habits
later in life become fixed habits, and the fake at thirty is
irreclaimable.

Parents are needlessly alarmed at the wildness of their
sons. Look at the young Cantabs and Oxonians, who,
after getting deeply into debt, learning more slang than
Greek, becoming first-rate " dragsmen," or incomparable
scullers, instead of senior wranglers, are pronounced by
parents worthless scamps, for whom no hope is possible. What do these young men become? Scamps?
No: good, upright, manly Englishmen ; specimens of the
finest race in the world—English gentlemen. A few
turn out badly, but they are the exceptions. Look at
the mass of English gentlemen—interrogate their youths,
and see from what youthful extravagances these men
have emerged to become the first of citizens.

Is this a defence of dissipation? No; it is simply saying, that as youth is foolish and exuberant, its acts will
be folly; but when youth passes away, it carries with it the
cause of all this folly, and parents should not despair.
Instead of despairing, they should observe. There is
a critical period in the young man's life, when he may be
turned to any thing that is good. It is then that his
future profession or avocation will have power to wean
him from his habits. It is then his character begins
to consolidate. Of all influences capable of directing
him into the right path, none is so powerful as that exercised by women. If he loves, he is saved.

Harry was saved by love. Isola's little Walter had
fallen ill, and the servant, despatched to the nearest surgeon, came to Edwardes Square. As Harry entered the
room, Isola was suddenly struck with a reminiscence of

his face. She had only seen him once, and that was on the occasion recorded early in this veridical history. She had, however, forgotten the occasion, and only remembered it after he had left the house. Her repugnance at the idea of meeting him again was heightened by her diffidence in his skill; a young man who had been *such* a student, could not be a good practitioner, she thought. She was on the point of sending for other advice, when the servant casually let drop Harry's name.

Isola started. She had often heard Percy speak of him, and speak of him in the highest terms. Could this be the same ? She trembled; but recovering from her fears by recollecting that Percy was in Germany, she determined to let things take their course.

That night Walter slept soundly, and the fever abated. Harry looked in to see how his little patient was going on, as he said; to see once more the lovely girl watching by that patient's side, he meant. He found his patient recovering, and the fair watcher grateful; she thanked him with tears in her eyes. He thought he had never seen any one so beautiful. The large lustrous eyes shining beneath that queenly brow, and the melancholy sweetness which overspread her whole countenance, strangely affected him. It was impossible to look upon her without interest. She seemed formed out of different clay from ordinary women; and there was about her an undefinable something which seemed to indicate that her life had a hidden romance in it. His visit was a long one.

His visits were daily longer and longer. Walter improved rapidly; and the conversation, which followed the medical inquiries and prescription, was to both full of charm. To Isola, because she so rarely saw a cultivated person, that his society was a luxury. To him, because he could have gazed for ever upon that melancholy face, and listened to her musical voice.

Walter at length became so strong, that even Isola's anxiety could not create a fear for him, and Harry was forced to cease his visits.

CHAPTER IV.

YES: HARRY IS IN LOVE.

He brushes his hat o' mornings: what should that bode ?
MUCH ADO ABOUT NOTHING.

Ella pelea en mi, y vence en mi, y yo vivo y respire en ella, y tengo vida y ser.

DON QUIJOTE.

HARRY began to have suspicions that he was in love; and these suspicions were not idly grounded. He thought of nothing but Isola; dreamt of nothing but her; heard the singular intonations of her voice always in his ears, had the magic of her beauty always before his eyes.

He determined to extinguish these sparks, and resolved to see her no more. But Byron says, that,

"When a woman hesitates she's lost."

Woman is necessary to the truth of the rhythm, but *man* would be equally good for the truth of the aphorism. What is hesitation?

Hesitation is the dalliance with a resolution never intended to be enforced—a sophistical flattering of our weakness — a patronage of reason, which we know to be harmless; in a word, hesitation is the *prudery of*

T 2

desire—the "and whispering I will ne'er consent, consented" of human incongruity.

When a man resolves to tear himself from the fascinations of a woman,—you may be sure that he is an epicurean, refusing a luncheon in order not to spoil his dinner. He stays away for a day—perhaps two—perhaps a week. He returns to her feet, only the greater slave.

Thus Harry, while vowing to see Isola no more, never could take any other walk but that up Nightingale Lane. The beauty of the lane was his excuse; which was the more suspicious, as he had never noticed it so curiously before. The reason also of his always keeping within sight of her house, instead of winding further up the lane, he never asked himself.

For two whole weeks, his walks were ungladdened by a sight of her, and his irritation at the disappointment increased every day. He had no right to call, and could forge no reasonable excuse. All this while she was shut up in her room, endeavouring to make up for the time she had lost in attending on Walter; and to be able to meet Mr. Cavendish's bill, which she was in daily expectation of receiving, and which she feared would be large.

One day, little Walter was swinging on the gate, as Harry came up the lane. Harry was delighted; Walter had a great fondness for him, and thought him such a "nice gentleman." They played and talked together; and Harry artfully elicited from him all the particulars of Isola's ways of life, and a great many interesting traits of her character.

While playing, they saw her come out of the house with a parcel in her hand. Walter ran up to her, exclaiming, "The Doctor!—the doctor!" who followed, feeling rather nervous. She again expressed her gratitude for the

cure he had effected, and asked him if she might venture
to take Walter into town with her; he replied, that he
thought it would do them both good, and recollecting that
he also was going into town, begged permission to accompany her. She smiled her acceptance, and passed her
arm within his.

As he felt the delicate hand of his beloved gently
resting on his arm, he experienced a sensation almost
equal to the first kiss; and he walked along, " as if he
trod on air."

Harry walked and talked; was fascinated and fascinating.
The turn of the conversation once lead him to mention
Ranthorpe. Isola trembled, and was silent for a few mi-
nutes, and then said:

" Did you know Mr. Ranthorpe, then ?"

" Yes," replied he, intimately; " we lived in the same
house together. Do you know him ?"

" I—that is—yes, I knew him in his.father's lifetime—
and—don't you admire his poems ?"

" I admire every thing about him, except—but, to be
sure, he has cured himself of that error."

" What—error?"

" Oh, nothing—nothing—not worth mentioning. Yes,
Ranthorpe and I have spent many happy hours together.—
But here is Mr. Jones standing at his own door."

They entered, and the subject of conversation was
changed. When Harry returned home that evening, he
confessed himself irretrievably in love!

CHAPTER V.

THE BETROTHMENT.

And in my heart, fair angel, chaste and wise,
I love you : start not, speak not, answer not.
I love you : nay, let me speak the rest.
Bid me to swear, and I will call to record
The host of heaven.

WOMAN KILLED WITH KINDNESS.

A CLOSER intimacy had sprung up between Isola and Harry : their meetings were favoured by all sorts of pretext. One was furnished by Walter's mother, who wished Isola would take Harry's portrait—that she might preserve the likeness of the saviour of her boy, she *said*—that she might throw the two together, she *meant*.

The subject was broached one evening, and Harry, who saw, prospectively, a number of delicious evenings, while the portrait was in progress, awaited Isola's reply with considerable agitation.

" You know," pursued Mrs. Williams, " he saved Walter, and we owe him a debt of gratitude."

" No debt can be more willingly paid than that," said Isola.

" Will it !" he exclaimed, catching her hand in transport. Suddenly recollecting himself, he stammered an excuse, and walked to the window. This action surprised her; and still greater was her embarrassment as she saw him turn round again, looking very agitated. He left the house after vainly endeavouring to keep up a conversation on commonplaces.

Isola was thoughtful. The last few minutes had opened tracks of thought before untrodden. She had known him only three months, and in that time he had completely changed from the wild, exuberant, medical student, into the gentlemanly, well-informed, enthusiastic, noble-resolved man he was at present. He had lost all taint of the medical student. She was struck with the amount of alteration. The transitions had been so gradual as to be unobserved: the changed man alone was recognised.

Whence this change?

Isola was no sophist, and therefore did not " reject with modesty" the idea which forced itself upon her, that *she* was the cause—that love for her had brought him, from the wandering extravagances of youth, back to his natural disposition. She contemplated the probability of this, and every thing occurring to confirm it, she acknowledged it as a fact. She was not displeased at it.

Did she then love him ?

She knew not. Her heart had for so long been shut, even to hope, that she had ceased to think of love ; and now that she was forced to interrogate her feelings, she found them so confused, that no conclusion could be drawn from them. That she was delighted whenever he came,—that she was fascinated by his conversation, so full of enthusiasm and fine feeling,—that she was thoughtful, and often weary, when he was away;—all this she knew, and acknowledged. But was this feeling love? At times she thought it was : at others she compared it with her

love for Percy, and a curious difference was perceptible.

This perplexity increased each evening as he sat for his
portrait: each night she went to bed with a surer feeling
that he loved her; but whether she felt for him the affection of a wife, she could not answer.

One evening, as they sat talking about their early years,
her voice faltered. She said that painful recollections
always prevented her indulging in long retrospections.
She paused—she knew not what she was about to utter,
and dreading lest she should commit herself, she stopped
abruptly.

Harry was breathless. She walked to the window, and
pulled aside the curtains. The young moon shone full
upon her face; she gazed on it in silence. There she
stood, trembling with vague, voluptuous, yet oppressive
thoughts, which crowded on her brain.

> " The holy time was quiet as a nun.
> Breathless with adoration."

She gazed upon the scene, unconscious of its beauty; but
her thoughts were not uninfluenced by it. She was in a
waking dream; the present and the past were dead, and
she was sailing down the sunny streams that intersect the
dreamland of the future. She was unconscious of Harry's presence. He sat gazing at her with aching eyes,
rapt in adoration.

Her quick thoughts gave a sudden flushing to her
cheek, and a sparkle to her eye; her lips were parted, as
by an eager breath, and a smile of ecstacy ran over them
from time to time. Her bosom panted quickly; she was
in a state of great nervous excitement, yet moved not, but
stood there in the moonlight, like a statue, gazing on the

moon, " that with so wan a face" rolled upwards through the sky. This continued only a few minutes, but those minutes were as years in thought. Her smile then died away; her eye became meaningless; and a long deep sigh told that her vision was at an end, and that she had fallen from the clouds to earth again.

He rose and walked up to her. She turned towards him with a faint smile, and extended her hand to him. He took it in both of his, and pressed it in silence. She returned the pressure.

" Miss Churchill—Isola—do you read my heart?"

" I do," she answered, again pressing his hand in that simple, truthful manner which characterized her; " but I am unworthy of it—I cannot give you in return the same devout affection—mine is a widowed heart."

She then related her past history. She told him of her early love, of Percy's coolness, of his ambition, and finally of his inconstancy. She told him how her heart had been sacrificed to the allurements of a coquette. Woman-like, she laid all the blame upon herself, excusing every way her lover.

Harry was speechless. He knew nothing of Percy's love for Isola. Such conduct from his best friend to one he most loved in this world, completely overcame him. He drooped his head upon his breast, and gave way to sorrow. A long silence ensued.

"Isola," said he at length, " you have indeed been wronged —but you have loved Percy—perhaps love him still."

" No," she said, shaking her head sorrowfully; " I do not love him—I have long been cured of that."

" Indeed; then you—?"

" I can offer you only a widowed heart—but that is

yours. I have been frank with you—I have been explicit, because on such occasions any misunderstanding is the cause of misery. I do not love you as *I have loved.* I ... esteem you; you are dearer to me than any one else in the world; but—but—"

" But what?"

" I have one condition to affix; that is one twelve-month's delay."

" Oh! why delay our happiness?"

" In order to secure it; not from mere caprice, believe me. Listen. As I told you, I have great affection for you; but whether as one dear friend loves another, or whether as a wife should love her husband, I know not. I have interrogated my feelings very, very often, but cannot get a clear, decisive answer. All that I can promise, therefore, is to be a faithful wife and companion. I cannot promise to return *your* affection. Duty *is* in our power; not so feeling. It is very important to our future happiness that you should be convinced that you would be contented with a widowed heart; it is important that, all the obstacles to your love being removed, you should render it amenable to reason, and calmly judge whether our union would be productive of the happiness you seek. In less than a year you may repent—"

" Impossible!" he interrupted.

" I do not say you *will*, but you *may;* it is well to guard against such things. If therefore on this day twelve-month you still desire our union, I promise to be yours; if before that you have reflected on all circumstances, and have come to the conclusion that your happiness would be uncertain without my love, then will we be as brother and sister, and never mention the subject again."

" But I am convinced; how could I cease to love you?"

" No; I am inflexible. A year's delay to procure a life's happiness, is surely a small sacrifice."

" I will not oppose your wishes, dearest love; but be assured that then, as now, as ever, it will be my pride, my rapture only to call you mine."

And thus they were affianced.

CHAPTER VI.

THE BIRTHDAY.

Lass diesen Blick
Lass diesen Händedruck dir sagen
Was unaussprechlich ist.

FAUST.

RANTHORPE remained two years in Berlin, supporting
himself by giving English lessons to the young ladies of
the upper classes, and devoting all his leisure to hard
study.   He lived a solitary life, but on the whole, a happy
one.   He knew that he was preparing himself for the great
combat with the world, and determined this time not to
fail from inconsiderate haste.   Many were his delicious
reveries when rambling through the wild Thiergarten,
which in winter, when covered with snow, looks so po·
etically desolate, and which in summer, forms a shady
retreat.   There, amidst its " leafy solitudes," he meditated
on the vexed problems of philosophy, or scrutinized the
mysteries of art.   There he was supremely happy.

He then went to Dresden, where he stayed some months
in almost daily communion with the master-spirits whose
immortal pictures grace the museum, and when he knew
by heart every tint of the Sistine Madonna and the Seggiola

of Raphael—the Maddalena, Notte, and St. Sebastian of Correggio—the Venus, and the Christo del Moneta of Titian—the pomp and magnificence of Paul Veronese, and the varied power of Rubens, Ranthorpe thought of returning to London. He had a tragedy in his portfolio, such as his most rigorous criticism could not throw any doubts on, and with that he hoped to achieve a name in literature.

He returned; went through the usual harassing preliminaries, which need not again be described, and at length had the satisfaction of seeing his labours crowned with success. His tragedy was an extraordinary work, and startled the public into enthusiasm. A great tragedy it was not; if we understand by the term, such a work as our magnificent dramatic literature has entitled us to expect from every ambitious aspirant. But though not proof against severe scrutiny, it had incontestible merits: power, passion, rapidity, and beautiful poetry. It drew crowds to the theatre nightly; it was read by every one; reviewed everywhere; was played in the provinces; and, in short, was a triumph. Ranthorpe from that day took his place amongst the literary men of England.

He had, in part, at least, realised the dreams of his boyhood. But although a proud consciousness of owing his success solely to his own energy and genius, from time to time made his heart beat with satisfaction, yet, on the whole, he felt no such delight as his boyish expectations had pictured. Success, after all, is not so gratifying as people imagine ; while failure is horribly depressing. Where then is the poet's reward? In activity—in creation—in the healthy employment of his faculties. There, and nowhere else, is his reward!

Ranthorpe might of course easily have been made a

" Lion" again—a " Lion," too, roaring in a far wider den than before. But he had seen through that folly. He was not a second time to be seduced. All invitations whatever were steadily refused. He was to be seen at the houses of a few friends—people whom he esteemed and admired in spite of their position, were it high or low—but he was " to be had," as the phrase goes, nowhere. He offended a number of people, who accused him of affectation—of wishing to making himself of consequence—but he never moved from the path he had chalked out for himself. He led a quiet, studious, meditative, melancholy life.

Yes, melancholy, for he had not forgotten Isola. His success seemed robbed of its charms, because she was not near him to share it. In his quiet, studious life he pined for the sunshine of her presence.

And Isola also thought constantly of him. She and Harry had been twice to see his play—had read it aloud to each other—and he often found her weeping over it. She knew it by heart; and yet there seemed a fascination in the page, which nothing could wear off. The heroine pretty much resembled her in character; so that when she read the impassioned love passages, she seemed to hear Percy uttering them to her: and her eyes would fill with tears of exquisite pain.

Harry grew fretful and uneasy. The calm delicious hours he had been accustomed to spend with Isola were now converted into jealous watchings of her countenance. She often spoke of Ranthorpe; and, although nothing betrayed to him a renewal of her former love, nor even a wish to meet Percy again, yet there was no concealing the very great interest she continued to take in his welfare. Every mention of his name jarred upon

Harry's feelings; every inquiry seemed to him tantamount to a wish for his presence. He asked her one day to consent to see him, in order that this suspense might cease.

" No," she replied. " It is better as it is: it is better for all sakes that I should not see him; at all events till I am married. I could not see him: it would open wounds now healed; it would lead to explanations as painful as they must be useless."

It was in vain that she declined seeing him. Harry saw too plainly that her thoughts were constantly in that direction. A painful sense of dread oppressed him: dread of losing her he best loved upon earth. He was willing to accept of her widowed heart: it would have made him the happiest of men; but her *estranged* heart he could not accept.

After many struggles with himself—after many plans laid down and broken as soon as made, he determined that his fate should be decided: he determined that Isola and her lover should meet again, and that if they loved each other still, he would relinquish his claim. If they no longer loved, all jealousy would be at an end.

" I forgive your jealousy," she replied, " it is most natural; but believe me it is groundless. Percy no longer loves me. It is impossible for me not to feel intensely interested in him. I cannot forget that my existence was once bound up in his. I cannot forget all the delicious associations of the past;—nor all the *pangs* which grew out of them. But do not let me see him. I have pleasant thoughts of him, for I think of him as he *was*. I have not seen him since that fatal day—the sight would awaken feelings—painful feelings, which you, dearest," she added placing her hand affectionately on his, " have caused me to forget."

" Bless you for those words !" he cried, in transport.

" Look at the drawing I have just finished," she said, holding one up to him, and anxious to change the current of his thoughts. " Are you pleased with it?"

" Mr. Herbert will be enchanted !"

" Never mind others—what do you think—does it quite satisfy you?"

" I think it exquisite—as every thing you touch must be. But now I look into it—you really have surpassed yourself! Those trees glistening with rain drops, look so cool! Those shrubs and the grass, so fresh and green, have just the appearance of a recent shower; and I seem to smell the keen perfume crushed from them by the rain. That little rivulet is charming, as it runs along there under those lush weeds, and turns down by the stile, on which that boy is sitting in perfect summer contentment, flinging into the water the pieces of stick he breaks off from the hedge.—I long to be in the rogue's place—with *some one* by my side."

" I'm so happy ! I have taken such pains with this picture. Look close at it, and see if you cannot trace its meaning."

" The clouds rolled away in the distance, and fringed with gold—the clear blue sky—glistening, radiant flowers—"

" My past life is in those clouds," she added, gravely, " my present happiness is in the sky and flowers. That boy is Walter; that rivulet is the stream of our happy days. The picture is for you, dearest."

" For me, Isola ?"

" Yes, to-day is your birth-day—this is my remembrance of it."

" So it is.—I had quite forgotten it. And how am I to thank you?"

" By being happy."

" I am supremely so."

" Not while you are jealous."

" I am so no longer.—Isola," said he, after a pause, " in four months hence you will be mine : can you not shorten the time ?"

" I told you to be happy," she said, laughing, " and you promised obedience. Is this the way you fulfil promises?"

There was no resisting this. Harry felt that she loved him. True, her love was very different from the eager passion which devoured him; true, she was calm, pensive, melancholy, though affectionate, with the love more of a sister ; but still she *did* love him, she *was* affectionate, and she loved no one else. She had made him comprehend her feeling for Percy.

" Remember," she said, " that although the wrong he did me almost broke my heart, yet it was the deed of a day, it was only one action; but the years of happiness, and constant love, which I passed with him *before* that,—the

> " ... little, nameless, unremembered acts
> Of kindness and of love.

which endeared him to me—these I cannot forget. If I remember the suffering he has caused me, I also remember all the pleasure. I love him for that pleasure: his image is the central figure of a world of sweet associations. But were I to *see* him now, he would only recal dark and bitter thoughts, and rip up wounds that bleed no longer."

" Sister Isola," said little Walter, bounding into the room.

" Well, my pet?"

" Will you go with us to Richmond to-morrow?"

" No, dear, I have work to do."

" Do you like work better than play?"

" No," she replied, laughing, and patting the inge-
nuous face that was turned upwards to her; " but, as I
often tell you, Walter, I must work, and very hard too, to
get my bread."

" You always say that," said the child. " *You seem
to think bread more valuable than pudding!*"

Isola caught him in her arms, and stifled her laughter
with kissing the young philosopher.

CHAPTER VII.

THE DREAM.

Oh ! come viva in mezzo alle tenebre
Sorgea la dolce imago e gli occhi chiusi
La contemplavan sotto alle palpebre !
Oh come soavissimi diffusi
Moti par l'ossa mi serpeano ! oh come
Mille nell' alma instabili, confusi
Pensieri si volgean !

GIACOMO LEOPARDI: *Canti.*

Quando in sul tempo che più leve il sonno
E piu soave le pupille adombra,
Stettemi allato e riguardommi in viso
Il simulacro di colei che amore,
Prima insegnommi, e poi lasciommi in pianto.

Ibid.

IT is a bright morning in spring. The lark is up, and cutting through the sky, pouring forth his joy in such a gush of song, that the rapid notes seem to trip each other up in eagerness of utterance. The trees and grass are spangled with the morning dew; all is bright, fresh, and exhilarating as the thoughts of youth.

Isola rises from her bed with slow, reluctant grace; for she has passed the night in dreams of ecstasy, from which it was a pang to awake.

She dreamt that she was in a thick, entangled wood. She was plucking the woodbine, and the fragrant flowers that grew up to her hand. Suddenly a rustle of the leaves startled her, and turning, she beheld Percy at her side. He was pale and care-worn; a strange light shone in his eyes; a radiant smile played round his lips, and around all his person there was a gleam of glory. She held out her hand to him in silence; in silence he took it, and gazed wistfully into her eyes.

" Do you forgive me?" said he at last.

His voice seriously affected her; it seemed like a stream of warm music; it seemed like music, and yet it seemed to pour along her nerves trembling and warm. She could not answer him.

He spoke again, and she found herself in his arms, thrilled with his kisses.

And they wandered through the wood, plucking the loveliest flowers, breathing the tenderest vows, and planning events for the future. Their hearts were indissolubly united in one delicious feeling. The pale moon smiled upon them through the enwoven branches ; the breeze sighed mournfully amongst the leaves, and answered to their sighs; they walked on air; a spirit seemed to permeate their beings, filling them with new life; and the soft murmur of each other's voice stirred their hearts strangely.

She awoke, and the dull white curtains met her enchanted gaze; she awoke, and her lover was afar. She endeavoured to sleep again, that she might feel the rapture of her dream; but in vain. Pensive and sad, she rose, and began her toilet.

She, nevertheless, *had* dreamed of him, and could again conjure up that vision, though knowing it to be a vision. She had dreamed of him, and that dream haunted her like a passion. Who does not know this feeling? Who is there that has not spent some blissful moments in a dream, with perhaps some person they have never spoken to, but of whom they continue to think, on waking, with unspeakable tenderness?

It is one of the subtle mysteries of our nature; it is one of the manifold, unappreciable *influences* which mould and modify the condition of the mind, how, or why, we know not. It is one of those things, trivial in their origin, but important in their effects, which make up that which (if I may venture on the phrase) I would call the *atmosphere of life* : for we breathe in it, we live by it.

More good will is generated in happy dreams than any one is aware of. If a coolness separates two friends, let one dream pleasantly of the other, and his heart will yearn for reconciliation. If lovers quarrel; a dream unites them again. The mind invests the reality with the splendour of its own imagination; it refuses to believe the object less good or great, than it has known it in those brief moments of communion. I have known a dream hang about me for days together; exciting me to actions which cooler moments have condemned. Who, when he thus interrogates his own experience, will wonder at the quick credulity, which, giving forms to its conceptions, believes the voices which resounded in a dream, were voices from above ; warnings or counsels addressed to no mortal sense, but *infused* into the immortal soul ?

Haunted by her dream, Isola was suddenly shaken by the sound of Percy's voice in the adjoining room, calling her to come to him. It was some moments before she could persuade herself that it was not an illusion; but his impassioned accents once more thrilled her with delight, and rushing into the room, she fell into his arms, uttering a scream of joy.

O joy! O rapture! It was indeed Percy;—it was indeed her lover! It was her dream realised! This was no vision; she felt it was not, as she felt his heart beating beneath her own, and his breath mingling with her own. They

> "Saw each other's dark eyes darting light
> Into each other—and beholding this,
> Their lips drew near, and clung into a kiss."

And thus they rested in each other's arms: speechless, because their hearts were full, and because both feared to break the charm. Much had they suffered since their last embrace!—fretful sorrow and sick disappointment; but here they were again united, with hearts untamed by sorrow, crowding an eternity into a kiss!

They were both much changed in appearance since their last meeting. Suffering, illness, and study, had thinned his cheek, and given a more spiritual delicacy to his brow. He had, moreover, changed from a boy into a man; and though perhaps scarcely so handsome, he had grown more interesting. Suffering, and brooding meditation, had also touched with melancholy lines the noble brow and meaning-full mouth of Isola, robbing her of some of that *naïve*, youthful charm which had so exquisitely tempered her august and queenly bearing. You could not look upon her without at once divining that she had long been a prey to some silent sorrow; but you also saw that if she had struggled, she had gained the victory at last.

She took his head between her hands, and gazed intensely at him, to convince her exulting heart that his presence was not a vision. She twined her fingers in his silky hair with a sort of impatience, and gazed upon his lovely face upturned to hers in ardent adoration. He pressed her to him, and kissed her luxuriant hair which fell in disorder over her shoulders, for she had not stopped to bind it up. And it was not till their first transports were over that he became conscious of not having asked her forgiveness of the past. He began to stammer his excuses:

" Dearest Percy," she said, " do not recal the past— not even to weep over it, as an error. You need no excuses— it is enough for me to see you here, to feel your hand, to tremble at the sound of your voice—oh! do not look back on the past!"

" Blessed one!" he exclaimed, " you forgive me then? you give me again that heart which this time I shall know how to prize? You are again my love—my wife ?"

" WIFE !" she shrieked, starting up, and recoiling from him.

" Are you not my Isola ?"

" *O ! it was a dream—and I am thus awakened!*"

She fell senseless at his feet.

Alarmed and surprised, he took her in his arms, and raised her to the sofa, chafing her hands, and kissing her lips. He called on her, implored her to answer him, but she heard him not.

" I have killed her," he frantically exclaimed.

A deep sigh heaved her breast, and she slowly opened her eyes. He was so overjoyed at this sign of life that he nearly stifled her with kisses. She pushed him from her, with a convulsive effort, exclaiming:

" Percy ! Percy !—do not touch me—I am another's !"

" Another's ?" said he, puzzled yet alarmed.

" Oh! yes," she sobbed, " it was a dream—a dream! Percy, *I am engaged.*"

" Impossible—you ?"

" Too true!—too true!"

A long silence ensued.

She gave way to her feelings of despair, and he to his of resentment. When he heard her pronounce those terrible words, he felt it as an insult. She was thinking of poor Harry; thinking of her folly, in believing that her love for Percy was dead, because it was silent.

" And you are engaged," he said, bitterly.

" Alas!—alas!—but hear me, Percy, before you judge me."

" No; it is enough for me to have lost you," he answered, rising from his seat. " I cannot reproach you—I ought to have expected this—I deserved it."

" Percy," she said; and he could not resist the plaintive reproachfulness of her tone ; so reseating himself, he listened to the history of her life since their last meeting up to the evening of her betrothment.

" He offered me his hand," she continued, " as he had given me his heart, frankly, but humbly. He knew I did not love him: he knew I loved another: still he offered me his hand. My position was perilous; I had lost you, as I thought, for ever. I had no friends. He, above all men, was the one I most esteemed—most loved: loved with a pure and lasting affection, quite capable of happiness in marriage. In his affection I saw a home of peace and content—and therefore did I pledge him my hand—I never repented it till now!" And she buried her face within her hands.

This simple tale of a suffering he himself had caused,

oppressed Ranthorpe with a dreadful sense of his treacherous
conduct; and he felt that he deserved to lose this priceless
treasure, as Harry deserved to win it. He was stupified
with this thought; he was as one crushed to earth, without
power of escape; he felt that the present moment must
decide his fate, and he felt that the decision would be unfavourable.

Tears came to his relief, and he wept like a child.
They wept together in silence, broken only by their
sobs. They were both devouring their misery—both
driving deeper in, with savage hands, the barbed arrows
of remorse.

And yet she loved him! Could he, then, renounce her?

"You cannot—shall not be another's!" he at length
exclaimed. "You are mine—mine only!"

She sobbed, but uttered no word.

"You love me, Isola—do you not? Answer me: is
not your heart mine?—your soul mine?"

Her sobs became hysterical, but still she spoke not.

"Isola, dearest Isola, I implore you, answer me. Tell
me that you do not love me, and—I will leave—leave you
at once." His voice faltered, but she trembled more beneath its tones, than he beneath his anguish.

She was silent. A sudden ray seemed to streak across
the darkness of her soul, revealing there a duty, and a
glimpse of hope. The duty of fulfilling her vow to
Harry commanded her to prevaricate with Percy. "If
he thinks I love him still," she thought, "I am lost."

She raised her head, and looked him steadfastly in the
face.

"Isola, decide my fate. Is there another tie besides
your vow which binds you to him?"

" There is !" she answered earnestly, glad of being able thus to escape a falsehood.

His lower jaw suddenly fell, like that of one smitten by death. He gazed upon her with a look of wonderment and sorrow, and sighing deeply, faltered out: " May you be happy—very happy !"—and moved towards the door.

As he placed his hand upon the door, he was startled by one convulsive sob, that seemed to burst her bosom— he turned round, and saw that she had fallen back upon the sofa, prostrate with grief, her face hidden in her hands; her sobs thrilled him, and he sighed heavily. She looked up, and beheld him gazing on her in inexpressible rapture.

" Percy !" she murmured, and closed her eyes again.

" Yes, your Percy—for ever yours ! We will part no more !—we will grieve no more ! You love me ! You are mine !—say that you are mine !—say that you will not foolishly condemn us both to everlasting sorrow—"

" Percy, I have pledged my hand to another—I must and will fulfil my vows."

" No, no, no—your vows are mine. I have a prior claim—a stronger, deeper claim: I have your heart ! Oh ! think well, Isola, before you act, and think upon the consequences of that act ! You love me—think of that ! Think of your lot, joined to one, and loving another ! Think of all the treasures of your life thus wasted, all the dearest feelings of your nature crushed, withered, turned back upon themselves. Oh ! think what it is that you are about to do !"

" My duty !" she replied firmly. " I may be miserable —I shall be so—but I shall be innocent—my conscience will be light."

"Light? Will not my fate burden it? will not my despair blacken it? Will not your own grief trouble it? You are mad—Isola, I love you! Is not that claim enough—does not your conscience bow to that? Are you not mine—mine in heart and soul? Have I not a husband's love, and shall I be debarred of a husband's right? Isola, I love you. Can *he* say as much? Has *he* loved you so long? Has *he* been tried in the fire of temptation. Has *he* known sickness and sorrow, and pined for your presence as the healing angel? Has he been influenced by adulation, intoxicated by vanity, dazzled by splendour, enervated by luxury—and, after all, returned to you and poverty, content to pass his life by your side? Isola, I love you! I have loved you from my boyhood—I loved you in my manhood: you, and you only! In a moment of distorted ambition I was deluded by a coquette. She dazzled me, she threw a mist before my eyes, that hid me from myself. This moment of delirious error I have bitterly repented; I have wept over it—I have borne the stings of remorse—but I have loved you through all, and have lived but in the hope of being pardoned by you."

Isola continued to weep in silence; at length she said:

"Percy, I did not need your words to picture what my fate would be, away from you. I felt it from the first, and, feeling it, resolved to bear it. I have borne misery ere now—worse, indeed, than any yet in store for me— and my greatest comforter in that misery was he who is to be my husband. I cannot forget his kindness; I cannot in wantonness bring sorrow to his hearth, who never brought it to that of others. No: I may have to bear a heavy weight of suffering—I will pray to God to give me strength to bear it."

" And you sacrifice my happiness—sacrifice your own."

" He *loves* me—has no other thought—no other hope, than that of calling me his wife."

Ranthorpe stamped with rage.

" Do not ask me to commit a *crime*," she continued, " for it would be one to wrong *him*."

" You are mad !" he shrieked.

" No, Percy, I am miserable ! But God will support me. I have devoted myself to the happiness of another; for that I live."

Ranthorpe looked at her, bewildered, awed by her calmness. That simple girl, covering a breaking heart with an heroic firmness, seemed to him so sacred in her grief, and in her virtue so sublime, that his own selfish promptings were silenced. Her deep voice was unfaltering—her manner fixedly calm; but the anguish which distorted her haggard face told terribly of the struggle she had endured. At all times there was a grandeur in the simplicity and majestic repose of her manner; but now, when the whole strength of her nature was summoned to vanquish the most fearful struggle that a loving woman could endure, she struck Ranthorpe with a sense of awe he could not overcome.

Gazing at her, he plainly saw that she might *regret*, but would never *waver*. Like the Indian wife about to ascend the pyre, and join her husband in the grave, she might regret the sacrifice of this fair world, but would not flinch from the accomplishment of her duty, because duty to her was more sacred than life was fair. Majestic in her sorrow, as in her motives, Ranthorpe then, for the first time, felt the immensity of his loss.

He took her hand with mournful tenderness, and kissing it with deep respect, said:

" Isola, I deserve to suffer—my wickedness has brought us to this strait—it is just that I should rue it. Your own great heart dictates to you this sacrifice, and what your heart dictates *must* be right. May it enable you to bear the burden lightly! Be happy! — I do not say *forget* me—but think of me as one who henceforth is to you a brother. We shall meet no more. But we shall be present to each other in thought." His voice became more and more husky as he proceeded, but making a sudden effort, he said, " God bless you, Isola,—God bless you."

And she was alone.

Sick at heart she sank upon a chair. She would have recalled him and unsaid her words—but she had not strength. A dizzy faintness overcame her: wild, bewildering, tumultuous thoughts oppressed her, and she could not speak.

When Harry came in, a short while after, he found her delirious. A brain fever, for some days, at least, kept her from her sense of desolation.

CHAPTER VIII.

WAKING DREAMS AND WAKING SADNESS.

> I did hear you talk
> Far above singing! After you were gone
> I grew acquainted with my heart ! and search d
> What stirred it so: alas! I found it love.
>
> BEAUMONT AND FLETCHER: *Philaster.*

> The sweet thoughts, the sure hopes, thy protested faith will cause
> me to embrace thy shadow constantly in mine arms, of the which by
> strong imagination I will make a substance."
>
> LYLY: *Alexander and Campaspe.*

> Bello il tuo manto, o divo cielo; e bella
> Sei tu, rorida terra. Ahi di cotesta
> Infinita beltà parte nessuna
> Alla misera Saffo i numi e l'empia
> Sorte non fenno.
>
> GIACOMO LEOPARDI: *Canti.*

WHEN Isola was sufficiently recovered, she told Harry
vaguely of having seen Ranthorpe (which Harry knew, as
it was he who had informed Ranthorpe of her retreat),
and that they had " met for the last time." Then begged
him never to refer to the subject again. From the manner
in which she spoke, he was completely deceived as to the nature of their interview. He believed that Ranthorpe's presence had only recalled a poignant sense of his treachery;

and that probably they had come to bitter altercations on the subject.

But she seemed shattered by the blow. She rarely smiled, and never laughed. She was perpetually plunged in reverie, from which she aroused herself by a long and painful sigh.

Poor Leo was neglected; but with the marvellous sagacity which dogs display, he seemed to understand her grief, to sympathise with it, and respect it. His large eyes were constantly fixed on her in mournful lovingness, and he would gently lick her hand as if to reassure and comfort her; but she seemed seldom aware of his presence.

Harry, deceived by her words, never interpreted these reveries aright, and seldom remarked them. He knew that she was melancholy—he knew her wounds were bleeding, and that time alone could staunch them.

She seldom wept, but the colour never rose into her ashen cheek; and there was an inward look about the eyes which betokened a complete withdrawal from the outward world, to contemplation of the inward. She lived, indeed, no longer with her senses. Her days were passed in reveries; her nights in fantastic dreams. Her language assumed a mystic colouring; and her paintings were so bizarre that people complained of them as unintelligible and unlike nature.

Unintelligible! why every leaf had its meaning, every tint its feeling! Those flowers that drooped so pensively —those weeds so tangled and torn—those lilies uprooted and thrown upon the bye path to be crushed beneath the foot of the passer by—those cottages so silent and deserted, with a lean and melancholy dog watching beside the door —those scenes of desolation and violence—had all to her deep meaning, for they were the symbols of her sufferings, as she found them expressed by nature.

In the midst of her work, she would often let her pencil or her needle fall, and with fixed but vacant eyes sit speechless for more than an hour at a time, absorbed in some painful or delicious reverie. She was then with her lover. His exquisite face was upturned to hers; his dreamy eyes were speaking to her soul a language only intelligible to her;—his voice whispering in her ear the music of a lover's flattery and a lover's hope. She was acting again that blissful dream wherein they rambled through the mystic wood. She spoke to him— and her heart framed his replies. She smiled on him, and felt the warm pressure of his arm about her waist. Thus to her was the ideal made real: she lived in dreams, her waking moments were feverish with sorrow and remorse.

Little Walter was forced to leave England with his mother. Isola wept for him, but not as she would have wept a little while before. She had almost lost her consciousness of external things, and mingled her grief for Walter with her own peculiar sorrow.

She had, in truth, overrated her strength: she had imposed a burden on herself no woman can bear. She was no longer in the same state of mind as she had been before. She *then* thought—believed that Percy had ceased to love her. A sense of injury and of maidenly pride, made her shut her heart against him; she *now* knew not only that he loved her still, but that she had never ceased to love him also—that her affection had slept, and was awakened by a touch. In the first belief she had only two resources; suicide or endurance: in the second, also, only two; duty or happiness; happiness purchased by the sacrifice of duty,

duty purchased by the sacrifice of happiness. As Schiller finely says:

> " O wie gross wird unsre Tugend
> Wenn unser Herz bei ihrer Uebung bricht !"

To evils, when there is no remedy, we make up our minds: we are not every moment irritated by hope deferred. It is when the remedy is possible, yet does not come,—it is when hope is strong, but never is fulfilled,—that the mind is racked with agonies of suffering. Put a bird into a cage, and (having tried all its fastenings and seen escape to be impossible) it will chirrup with content, and take its daily food in peace: but tie that bird's leg by a string, and it will flutter to be free; refuse all food; all consolation; and break its yearning heart. The bright Heaven and the free air are above and around it, inviting it; one petty barrier alone prevents its springing into the air. It feels the power to fly—it rises and flies—to the length of the string! This constant endeavour, and this constant failure, is the misery. Affliction may be borne; but it must be irremediable, before it can be borne with patience.

Isola was fast sinking under this wearing struggle of her conscience with her instincts; and even Harry at last remarked that some secret sorrow was consuming her. He could not believe it to be grief for Walter's loss—could it be for Percy's loss?

One evening as he passed beneath her window, he heard her singing. The pathos of her voice arrested him, and the tears rose to his eyes, as he distinctly caught this verse:

> " A present à peine j'endure
> Ce qui me charmait autrefois;
> Du ruisseau je fuis le murmure;
> Je crains l'ombre triste des bois;

> Je maudis l'épine piquante
> Du rosier que ma main planta;
> Tout m' importune, tout me tormente—
> Rien ne me plait—il n'est plus là!"

Her voice was broken by her sobs as she reached the last line; and he moved away dizzy with the horrible thoughts that crowded on his brain.

CHAPTER IX.

THE SACRIFICE.

Oh je t'ai aimée, simple fleur que le vent brisait sur sa tige, pour ta beauté délicate et pure, et je t'ai cueillie espérant garder pour moi ton suave parfum, qui s'exhalait à l'ombre et dans la solitude. Mais la brise me l'a emporté en passant, et ton sein n'a pu le retenir! Est ce une raison pour que je te haisse et te foule aux pieds? Non! je te reposerai doucement dans la rosée où je t'ai prise, et je te dirai adieu, parceque mon souffle ne peut plus te faire vivre, et qu'il en est un autre dans ton atmosphère qui doit te relever et te ranimer. Refleuris donc, ô mon beau lis! je ne te toucherais plus!

GEORGE SAND.

HARRY from this time suffered all the miseries of doubt and dread. He began by suspecting that, in spite of her assertions, Percy really had her heart. He watched her narrowly. He scrutinized the events which had occurred—her wrong—her second betrothment—her meeting with her first love—her subsequent sorrow.

"She loves him!—Yes—yet she would spare me! Yes, that must be the cause of her grief. Oh, God! what a thought; to owe her to a sense of duty—pity!"

Men are rarely moved to tears; and *his* grief was too dull and stupifying to find relief in tears. But he walked up and down his room like a criminal awaiting execution,

x 2

who knows his doom is inevitable, and yet cannot believe that he must die.

A terrible struggle took place in his breast. But it ended in virtue subduing instinct. He resolved to relinquish his claim, and purchase her happiness at the sacrifice of his own.

But he found it impossible to speak on the subject with Isola. Whenever he alluded to her melancholy, she asked him if she had not cause? Whenever he approached the name of Percy, she put her finger on his lips. By the sudden shiver that ran over her frame when it was alluded to, Harry saw how full of anguish the subject was; and at times doubted whether she really did love Percy.

In this state of fluctuation he remained until the event recorded in the last chapter brought things to a crisis. From a narrow scrutiny of her countenance and manner, he divined pretty well the history of her grief. Unable longer to doubt, he was resolved to act.

After quitting Isola on that memorable day, Ranthorpe returned home broken-spirited. He could no longer work—he had no object. What was popularity to him? Noise, mere noise!

And yet so little is a poet master of his own faculties, so little can he resolve to write or to be silent, that Percy, convinced of the nothingness of popularity, feeling that he had no object in life which should make him court the suffrages of the world, nevertheless was soon afterwards enthusiastically pursuing the plans of a new work, with the same eagerness, the same delight, as if his existence depended upon its success.

He was one day sitting in his study with Wynton, fondly detailing to his faithful friend the nature of the work upon which he was then engaged, when Harry walked into the room. Percy rose surprised; and answering the frank gesture of Harry's outstretched hand by a cold bow, motioned him to a chair. Harry understood the reception from a rival; but he was sorely hurt at it nevertheless.

Ranthorpe was determined that his visitor should begin the conversation. Wynton looked on in uneasy amazement, and knew not what to conclude from Harry's altered appearance; for his cheeks were burning with a hectic glow, and his eyes had a strange wildness in them Wynton had never seen before.

After a few minutes of this chilling silence, Harry said:
" Can I speak with you alone?"

Wynton rose ; but Ranthorpe checked him, saying:
"Don't stir; there is nothing Mr. Cavendish can say to me that you may not hear."

Then turning to Harry with exasperating coolness:
" You were about to observe—"

" What I have to say is entirely a private matter."

" You must excuse me then if I decline attending to it."

" Percy," said Wynton, " I *must* go; my presence is positively indelicate."

" Your presence is indispensable. I wish to have some one by my side who will be some *restraint* upon me."

Harry was galled; he knew not what to say, or what course to take.

" Percy !" he exclaimed.

" My name is Ranthorpe, sir."

" You shall not irritate me, do what you will. I came to speak with you about Isola—now will you listen?"

" Nothing you can say to me respecting Miss Churchill can have any interest for me," replied Ranthorpe, the beating of his pulse belying the coldness of his manner.

A thought flashed across Harry's mind, that possibly he had been mistaken with respect to Isola's grief—perhaps Percy did not love her after all.

He started up, and hurriedly saying, " Good day," left the room.

" How could you treat him so, Percy?" said Wynton.

" I hate him !"

" Your old friend?"

" My rival. My ungenerous rival. He knows—he must know Isola loved me; yet he has her word—she is engaged to him—and——"

Here the door opened, and they both started as Harry again appeared before them.

" I will not be frustrated, " he said, " I will learn the truth. Since I must speak before Wynton, I here solemnly ask you if you still love Isola? Your answer I can read in your face. As you value her happiness and your own I charge you, tell me whether at your last meeting you talked with her of your love; and whether she told you of her engagement."

Ranthorpe got up from his chair, and with intense scorn, answered: " Jealousy has many ingenious devices —could you not hit upon one which would answer your purpose quite as well, and not be *quite* so insolent."

" Jealousy?" echoed Harry, while a bitter smile faded on his quivering lip.

" Rivals," added Ranthorpe with increasing scorn, " are usually *defied*, not interrogated !"

" Percy, Percy, have you not nobility enough at heart to understand me? Cease that scorn—do not make me forget myself ! I am not jealous. *Jealous,* indeed !—

Well, well!—I ask you whether you spoke of love to her, and whether she rejected you because she was affianced to another. I *feel* she did; but I ask you that I may be sure that when I yield up my claim to be her husband, I am acting uprightly. You stare. You look incredulous? —Why, man, I *love* her—love her better than myself! Now do you understand me? I, who would die for her, shall I do her an irreparable wrong? I, who worship her, shall I permit her to waste her life on me, she loving another? No, no, no! Tell me that she rejected you, because her word was pledged to me—and she is yours! Now do you understand me?"

Ranthorpe gazed at him for a few seconds as if bewildered. Then recovering himself he walked up to him, holding out his hand in silence. In silence it was taken, and one long significant pressure was all these two bruised hearts could find to express their emotions.

CHAPTER X.

RECONCILIATION.

Alli, el silencio de la noche fria,
El jasmin que en las redes se enlazaba,
El cristal de la fuente, que corria,
El arroyo, que à solas murmuraba,
El viento, que en las hojas se movia,
El aura, que en las floras respiraba
Todo era amor.

CALDERON: *Cisma de Inglaterra.*

Qué causa puede haber sido
La que llegó á separar
Dos corazones tan finos?

MORATIN.

ON that wedding-day which had so strangely been
fixed upon by Harry as the day which should witness his
sacrifice; on that wedding-day which had approached
without either Isola or her betrothed being aware of it,
so little had their thoughts for some weeks been fixed
upon marriage; on that day Isola had been deeply engaged with a drawing of more than usual mysticism. It
was wild as a Salvator, tender as a Claude. It was a
mere nothing—and yet every thing—a " study," and yet
full of meaning. To ordinary eyes it was but a rocky

pass, with trees, flowers, weeds, and fragments of fallen stone, all in inextricable confusion. But as you looked closer its meaning gradually unfolded itself. There was desolation in those blasted jagged crags around which grew such luxuriant vegetation; in the sombre blackness of the earth, from which the lush weeds grew—the weeds themselves confused and suffering, entangled, bent, and broken—tortured by overgrowth, yet full of beauty; there was desolation in the booming, roaring, flashing waterfall, writhing and hissing from a melancholy cleft; in the trunks of ancient trees twisted into fantastic shapes. branchless, hollow, scathed with lightning. And above all was the calm blue heaven, cloudless and windless, a solemn mockery of the desolation upon earth. There was a sombre irony in the picture. It showed the hideous skeleton beneath the mask of life. It was the symbolised sadness of one who had peered too curiously into the depths of her own heart.

And yet this bitter mockery of life—this ghastly analysis of irony, which displayed the skeleton beneath the beauteous form—this consciousness of her wound and scornful laying of it open, was not without its fascination to the artist. There is a dalliance with misery, which has its voluptuous orgies, powerful as those of the senses. There is a passion for rising above sorrow, and looking down upon it in painful scorn: playing with it, smiling at it—smiling amidst tears.

In this mood Isola touched and retouched her picture. Her brush seemed as if it would never quit her hand; each stroke served only to bring out more fully the contrast of life and death—beauty and deformity—enjoyment and torture—contained in her conception. No clump of moss but had its meaning; no blade of grass rose higher than

its neighbours without some ironical intention. The very
masses of rock which encumbered the valley bore in one
way or another the impress of this irony: here, one fragment was richly covered with lichens, while its side, partly
exposed, was black and scathed; there, another fragment,
rugged and barren, had green and speckled lizards crowding from its fissures.

In the evening Harry came and found her still occupied
with her picture. She was greatly excited, and talked of
little but of Art.

"Art enshrines the great sadness of the world," she
said; "it purifies, elevates, incarnates sadness in beauty,
and thus preserves it. Without Art man would forget the
sufferings which humanity has endured. Suffering, being
disorder, is perishable; yet it does not deserve wholly to
perish, and Art enshrines it."

"Should we not rather wish it to perish?" said he.

"No; we need it constantly with us, to teach us charity
—we need it to teach us fortitude. I should go mad, if
I could not read in the pictures, poems, and melodies of
great artists all that I endure! I see they have endured them, and yet lived on. I trace the sadness of the
artist in his lines, or in his faltering rhythm. I see his
sadness underneath the gaiety with which he strives to
mask it."

"Does not this depend rather upon your mood, than
upon their meaning?"

"No; sadness is everywhere written on their works as
it was engraven on their hearts. What sorrow is implied
in the ever-present irony of Shakspeare! What sorrow
renders touching the measured stateliness of Milton! Then
think of Dante, grim with a thousand woes! Think of
the pensive sadness of Raphael, the austerity of Fra Bar-

tolomeo, the irony of Albert Dürer ! And oh ! the infinity of sorrow in the works of Beethoven; piercing, plaintive, exquisite, unalterable ! It is no common spirit, struggling with no common pain, which pierces his melodies with such plaints of woe ! And then Mozart—what quiet pathos amidst his smiles—what settled melancholy diffused through all his beauty."

There was a pause. Her brush again struck out a few significant tints. She set it down again, and said:

" It is in Art that I commune with those subtler portions of experience which words have no power to express. Art gives enduring form to the supersensuous in life. It gathers to its bsoom all the sufferings of Humanity, soothes them, embalms them, and thus becomes an everlasting monument of human experience."

She stopped, but her lips continued to move, as if endeavouring to speak. She rose and walked to the window, and threw it open. The moon was hidden behind a cloud, and the foliage which spread before her window, was dark as night; nothing but an indistinguishable mass of foliage met her gaze. The sweet scent of flowers entering at the window, had a peculiar effect upon her nerves, and awakened strange associations.

All was so calm, nothing interrupted the current of her thoughts.

Harry watched her in silence; listened to her gentle breathing ; watched the rise and fall of her exquisite bosom as it panted beneath her dress; and puzzled himself as to how he should break to her his resolution.

While she stood there wrapt in thought, the moon slowly emerged from the cloud, and streamed upon her. She was thinking of Percy, when a rapid association carried her back in thought to that evening when, standing at the same window, and under the same moon, she plighted her vow to Harry. And this was its anniversary.

" Come here, dear one," she said.

He rose, approached, and took the hand she held out to him.

" Have you forgotten this day?" she asked. " It was to be our wedding-day."

A strange and sickly smile passed over his face.

" You do not answer me."

" Isola, dearest Isola, forget that evening."

She started, and looked eagerly at him.

" You promised me a widowed heart.—I should have been the happiest of men!—but your heart was not widowed ! — I — don't heed these tears — I'm agitated. Well.—In a word, I forego my claim!—I ask no fulfilment of a vow—how could I ask it?—rashly made, and bitterly repented. You love Percy Ranthorpe—he loves you. Be happy with him—it is all I wish. Let me be your friend—a brother whom you love. All I think of, all I care for, is to see you happy."

She stared at him with vacant eyes, as one who rather felt than comprehended his meaning. Speechless and motionless for a few moments, she then touched his forehead with her cold and quivering lips, murmuring:

" You humiliate me—I am very wicked !"

" You are an angel, whom I love too well to see unhappy."

" I did not think," she sobbed, " that I should ever give pain to one who has been to me what you have been."

" Isola, Isola, let me have my reward; let me see you happy !"

She raised her tearful eyes to him, and after one long look of unutterable gratitude, gave vent to her tears.

She wept over the duty she was sacrificing to love; he wept over the love he was sacrificing to duty.

A carriage drove up, and put an end to this painful scene. Fanny Wilmington stepped out, and was soon beside her friend; and soon made confidante of what had taken place. Why did she suddenly feel so elated? and why did she gaze at Harry with such intense fervour? and why was she so eloquent in his praise? She knew not; all she knew was that the communication just made seemed to remove a load from off her heart. And it was with a strange flutter that she accepted his invitation to take a turn in the garden with him, so as to leave Isola with Percy, whose knock then announced him.

Over the meeting of the lovers I draw a veil. The burst of rapture with which they clasped each other in a wild embrace—the many inquiries—the fond regrets and thrilling hopes—it is out of my power to convey. Let me, therefore, leave them to their happiness.

CHAPTER XI.

LOVE IS BLIND; COUCH NOT HIS EYES.

> There are a sort of spirits fall but once,
> But that once is perdition.
>
> GUIDONE.

> Per me si va nella città dolente;
> Per me si va nell' eterno dolore;
> Per me si va tra la perduta gente.
>
> DANTE.

> O God! O God! that it were possible
> To undo things done; to call back yesterday!
> That time could turn up his swift sandy glass,
> To untell the days, and to redeem these hours!
> <div align="right">HEYWOOD: <i>Woman killed with kindness.</i></div>

HAVING thus seen Ranthorpe's battered boat at length put into port; let us see what fate awaits Florence Haw-bucke, whom we left battling with the waves.

Florence was in love; and her husband had no suspicion of it! His jealousy had indeed somewhat abated, but its embers were still burning. What made him blind to Florence's love was the absurdly mistaken notion he had formed of her. He thought her frivolous, and that, *therefore*, she would only love a frivolous man: strange error! He knew her first complaint against him had been his want of liveliness, and imagined that she would only love some gay and lively man who could amuse her.   This, which at no time would have been true, was singularly false under present circumstances.

Florence was wretched, and needed sympathy, not live-liness.   Shakspeare, who has sounded every note of human feeling, has not left this one untouched.   The officious waiting-woman would charm a queenly sorrow with music, but the sufferer replies:

" Thou shouldst please me better wouldst thou weep."

Song may distract the gay, or lay its heavy burden of delicious pain upon the spirits of the happy; but grief demands sympathy—tears seek for tears—and sorrows love to jostle with sorrows greater than themselves, to learn, in the contact, humility and comfort.

While, therefore, her husband would assuredly have shot the first lively young man who had the bad fortune of attracting much of Florence's attention, he witnessed without the shadow of a suspicion the intimacy growing between her and Bourne.   The melancholy and unsuccess-ful dramatist, whose plays Sir Frederick had read with merited contempt, was, however, the only really danger-ous rival admitted to Florence's intimacy.   Sir Frederick had too profound a contempt for him to fear him.   Besides, it never occurred to him that a heavy melancholy man could interest the frivolous Florence.   But that melan-choly man interested the *wretched* Florence !

Bourne was naturally of a bilious temperament; and continued ill-success, acting upon an idolatry of Byron, had fostered in him a very respectable amount of misan-thropy.   He was intensely vain; and was incessantly en-deavouring to assume some imposing attitude before the world. As an orator, a legislator, and a poet, he had ludicrously failed. As a misanthrope he had gained tolerable success in society: for people avoided him with unfeigned alacrity.

Florence was attracted to him by his sorrows. They spoke vaguely of woes which had, in both their cases, embittered an ardent youth—of deceptions which had blighted a believing heart. They were eloquent in scorn of the pretended force of love. In this Florence was serious, Bourne acting. Strange that this actress should in turn become a dupe!

Bourne, gratified at so credulous a listener, made up a history of his life, smacking greatly of the circulating library, but avidly listened to and believed by Florence. He had at first no motive in this beyond the mere delight of making himself the hero of a fictitious narrative—of placing himself in an effective attitude. But when she confided to him her history,—when he had shed tears with her over that confidence,—new thoughts, wild and turbulent, hurried across his mind. He felt that when man and woman exchange confidences, there is but one step more for them to take; and that is to exchange vows.

Florence, as I have more than once intimated, was not possessed of much heart. She had more sensibility than depth of feeling. Her nervous temperament and her education together had made her somewhat romantic— that is to say, avid of emotions; but hers was not a loving nature. She loved with her head more than with her heart. And it was owing precisely to this distinction that she was led away by the vulgar acting of Bourne. Her imagination was inflamed. She seemed in his history to have read the narrative of a life which she was made to render glorious and happy. Bourne was the loving, sensitive, suffering heart, she had been seeking all her life. With him she would fly away from the odious tyranny of her cold-hearted husband. She but awaited Bourne's avowal.

That avowal was made one night at a ball. Bourne, who was a great coward, approached the subject in the most guarded manner; but her encouragement soon dispelled his fears. He returned home that night in an intoxication of vanity he had never known before. She loved him! She was his! The beautiful and admired Lady Hawbucke, his!

He could not sleep that night. Nor could she: but for a different reason. The crime she was about to commit—and fears of her husband's vengeance—tortured her all night. Often did she resolve to write to Bourne entreating him to think no more of her; or thought of quitting London, and giving him no clue. But the uselessness of these steps soon occurred to her; the terrible figure of her husband was ever before her, and the prospect of escaping from him was too tempting.

A prey to contending emotions, she lay shivering in her bed, uncertain how to act, yet feeling that some dread fatality urged her to ruin.

Bourne got up next morning in a state of smiling complacency. He sat down to breakfast, smiling; he broke the eggs, smiling ; he buttered slips of toast, smiling; he opened the newspaper, smiling; and failing in an attempt to read it, threw it on the sofa and poked the fire—still smiling.

Breakfast finished, he drew his chair in front of the fire, and placing his slippered feet upon the fender, commenced a mechanical poking of the fire—serenely smiling all the time. Now was the poker suspended in the air as if the blow was intercepted by a thought. Now was it thrust with vigour into the centre of some glittering lumps of coal. Now it rested in the fire till it became red hot. Now it rested on the hob to cool, and Bourne regarded it with an indefinite smile.

He was chuckling over the success of his acting, and framing plans of future delight. He was picturing to himself her tenderness and jealousy—who can wonder that he smiled?

But this self-gratulation was not of long duration, for in the midst of his smiles, he was startled by the appearance of his victim. Florence, pale with fatigue, terror, and the emotions of last night, stood before him.

" Good God !" he exclaimed, letting the poker drop, but never rising from his seat.

She rushed into his embrace.

" You are surprised, Henry?" she said, throwing her arms round him. " Did you fancy, then, that I could keep you in suspense? Did you think me coquette enough to enjoy your torture?"

He wished from his heart she *had* been that coquette; but he remained silent.

" Why, Henry," she resumed, " you do not speak to me; you do not even kiss me! One would say that you were not glad to see me !"

" To confess the truth," he replied, " I would rather have seen you at your own house. You have been very imprudent. You may be seen—recognised."

" Well !" exclaimed the astonished woman.

" We should both be lost. You must be mad to brave the danger.

Florence looked at him steadily; his eye shifted from her scrutiny, and her face contracted with agony.

" Do you not love me ?" she said, coldly.

" I do—I do," replied he, rising; " believe me, dearest Florence, it is my love that dictates this prudence.   I tremble for you every instant you are here; suppose any one should call?"

Without answering, she rang the bell.

" Mr. Bourne is at home to *no one*," she said, to the servant who entered.

" Now, then, your fears are set at rest."

" You will drive me mad !" he exclaimed, pacing the room with restless agitation.   " How can you be so imprudent !"

The coward heart of the man was crushed by this event ! He had calculated on a quiet intrigue; but the recklessness of this first imprudence awakened bitter fears for the future.   If the present visit should pass unnoticed, yet he could not hope that the succeeding visits would be equally fortunate; and then the husband, publicly outraged, would avenge his dishonour !   This idea distracted him; it poisoned all his feelings; it ruined all his hopes. He bitterly cursed himself for having chosen so violent a woman; and vowed to leave London the next day, and to escape the consequences of an intrigue with her.

She watched him for some time in silence; at length she said:

" Henry, did you not bid me come?"

" I ?" exclaimed Bourne, amazed.

" Yes, you.   Did you not tell me that you loved me ? Did you not curse the fate that separated us?   Did you not say how sweet it would have been to pass your days for ever at my side? Did you not swear, that should I be a widow, your hand was ready to confirm your oaths?"

These were so many thrusts of a knife into his breast. This rapid turning upon him of oaths, sworn in the heat of successful acting, was overwhelming.

" Did you not say this?" she repeated, vehemently.

" I did!—I did! I say so still."

" Then be happy—*I am a widow!*"

" Great God!" said he, thunderstruck. " Is he—is *he dead?*" he faltered, overcome with the terrible idea which had entered his head that she had murdered him.

" No, Henry, not dead. But I am a widow ; I am no longer a wife; I have left him; I have dishonoured him; I have broken my vows—I have ceased to be his wife, to become your mistress!"

He sank upon the sofa, prostrated with terror. Then suddenly springing up, he exclaimed:

" It is not too late; your absence will not have been remarked; you have been shopping—visiting—any thing. Fly, fly—go home. I will see you this evening. Quick! quick!—home !"

" Home? I have none, but beneath your roof. I have left my husband for ever. By this time he knows it."

Bourne's face became livid with horror, as she pronounced these words, and it was with difficulty he could articulate.

" *He*—knows —it !"

" Why are you so agitated?" she asked, wonderingly. " Did you not expect me?"

A savage smile played upon his lips, as he murmured, " Expect you ?"

"Yes, expect me! You swore you loved me. Did you suppose that I could listen to your vows, and remain with my husband? Did you suppose—"

"Oh! how could I suppose you mad!" he interrupted —"how could I suppose that you would fly in the face of the world, and ruin yourself and me, and dishonour your husband, by a mad revolt? How could I suppose you would have acted differently from other women, and drag down unnecessary ruin on us both?"

"Would you then have waited till *he* discovered our love? You know *him*—you know what the consequences would have been. He who killed an innocent man on mere suspicion!"

Bourne shuddered.

"I have written to him," continued Florence, "to say that I have left his roof for ever, and that in America I hope to find a home."

"He will not believe it—he will discover all. He will not rest. Oh God! what a fool! what a fool!"

He beat his hand against his forehead as he said this.

She burst into tears. He paced up and down the room, fear and remorse beating at his heart.

And all this while the husband was pacing up and down the street, undergoing a struggle almost as fierce, though of a different kind!

He was returning home just as Florence left. Surprised at seeing her go out at so unusual an hour, and without the carriage, without a footman, his jealousy was at once alarmed. He followed her at a short distance, and saw her enter Bourne's house. He was now struggling with contending passions.

Florence but too clearly saw that she had been deceived:

that Bourne was a despicable coward, who trembled for himself, and therefore would not protect her. But unwilling to relinquish her last illusion, she said, timidly,

" Dearest Henry, am I to blame? If you loved me, did you not wish me to come and be your companion?"

" No!" he retorted, brutally.

A low shriek was her only answer.

" No! not at *such* a cost; you must have known it."

Having vented his rage in this brutal speech, he resumed his restless walk, absorbed in plans for escaping from the consequences of the act for whose immeasurable folly he now cursed himself. Nothing is so cruel as cowardice, and Bourne was an utter coward.

Florence stood motionless, as if endeavouring to collect her ideas, which had been scattered by this blow. There are moments of mental paralysis in which the brain has only a dim consciousness of all around—a heavy stupor oppresses the faculties, and blunts all mental pain. In such a state stood Florence. Her eyes were couched, and she had read the heart of her seducer. She knew herself to have been his dupe. He had only acted love!

A street-organ at that moment began playing the duet from " *L'Elisire d'Amore*," which Florence had been accustomed to sing with Ranthorpe. In an instant, the whole drama of her coquetry, and his love, again passed before her mind.

" This is my second punishment for that wickedness," she said, in a mournful under tone, speaking to herself. " I did not think my crime had been great. But it must have been. The measure I meted out to him, is now meted out to me."

Slowly and mechanically she turned to the door. Bourne looked up at her. One withering sneer was all she deigned to avenge herself with ; and in another instant he was alone. A deep sigh seemed to remove an intolerable load from his breast. He instantly commenced preparations for quitting England.

She descended the stairs slowly, opened the street-door, and found herself face to face with her husband.

CHAPTER XII.

DENOUEMENT.

And greadie wormes had gnawen this payned heart
Without its feeling pain.

FERREX AND PORREX.

WHATEVER astonishment Florence might have felt at this unexpected apparition of her husband, was merged in terror as she accepted his quietly proffered arm, and walked with him down the street. She had such an opinion of his remorseless vengeance, that all present suffering was for a moment arrested; she could only watch his countenance, and seek to divine what was going on in his heart. He was deadly pale, and his lips were compressed together by an effort. But his face was otherwise impassive, and gave no indications of what was passing within.

Some fearful retaliation was apparently concealed beneath that stillness, and her flesh crept as she watched his pale, calm face.

They reached home. Sir Frederick gave the servants some trifling orders in his usual tone; and on being left alone with Florence in the drawing-room, he sat himself at the further end of the room, and said:

"Lady Hawbucke, if the irreparable wrong that you have done me, has not quite corrupted you—if there is any particle of truth and honour left in you, answer me truly: How long have you and *he* understood each other?"

" We have never understood each other."

He frowned, and almost shook with rage. Collecting his ideas, he rose and said:

" I might have expected this."

" You misapprehend. When I said we had never understood each other, I spoke truly—*he* never understood me, and I—oh God, what a fearful mistake did I make! But I know what you mean—and I will answer. You ask me how long he has known that I loved him. Since last night.—Would that I had died before that night!"

He started, and then looking incredulously at her, repeated:

" Since last night!"

" Yes; did you not get my letter ? But I forgot— there was nothing of that in it."

" Your letter? Where? when?"

" Go into your dressing-room. Read, read."

He went; found the letter, read it, and returned.

" And will you swear?" he said, " that last night was the first time you had spoken of love to him?"

" I swear it."

" Your intention was then to quit me at once ?"

" It was."

" Thank you for *that*." He paused awhile, and then said, " But why do you quit *him* ?"

" Because he is a despicable coward—a selfish hypocrite; because I found that I had been his dupe; because his fear of you betrayed him !"

" Yet you loved him!" he bitterly murmured.

She wept, but made no reply. A long pause followed. The scene which had just taken place had altogether altered the current of Sir Frederick's thoughts. If Bourne was such a coward, that he would rather brutally repulse a lovely woman who threw herself into his arms, than run the risk of braving her husband's vengeance, it was quite clear that he would never insinuate any thing in the remotest way connected with the affair. His silence was certain. As their understanding had been so recent, no one else could as yet have been informed of it. On this score also, Sir Frederick felt relieved.

Florence was eagerly, though furtively, watching him, and augured well from the comparative brightness his face assumed. Her terrors began to diminish. They were renewed, however, as he began to speak again; the glacial tone of his voice was more terrible than any vehemence.

" You have done me a wrong; you can in some degree repair it. Are you willing ?"

" My life is yours—take it."

" I have no need of it. I only ask you to save your character, and mine. As society is at present constituted, your acts may dishonour me; though mine cannot affect you. I may be dissolute, degraded; and your name is uncontaminated by my acts. But the slightest of your acts touches me nearly; and when you forget your own self-respect, you drag my honour with you into the mire. Pray allow me to proceed. I will hear you afterwards. *We can no longer live together.* I relinquish the combat. I cannot defend my own name. I withdraw. But, mark me, the wish for separation must spring from you—the cause from me. You must continue to act the pure wife— I must be the unfaithful husband. You must be above suspicion."

" What do you mean ?"

" If we part now, or if we part from any cause alledged by me, your character will be stained—and mine with it. If I give the cause, both our characters will be untarnished. In one month hence, you shall discover in my desk letters written to me from some abandoned woman. These you will take to your mother, heart-broken and indignant. You are actress enough for that. You will insist on a separation. You will be inflexible. The separation will take place, and all the world will say, ' Poor thing, she has been dreadfully used!' "

" And what will they say of you?"

" Nothing—except perhaps to wonder at my taste. But let them say what they please, I preserve my name spotless. Are you prepared to play this little farce ?"

" If you insist."

" I insist."

" Then I have no will."

" That shall be my vengeance."

He left the room. She remained almost bewildered at what had passed. For a long while she was incredulous. Could he be devising some fearful vengeance under this; or was it simply, as he said, a plan for the preservation of his name from suspicion?

Her terrors once banished, her grief returned. But it was a silent grief—a stupor, not a passion.

———

A few months after the events just recorded, Sir Henry Varden came home one day, and said to his wife:

" Really, my dear, Catholicism is making alarming progress in England. Who do you think has recently become a convert ?"

" Who ? Don't tantalise me."

" Lady Hawbucke. I have it from her mother, who is inconsolable, and highly indignant with her daughter. It seems but the other day she was separated, and now she turns Catholic !"

" As a refuge, I suppose, from her sorrows."

" Egad, if all the women whose husbands are incon-stant threw themselves into the arms of the Church of Rome, England will soon be under the thumb of the Pope."

" Don't talk so, my dear Sir Henry. I quite wonder at you. Poor Lady Hawbucke ! Well, who would have thought it ?"

CHAPTER XIII.

THE LOVERS.

Wenn alle Menschen ein paar Liebende wären, so fiele der Unterschied zwischen Mysticismus, und Nicht-Mysticismus weg.

NOVALIS.

What is love? Ask him who lives, what is life? ask him who adores, what is God?

SHELLEY.

AND now the little circle of our friends is happy again: greatly to my relief, as doubtless to that also of the reader. We have had nothing but tears for some time: every thing seemed to go wrong, and every body to be miserable.

Now, although misery is a good condiment, it is a bad food. It may leaven our daily life; it may heighten it with glimpses of something above and around it, of which the senses give no intimation; it may help to sharpen the gusto of pleasure; it may add a tenderness to content: but it will not suffice for the staple of life, nor of fiction, which pretends to image life. The reader gets tired of tears: his sympathies become exhausted. The writer also gets tired: his vocabulary becomes exhausted. Thus it is fortunate for all sakes, that our friends happen to be all smiles and hopes just now.

Isola and Percy were supremely happy—happy as lovers
in their height of bliss.

Harry was happy.   At first, indeed, a shadow of melancholy darkened his soul, but the glory of a virtuous action supported him.   It delighted while it pained him to
see Isola happy; he felt that he had done well, but he
was human, and could not altogether repress a feeling of
jealousy.   I am not sure that he would ever have been
perfectly reconciled to his act, had he not found consolation in his love for Fanny.

Yes, reader—for Fanny!   There is deep meaning in
the proverb, " Many a heart caught in the rebound."
No want is more imperious than the want to love.   And
Harry had, for the last two months, been constantly thrown
with Fanny, to be consoled by her, to be sympathised
with by her, to talk *of* love to her, and finally to talk love
to her.   *Parler l'amour c'est faire l'amour:* another
true proverb !

If any reader should accuse Harry of inconstancy, levity,
or want of true affection, he will be grievously mistaken.
It was owing to the very overflowing excess of his affection that he loved another.   His heart could not be void.
He saw the hazel eyes of Fanny full of love for him, and
he was subdued by them.   Isola was lost to him; Fanny
was there, ready to console him.   Did he not act wisely
in allowing himself to be consoled?   He did.   Or rather
he could not help it.   He glided imperceptibly into
love !

And Fanny !   She had seen much of him, and
learned to prize him dearly, before the flattering idea of
one day gaining his love ever crossed her mind.   She
knew him as the noble, generous, affianced lover of her
friend; and this knowledge had removed all the constraint

in her manner; she could talk to him without fear—but not without danger! Poor Fanny! hers was a heart made to love; but her natural shyness had kept her a stranger to the feeling, until she indulged it for Ranthorpe, and after that illusion had been dispelled, she had never dared to raise her eyes to another. But Harry she had known in all the intimacy of exquisite unreserve. A brother could not have been more dear to her. And it was not until his disinterested renunciation of Isola had broken the relation which formerly subsisted between them, that she became at all aware of the condition of her heart: she was then too far gone to retract, even had she desired it.

These too creatures loved each other; but there was something strange and feverish in their affection. They had both occasional twinges of jealousy. Harry could not always see without a pang the silent adoration with which Isola gazed upon Percy. Fanny could not fail to remark it.

In spite of this little occasional twinge our four lovers spent a delicious time of it. Percy and Isola saw clearly enough the state of their friends' hearts, and only awaited the avowal. That came at last. They used always to assemble at Isola's in the evening, and the twilight was prolonged to the utmost; and when candles were at last inevitable, they consoled themselves with music for the loss of those mysterious feelings which seem only fitted for the vague and dreamy twilight. And what hours were those of twilight!

In one of them, Percy and Isola were seated in the window recess, hand clasped in hand, speechless from unutterable emotion, gazing into each other's eyes, his cheek gently brushing her silken hair, whose perfume thrilled his soul with vague voluptuous ecstasy. Fanny gently ran her fingers over the chords of the piano, producing wild and plaintive sounds like those ravished from an Æolian harp; and Harry sat close to her, his elbow leaning on the piano, his head resting on his hand, gazing at her in silent adoration. The plaintive chords moved him strangely. He begged her to sing; and in a soft, small, but touching voice, she sang Paisiello's *Il mio ben*. He had heard Isola sing this; and her magnificent voice, every intonation of which made the hearer vibrate beneath its mysterious power, would have made the singing of a Malibran or a Grisi ineffective in comparison; but Fanny's small, veiled, yet pathetic voice had a charm of its own, which if not greatly musical was intensely affecting.

The tears came into his eyes. He could not thank her. He continued to gaze at her, and she turned her hazel eyes upon him: their light shone through the darkness, and he read their meaning. Then, for the first time, did he read their meaning aright—then did he feel she loved him! No word of love had crossed their lips; and yet in this sudden inspiration all their passion was revealed. He gently placed his hand in hers: a burning pressure was the reply. He bent forward, and their lips met in one long fervid kiss. In that moment they were affianced!

The happiness of Percy and Isola now was complete. The engagement of Harry and Fanny, which they had quickly foreseen, removed the only obstacle to their perfect happiness. New feelings had sprung up in Percy's breast during the last month, which made him regard marriage with peculiar solemnity. In fact, he had not *loved*, properly speaking, till now. His senses had been inflamed, his imagination dazzled, and the yearning, eager, all-curious heart of the boy had been occupied; but his love had been the love of a boy.

The love of a boy differs from that of a man in this— it is the wanton enjoyment of a present imperious feeling, from which all serious consideration of the future is excluded. It is mere blind activity of newly-awakened emotions. Hence the rashness of early loves. The boy wants to love; almost any woman will suffice. Hence he is violent, capricious, inconstant, because he only seeks an excitement; he tries his young wings. The tender feeling of *protection*, which enters so largely into the love of a man,—the serious thoughts of the duties he owes to the girl who gives up her life to him, and to the children she may bear him,—these, and the thousand minute but powerful influences which affect the man, are unknown to the boy.

Percy Ranthorpe felt that he was entering upon the most important epoch of his life. Already had many things become clearer to him. He could say, with Shelley,

> "In no communion with this purest being
> Kindled intenser zeal, and made me wise
> In knowledge which, in hers my own mind seeing,
> Left in the human world few mysteries."

CHAPTER XIV.

THE COURSE OF TRUE LOVE.

Let them anatomise Regan, see what breeds about her heart. Is
there any cause in nature makes these hard hearts?

SHAKSPEARE.

THE insolence of lovers! They always imagine that
when they have avowed their love to each other, the
whole business is completed. Parents are nonentities,
settlements are figments. Whoever thinks of one or the
other?

But, alas! Fanny and her lover were somewhat rudely
awakened to the existence of parental authority by the
plain, unqualified refusal to the marriage, with which her
mother answered Harry's application. It was more than
a refusal—it was an insult. Indeed, when Lady Wilmington heard of her daughter's engagement with an
obscure surgeon, the reader may imagine her indignation,
and the vehemence with which she protested the marriage
should never take place. Unfortunately, Fanny, though
almost broken-hearted at her mother's refusal, could not
be persuaded to dispense with her consent. She dared
not brave her mother's anger; not from any love she felt
towards her, but from an exaggerated sense of duty and

gratitude. Her mother had always treated her with marked indifference ; but she was, nevertheless, her mother.

The reader is already somewhat acquainted with Lady Wilmington's character; one or two touches more are necessary to complete the picture.

Lady Wilmington was considered irreproachable by her friends, and invulnerable by her enemies. If the term " respectable," could consistently be applied to any one of the class to which she belonged, one would say that she was eminently " respectable." She had preserved her virtue (!) from the breath of slander—a breath which Shakspeare says a woman cannot escape, though " chaste as ice, as pure as snow,"—but I never said Lady Wilmington was chaste as ice. She had never opened her doors to any woman whose frailties had been openly canvassed. She went to church—once a month. She gave her name to subscriptions to several charitable institutions: her *name*, indeed, but rarely her money. Generosity, charity, and other Christian sentiments, were for ever on her lips: a fact which, perhaps, accounted for their absence elsewhere.

A character like hers, reduced to its strict formula— without heart as without intellect—appears, at first sight, the mere exaggeration of a novelist, and the reader refuses to believe that such a woman could anywhere be tolerated. But, good and gentle reader ! I have not been thus minute in painting a mere exaggeration. It is a portrait —taken at many sittings, and under many different lights —a portrait, unfortunately, that might be hung up in many a drawing-room, and pronounced " most like."

And yet is it not strange that the reader should doubt its truth, because, although the features themselves are

z 2

neither untrue nor exaggerated, yet inasmuch as the *expression* is absent, so the face seems revolting. I have given the moral characteristics of Lady Wilmington: but the *manner*, which was as drapery to her worthlessness— manner by which most people are judged—this I could not give.

Not that her manner was more winning than that of ordinary people; but such as it was, it served to cover a hideous skeleton. Perfect in all those movements which nothing but long habit can successfully assume, and which demarcates the aristocracy from the rest of society, her very affectations seemed to be natural to her. Soft, languishing, low-voiced, and indifferent, she was almost made up of negations, and thus never offended. There was an absence of every thing positive in her manner, which presented any single point either for approval or dislike; except when she startled by a sarcasm, and then, indeed, she seemed to compensate for previous langour by the sparkling malice of her eyes. The most cold and cruel things were uttered with a gusto which made you start, especially in so languid a person: it was, indeed, revolting to see this soft-mannered woman suddenly aroused to eager cruelty (which alone seemed capable of arousing her)—it was like looking on the sleek, velvety paws of a tiger, out of which softness suddenly spring hideous talons!

Fanny, with her opposite sentiments, soon detected her mother's adoration of the world, and the world's ways, and thought she sacrificed too much to it ; but she had not the slightest suspicion of her insincerity; and had heard her so often attribute to herself the virtues of generosity, charity, self-sacrifice, and religion, that she received the existence of these as matters of course.

Affection there was none between them: all her advances to her mother had been repelled; all her sentiments opposed; and all her sympathies ridiculed. But Fanny could not forget the relationship; and her mother hoped, she said,

" That no daughter of *mine* can ever forget the *immense debt* of gratitude she owes to me—never forget the *sacrifices* I have made for my children—sacrifices which *no* other mother would have made."

Fanny did not clearly comprehend in what this debt consisted, but as her mother was always referring to it, she could not doubt that it had been contracted. The " sacrifices" having never been specified, were equally received upon trust ; and the deed, or deeds, which no other mother would have done, were left to her force of imagination. In sober seriousness Fanny believed herself bound, more than any other child had ever been, to sacrifice herself for the parent who had done so much for her. So that in spite of the want of filial love, there was a strong sense of filial duty in poor Fanny's breast; and when her mother wept with her at the mention of Harry—when she declaimed in her usual style on the sacrifices she had made, and which were thus to be requited; when she painted the horror she should suffer from such a disgraceful alliance; when she told her what the world would say, already too busy as it was with her unfortunate sister, Florence ; how it would blame the parent who consented, more than the child who lost herself ; and how this " would infallibly shorten her days," —can we wonder that Fanny's heart sunk within her, and that she determined not to act in outrage to the feelings of one " who had done *so much* for her?"

She trusted that time would soften her mother's objections ; trusted that when her mother saw how real and unshakeable was the love she bore him, consent would not be long withheld. She little knew her mother!

Percy and Isola, as may be expected, were deeply distressed at Harry's situation. On finding Lady Wilmington so opposed to the match, Percy called on her. He had not been within her doors since that day on which Florence rejected him ; and it was with violent agitation that he ascended the staircase. He mastered his feelings sufficiently to meet Lady Wilmington with becoming suavity. She was delighted to see him, for he was celebrated, and she had been often foiled in her attempts to allure him to her house. She upbraided him with his fickleness towards " old friends," and told him that she must positively keep him to dinner. He accepted; made himself immensely agreeable, and having stayed till all the guests had departed, he opened to her the real purpose of his visit. She was indignant at the idea of the match. He was eloquent—earnest—but he had to do with Lady Wilmington. He left the house, bitterly convinced that her consent would never be given.

On hearing this, Wynton, who had been powerfully affected by the noble generosity displayed by Harry, told Percy that he thought of going himself to Lady Wilmington, and interceding in his friend's behalf.

" I have a strange suspicion that she will be in some way influenced by me."

" I fear not, Wynton. But you can try."

" It will be extremely painful for me to see her—I have not seen her since the day on which she became Lady Wilmington! Yet, for Harry, I would do a great deal.

Indeed, I should be ashamed to consider my own feelings in a case where he is concerned—he, who so little considers his own!"

On the following day, Lady Wilmington was sitting in her drawing-room, really vexed. She was not apt to be angry; but she had that morning suffered a shock in her tenderest point. Fanny had refused—positively refused— a brilliant match. The girl's head was completely turned by silly romance. She had thrown away her best chance of happiness; and thrown it away out of some nonsensical feelings for an adventurer. Lady Wilmington almost stormed. What could the girl expect ? What could she come to ? Was that the way to gain a mother's consent ? Was that the way to gain a mother's pardon?

Lady Wilmington was astonished.

Still greater was her astonishment and agitation as the servant handed her a card on which she read Wynton's name. Scarcely conscious of what she was saying, she bade that he should be admitted; and before she had recovered her self-possession, her former lover stood before her.

Wynton was deadly pale. His countenance betokened the mastery of a dreadful struggle passing within. His bearing was haughty and cold: the perfect reverse of his usual manner. He had struggled; he had conquered; and he was there;—there, in the presence of her whom he had not seen for twenty years! The sight would at all times have been painful to him; but to see her so changed—to see the giddy, lovely, heartless, but fascinating girl, grown into the sedate, heartless, and repulsive woman, was what he had not prepared himself for.

He, too, was changed, and she noticed it. Twenty years of struggle and improvidence had robbed him of his personal advantages; but it had not robbed him of his intellectual superiority; and in the careworn, intelligent, haughty man who now stood before her, she saw little change for the worse.

She rose and held out her hand. He remained motionless, at if disdaining to notice her advances. She walked towards him, and, with sudden warmth, said:

"Let us be friends."

He fixed his eyes steadily upon hers; they did not waver beneath his glance. He answered coldly, while a slight sneer quivered his lip:

"Your ladyship forgets I was your brother's tutor."

She was piqued, and said reproachfully:

"I only remember that I once loved you."

"Loved?"

"Yes, loved. Ah! I know how shockingly I behaved to you. But, indeed, it was not my fault. I had not courage to go through with my part. When I saw all my friends assembled—when I heard myself called upon to pronounce the fatal 'Yes,'—I was frightened, and pronounced it. Had you been there—had I but caught a glimpse of your eye, I should have braved them all. But I was alone, and I was hurried into a marriage I abhorred."

She spoke with warmth; a bitter sneer was all the answer he could give. She perceived it, and sinking into a chair, covered her face with her hands, and wept. She was acting. Yet, as so often happens with persons of keen nervous sensibility, she felt something of that passion which she was portraying. Above all, she wished to impress him with belief in her sincerity. The more incredulous he appeared, the more she redoubled her efforts. At that moment she would have given any thing to see a tear in his eye, to hear the words of pardon from his lips.

She had nearly succeeded, when he broke to her the object of his visit. " You can remove my doubts at once," he said. " Give your consent to the marriage of your daughter with the man she loves, and you will best convince me that you really prize affection above wealth."

" Consent to Fanny's marriage?"

" Ah! I see—you shrink from it."

" No, no, no. Believe me, no. If she really loves him. There.—I will consent. Now, are you convinced?" He took her hand, and kissed it.

" You have made me happy," said he.

" Then you forgive me?"

" I do." Wynton did forgive her at the moment. He had not, however, long left the house before his old opinion of her returned, and he looked upon that scene as a well-acted piece of sentiment. But the motive he could not fathom.

Let me endeavour to explain it. Lady Wilmington was, as I said, a creature of sensitive nerves, but small brain. She was consequently a creature of impulses. The impulse to convince Wynton of her not being the worthless creature he must necessarily think her, was naturally a strong one. To convince him, she was reckless as to the means. Besides, the fact of Fanny's refusal of a brilliant match, seemed to indicate an obstinacy her mother had little hope of conquering. And if Fanny would not make a good match, there was less harm in her making a bad one. This had some influence with her mother.

And thus the cold, heartless woman, who would never have consented to " a degrading alliance," although her daughter's happiness depended on it, consented to it for the sake of a little triumph in acting.

This would be incredible, did we not know that to such

an egotist, a daughter's happiness was nothing; but a successful piece of acting was an intense gratification. It is frightful to think that there are such people, and that those people should be parents; but it is unfortunately too true. I, who paint this portrait, seriously and soberly declare that I *subdue*, rather than exaggerate, the colours. Had I drawn in all her hideousness the original who sat for this picture, the reader would have turned away in incredulous disgust. Let him profit, if he can, from the feeble sketch.

CHAPTER XV.

PEAL THE MARRIAGE BELLS.

Come home, home to my heart, thou banish'd peace ;
Hymen shall now
Set all his torches burning to give light
Throughout the land.

FORD : *Lover's Melancholy.*

AND now our hero's troubles are o'er. He is happy ;
his bride stands at the altar beside him. Behind him are
Harry and Fanny, waiting also to be united by the same
priest.

Privately, in Kensington Church, were these four married ; and seldom has any church been graced with four
nobler beings. Isola was magnificent. The flush of
modesty, the bride's delicious colour, had given her cheek
that tinge which at other times it wanted, and had given
to her calm, deep eyes, a passion and a brilliancy which
stirred the depths of the spectator's soul. She was incomparably beautiful at that moment. Ranthorpe gazed
upon her with passionate pride ; and felt his heart too
full, as he thought how, after so many struggles, he had
found at length the path of peace ; how, after many wanderings on the rugged highway, he had reached the
Happy Valley.

Only second to them in charms were Harry and Fanny. She looked as beautiful on that occasion to strangers, as she was always to those who loved her. Shy, and tremblingly happy, she formed a pleasant contrast to her friend; and as she looked up into the noble countenance of her lover, and met his fond, protecting gaze, she made as sweet a picture of the timid gentlewoman as painter or poet could desire. But although there was little pomp displayed at the wedding, it had a splendour of its own in the warmth of the affections therein engaged. All our hero's old friends were present. Joyce looked more sunny than ever, and Wynton gave Isola away. Lady Theresa and Lady Wilmington were both stiffly present; and an uncle of Fanny's, a bright, good-humoured creature, gave her away.

Were mine a female's pen, I would delight you with a minute and vivacious account of the whole ceremony, dresses and all. I would tell you how every one behaved, from the bride down to the pew-opener. I would introduce you to the breakfast, and its exhilarating festivity. In a word, I would place before you, imaginative reader, all that I must now leave to your imagination. But my pen has no such power.

EPILOGUE.

> Then gently scan your brother man ;
> Still gentler sister woman.
> Though they may gang a kennin' wrang:
> To step aside is human.
> One point must still be greatly dark —
> The moving *why* they do it;
> And just as lamely can ye mark
> How far, perhaps, they rue it.
>
> BURNS.

> He was a man who preached from the text of his own errors; and whose wisdom, beautiful as a flower that might have risen from seed sown from above, was, in fact, a scion from the root of personal suffering.
>
> WORDSWORTH (of Burns).

RANTHORPE is now exquisitely happy. Two children are playing round his knees, and twining their embraces round his heart. Isola grows more lovely every time I see her, and not even maternity, and increased experience of the world, seem to brush off the bloom of that simplicity and ingenuousness which makes her a godlike child. Harry is also a happy husband and father ; and Fanny the happiest of wives, and most anxious of mothers.

Ranthorpe's life is now one of activity and happiness: the true ideal of an author's life. He has bitterly expiated his early error; and in that expiation recovered the purity and independence of mind, the confidence in his mission, and reliance on his means of fulfilling it, without which a man may indeed become rich and popular, but no man can become a great author. How much of his present serenity of mind he owes to Isola, let those answer who have known the gentle influence of a woman! Certain it is, that if those who remember his early efforts compare them with his later works, they may marvel at the delicacy and gentleness, wedded to strength and solidity, which present such a contrast to the turbulence, inequality, and exaggeration of his " Dreams of Youth," and " Quintus Curtius."

He has won his spurs. His genius has begun to take its magnificent flight far above the reach of other wings. He is in his twenty-fifth year, and his genius is free to operate untrammelled upon the materials afforded him by experience. He has felt, and he has thought: he has dreamed, and he has suffered. He is now to " preach from the text of his own errors"—to make his experience incarnate in song.

After many a giddy faintness, and many a sick despondency, he has reached a table land, from whence he can look down calmly on the path before him. He has walked up through mists, but has reached a certain height. The storms are below him. The poor attorney's clerk has become an honoured author. He is no longer vulgarly lionised; he is respected and courted. His footing in society is no longer dependent upon the caprice of a drawing-room. It is the security of that intellectual power which forces the world to bend the knee. The poor, dreamy boy, self-taught, self-aided, has risen into power. He wields a pen. And the pen, in our age, weighs heavier in the social scale than the sword of a Norman Baron!

THE END.

C. WHITING, BEAUFORT HOUSE, STRAND.

NOTES

Ranthorpe, despite a relatively cordial press, seems
to have lacked popular appeal, for it was remaindered
with the Chapman and Hall title page intact but in yellow linen boards bearing the imprint of Ward and
Lock, 158 Fleet Street, together with advertisements
for "Popular Standard Books at Greatly Reduced
Prices." A Tauchnitz edition in 307 pages, also dated
1847 but with Lewes named as author, appeared as
volume CXXXIII of Tauchnitz's Collection of British
Authors. The Newberry Library possesses a copy of
an edition in 326 pages published by the New York
firm of Gottesberger in 1881, and The Library of Congress lists *Ranthorpe* in 172 pages issued in New York
by G. Munro in 1885 as number 442 in the company's
"Seaside Library, Pocket Edition."

Lewes employs quotation with such fantastic profu-
sion that identifying and translating such items in the
notes would add measurably to the cost of this book
without appreciably enhancing its usefulness. As Charlotte Brontë was to observe regarding Lewes's second
and only other completed novel, *Rose, Blanche, and
Violet* (1848), the author's display of his acquirements
in foreign tongues "awes and astonishes the plain reader" but represents superfluous "embroidery" rather

353

than anything integral to his work (*The Brontës: Life and Letters*, ed. Clement Shorter [1908; New York, 1969], I, 411). George Eliot was to select (and often to create) her mottoes with obvious care for their function, but Lewes's seldom have more than a very general appropriateness to the pages they introduce. He uses them often by two's and not infrequently by three's, and for Chapter VIII of Book IV he attains a record six. Lewes was proud of his fluency in languages, but he seems to have exercised caution (possibly at the urging of the eminent friends who, he tells us in his preface, guided him in revision) in seeing that Florence Wilmington keeps to simple usages in her penchant for decorating her repartee with French phrases.

5. *His hunger was for knowledge*: George Eliot wrote Sara Hennell in 1869: "Mr. Lewes has a singular faculty for remembering what is advertised, and what forms the common or exceptional material of Book-catalogues. It comes of his diligent, hungry search in his days of youthful penury, when he dined on a sausage in order to buy a longed-for book" (*The George Eliot Letters*, ed. Gordon S. Haight [New Haven, 1954-55], V, 69).

6. a *mixture . . . Mohock*: Member of a gang of young aristocrat ruffians who terrorized citizens of London in the early eighteenth century.

8. to *gratify Mr. Martin's feelings*: Richard Martin (1754-1834), known as "Humanity Martin," was the chief sponsor of legislation for protecting the rights of animals. He was one of the founders of the Royal Society for the Prevention of Cruelty to Animals (1824).

25. *Ernest Maltravers*: See section II of the Introduction for a discussion of the considerable parallels of plot between *Ranthorpe* and this novel by Lewes's

friend Bulwer-Lytton, published in 1837, and its sequel of the year following. The particular quotation
Lewes chooses here, however, is of special interest. It
is Bulwer-Lytton's phrasing of an idea that, as Alice R.
Kaminsky observes (*George Henry Lewes as Literary
Critic* [Syracuse, N. Y., 1968], p. 89), figures importantly in the theories of literature of both Lewes and
George Eliot. Lewes in his "The Lady Novelists" for
the *Westminster Review* in 1852 (LXXX, 130) was to
build his argument for reality as the only proper basis
for good literature upon the assumption Bulwer-Lytton expresses in the motto: "All poetry, all fiction, all
comedy, all *belles lettres*," Lewes declares, "even to the
playful caprices of fancy, are but the expression of experiences and emotions; and these expressions are the
avenues through which we reach the sacred adytum
of Humanity, and learn better to understand our fellows and ourselves. In proportion as these expressions
are the forms of universal truths, of facts common to
all nations or appreciable by all intellects, the literature which sets them forth is permanently good and
true." Four years later George Eliot in "The Natural
History of German Life," one of her finest essays for
the *Westminster Review* (LXVI, 51-79), was to make
the widening of our sympathies the basic function of
all the arts: "Art . . . is a mode of amplifying experience and extending our contact with our fellow men
beyond the bounds of our personal lot. . . . The greatest benefit we owe to the artist, whether painter, poet,
or novelist, is the extension of our sympathies."

33. *a kinder man, nor a crueller critic*: Pungent
may well owe the special paradoxes of his nature to
William Smith Williams (1800-1875), formerly fine arts
critic for the *Athenaeum* but by 1847 a publisher's ad-
viser for Smith, Elder and Company. Eliza Lynn Lin-

ton (not, it is true, the most reliable of witnesses) in *My Literary Life* (London, 1899, p. 16) describes him as she knew him in 1845 when, like Lewes, he frequently took part in the social gatherings at the Phalanstery (see Introduction, section I): "I remember Smith Williams, the reader for Smith & Elder, a man who fulfilled the Spanish proverb about him who speaks softly and writes harshly. In voice, manner, and conversation he was the gentlest creature imaginable; but his letters were harsh and acrid, and no one could think more cruelly than he—no one wound more deeply when it came to the pen and ink contradiction of his mild words and half-hinted promises."

George Eliot, as Richard Ellmann observes ("Dorothea's Husbands: Some Biographical Speculations," *TLS*, 16 February 1973, pp. 165-168) seems to have worked habitually from live models, a practice Lewes had followed throughout much of *Ranthorpe* (see Introduction, section I, and his frank avowal in regard to his source for Fanny, Lady Wilmington, in pages 339-340 and 346). In his critical writing Lewes vehemently urged novelists to paint from life at the same time avoiding (as he had sought to do in *Ranthorpe*) a recognizable rendering of their originals. Speaking of Lady Bulwer-Lytton's scandalous roman à clef *Nélida* as a case in point, but framing an important generalization on the subject as well, Lewes states in "The Lady Novelists" (pp. 139-141): ". . . it may be pertinent to distinguish between writing out your actual experience in fiction, and using fiction as a medium for obtruding your private history on the sympathies of the public. We hold that the author is bound to use actual experience as his material, or else keep silent; but he is equally bound by all moral and social considerations not to use that experience in such forms that the public will recognise it, and become, as it were, initiated into the private affairs of his characters." George Sand and Madame d'Agoult had sinned in making their originals easily identifiable. Though they were "bound to go back for material to their own personal experience, it is quite clear that, in so doing, they were bound by the very notoriety of their histories to work up that material into shapes so unlike the outward form of these histories, that no one should detect the origin."

34. *Leda's egg*: Helen of Troy, in a variant of her history employed by Euripides for his *Helena*, is hatched from an egg laid by Leda rather than, as in other forms of the legend, by Nemesis, child of Night.

38. les coulisses *of the great theatre*: In Ranthorpe's exuberant figure of speech, the murky paraphernalia of his present pursuit of journalism seem attractive to him rather than ugly because they will, he believes, serve him as a means of making an entry from the wings of the great theater of literature on to the central stage itself.

49. *Grisi*: Giulia Grisi (1811-1869), a famous Italian operatic soprano who appeared in London frequently from 1834 to as late as 1861.

53. *the supreme poet of albums*: The most popular producer, that is to say, of light effusions for the ornate gift books that were fashionable in the earlier decades of the nineteenth century under such titles as *The Keepsake, Friendship's Offering, Love's Souvenir*, and the like.

59. *a second Petrarch, crowned in the Capitol*: Petrarch, a native of Arezzo by birth, was crowned poet laureate by the Roman Senate in 1341 mainly in recognition of his epic poem *Africa*.

64. *the opinion of medical students*: Harry Cavendish, Lewes's most extensive study in the species, is to

play a prominent part in the later chapters of *Ranthorpe*. Lewes had himself "walked the hospitals" as a medical student for some time as a youth but had given up the idea of a medical career because of his unusual sensitivity to the pain of others. He had also, he recorded in his journal in 1857, felt extreme revulsion in dissecting a dead puppy—a curious fact in the light of his later extensive biological researches. See Edgar W. Hirshberg, *George Henry Lewes* (New York, 1970), p. 20. Lewes had a brother who in 1837 was also a medical student (William Bell Scott, *Autobiographical Notes* [New York, 1892], I, 130 n.).

83.   *Arden of Feversham*: A tragedy published by George Lillo in 1736 and first played in 1759. It is based upon *The Tragedy of Mr. Arden of Feversham,* an anonymous play first printed in 1592 and sometimes attributed to Shakespeare.

86.   *I sent articles, tales, and poems to every magazine*: Lewes's character Wynton strongly reflects his own experiences, both in Wynton's struggles to secure a foothold in the world of literature and in his serving a family as tutor, falling in love the while with a daughter of the family. See Introduction, section I. See also Hirshberg, pp. 22-23, and Scott, I, 129-134: "I am a student living a quiet life," Lewes at twenty wrote Scott in a letter introducing himself, "but have a great gusto for intellectual acquaintance, with which, I am sorry to say, I am not overburdened." Lewes was at the time living with his mother and "quite in his infancy as a professional literary man." Scott writes amusingly of young Lewes's reading aloud some months later from a tragedy he had composed on the unhappy love of Tasso for Leonora d'Este.

88.   *She flattered every body and cared for none*: For the considerable parallels between Lewes's sketch

of Fanny, later Lady Wilmington, and George Eliot's consummately finished portrait of Rosamond Vincy in *Middlemarch*, see Introduction, section III.

108. *a Diocletian, a Pertinax, a Probus, or a Vitellius*: As the context suggests, they were all Roman emperors who rose from relatively humble origins.

116. *a first floor in Hans Place*: Lewes's attempt here to create the atmosphere of rented rooms anticipates his more elaborate experiments in minutely detailed realism in *Rose, Blanche, and Violet* (1848), his only other completed novel. Especially notable in his second novel is his thirty-one page description of Mrs. Tring's Boarding House (II, 121-131), which seems to bear special resemblances to the similar chapters at the outset of Balzac's *Père Goriot*. Lewes's intense interest in Balzac, reflected in *Ranthorpe* not only in his mode of describing Harry's first-floor rooms in Hans Place but in his way of treating such interiors as the unsavory coffee house the impoverished Ranthorpe patronizes (19-20) and the manager's waiting room at Covent Garden Theater (139-141), had been in Lewes's thoughts at least as early as 1842. In that year he had written a ten-page article on Balzac for the *Monthly Magazine* (VII, 463-472), and in 1844 he had given a large part of another to the same author ("Balzac and George Sand," *The Foreign Quarterly Review*, XXXIII, 141-163). A portion of Lewes's *Fraser's* critique in December 1847, devoted centrally to *Jane Eyre* (see Introduction, section II), is given to *Cousin Pons*, the earlier half of which Lewes considers to be in "Balzac's best style, with that minuteness of detail, that prodigality of observation, that Gerard Dow truth and finish, which make *Eugénie Grandet, Le Curé de Tours, Pierette*, and in general his scenes of provincial life so interesting." Though the second half of *Cou-*

sin Pons was marred by its melodramatic intrigues,
Balzac had once again displayed "the astonishing faculty of observation, and the patient power of depicting
what he observes" that have signalized his writing for
many years. "Wonderful it is," Lewes declares in this
critique of late 1847, "to see with what marvellous power such a simple subject is wrought into a story of deep,
unceasing interest."

Some five years earlier, in the *Monthly Magazine* essay of 1842, Lewes had been much less laudatory in
his estimate of the qualities that had made Balzac one
of the world's wealthiest and most imitated of authors.
The piece has special interest because it represents in
miniature the position of Lewes at the time of his writing the bulk of *Ranthorpe*—the time, as he tells us in
his preface, of composing in three volumes the novel
that in its final form he has reduced, under the guidance of his friends, to a single volume. In 1842 he is
still strongly drawn toward romantic values. Fielding
is already for Lewes a great novelist, but George Sand,
whom Dumas had accused with much point of giving
her readers *"du lord Byron au kilo,"* is also one of his
particular idols. Balzac, Lewes feels in 1842, has no
claim, despite his great popularity, to a place beside
her. Devoid of the highest gifts of the novelist, without
any "divine instinct truer than logic," Balzac must depend upon his unaided reason: he has "nothing but his
own intellect and its conclusions to guide him—and
that intellect not of the soundest." He has concentrated
on the *"outward case"* at the expense of the *"inward
spirit."* Wealth and popularity have resulted, Lewes
concludes in a final address to the author, "—but Fame,
we fear, is inexorably denied thee!"

And yet it is clear in the same essay that Lewes is
half inclined to concede that there may be more merit

in Balzac's minute realism than his own critical tenets at the time can account for: "And truly is De Balzac's success a phenomenon it were worth our while examining . . . ." If Balzac's graphic scenes are lacking in elevation and often not in the best taste, they are nevertheless exciting "from the elaboration of their intensity." Such "minuteness of observation is often full of effect," as in such an unpleasant but on the other hand remarkably clever story as Balzac's *La Vieille Fille*.

Two years later, in his *Foreign Quarterly Review* essay of 1844, Lewes still prefers George Sand to Balzac (the "one gives you her experience; the other his observation"), but he has obviously arrived at an increased admiration of Balzac's powers. Lewes is already traveling toward the attitudes conveyed in his *Fraser's* critique of December 1847, in his letters to Charlotte Brontë (see Introduction, section II), and in his extended practice of a similar kind of realistic detail as in the boarding-house scenes of *Rose, Blanche, and Violet* (1848): Balzac's "vast gallery of portraits, in which almost every species is represented," Lewes tells us now, is "wonderfully executed." We follow his "curious minuteness" with untiring interest. Despite his lack of poetic depth of the sort that renders George Sand's novels so admirable—her lyrical conveyance of her own passionate experience in the experience of her characters—Balzac's "merits are great enough and rare enough to outweigh his faults." Balzac's unusual devotion to detail of scene and sifting of motive, his microscopic examination of "all the intricate obscurities of egotism" as in the *Curé of Tours*, have obviously come to appeal to Lewes more and more strongly.

By 1846 Lewes has altered his tone regarding George Sand's recent novels. The "author was once a great poet," he remarks concerning her *Jeanne, Isidora, Le*

Péché de M. Antoine, and *Teverino*. "It is a sad fall this poet makes when dropping into the conventional agonies and unreal passions of the circulating library" ("George Sand's Recent Novels," *Foreign Quarterly Review*," XXXVII [1846], 36). In the *Fraser's* review of 1847, which so vehemently praises the "marvellous power" of Balzac's *Cousin Pons*, George Sand's *Piccino* is dismissed as "an improbable bandit story" of three volumes' duration, whose chief virtue is that it does not have "the drawback of most of her novels: it is not a social manifesto." Two other recent novels of hers, *Lucrezia Floriani* and *La Mare au Diable*, serve to reassure him (though he does not choose to discuss them); otherwise "we might fear she had exhausted herself." Some months later Lewes was to send Charlotte Brontë copies of Balzac's *Modeste Mignon* and *Illusions Perdues* (*The Brontës*, II, 175). Lewes continued to place George Sand high in his estimates of woman writers. She was still, on the basis of her best work, the supreme poet of the emotional depths of human experience. His emphasis in his criticism, however, was increasingly given to feminine novelists of a less poetic turn—above all to Jane Austen. "Of all imaginative writers she is the most *real*," he declared in 1852 ("The Lady Novelists," *Westminster Review*, LVIII, 135). "Never does she transcend her own actual experience, never does her pen trace a line that does not touch [i.e., strike a responsive chord in] the experience of others. Herein we recognise the first quality of literature." It was Jane Austen who formed the subject of one of the most memorable of all his essays as an exponent of realism in English fiction ("The Novels of Jane Austen," *Blackwood's Magazine*, LXXXVI [1859], 99-113), an essay in which Lewes speaks of "a striking passage" (quoted at the end of section II of my Introduction) "from one of the works of Mr. George Eliot," a writer who in *Scenes of Clerical Life* had not yet mastered a technique comparable to Austen's but who was already her equal in truthfulness and her superior in culture and "reach of mind." Whereupon Lewes gives at length Eliot's first manifesto as novelist for faithfully rendering the lives of commonplace people with all their imperfections completely visible. (She was to make a notable parallel to it in Chapter 17 of *Adam Bede.*) In *Ranthorpe* we can see Lewes, in such scenes as his description of Harry Cavendish's rented quarters, already experimenting in the direction of out-and-out detailed realism but showing still in other parts of his novel the powerful gravitational force upon him of romanticism as it figured in the novels of George Sand—or, more specifically, in Bulwer-Lytton's *Ernest Maltravers* (see Introduction, section I).

126. *inveighed against Macready*: William Charles Macready (1793-1873), the eminent tragedian, had as manager of Covent Garden Theater (1837-1839) struggled to elevate the quality of English acted drama. In addition to producing a good deal of Shakespeare, he had challenged popular tastes by performing new plays by aspiring authors, including, for example, Browning's *Strafford* (1837), losing money on most of them. He tried again as manager of the Drury Lane Theater (1841-1843) without better success.

139. *Covent Garden . . . the manager*: Macready (see the previous note) was manager of Covent Garden at the time, so far as Lewes's somewhat vague chronology for his novel seems to indicate. (Harry Cavendish at a later point [p. 218] attends the Adelphi Theater to witness the acting of John Reeve, who died in 1838.) Such frustrations on the part of both manager and play-

wright as Lewes presents in the next chapters have ample parallels in the two volumes of *The Diaries of William Charles Macready, 1833-1851,* ed. William Toynbee (London, 1912). However, Lewes seems bent on keeping the particular character of the manager composite and indeterminate. It was Alfred Bunn (1796-1860), and not Macready, who in 1840 as manager of Covent Garden appeared before the Commissioner in Basinghall Street to seek "release from his creditors" (p. 158) by resort to the bankruptcy laws; and it was hardly Macready that Lewes had in mind when he made his manager (p. 158 also) resolve forever to abandon the legitimate drama to "spend his money upon spectacles and ballets."

148. *To have a play in rehearsal!* Lewes himself, so far as is known, had not yet experienced the "glory and delight" he speaks of so wistfully in this paragraph. He had written at least three plays, probably a good many more, by 1847. His *The Noble Heart*, composed around 1841, was to be given seven times in Manchester in April and May 1849, two years after the publication of *Ranthorpe*, and was to be performed at the Olympic Theater in London in 1850 after several major changes had been made in it. At Manchester Lewes himself had acted Don Gomez, the elderly hero. Lewes's unacted play *Pretension*, the manuscript of which is in the Beinecke Library at Yale, was written before November 1843. See Hirshberg, pp. 122 ff. and 210 note 53; Francis Espinasse, *Literary Recollections and Sketches* (London, 1893), pp. 284-286. Lewes writes feelingly of the grievances of unacted dramatists in his 1842 article "The Drama: Authors and Managers" (*Westminster Review*, XXXVII, 71-97) but speaks temperately regarding the managers' responsibilities in the matter. "Bad, then, as the judgment of managers may be, it must be abided by" (p. 74).

158. *till Basinghall Street released him*: See above, note for page 139.

162. *Chatterton! Gilbert! Haydon!* Versions of Chatterton's death are conflicting (though in 1847 he was unquestionably considered a suicide). William Gilbert, author of *The Hurricane* (1797), went insane before his death. Benjamin Robert Haydon (b. 1786) had committed suicide on June 22, 1846, within a few months of the completion of *Ranthorpe*.

167. *whole . . . Philharmonic orchestra*: The answer to Mr. Thornton's rhetorical question would probably have to be No, though Beethoven's Third, or *Eroica*, Symphony offended many musicians by its revolutionary innovations and continued to be disparaged for years. Later Beethoven's F Major Quartet (Opus 59, Number 1) so amazed its first hearers, according to Carl Czerny, that "they laughed and were convinced that Beethoven wanted to play a joke and that this was not the promised quartet at all" (H. C. Robbins Landon, *Beethoven: A Documentary Study* [New York, 1970], 208-209).

170. *Mr. Thornton . . . had known Göthe*: Hirshberg (p. 38) observes that Lewes's Richard Thornton bears resemblances of appearance and manner to Leigh Hunt, whose son Thornton was one of Lewes's closest friends. It is likely, however, that Lewes intended a general likeness of his friend Dr. Neil Arnott (see the note following), though Richard Thornton's demise by murder in a later chapter of *Ranthorpe* makes the compliment somewhat awkward. Lewes's *The Life of Goethe*, first published in 1855, was to become a classic of Victorian biography that was to run through at least seven editions by 1908.

173. *Dr. Neil Arnott*: As Lewes's quotation and paraphrase would suggest, Neil Arnott (1788-1874), a physician in ordinary to the Queen, seems to have been

a friend of humanity in general and of Lewes in particular. Like Lewes's Richard Thornton, he was in 1847 an elderly bachelor (though he was to marry nine years later). He had been one of the witnesses at the Leweses' wedding in 1841, and their second son (born in 1844) was named Thornton Arnott Lewes. George Eliot came to know Arnott and to like him. He was "nice Dr. Arnott" by June 1853 and her "especial favorite" a few months later (*George Eliot Letters,* I, 342; II, 104, and Gordon S. Haight's notes to the same pages).

178. *Holland House*: A Kensington mansion built in 1607, it was a social gathering place of great prominence for artists, writers, and statesmen.

182. *Ithuriel spear*: In *Paradise Lost* (IV, 788 ff.) the spear of Ithuriel, one of the cherubim, possesses unusual properties enabling its owner to search out Satan, though he is disguised as a toad:

> Him thus intent Ithuriel with his spear
> Touched lightly; for no falsehood can endure
> Touch of celestial temper, but returns
> Of force to its own likeness.

192. *George Robins' advertisement*: George Henry Robins (1778-1847), an auctioneer, was the object of much humorous comment because of the florid character of his language, especially in his elaborate advertisements of sales. He had conducted in April and May 1842 the auction of the contents of Horace Walpole's collections at Strawberry Hill, a sale that required twenty-three days and attracted widespread interest and discussion.

203. *The idea of murder*: Lewes's endeavor to trace the patterns of a murderer's mind anticipates such later more ambitious fictional studies as Dickens's of Bradley Headstone in *Our Mutual Friend* (1865) and

of John Jasper in *The Mystery of Edwin Drood* (1870).
Harry Cavendish's considerable appearance in the role
of pursuing detective in Chapter VI of Book IV of
Ranthorpe anticipates such more elaborate portrayals
as Wilkie Collins's Sergeant Cuff (*The Moonstone*,
1868), often referred to as the first detective in the English novel.

218. *The Adelphi . . . Reeve . . . Buckstone*: Thackeray had seen Reeve and Buckstone perform at the
Adelphi as early as 1833 (*The Letters and Private Pa-
pers of William Makepeace Thackeray*, ed. Gordon N.
Ray [London, 1945], I, 260 n.). John Reeve (1799-
1838) was a popular low comedian as was also John
Baldwin Buckstone (1802-1879), who was in addition
a writer of comedies, *Married Life* (1834) and *Single
Life* (1839) being among the best received of them. In
1855 while Buckstone was manager of the Haymarket
Theater, Lewes was to write a farce for him entitled
Buckstone's Adventures with a Polish Princess.

225. *Shakespeare*: A misidentification for the last
line of Milton's *Lycidas*.

229. *The Miseries of Genius*: Lewes, who had experienced his share of unhappiness in the pursuit of
literature, obviously feels deeply on the subject of this
chapter. He had written "A Word to Young Authors
on Their True Position" (*Hood's Magazine*, III [1845],
366-375) with a good deal of the same substance and
two concluding paragraphs with, in fact, many of the
identical sentences he employs in the final four briefer
paragraphs of the chapter, including the two quotations.

230. *a Nessus-poisoned shirt*: The bloody shirt of
Nessus, a centaur slain by Hercules with a poisoned ar-
row. His wife Deianira had sent it to Hercules to win
back his love, having been told by the dying Nessus that

it would possess such properties. Instead it clung to Hercules' body and could be torn off only by tearing away strips of flesh as well.

233. *Marcia sulla . . .* : Beethoven's inscription on a manuscript page of the funeral march in his *Eroica* Symphony.

239. *The Hawbuckes*: For the considerable parallels of subject and treatment between Lewes's Florence-Hawbucke subplot and the Gwendolen-Grandcourt half of Eliot's *Daniel Deronda*, see Introduction, section III.

247. *Hercules spinning with Omphale*: Hercules was required by the Delphic oracle to serve Omphale, a Lydian queen, dressed in women's clothes, a form of expiation for his having slain Iphitus in a fit of madness.

247. *but for the Exhibition*: The annual exhibition of work by living artists at the Royal Academy of the Arts, a social event of much importance.

248. *Chalon*: Alfred Edward Chalon (1781-1860), a fashionable portrait artist who had been born in Switzerland but educated in the schools of the Royal Academy of the Arts in London.

311. *I, who worship her*: Harry's magnanimous sacrifice follows a general pattern Lewes had used for his drama *The Noble Heart*, probably written in 1841. When the lover to whom his wife had been originally betrothed reappears, the elderly husband gives up all claims upon her, has the marriage annulled, and retires to a hermitage.

326. *L'Elisire d'Amore*: Donizetti's comic opera *L'Elisir d'Amore* contains in Act I a duet appropriate to the situation Florence is recalling. The lovesick Nemorino pleads with the coquettish Adina to return his affection while she announces her preference for flirting with large numbers of suitors.

336. *Paisiello's* Il mio ben . . . *Malibran* . . . *Grisi*: Giovanni Paisiello (1741-1816) was an Italian composer of nearly a hundred operas. Lewes, or perhaps Harry, is probably guilty of exaggeration in preferring Isola's singing to that of Malibran or Grisi. Maria Felicia Malibran (1808-1836) was a celebrated French operatic contralto who was sensationally popular with London audiences from 1825 until her untimely death. Grisi (see note to page 49) was equally celebrated.